AUTHOR	CLASS
NICKELL LJ	F

TITLE	No.
The White Queen	17900989

THE WHITE QUEEN

The White Queen

Lesley J. Nickell

THE BODLEY HEAD
LONDON SYDNEY
TORONTO

01084182

To my mother and father

ƒs 3.79

17900989

British Library Cataloguing
in Publication Data
Nickell, Lesley J
The white queen.
I. Title
823'.9'1F   PR6064.12/
ISBN 0-370-30132-3

© Lesley J. Nickell 1978
Printed in Great Britain for
The Bodley Head Ltd
9 Bow Street London WC2E 7AL
by Redwood Burn Ltd, Trowbridge
set in Monophoto Baskerville
by Keyspools Ltd, Golborne, Lancs.
First published 1978

CONTENTS

PART I
Daughter

HOME

Anne was a timid child. She was frightened by the sweaty reek of the soldiers clattering through the fortress, and the great horses that lumbered into the courtyard striking sparks from the cobbles with their iron hoofs. Although she slept in the same bed as her sister Isobel she was terrified of the dark, and she had nightmares about being drawn up with the draw-bridge and impaled by the portcullis. She was afraid of the sharp-nosed hounds which followed her father around, lashing their tails like whips, and she hated it when he picked her up and threw her into the air, shouting that she still weighed less than a feather. He always caught her safely, but there was that panic-stricken moment every time when she could see the floor far below and feel herself plunging fatally towards it.

Her father did not so much scare as overawe her. He was a very important man. Not only the hounds fawned on him. The bright gentlemen who sauntered about the hall stopped whispering and sniggering whenever he came in and bent towards him with loud rustlings of silk and brocade. Anne and her mother and sister had to curtsey to the ground as he appeared, and not stand up until he commanded them. Once she had mixed up her foot with the hem of her kirtle and instead of standing up she fell over. He was not cross with her, but neither did he laugh like her least favourite among the gentlemen. He had looked at her thoughtfully for a moment as she struggled to her feet, and then turned away with a slight shake of his head. Later her nurse scolded her for her clumsiness.

'It's bad enough as it is, lady, without your making it worse.'

Anne tried unsuccessfully not to cry. What was bad enough as it was she did not know, but she was sure it was her fault.

Everything seemed to be well when she went out into the streets. Roars of enthusiasm greeted her, which were twice as loud when her father was there. His eyes would light up as he waved right and left to the motley groups of townsfolk, but Anne went stiff among the cushions of her litter, her stomach a hard lump of lead, dreading the grinning faces and dirty hands which thrust through the curtains.

Once a week at least the whole family left the fortress and progressed through the raucous streets to hear mass in the church. This was quite beyond Anne's comprehension, since there was a snug little chapel inside the fortress with coloured paintings of angels on the wall and a shiny golden cross on the altar, and a ceiling low enough for her to see. The town church had a roof so high and gloomy that it was out of sight even when she dared to look up, which was not often. Although her confessor had told her reassuringly that devils lived underneath the earth and would only come and take her away if she was very wicked, she was convinced that some of them lived up there in the roof of the church, echoing mockingly the words spoken by the distant priest on the steps of the sanctuary. Sometimes the thought of those monsters with staring eyes and scaly wings and forked tails sitting up above leering at her drove every word of the mass out of her head and she could not even remember her Pater Noster. One Sunday she foolishly glanced upwards as they left the church, and caught a glimpse of one of them. It was hunched on the corner of the porch, grey and still, its mouth wide open showing jagged broken teeth – broken, she supposed, by the number of lost souls it had chewed up. She never told anyone about that.

Indeed there was no one to tell. It would not have entered her head to confide in her father. He was often away, doing wonderful things, she gathered dimly, like sweeping the Dons' fleet from the seas, whatever that meant, defeating murderous mobs single-handed, and escaping miraculously from disasters. When he was there she hardly dared open her mouth in his presence, even to answer his enquiries as to how she fared.

Her mother, on the other hand, seldom stirred from the fortress. She spent her days sitting over a large embroidery frame in the solar, and her evenings seated on the dais in the great chamber. She smiled kindly at her daughters, and came to see Anne when she was sick and laid her long cold hand on her hot forehead, but she never said very much. And her face was so sad that Anne did not like to add to her sorrow with her own little worries.

Apart from the nurse, whose chief duty was to remind Anne that she was the youngest person in the fortress and should behave with corresponding modesty, that left Isobel. Isobel was four years the elder, and lived in a different world. Anne did ask her questions occasionally, which she answered, if she chose, with great condescension. She always knew exactly how to cope with things, and seemed surprised that her younger sister did not. If Isobel caught a cold, she managed her handkerchief so cleverly that her nose neither dripped down her chin nor turned bright red. Sniffing and scrubbing her nose on her sleeve, Anne was condemned to winters of sodden sleeves and raw sore noses. There was a wistful hope in her mind that some day she would catch up with Isobel, be just as tall and pretty and sure of herself, and not trip over her kirtle any more or feel breathless when climbing the twisting stairs. But that was impossible, Isobel informed her crushingly when in a rash moment she revealed her hope. There would always be four years between them, and if they both lived to five hundred Anne would still be four years behind. Mutely, Anne took the pieces of her dream away.

One creature in the fortress had been smaller than herself, a kitten she found in the courtyard beside the body of its mother which had been savaged by the hounds. She took the wretched scrap of fur up to her chamber in the pocket of her pinafore, and when she had cuddled and stroked it for a little while it stopped shivering and, wonder of wonders, its body was shaken instead by a remarkably healthy purr. Only half believing in the miracle, Anne carried it everywhere in her pocket, until it grew too big and then she kept it hidden in her bed all day. Feeding it on scraps saved at mealtimes, she lived for the odd minutes she could pass petting and talking to it. The nurse tut-tutted and said it was unseemly; Isobel flatly refused to share her bed with a mangy cat. In vain Anne pointed out that it was not mangy and proudly showed her sister how cleverly the kitten had learned to wash itself; she would not even look. So it slept under the bed on a pile of rags, within reach of Anne's hand if she rolled right to the edge. There was untold ecstasy in stretching her arm down into the darkness to receive the caress of that rough little tongue.

Then one day the kitten disappeared. Although Isobel said it had simply run off as cats do, Anne did not believe her. She searched, without optimism and without success, for several days.

At about the time of the kitten there were some newcomers to the fortress. There was much excitement, for they were both great men – earls like her father and almost as famous. One was her grandfather, an old man who walked as if he were still on his horse and who took as little notice of Anne as everyone else. The other took rather more notice of her, and although she sensed that he meant it kindly she was overwhelmed by his attentions. He was, they said, her cousin Edward, but to her he was more like the Archangel Michael from the wall of the chapel. Descending from the skies above her, this magnificent personage came down to her level and said, 'Give you good-day, little cousin.' Even squatting on his heels he looked like an archangel, and Anne was so thunderstruck by the visitation that she merely stared at him with her mouth open. Cousin Edward-Saint Michael laughed. 'Why, you're as silent as Dickon,' he said, and tweaking one of her plaits he rose out of her ken and up into heaven again. Through her daze she wondered what a dickon was.

The arrival of the earls brought a change in the atmosphere of the fortress. There were more comings and goings, more soldiers in steel helmets and leather jerkins, more busy lords hurrying to her father's closet with important faces, a growing bustle of preparation for something. And through the winter and the following spring, shivering in bed or pushing crumbs around her platter, Anne heard recurring with increasing intensity, from servants and lords and men-at-arms, the same word. Home. They were going home.

Somewhere back in the mists of the past, last summer at least, she thought she had heard it before, spoken with the same eager expectancy, whispered from person to person like a secret that everyone shared except the Lady Anne. But suddenly the whispers had ceased, and everyone had assumed a tight anxious expression instead, until her father came back with her grandfather and cousin and the smiles reappeared.

Home, apparently, was more distant than the town church, beyond the town walls, beyond even the flat brown land that Anne had glimpsed once or twice outside the walls stretching to meet the sky. To have left the fortress for that vast emptiness would have been bad enough; she was dizzy at the thought and had to sit down. But the place where they all wanted to go lay in another and more perilous direction. Across the sea. The mere sight of that heaving sheet of grey made her feel unwell, and the prospect of actually launching out on to it, in one of those little ships that she had watched being tossed and buffeted, growing tinier and tinier until they fell over the edge, made a great well of blackness within her in which she struggled not to drown.

The fact that she had crossed the sea before, further back in her life than memory would reach, was no comfort. Isobel could remember perfectly (she said) leaving the castle of Warwick where they had both been born, riding along miles and miles of roads, and then spending days shut up in an evil-smelling box that pitched about all the time and made them ill. Anne was not sure whether to be glad that she had forgotten such an ordeal, or sorry that she had no forewarning of what a similar journey might be like. There was also something vaguely disturbing about having been born in a place called Warwick of which she could recall nothing.

Perhaps it would not happen. She closed her ears to all the murmurs of change, and pretended that they had stopped. Her father was unmistakably planning a new expedition; but then he always was. On a raw day in March she stood with Isobel and her mother on the quay and waved her handkerchief in the direction of her father's ship, which was edging cautiously out of the harbour towards the angry white breakers beyond. Like the red flag straining at the masthead with its white bear and tree-stump, her handkerchief slapped against her hand, trying to tear itself away into the ragged clouds and balancing seagulls. She did not know where he was going, but the main thing was that she was still here.

It was full spring before he returned, bringing Anne's grandmother with him, so that the entire family was in the fortress, and there was one more person to curtsey to at dinner time. The town was bursting with soldiers; the harbour was full of ships, large and small, with sailors swarming over them and up into the rigging like a plague of ants. Anne could not close her eyes as well as her ears to the crescendo of industry. Chests were humped with great difficulty down the spiral staircases; pieces of bed and bundles of arras were carried out to the courtyard and loaded on to wagons. Each time Anne returned to her chamber she dreaded to see the walls bare of their blue trees, prancing horses and fleeing deer, the bed dismantled and the chest which held her clothes disappearing to join the outward-flowing stream of baggage. She almost expected the walls of the fortress to be taken down, stone by stone, and stacked neatly on one of those wagons that rumbled off in the direction of the harbour.

All the earls were going, and most of the other men were going with them. But not, as yet, the ladies.

There came a day in summer when Anne was in bed with a headache – a bed that remained intact – and unusually her father came to her room, with her cousin Lord Edward. Their spurs clashed as they came in, as if the noise were inside her head. The open door let a shaft of sunlight into the darkened chamber, striking splinters of gold from the chains around their shoulders. On her father's breast was the white bear and tree trunk he wore when he was leaving on his expeditions; Cousin Edward wore a silver falcon, rousing its feathers and opening its beak in a most lifelike manner. Anne found she could never look higher than Cousin Edward's chest. Her father leaned down and pecked her on the brow.

'Be good, and don't disgrace your lady mother,' he said. 'I'll come back for you soon.' His voice battered at her throbbing head, and she knew she ought to have got up and curtsied to him but she did not have the courage to risk making the pain worse. Then Edward bent over her, swooping from the sky. Instead of kissing her forehead, he took up her hand which lay on the coverlet and she felt his warm moist lips on it. Her heart started fluttering, and as soon as he let go she tucked her hand hastily beneath the covers.

'What a coquette she is, Richard!' he cried to her father. Bending down again, he said, 'Well, sweeting, the next time I see you, we'll be at Westminster, God willing. There you can flirt to your heart's content.' He laughed heartily, and as they turned to go Anne looked up under her eyelids to see if her father was laughing too. No, there was nothing but a rather absent smile. She thought that perhaps he did not understand what her cousin was laughing at either.

The door shut behind them and the restful dusk filtered down once more. Muffled by the thick walls she heard their departure, the hoofs scuffling, the wagons rumbling, the spatter of cheering as they emerged from the gatehouse, and then fading away into the distance. Everyone had gone down to the harbour to see them off, and as far as she could tell there was nobody left in the fortress but the Lady Anne, in bed with her headache. And if they all climbed into the waiting ships and sailed off to Home leaving her here, she would not know, and she would stay here for ever on her own until she died of her headache. The silence was so good for the beating in her head that she did not care.

And anyway it was no good pretending any more. Her father had delivered the sentence himself. Wherever he was going, and however long he was away, he was coming back for her. Soon. She lay in the gloom with her eyes closed, and the ache behind them was no worse than the ache in her heart.

He was as good as his word. Having felt sick continuously since he left and regarding with fear every potential messenger who cantered his horse through the gates, Anne saw the reappearance of her father to fetch his family as almost a mercy. Isobel was positively pleased, though the only reason she would give her sister was that they were to be presented to the King. Anne had not heard of the King before. Of the Queen she had caught an odd word here and there, mostly accompanied by sour faces and, in the case of servants and soldiers, spitting or a curse. Why Isobel should want to meet anyone connected with this unpleasant person was not clear. Her only answer to Anne's tentative questions was, 'Because he's the King of course.' Since she could not bring herself to ask if they were to meet the Queen too, Anne's vision of Home was further darkened by the shadow of the wicked woman who was her father's deadliest enemy.

She watched her chamber emptying, the clothes-chest, the

15

tapestries, the furniture, and then she was following them down to the harbour. It was raining steadily, as so often that summer, and the sea was a dull sheet of lead pitted by numberless drops of rain. The sails, ready spread, hung wetly from the spars. Shepherded on board by burly sailors, Anne clung for a moment to the head of the ladder which led down into the dark belly of the ship, gazing back bleakly at the crowding roofs of the town where she had spent all her conscious life. It was indistinct already, separated from her by a sullen veil of drizzle. Someone prodded her on, and she slithered down the steep rungs, too numb to mind if she reached the bottom safely.

All the ladies and their women were herded into one cabin with a low ceiling and no windows, lit by a hanging lanthorn which swung slowly to and fro for no apparent reason. Isobel was right about the bad odour. It was nothing like the garderobe tower in the fortress, or the midden-heap in the courtyard, but it made Anne feel slightly sick as soon as she went in. She rapidly felt worse. Women she had known as aloof and poised, with never a wrinkle in their coifs or a spot of grease on their gowns, were slumping on to the floor, groaning and writhing, vomiting down their own gowns or their neighbours', all dignity gone. From the corner where she had tucked herself Anne looked on with round horrified eyes, the bench heaving beneath her, the lanthorn swinging above her, her hands pressed to her unquiet stomach. Even Isobel, the grown-up, the assured, was weeping and retching loudly with her head in somebody's lap. Closing her eyes did no good as long as the sounds and smells still attacked her, and after a while Anne curled herself up into a ball, pulled her cloak and hood round her, and tried to cut herself off from the terrible little world which had entrapped her.

When she dared to uncover one eye again, the lanthorn was hardly moving. Cautiously she uncovered an ear as well, and the bedlam of distress had changed to a hubbub of normal conversation. Deciding that it was safe to come out, she began to uncurl and discovered that both her feet and one of her arms had gone to sleep, and there was a painful crick in her neck. She rubbed her neck with the hand that was awake, and shook her other limbs anxiously to assure herself that they were still there. As feeling tingled back into them, she saw that although the stench was no sweeter and the cabin was still in chaos, her fellow-prisoners were behaving in a much more recognisable way. Dishevelled and soiled as they were, they had found their small steel looking-glasses and combs and were prinking and smoothing and scrubbing themselves for all they were worth. There was an air of excitement about them, and several pale green faces were lit by smiles. Baffled by the sudden reversals of fortune, Anne smoothed her rumpled dress and waited. She was aware that Isobel was casting unfriendly glances at her, and noticed that her admired sister looked positively ugly.

They were released eventually, and Anne's confusion increased as she scrambled up the ladder into the daylight. It was still raining; the sea was still grey and flat; the same ships lay at their moorings in the same harbour, with the same jostling houses on the quay. Had she dreamed that ordeal in the cabin, and was it all to do again? As panic began to build up inside her, she cast about for reassurance. And then the rain curtain drifted aside a little, and high above the harbour there hovered the ghost of a castle, which gradually revealed itself to be attached to an equally ghostly hill. Other contours loomed out of the mist as she watched. The harbour was guarded at each side by lofty cliffs such as she had never seen before. This was no familiar landscape. Beyond the commonplaces of the port, it was crushingly alien. This must be Home.

When she stepped on to the quay she stumbled and nearly fell; the solid stone seemed to be trying to heave her back into the sea. There were crowds of people waiting for them, and Anne's father strode forward fearlessly to meet them. He was engulfed by flailing arms and howls of enthusiasm, and then he rose above them as he mounted his horse, still mobbed by his assailants. They were milling about the litters which stood ready for the ladies, and Anne realised that she would have to run the gauntlet of that mass of boisterous humanity to reach her place.

It was the beginning of another nightmare.

They were always moving, the litter swaying and lurching over cobbles and potholes, surrounded by the rumbling of baggage wagons and the clatter of hoofs, the red jackets with their bear and tree trunk bobbing alongside, always hemmed in by the mobs with their wide-open mouths and uncouth yells of welcome. It was like journeying to the church on Sundays, but going on for ever. Weary and nauseated from the motion of endless travel and not enough rest, Anne marvelled that her father could take so much pleasure in the journey. She had never known him in better spirits, exuding energy and happiness, sparing some of his good humour even for his younger daughter, who rather wished he would not. Her mother too had lost something of her careworn expression, and Isobel had recovered from her seasickness far enough to wave quite gaily to the crowds which beset them. Anne would have liked to share in the universal joy, but she could not; she could only cower behind the curtains of the litter and endure.

There was an interlude in the nightmare, like an intrusion from another dream. The blur of faces and noise and movement slowed to a pattern of hushed order and courtesy which was almost familiar. They had come to a place called Greenwich, a large building that lay beside a wide river. The mob was left outside the walls, and it was inhabited by ladies and gentlemen who seemed to have nothing to do but stand around and decorate the spacious rooms. No trace here of the bustle that had filled the fortress. Even Anne's father restrained his purposeful stride as he led his family through a daunting succession of chambers.

In one of them he paused, and an exceptionally tall gentleman detached himself from one of the formal tableaux and came towards them. Anne recognised her cousin Lord Edward, and was surprised to see that her father, as well as the rest of his party, deferred to him. His voice, confident and vigorous, vibrated into the rafters.

'Faith, cousin, you don't waste any time.' This to her father; then, turning to the ladies, he said smiling (Anne could hear the smile in his voice, for of course she did not raise her eyes to his face), 'Welcome home, ladies. England has lacked your beauty for too long.' He proceeded to kiss their hands, beginning with Anne's grandmother, concluding with Anne herself. As he humbled his august height before her, she could not help glancing at him. His eyes, on a level with hers, were dark blue and sparkling, and the smile was in them too. 'Not quite Westminster,' he said, so low that only she could hear, 'but nearly as good. Don't break too many hearts.' Anne felt herself go hot all over. She would almost have preferred the obscurity of the jolting litter.

Lord Edward had returned to her father.

'The King is most anxious to receive you.' There was a strange intonation in the simple words. 'I'm sure he'll give you audience at once.'

They left Edward and went on. Nobody had said anything about the Queen. Fear breathed on Anne. But surely everyone would not look so cheerful if the terrible Queen were about.

The throne room was musty and damp, as if it were not much used. It was also empty. Anne was taken aback, since the only kings within her knowledge, who hung on the walls of the great hall in the fortress, were seated stiffly on tapestry thrones wearing their embroidered crowns and carrying embroidered sceptres, and surrounded by banks of stiff embroidered courtiers. There was no one here at all, only a goldfinch in a cage which began to flutter about and chatter as its peace was disturbed.

And when someone did come in, it was a tall stooping man in a homespun gown, with a creased purple mantle huddled round his shoulders. He shuffled on to the dais and sat diffidently in the gilded chair. The soldiers who had followed him in took their places at each corner of the dais and grounded their halberds. Any man less like the kings in the tapestries, resplendent in their majesty, was hard to imagine.

Yet it was the King, for Anne's father strode the length of the chamber and knelt before him, and he would have knelt only to a king. Extending his hand, the King said, 'My lord of Warwick, we are graciously pleased to receive you again in our court.' Anne could hardly hear the quiet greeting, and the rest of the King's speech was lost somewhere in the chilly reaches of the throne room.

Then they were all before the throne, and kneeling in their turn to kiss the long thin fingers, on which hung several rings that looked too heavy for them. When it came to Anne's turn she found she was not afraid to gaze up into the King's face. A gentle face, and the eyes were dark and mild and a little frightened. Something moved inside her, as it had for nobody before, only, oddly enough, as it had when she touched the abandoned kitten and felt its trembling. Without thinking she smiled at him, and in reply she saw his lips widen, though his anxious expression did not change. Her father was ready to shepherd them all away, but the King had reached over to the cage beside him and taken out the goldfinch. For a moment it was a frantic bundle of brilliant feathers, but soon it settled into the King's soothing hands, and he held it out towards Anne.

'Look,' he said, 'it's my little bird.' She stroked it with one finger, and it swivelled its head comically to look up at her.

They led her away, and from the door she saw the King bent over the bird, talking to it.

After that it was back to the endless road, and the strange meeting with the King faded behind the rumbling and creaking and shouting of the present. All jumbled up with the discomfort were shrill hordes of children in fancy dress at the gates of London, shrivelled heads like mouldy walnuts on London Bridge, the candlesoft hush of the shrine of Our Lady of Walsingham, the sharp scent of danger as the whisper of ambush rustled through the cavalcade.

And at last it did end, with a climbing road towards some round turrets in a bank of trees which they said were those of Warwick Castle, her birthplace.

She had no recollection of it, and neither, she could tell, had Isobel. It was a vast pile, quite dwarfing the fortress across the sea. On the day after their arrival, Anne was lost for fifteen heart-stopping minutes in the warren of passages and spiral stairs, and she conceived a horror of being forgotten somewhere in the castle and wandering for ever in its stony half-light. There was no sea within sight or sound, although she thought at first there was. But the perpetual roaring under the windows of the great hall was the River Avon, swollen by the summer floods, hurling itself over a weir. Having once climbed on to the window-seat to look at it, frothing angrily round the rocks many feet below, Anne decided that it was worse than the sea and did not look again.

Apart from the increased scale of the surroundings, life soon settled down into a familiar pattern. Her mother's embroidery frame came out, her father set off escorted by a train of red-jacketed soldiers, and Anne went down with a fever. Her bedchamber was bigger than that in the fortress, and the arras did not quite cover the walls. Also there was a draught from under the door which made the tapestries quiver slightly as if there were something hidden behind them. At the height of her delirium she caught sight of hands and claws, stealing into view for an instant before they withdrew to their refuge. Once there was a face too, and she screamed, but nobody heard her.

She was in bed again, though probably with a different bout of illness, when a thrill of alarm ran through the castle, echoing even in her remote sickroom. Her nurse, unusually communicative, told her with red eyes and many sniffs that her great-uncle the Duke of York and her grandfather and her uncle Thomas had all been butchered by the barbarous Queen. The Queen again! What inhuman kind of monster could she be, not only to murder so many important men, but also (the nurse went on in a sepulchral whisper) to nail their heads up on the gates of York. Anne thought of the mouldering walnuts on London Bridge, and her blood froze. The Queen would surely not dare to do that to her father, but what if she caught her mother? Or Isobel? Or her? She shrank beneath the bedclothes, and all the carefully-husbanded warmth had fled.

A mass was said for the departed members of the family, and Anne was hustled down to the chapel from her bed to hear it. It was cold in the chapel, where the wilting Christmas greenery still stood on the altar, but not all the shivering of the congregation was due to the temperature. Although her mother's expression was as patient as usual, her fingers moved rather fast on the beads of her rosary; a few people were weeping openly, and there were many apprehensive glances towards the door in the course of the service. Evidently Anne was not the only person to wonder how far the malevolence of the Queen could reach.

The castle was pervaded by uneasiness. There was no dividing ocean here to protect them from peril. The river and the dry moat, the stout walls and the many soldiers, were puny defences without the powerful presence of the Earl. He did not come back. Apparently he was holding London against the Queen, although, Anne heard one of her mother's attendants mutter, that was precious little help to his household in Warwick. It was no comfort to Anne to sense that everyone was as anxious as she was. Grown-up people should be as sure and fearless as her father, even if they ignored her completely – not sneaking down to the chapel and burning nervous candles to their favourite saints, and jumping edgily at every slight noise, and forever gazing over the northward-facing battlements. For her part, whenever she passed a window which gave on to the outside of the castle, she sedulously averted her eyes for fear of what she might see approaching.

It was from the south that someone approached, a tired man flogging a tired horse. He dragged his feet as he came into the great hall, and Anne thought that he looked very untidy. One of his sleeves was torn right off, and the tree trunk on his surcoat was stained brown. She saw her mother, with a swift movement quite unlike her, press her hands to her stomach; then she and Isobel were hurried away by the nurse. Later she heard that her father had been defeated by the Queen.

Life came to a standstill. Everybody stood around, saying nothing, doing nothing, only her mother's eternal needle flickered in and out of the fabric. Isobel took to crying in bed, and sobbed out one night that they would never see their father again, and that the Queen would come and murder them all. Since she was voicing Anne's secret dread, long after she was asleep her younger sister lay staring into the darkness, listening to the faint rustle of the tapestry and waiting for the Queen's hands to reach out from behind it and strangle her.

But Isobel was wrong. Only a few days later the Earl came briefly, trailing a sorry band of cripples, some limping and helping each other along and others on carts. They were untidy too, and Anne found that they were the wounded refugees from the lost battle. But her father did not look untidy or defeated. On the contrary he was in wonderful spirits, and the despondency in the castle lifted immediately. Isobel wept no more, and mocked Anne's long face. Her change of mood had something to do with a cryptic remark which the Earl had made, pinching her cheek in passing.

'How would you like to marry a king, eh, Isobel?' Since the King was the kind man with a bird, and he was married to the monster Queen, Anne did not attempt to understand.

The mystery deepened on a morning in spring when all the bells in Warwick began to peal, and an excited Isobel told her sister that it was for King Edward. Who was King Edward? The king with the bird, Anne knew, was called Henry.

'Our cousin Edward, you goose,' said Isobel impatiently. 'First he was the Earl of March, and then the Duke of York, and now our father has made him King.' Anne did not see how there could be two kings at once, but she could not bring herself to ask what had happened to King Henry. She went away and sat in a corner of the solar, hugging her knees and listening to the clangour of the bells, wondering about King Henry and King Edward. Of course Cousin Edward would look right wearing a crown, because he was so beautiful, much more beautiful than the stooping homely man who had let her stroke his little bird. But it was her father who had brought about the change. Suddenly Anne was swept by a wave of awe which made her feel very small. He had made a king, and she had thought that only God could make kings. The Earl of Warwick must be the most powerful man in the whole world.

The Queen had been driven away by the Earl and his new King. Now the sentries leaned on their pikes gossiping in the sunshine, and the drawbridge remained lowered all day. They seldom saw the Earl, who was busy riding about the country keeping it safe for King Edward. Summer came; Anne stopped shivering in bed, and the weir beneath the hall windows lost some of its ferocity. Soon after her birthday her father paid one of his flying visits, and when he had gone she began to notice sinister changes in the daily routine. Large numbers of empty wagons were assembling in the courtyard. Bare stretches of wall appeared in the castle chambers and rolled-up tapestries descended to fill the wagons. There was a constant tapping and stench of burning hoof from the direction of the stables. Anne could not mistake the signs. They were moving again. She thought that she would on the whole rather face the hazards of Warwick's maze of passages than another journey.

For once Isobel was upset too. While Anne kept her lips pinched tightly together to contain her apprehension, her sister gave way to hers. It was not, however, the travelling that worried her, but the destination.

'I thought we would go to London,' she wailed, 'so that I could be near the King.' Personally, Anne could well do without the attentions of Cousin Edward, who must surely be even more awesome now that he was King.

'Where are we going?' she ventured to ask.

'Miles and miles and miles away,' said Isobel graphically, 'up into the north where it's wild and nobody lives at all, because of the Scots and other savages.'

'Oh.' Anne's heart sank. She did not mind if there were no cheering crowds, but the Scots and other savages did not sound a good exchange. As usual she was sorry she had asked the question at all.

It was miles away. The long cavalcade wound down Castle Hill and lumbered northwards for several weeks. There were no crowds. Occasionally, passing through towns, curious knots of people would gather and raise a huzzah at the red-and-white pennants; ragamuffins would slide alongside the ladies' litters, whining for alms, until the soldiers beat them off. But the Earl was not with them, and the mob followed him. Anne hardly noticed what was happening or not happening beyond the leather curtains. For days before their departure her stomach had been tying itself into knots; on the journey it was occupied in violently untying the knots. She was either feeling sick, or being sick over the side of the litter if she could reach it, several times over herself, once, to her great shame, over her mother. In between she dozed, and woke to be sick again. She was sometimes unsure whether they were travelling or had stopped for the night – nothing under her was solid and everything made her ill.

There was one place she remembered, because she had heard of it before. The city of York, where the Queen had chopped off her grandfather's head and stuck it on the gate. She could not help looking as they approached the barbican. There were no heads, and in her relief Anne warmed towards the city, despite the imposing scarlet men who greeted them outside with long speeches in an unintelligible tongue.

And that was nearly the end of their journey. Only one more day on the road remained, and although it was a long day Anne did not suffer as badly as before. The highway was so rough that they had to go very slowly; during the afternoon they abandoned the litters and Anne was taken up before one of the horsemen. She did not mind sitting on a horse, especially with a stout pair of arms steadying her; up there she was safe from the danger of plunging hoofs. The weather was fine, and she watched with comparative interest the sun sinking towards the hills on her left.

It was dark by the time they reached Middleham, and beyond the bobbing torches carried by the foot-soldiers only the faintly luminous sky was visible. Anne's head was nodding against the broad chest behind her, and as the horse began to climb toward the darker mass which stood against the sky, she thought drowsily, as she had once thought before, that they were back where they started. But when she had been put to bed and the candle had been blown out, she could not hear the muffled roar of the Avon weir below the castle walls. There was nothing but the breathing of Isobel beside her, and she fell asleep listening to the silence.

2

RICHARD

At the top of the slope on the south side of the castle was a curious piece of hummocky land, crowned by hawthorn bushes and thistles. Beyond it the sparse fields rose to the vague heather of the skyline. Anne could see it from the battlements above her room, which she could reach by a spiral stair if the door at the top was open. For some reason she never tired of looking at it, and she would stand for hours, her chin and cheek resting on the stone embrasure, gazing at the tangle of leaves and weeds, and thinking. They were not clear thoughts, just a slow pleasant procession of unformed ideas circling round the jumble of hillocks. She had been up on the walls once, dreaming, and never noticed that it was raining until the water began to run down her neck. The leaves on the bushes had been green when she first discovered them, but gradually they had reddened and turned brown, and now they were blowing away, leaving the twigs clad brazenly only in their clusters of scarlet haws.

There were always swarms of birds around the place, and today they were squabbling over the berries so shrilly that Anne could hear them, though she told them that there were quite enough for all. Her nurse's heavy step on the stairs brought Anne back abruptly to the castle ramparts. The climb from the floor below had not agreed with her.

'So here you are, lady! Where have you been all this time?' Anne took it as a rhetorical question and did not answer. 'There's your sister all clean and ladylike in her best kersey for our visitor, and you hiding up here as slovenly as a gipsy. Look, there's a green stain down your smock and a smut on your cheek.'

She continued to scold as she hurried her charge somewhat

dangerously back to the nursery, although as far as Anne could remember nobody had notified her of an important occasion this afternoon. Trying not to flinch as the nurse brushed the tangles from her hair, she learned from Isobel what a momentous event she had not heard about.

'How could you *forget*, Anne! His grace the King's own brother coming to live here and you say you didn't know! He's a duke now, the Duke of Gloucester, so he's very important.'

'Not as important as our father?'

'Oh no, of course not, but one day he may be nearly as important. That's why the King has sent him here.' Isobel continued to talk, twisting her fingers together as she did when she was excited, while Anne was stripped and dressed again in something presentable, a close-fitting brown woollen gown which cut her under the arms. So there was another like King Edward. A second Cousin Edward, permanently striding through the quiet castle and laughing loudly at inexplicable jokes, touching her and glancing at her in his disturbing way; the prospect was unnerving. A brown velvet cap was pulled over her hair, and the girls were driven along the passage to their mother's withdrawing chamber, where they were patted and tweaked anew for the Countess's benefit. Then they followed her over the wooden bridge, which made Anne a little queasy each time she crossed it, into the keep.

In the great hall her father was pacing impatiently, and although no one actually said that it was Anne's fault they were late, she felt every eye on her accusingly. She could not help seeing her father – she would have known he was there with her eyes shut – but she kept looking at the floor as they went to meet him. The presentations were made: his grace the Duke of Gloucester, my lady the Countess of Warwick, the Lady Isobel your cousin; and Anne spied a chicken bone and a bead from a broken rosary half submerged in the rushes. She put out her toe to find if there were any more beads.

'The Lady Anne your younger cousin.' Anne thumped ungracefully to her knees, and a pair of dusty boots stepped before her.

'His hand,' Isobel hissed from above, 'you must kiss his hand.' And there it was, quite a small hand, without any of the rings which adorned his brother's. As she saluted him her gaze travelled upwards, not very far, over the grey hose and sage-green tunic, to the chain of office which was too big for the narrow shoulders, and the thin pointed face. But surely it was her own sensation of startled relief reflected in those serious eyes. He was only a boy, older than she but not by many years, and as different from his opulent brother as this castle was from the galleries of Greenwich. Her father was making his speech of introduction.

'My lord the King has done us great honour by entrusting his grace of Gloucester to our care. His grace is to live here as part of our household. You are to treat him with the deference due to a brother, as he will serve you with the duty of a squire.' Other people made suitable replies – the Countess, the Master of Henchmen who would be in charge of the Duke's training, the tall dragonfly of a chamberlain. His grace of Gloucester said nothing. That too was unlike his brother Edward.

His arrival brought into focus the other preparations of which Anne had hardly taken account, since they were clearly for comings and not goings. The tiltyard had been weeded and sanded, the dilapidated quintain painted in shiny new colours, and straw targets were set up in the outer bailey. There were extra musicians to play to the company dining in the great hall, and extra faces at table too, although Anne had been too shy either to take them in or to ask about them. Several were boys of roughly the Duke of Gloucester's age, and Anne now realised that they had come to share his schooling.

She and Isobel also formed an essential part of the curriculum. There was less time for her favourite occupation of standing on the ramparts and thinking. The girls were required as appreciative audiences at archery contests and tilts, they were trodden-upon partners at dancing lessons, and subjects for experiments in table service. They began learning on their own account also: reading, embroidery and playing the lute. The private lessons Anne found quite tolerable, although Isobel complained; with the public appearances it was different. Isobel was not at all averse to playing knights and ladies. For Anne, who had always been left in the shadows to her own devices, this regimented thrusting into the limelight was new and uncomfortable. Every dance and combat was something of an ordeal.

There were only half a dozen lads in the Earl of Warwick's school of chivalry, but so reluctant was Anne to look at them that they seemed at least double that number. Despite their names ringing round the great hall and tiltyard, she could identify none of them, except of course the Duke of Gloucester. Perhaps because Isobel was taller than the Duke he was paired with his younger cousin quite often. And she could not forget, boy though he was, that he was King Edward's brother. He showed no trace of Edward's charm, of his embarrassing forwardness; he had never addressed a single word to her beside the formal exchanges which were part of the code of courtesy. Yet she could not escape the inner knowledge that he was among the greatest in the land and she was unworthy of him.

On odd occasions she would still escape to the corners of the castle where she could be sure of solitude. Winter was drawing on and her favourite spot on the walls was too exposed for long vigils; there was another place overlooking a small neglected outer courtyard where she could wedge herself between two buttresses in comparative shelter.

She made her way there on a chilly morning a few weeks after the Duke's arrival. Bundled up in the miniver border of her cloak was the precious billet of wood which she took to bed with her and talked to when nobody was listening. Before she could settle down to a quiet conversation there was a noise below her. In a spurt of annoyance at the intrusion on her refuge, she saw that someone was down in the courtyard, where no one ever went, playing with a sword.

No, not playing, for it was a full-sized broadsword, and the child who was handling it – he was no more than a child – could hardly lift it with both hands. Even from a distance Anne could tell the effort which was involved, the feeble straining muscles, the panting breath. It was the Duke of Gloucester. Suddenly Anne knew that she should not have been there. It was as if she had stumbled into a confessional and overheard thoughts so intensely private that only God should hear them. And in the wake of that instinct to run away came an uprush of the same emotion with which her kitten and deposed King Henry had touched her. This time it was so strong as to be a physical pain, which brought tears to her eyes. Catching up her billet she blundered away, leaving the King's brother to his lonely exercise.

He was far from an outstanding pupil. Being the smallest and most slightly-built of the lads, he had little of the sheer physical strength needed to control a horse or draw a bowstring. What to the other boys was an exciting challenge was to him an arduous labour. It was this, and not his rank, that set him apart. No longer dazzled by awe, Anne was aware for the first time of someone beside herself who did not fit effortlessly into the expected pattern of life. She noticed how he took criticism without comment and, instead of discussing it with his companions, went off into a corner to work at correcting his fault. In recreation time after supper in the great hall he did not join the groups playing chess, or romping like puppies, but sat alone. Sometimes a long-legged boy called John kept him company; though they talked a little, in the main they were a silent pair. From a stool beside her mother on the dais, clutching her grubby piece of embroidery, Anne watched him. She wondered whether John shared his secret; and if he would be angry at knowing that she did too.

The first of December brought snow. For six days without pause they were marooned amid the aimless and inexorable flakes. If Anne stared long enough out of a window the castle seemed to be floating slowly upwards into the whirling grey sky. Outdoor activities were abandoned, and the great hall was rather louder than usual with boys venting surplus energy. On the feast of St Nicholas the snow stopped, though the heavy sky promised more, and Anne took the opportunity to slip up to the ramparts above the nursery. She was intrigued to find out what so much snow had done to her favourite view.

It was transformed. In the wonder of that smooth white coverlet which lay over the broken land she forgot to shiver at the icy air. And her special place was the most beautiful of all. It was a confection of whipped-up meringue peaks, decorated with crystallised sugar tracery, like the subtleties that adorned the high table on feast-days.

'Look, Kat.' She poked the head of her billet out of her cloak; not too far, in case it caught cold. 'How pretty our place is. Like a magic castle.'

'Yes. I expect it was a castle once.' Kat did not usually

answer aloud nor with such originality. Anne glanced down at it in surprise. But the billet had remained mute, and it was a human voice which had responded to her thoughts. The King's brother was standing behind her, gazing as raptly as she had been doing at the snowy landscape. 'That hump in the middle, you see, was the keep, and then there was a moat in the dip, and the bumps all round it were the outer fortifications.' He pursued his theory, pointing out the features as he mentioned them.

'It must have been a very small castle,' said Anne shyly, half caught up in his enthusiasm.

'That's because the people in the old days were small – like the fairy folk,' explained the Duke with conviction.

'Were they as small as us?'

'I expect so. But they were valiant fighters and good at building things.' He paused, and they both stared at the snow-castle built by fairy folk. Then he said diffidently, 'Would you like to go up there with me one day? Then we could look at it properly.'

'Oh yes! Kat would like that.' Anne had not stopped to consider that no one in the world knew about Kat except herself. 'And so would I.'

'When the snow is gone, then.' The Duke did not ask who Kat was.

Random flakes of snow were meandering about their heads, and he said suddenly, 'You must go in now, or you'll take a chill.' Although Anne's nurse had used the same words a hundred times she did not feel at all chastened, but rather gratified that someone should have noticed she was shivering.

So now they both shared a secret: Anne had watched the Duke's practising, and he had heard her talking to Kat. Neither mentioned it to the other, indeed they spoke no more in public than they had done before, but they sensed it between them each time he took her hand for a dance or knelt beside her at table with a finger-bowl. And there was the promise of the expedition to the castle when the snow went away.

There was no sign of its going. After the lull at St Nicholas snow fell every day until the last week of Advent. When at last the clouds lifted their swollen bellies from the hills, the bailey was suddenly swarming with men in bright hoods and mufflers, and there was the scraping of shovels as they cleared the drifts away.

It was nearly a week before the roads to Richmond and York were passable. On the day when the first messenger from her father arrived Anne suffered a major loss. She should not have taken Kat to the garderobe, but she had forgotten that the billet was wrapped in the corner of her cloak until it slithered out and rolled, very gently, over the side of the stone ledge. Peering after it she was met with thick darkness and an acrid odour. There was no chance of recovery. All the way to the nursery she held back the tears, but by the bed in which she had so often fallen asleep with the hard pressure of Kat under her chin, she let them flow. Neither the scathing glances of her sister nor the disapproval of the nurse could stem them, and finally the Countess was called to her errant younger child. Having laid her hand on Anne's forehead, she pronounced her daughter sick and ordered her to be put to bed, and bled if she was not better by evening. Then she returned to her embroidery. The threat of bleeding nearly scared Anne out of her grief, but after she was left in the darkened room with a cold compress on her head, it came back in full force.

Several hours later the tears were exhausted, and since the only signs of illness now were occasional dry hiccups, she was declared cured and haled down to supper. Of course she could not eat a thing. She sat and stared at her platter, seeing nothing but the slow inevitable roll of Kat towards the precipice.

Submerged in her sorrow, she was unconscious of the concerned regard of the Duke of Gloucester beside her. Later on he came to her when the other children were involved in a noisy game.

'Is there anything I can do?'

'I've lost Kat,' she said bleakly.

'Perhaps I can find her for you.'

Anne shook her head. 'No. It's gone.'

The Duke frowned at her for a moment, his wide mouth compressed. Then he said, 'I have an idea. But we should have to ask John. Do you mind?' Anne looked at him. He was not making fun of her. His face was very serious. She decided to trust him.

'No.'

'I'll ask him tonight.'

Although he did not approach her again that evening, she was so curious as to what he would do with John's help that she only thought about Kat every other minute, instead of all the time.

The snow had frozen, and outdoor activities were still curtailed. Hunting, however, was possible in all weathers, and the following morning the lads rode out to chase foxes, rabbits, or deer if they could find them, up the blanketed dale. But Anne was not forgotten. Before dawn she was sitting in the nursery with Isobel, having her hair tugged into plaits, when the Duke came in. The girls' attendants looked askance at each other, but because of who he was they withdrew.

John was with him, and they were both cloaked and booted ready for the hunt. After apologising formally for interrupting her toilet, he said, 'Show her, John.' The other lad produced something from beneath his cloak and put it into her hands. It was a miniature horse, carved in wood, unpolished and naïve but definitely a horse, its neck and tail stretched expectantly. 'He carves with his dagger,' explained the Duke, 'when he has nothing else to do.' The wood-carver stood and nodded, his long sombre face trying not to show his pride in his work. Evidently the King's brother had found a friend yet more silent than he was himself. 'If you like, he'll make you a poppet.' Anne turned the little horse over, touching the mane and heavy fetlocks. Then she looked up at the two boys, who were waiting almost apprehensively for her answer. With a flash of insight she guessed that John's carving was another secret. She smiled, for the first time since yesterday afternoon.

'Thank you.' They smiled too, at each other and then at her. The horse was returned to its creator, and the boys went off to their hunting.

As soon as they were out of the room Isobel rushed at her, blonde hair, not yet braided, flying across her face. 'What did he want? What did he say to you?' The women's expressions asked the same, though etiquette would not let them speak. Anne shrank back on to her stool, her face closing. She had no inclination to tell Isobel what was happening, and she was sure that the Duke of Gloucester would not like it either. But Isobel was not taking silence as an answer. 'Tell me, Anne. You must tell because I'm the elder and you're only a child.' The logic was irrefutable: never before had Anne failed to accord to her sister the rights due to her. Yet now there was a stronger claim on her obedience.

'It's a secret,' she said.

Isobel was shocked. 'You can't have a secret from me. Specially when that boy John Wrangwysh knows it. He's only a merchant's son.' That surprised Anne a little; she had assumed that John was, like herself and the other henchmen, from a noble family. In any case, she had only the vaguest idea what a merchant was, and she did not see that it made any difference to keeping or sharing secrets.

'He's my lord Duke's friend.'

'And I'm his cousin,' countered Isobel. But though she felt wretchedly that she was being stupid and wicked, Anne would say no more. Disconcerted by this unexpected check to her curiosity, Isobel went away and had her hair brushed. While Anne was pushing her cold feet into fur-lined slippers she came back. Her smug expression was ominous. 'If you won't tell me, I shall ask his grace our cousin myself.'

'No, no, you mustn't!' Her sister's threat threw Anne into an agony of fear. The precious circle of confidence between her and the Duke and John would be broken irrevocably if Isobel were to join it. There was only one way she could think of to stave off the possibility. 'Let me ask him.'

'As soon as he's back from the hunt?'

'Yes.'

'Do you promise?'

'Yes.'

'Very well. But don't forget.'

'No.' Satisfied, Isobel flounced off to finish dressing, leaving her sister shaken and apprehensive. She hated the idea of asking for anything, let alone from the Duke. Not that she stood in awe of him any more, but he was already doing her a favour and she wanted to be grateful, not to demand more.

Nevertheless, when the henchmen came in she was waiting in the great hall, out of sight of the trophies they brought back, which she did not like very much, but near enough to the spot where the Duke's attendant was standing ready to take his master's cloak and gauntlets. The lads were stamping around,

34

breathing clouds of steam as if still out in the wintry air, calling to each other in the loud relaxed voices of men taking ease after a hard morning's sport. As usual Gloucester did not join in the chatter, though several admiring remarks on his prowess were thrown his way and quietly acknowledged. He allowed his man to divest him of his outdoor garments, running his hand over his hair to smooth it as the hood was removed. By the time Anne had summoned the courage to approach him, he was fastening the buttons on a long woollen houppelande. Yet when she stood before him and his sober gaze was on her, she could not say a word. Reaching the bottom button, he regarded her a moment longer, then said as if in answer to a question, 'John has a good piece of wood. We're free this afternoon so he can start then.'

'Thank you,' Anne whispered, and continued to stare up at him beseechingly, wishing he could read her thoughts.

At length he asked, 'Is something wrong?'

'Yes . . . no . . . Isobel wants to know,' she said in a rush.

'Oh. Is that all?' Anne nodded, looking at the floor. 'She can watch if she likes. John won't mind.' He left his small cousin trembling with relief. Somehow, by the easy way in which he had let Isobel into their conspiracy, he had kept it intact. Isobel, however, was not overgrateful for the privilege Anne had won her.

'He says you can watch.'

'Watch what?'

Anne would presume no further than the Duke had conceded.

'This afternoon, he said.'

'Watch *what*?' No answer. 'Anne, you are silly' And you must call my lord Duke "his grace".'

'Yes. His grace said you could watch this afternoon. John won't mind.' And she ran away before her sister could pester her further.

It was unusual for the children to be given an afternoon off. Their régime was very strict, accounting for each hour of the day from rising to bedtime. When the trestle tables had been dismantled they gathered in the great hall, where there was a fire. Though the heat from the burning logs did not spread nearly as far as the smoke, it made a cheerful core to the big chamber. Tired from their morning exercise, the hounds nosed half-heartedly through the rushes in search of scraps, then turned round several times, curled up and went to sleep. Most of the boys, uncertain what to do with their leisure, did much the same, wandering about aimlessly before settling down for a lazy afternoon. The Duke, however, took charge of Anne and her sister, and wasted no time in setting up their entertainment. Squatting by the fire, John was prepared; his lump of wood was already cut into a rough pear-shape, and with the three other children ranged round him in a semicircle he began his demonstration.

Nobody said anything, although Isobel was only restrained by manners from asking what John was making. Anne was fascinated by every sliver of wood which flew from his dagger, warmed by the knowledge that it was all for her benefit. In her opinion no real baby could have been more beautiful than the poppet emerging from the block of elm wood.

It was nearly completed when out of the tail of her eye she caught a movement by the entrance. Three people were standing inside the leather curtain: Master Barton the chamberlain and two strangers well wrapped in furs. One was a girl in a widow's cap; the appearance of the other immediately drove Anne to take refuge behind her sister. He was a big man, and she knew at once that he was just the type of person who most frightened her; confident, assertive, like her father and King Edward, raking the hall with keen eyes which she hoped might miss her, but was sure would not. The apparition had an unexpected effect on John. Roused from his concentration by Anne's retreat, he sprang to his feet with a yelp and flung himself at the girl, who hugged him joyfully. Then the big man cuffed him, which John did not seem to mind at all. Peeping at them from behind Isobel's back, Anne wondered at their strange behaviour.

John led the newcomers over to the fire, and she was forced to emerge and face them. This was John's father – the girl was his sister Janet – and Anne remembered what Isobel had said about John being only a merchant's son; she did not look quite so superior now. For Master Wrangwysh considered himself the equal of anyone. Although he knelt and kissed their hands most correctly, there was no humility in his courtesy. When the

36

merchant advanced on Anne she would have run away had she had the strength; as it was, with his great hand engulfing hers, she very nearly fainted.

Not quite, because Richard of Gloucester was beside her, proffering the wooden baby which his friend had carved for her. He laid it in her arms, and it was still warm from John's grasp. The slight roughness of the wood was soothing, as soothing as Kat had been, and as the Duke guided her back to the fire and sat her down on a cushion, her fear subsided.

Soon Master Wrangwysh and his daughter departed to be presented to the Countess, and John borrowed back the poppet to finish it off before he went home to York for Christmas. The Duke had noted his elder cousin's covetous glances at it, and tactfully suggested that on John's return he should carve her a poppet as well. Isobel wavered between desire and pride. Pride won; she declared that she was much too old for poppets, and honour was satisfied all round.

Somehow that winter was not so cold for Anne as all the others she remembered. Snow, frost and rain pursued their dreary cycle, and she spent a large proportion of the time in bed, sniffling and coughing. Her toes and fingers and nose were always purple and numb. But there was New Kat to cuddle through her sickness, and there was the Duke of Gloucester to ask how she was.

John also talked to her sometimes, ducking his head respectfully, and she came to learn the names of the five other lads. The Duke had been supplanted at bottom of the class by Francis, Lord Lovel of Titchmarsh, better known to his contemporaries as Frank. He was a sturdy lad with a mop of yellow hair that did not seem to know which way to grow. His slow progress was not due to lack of ability but to the faraway look in his wide-set eyes. What he could do superbly was to play the lute, and it was this, and the composition of new lyrics to sing to it, that took him away from the tiltyard. Robert Percy, who came from the Border, scoffed at the wayward musician and said that the only instrument for a man was the pipes. Since, when challenged, he proved not to be able to play them, his argument lost its force and there was a fight instead. These were the squabbles inevitable in a litter of hound puppies. In general they were a happy band. As the Duke's acknowledged partner and protégée, Anne found herself accepted by them without question.

In the first mild spell of the spring Richard took her up to the old castle. She sat contentedly on the central mound, nursing New Kat, the sharp scent of blackthorn flowers drifting past her nostrils, and watched her guide marching round purposefully to investigate. After the survey he came to sit beside her, breathing quickly. For some time he ran on about his discoveries and she listened attentively, liking the brave sound of the long words he used. Then they fell silent and looked down on the newer castle where they lived, which squatted comfortably in its nest of small houses. Years later it seemed to Anne that she had spent most of her life at Middleham sitting on the slope of the earthworks, with Richard beside her drawing a piece of grass through his teeth, the sloe blossom creaming the bushes and speckling the grass. Only the occasional blink of red as the Neville standard stirred in the slight breeze; otherwise everything was green and brown and blue, the river in its valley an errant ribbon of the sky, and the buds shiny on the trees.

Nevertheless Richard was away sometimes for long periods, and it was difficult for her afterwards to recall Middleham when he was absent. She was too nervous of stumbling to dance with anyone else, and Isobel, who was generally amiable when the Duke of Gloucester was present, tended to scold. Her most memorable moment, Richardless, was the arrival of the first letter she had ever received, complete with pendent seal. And her pride in the letter was increased by her ability to make out, in the Duke's own handwriting, the resounding greeting: 'To our right well-beloved and noble cousin the Lady Anne.' Isobel would not speak to her for days afterwards.

Yet even in the security of the fortress in Wensleydale she could not fail to hear of outside events. As she grew older she was able to connect them together more readily and begin to understand why it was that her father was the greatest man in England. On his brief visits to his family, the Earl of Warwick was generally on his way to or from a victory over the Lancastrians. King Edward was firmly on his throne in London, but the terrible Queen Margaret would not quite relinquish her hold on England. Time and again the Border fortresses fell into her hands, and time and again King Edward's champion marched north to wrest them away from her. Anne could not help resenting a little, on her father's behalf, the way in which the King took his ease in the south and left to his mentor the endless toil of safeguarding the kingdom. But this was one case in which her cousin Richard did not agree with her. If he worshipped Warwick, turning quiet and unobtrusive to the point of invisibility in his presence, he idolised his eldest brother. When he rode off one Christmas to join Edward in Durham, he burned with such eagerness that Anne knew a pang of jealousy; he had never turned a gaze of such intensity on her. And when he came back, months later, he talked of nothing but the King for days. He had quickly discovered that Anne did not share his enthusiasm, and set about with great patience to explain Edward's policy.

'My brother has already proved himself a leader in war. Now he leaves it to us to keep England safe while he learns to rule it in peace.' She could tell that he was repeating words that the King himself had spoken to him, although she could not picture the glittering royal jester saying anything so serious. Did he never make fun of the Duke of Gloucester? she wondered; she would have thought that her grave companion would have shied away from his boisterous sense of humour even as she had.

But she was forced to accept Richard's admiration of his brother, despite her inability to understand it. It was that, she came to realise, which swayed his life. He once let fall the remark that at the age of ten Edward had been able to wield a full-sized battleaxe, and another time that he had fought his first battle, with Warwick beside him, when he was thirteen. There was such a world of longing in Richard's face as he spoke that she comprehended the reason for all his secret exercise.

It was paying off. Instead of lagging behind the other henchmen he was fast overhauling the best of them. He had always been good on a horse; the animal seemed to respond without reserve to the will of its young rider. Now he had discovered the trick of balance and timing which served him better than brute strength, and he could handle a sword and bow with confidence. At the gentler arts of dancing and music he remained awkward. Apparently, matching his brother in grace and courtliness was not one of the goals he had set himself.

But Richard's devotion was due for its first test. In the year of Anne's eighth birthday Warwick went to France to conduct negotiations for the King's marriage. News came infrequently to the castle when the Earl was not there, and it was a particularly peaceful summer for the household, unruffled by several skirmishes farther north which disposed of the last Lancastrian resistance. The children were playing nine-men's-morris in the outer bailey on an evening in September. It had been a cloudless day and not much energy was left for the game. Between turns the boys sprawled on the grass; Anne wished that her nurse had not made her wear a linen pinafore. The page sprinting through the postern from the castle broke into their indolence. He was a pretty, round child, whom Anne distrusted because he never looked straight at her, and he was very excited.

'The King is married,' he blurted, without any of the formalities due to the lordlings he was addressing.

'Married? Who to?' It was Robert Percy who confronted him, standing squarely before him with arms akimbo. Laziness forgotten, the others were all sitting bolt upright.

'To a Lancastrian widow, sire.' The page caught up on his courtesies with satisfaction at the effect of his announcement. There was a shout of protest from the henchmen, Yorkist to a boy. Above it rose Robert's voice again, gruff with coming maturity.

'My lord will never allow it. When he comes home—'

'He is home, sire.' The page was swelling visibly. 'And he's given his approval. Though it's said he's not best pleased.'

There was a vigorous chorus of agreement with the Earl of Warwick's sentiments, but it died away as Richard stepped up to the messenger and asked very quietly, 'Is this true?'

'Oh yes, your grace. Master Barton told me in confidence and he spoke to my lord's own man, who's come direct from Reading to my lady.' The revelation of his source of information rather spoilt the gratifying reception from his betters. Derisory remarks about Master Barton's lap-dog started to fly, for the chamberlain's sudden fondnesses were a standing joke. Uncertain of how to regain their attention, the child launched into a description of the council meeting at Reading where King Edward had announced to his astounded peers his four-month-old secret marriage to Lady Elizabeth Grey. Several of the henchmen continued to scoff, and two went off for a private tussle over one of the morris pieces. The nine-minute wonder was passing when Isobel pushed to the front of the group and slapped the page across the face.

'How dare you tell such lies!' she said in a hard shrill voice. 'It's a wicked falsehood and I don't believe it!' To the consternation of all she burst into tears. The Lady Isobel in tears caused almost as much of a sensation as the news of the King's marriage. Attendants converged on her with kerchiefs, the page fled snuffling with bright red marks on his cheek, and the boys were all talking at once.

Except for the Duke of Gloucester. Anne had been watching him ever since the name of his brother had been tossed into the lazy evening. Apart from the one question he had taken no part in the vigorous crowd reactions, standing among the irregular patterns of the nine-men's-morris with his head thrown up, listening intently. As Isobel staged her scene, he turned and walked away. Anne followed him. He made for the stables, and putting an arm briefly round the neck of his own bay gelding he climbed the ladder to the loft and sat on the edge of the new hay, dangling his legs. When his cousin appeared at the top of the ladder, a little puffed from the effort of scrambling up in a long kirtle, he turned his head but said nothing. Anne saw no invitation in his face, but neither did she see rejection. Crawling clumsily into the hay she sat down beside him. He did not move for a long time, staring down at the polished stone he had carried away from the game, his lips compressed into a thin straight line. Anne waited, feeling for his mute distress, yet content to be able to share it. The rich open-air scent of the hay was all about them, pricked through with the sharper odour of the horses. It was nothing to her whether Edward married a Lancastrian widow or the Empress of Cathay, but it was terribly important to Richard.

'Why didn't he tell him?' he muttered at last, and she understood at once that it was not so much the act itself that

41

upset Richard, but the King's deceit in concealing it. When he seemed to be finding no solution to his query, she ventured what was to her the most logical explanation.

'Perhaps he was afraid of what my lord would do.' The Duke threw her a glance which was distinctly hostile; she wished she had held her tongue.

'My brother is afraid of nothing,' he said stiffly. Then he saw her biting her lip, and added with almost a smile, 'It takes a brave man to cross my lord your father.' Back in favour, Anne resolved to make no more helpful remarks. 'But to take a Lancastrian queen. . . .' Richard went on, talking to himself, and for the first time Anne felt a flicker of fearful involvement. Had they just rid themselves of one monster queen to acquire another? Following her own timorous train of thought, she remained aware that beside her the Duke of Gloucester was trying to square the King's behaviour with the image he kept of him. Finally he looked up with a short sigh. 'It must be for the peace. The King told me he wanted no more battles, but to win people by love. So he's shown the way by marrying a Lancastrian himself. After all, we've had enough of French queens, and this one is English.' Thus far he was sure of himself, but anxiety was creeping in. 'Maybe he didn't think my lord would understand, after fighting Lancaster for so long.' His voice trailed off, almost on a question, and his mouth tightened again. Anne knew she must say something to set his mind at rest.

'But he understands now. That the King did it for the best.' She was not sure that it was for the best, but she had chosen the right words this time. In a rare spontaneous gesture, Richard put his hand on her arm. His face relaxed.

'Yes. Yes, whatever he does must be for the best. He would never do anything wrong.' Without further delay he stood up, and helped Anne to her feet. 'Come, we must finish the game.' He saw her solicitously down the ladder, but he did not forget to clap his horse on the rump as they passed its stall. Outside in the levelling sunshine John was loitering, haloed with a golden cloud of mosquitoes.

'They're all looking for you. I said I'd find you.'

'How is the Lady Isobel?' asked Richard.

'Better, I think. But she has gone to her chamber.' Anne's

conscience tweaked her; she had not thought of her sister since leaving her.

'I'm afraid she's suffered a sad disappointment,' the Duke said, and flicked a mosquito off his neck. He made back to the nine-men's-morris while Anne and John fell in behind.

Although at the time she had not guessed, as Richard had, why Isobel had taken the news so badly, Anne was not left in the dark. Long ago, it seemed, when they were still at Warwick, their father had promised that she should be Queen. Anne had forgotten – or perhaps had never noticed – but Isobel remembered. For three years she had cherished her hope, even in the fastness of Wensleydale, even against the Earl's forays into France after a French wife for King Edward. And now, loudly and ceaselessly, she mourned its passing. She told her attendants about it as they dressed her, she complained to her mother at table, and kept Anne awake at night. In vain they conjured up streams of powerful young lords as alternative suitors; Isobel was inconsolable.

She remained so until, late in October, Warwick returned to Middleham. The usual buzz of activity heralding his approach woke up the somnolent household, to the extent of changing the rushes in the solar and great chamber – unprecedented at that time of year. Even in peacetime his train looked more like an army than a great lord's retinue, but it was bright enough with Neville pennants and devices. The Earl rode a glossy grey stallion, which turned out to be a present from the King. The narrow inner ward between gatehouse and keep did not seem large enough to contain them.

The next day a message came to the nursery: the Earl wished to see his daughters privately, in the solar, one after the other. Isobel departed, pale but brave, and Anne was left quaking in the hands of the attendants, who had already fussed around her for an hour and would not let well alone. They were like flies worrying at her when she needed all her concentration to keep her hands from trembling and her mind from her great terror; that he would send her away from Middleham. Hours of suspense seemed to drag by before Isobel came back, her customary tragic expression radiant.

43

'You are to go now,' she said, as though speaking from a different element.

'What is it? What did he say?' Anne found the voice to whisper.

'Oh, I can't tell you. It's a matter of state. I had to take a solemn oath not to speak of it.' Not attempting to probe further, Anne hitched up her kirtle and set off on the long walk to the keep, plunged even deeper into apprehension by her sister's joy.

This was the first time she had set foot in her father's solar, the holy of holies beyond the great chamber where he normally gave audiences. The fragrance of the fresh rushes came to her as the squire ushered her in, and she was grateful for it because it made her think of outdoors and spring. Her father, in a long russet velvet gown, was striding about the room; she had never known him to sit down except at mealtimes. Behind him the red and white bedhangings, still crumpled from travelling, sprang out of the shadows, and the Countess, in a carved chair, merged into the gloom.

Anne fell to her knees, and the Earl's hand descended on her bowed head, weighing heavily for a moment before he removed it and told her to rise. As she obeyed him she looked into his face, which she did rarely enough to be disturbed at what she saw. His forehead was deeply ridged, and the cropped hair rubbed away at the temples by constant wearing of a helmet. His mouth bore a faint formal smile which did not reach the eyes, and over all was that vague disappointment which was always there when he looked at her, and which always gave her a sense of rejection. For a long time he surveyed her without speaking further and she could not help, despite her resolution, squirming a little under the critical gaze. When he did speak, it was to the Countess.

'Has the child no becoming gowns? That stuff drains all the colour out of her.' Anne was wearing her best dark blue costume, with a high tight waist that restricted her breathing. Her mother said something in a muffled tone about leaving the children's gowns to the Master of the Wardrobe.

'Then dismiss him. And see that Master Barton orders a length of sky-blue velvet for her. That should bring out what light there is in her hair.' The Countess agreed, and Anne felt guilty on her behalf and on that of the Wardrobe Master, who had spent a great deal of effort on the fitting and sewing of her scorned and uncomfortable garment. Warwick returned to his scrutiny, rubbing his knuckle across his teeth.

'And how is her health these days?'

'She has been well enough this summer, my lord. But winter usually indisposes her.'

'Hmm. She doesn't look very robust.' He threw an accusing glance over his shoulder at his wife, who coughed deprecatingly. 'Well, but neither is he.' At last the searching eyes swooped down to meet Anne's. 'What do you think of your cousin the Duke of Gloucester, child?'

'He is my good and loving lord, sire,' murmured Anne. They were the first words that came to her disordered mind in the shock of the question. How could she possibly describe to anyone, least of all her father, what Richard meant to her? She did not know herself, except that she could not remember what life had been like without him. But the Earl had taken her faintness for lack of enthusiasm.

'Is that all?'

She could summon up no more sense for the wild entreaty that was filling her head, 'Don't send me away, please, don't send me away!' Somehow she did not say it, only shaking her head and staring at her father's golden suede shoes with their long soft points.

'Then you must study to like him better. It is my wish!' His tone was pleasant, almost jocular, but it was none the less a command. Unable to grasp his meaning, Anne memorised the phrases and stored them away to examine later, when she was less confused. Once more she was on her knees, perhaps because there was dismissal in the air, perhaps because her legs would hold her up no longer. 'You're old enough, my daughter,' he said as she kissed his square fingers, 'to be discreet. Keep my counsel.'

The sky-blue gown, which was ready by Hallowmas, was beautiful; too grand for her, Anne thought, gingerly smoothing the bodice. The hem and neck were embroidered with seed-pearls, and there was a coif to match. She wore them on the feast-day with her hair loose instead of plaited. It made her feel grown-up and very self-conscious, especially after the Earl gave her a curt nod of approval in passing. There had been none of the expected jealousy from Isobel, who had no new gown; since the interview with her father she had existed on an exalted plane, noticing Anne even less than usual. And so, apart from the Earl, only her cousin Richard acknowledged the addition to her wardrobe. He did not say much. On the way into chapel for mass he had glanced at her with unwonted animation, caught her eye and smiled. Later on, escorting her into dinner, he simply said, 'It's very pretty,' and squeezed her hand. That pleased her more than a dozen flowery compliments from anyone else would have done.

Moreover it was, she supposed, fulfilling her father's orders. Every night she brooded over what he had told her, and had come to the conclusion that Warwick was trying to make amends to the King for his ill humour over the marriage by special consideration towards his brother. Certainly the Earl himself was showing favour to the Duke of Gloucester, singling him out for attention from the other henchmen, letting his hand rest familiarly on Richard's shoulder, applauding his efforts at the quintain. Embarrassed and a little dazzled, Richard submitted. As for Anne, she was at a loss how to carry out her instructions. She did not see that she could increase her liking for her cousin by studying, when her Latin and French lessons were conducted quite separately from his, and seemed to bear no relation to him anyway. They were perhaps thrown together a little more than usual, but nobody remarked upon it. He did not change towards her, so she behaved as before, and was thankful. His companionship was all she wanted.

The winter came, and she retained no memory of it afterwards except that Richard had been there all the time. Christmas was spent in York, turning the priory in Lendel where they lodged into anything but a quiet devotional retreat. And hard on the heels of the mummers and figgy pudding and the slippery journey back to Wensleydale came spring. Already in March there was expectancy in the air; the slim brown branches of the trees stood very still, as if waiting to burst suddenly into life; the cry of new lambs reached Anne's ears at night from the pens on the hill. But the draught under the door of the Countess's chamber was still icy. With her feet under the brazier, Anne was blowing on her mittened fingers between stitches when Richard came to her. His fur cap was pulled down over his ears, but his face was warm enough for midsummer. The Countess's ladies moved their stools away from the brazier with reluctance, although he did not really notice them. To Anne he said, 'The King has sent for me.' She had learned by now to show pleasure for his sake even when she did not feel it. 'He wants me to be with him and George in London.' George was his second brother, the Duke of Clarence, and another of his heroes.

'Will it be for very long?' Anne tried to sound casual and delighted.

'Oh, yes. I've finished my training now. There are duties for me to take up; it will be for good.'

For the King's good, perhaps, and possibly for Richard's good, but not for hers. Not allowing the significance of his sentence to sink in, she asked, 'When will you be going?'

'Next month. There are arrangements to be made first. John and Frank and Rob are going with me.'

Anne took another stitch in her embroidery, stuck the needle in her finger, and did not wince. 'I'm very pleased,' she said, and wished he would go before she cried.

'Yes. I told you first. I thought you'd want to know.' For a second, distant concern dimmed the brightness of his face. She quickly ducked her head so he should not see her trembling lips. 'I have to tell the others,' said Richard a little apologetically, and he went away, walking on air. Outside a thrush was shouting into the milky sky. Anne stared down at the half-finished popinjay she was working. The vivid colours quivered and blurred in a maze of tears.

If winter had passed quickly, the days of March fled by. It was no use trying to hold them back; as soon stand in a swift river and try to stem the current with one's fingers. At first Richard made it worse by talking constantly of 'When I am in London' and of how slowly the time was passing. But Anne could not disguise her unhappiness from him, and as soon as he realised its cause he stopped. There was still an air of contained excitement about him; when he was with the elect among the henchmen she could see it from afar, possessing them all; yet with her he was as he had always been, quiet, considerate, speaking about the things that interested them both. Only when he went back to his companions did she see that it was a sham, and feel betrayed by his very kindness.

The imminent departure of the Duke did not ruffle the routine of Middleham and required no major upheaval as when the Earl was moving on. His few possessions and those of his followers would fit into the saddlebags of their horses. He would have gone without ceremony had not a troupe of French musicians been passing through Yorkshire in April, on their way to King James's court in Edinburgh. Warwick invited them to break their journey in Wensleydale, and in return for his hospitality they performed in the great chamber after supper. While the other henchmen squatted in the rushes, Richard was given the chair on the Earl's left, and although his wife was at his other hand Warwick's attention was all for the Duke. Anne, who was on a cushion at their feet, could catch little of the conversation, but she knew that her father had never been so gracious or so relaxed.

The pure boneless voice of the singer picked its way among the French words and the weaving notes of the recorder, and Warwick's voice murmured on. One phrase she heard, in the pause between two chansons: 'Remember, my dear cousin, that it is I who am your good lord. That will not change.' Afterwards he made a special point of introducing the leader of the musicians to the Duke. 'I met him in the service of the dauphin before he became king, your grace. Among other wonderful works, King Louis has made French music supreme in Christendom – and only the Burgundians dispute it!' The Frenchman touched the bow of his viol to his heart and smiled modestly.

'My master could not wish for praise from more exalted lips, monseigneur,' he said in remarkably good English.

'Know Bertrand de Josselin again, my lord,' Warwick said to Richard. 'He is worth the acquaintance.' And in an access of geniality the Earl conducted de Josselin into his solar for a private cup of wine.

The lesser mortals were left to their own devices; Anne watched the household dispersing to its evening duties or recreation, the musicians wrapping up their instruments with loving care and chattering lazily in a rapid birdlike tongue. A fragment of melody was running through her head. When she tried to hum it, it melted away and returned to her imagination in the unreal voice of the French singer. Richard touched her shoulder and said, 'Will you come up to the old castle after mass tomorrow morning?'

The elusive tune still haunted her as she mounted the grassy slope with her cousin the next day. The rising sun threw long spidery shadows across the mound, glittering on the frost and turning it to dew. On the highest hillock he spread his cloak for them to sit on. Breathless from the ascent they rested and stared out over the valley, hazy and indistinct in the early light. It was three years since they had first come here, on that day when the blackthorn was dropping white petals over the ancient earthworks. And although they had been many times in the interim, at all seasons, the years seemed to telescope and make the first day only yesterday. Down there Warwick's standard still hung limply against the flagstaff on the keep; his men-at-arms were still pacing the battlements, the Ure still reflecting the sky. But the day after tomorrow was St Mark's Day, and the Duke of Gloucester was leaving for London.

'What is it you're singing?'

'They played it last night. It won't come right.'

'Yes, I've heard it before. At Westminster, I think. It's a popular song at court, although most of the King's musicians are from Burgundy, not France. I can't sing it either.' The tune had broken their silence, and the taboo on talk of London. 'Anne, I will come back. My brother needs me in the south, but my duties are bound to bring me to Yorkshire sometimes.'

'Will they? Really?'

'And I'll write to you. My lord your father has promised to stand my friend always, and he said that I might.'

'My father?' It was hard to believe that the Earl had actually spoken of her to Richard.

'Yes. He's sorry I'm going. He would have wished me to stay longer, because there are other things to be learned.' The question was on Anne's lips before he crushed her faint hope. 'But I must obey the King. He is my liege lord, you see.' Anne nodded. King Edward's summons, for his youngest brother, was like a call from God.

'You've been waiting for it, haven't you?'

'Yes, for a long time. I only hope I'm worthy of it.'

'Of course you are,' Anne assured him warmly.

'And of you.' Richard turned his attention from the landscape and the future to his cousin. Reaching inside his shirt, he drew something over his head and held it out to her. 'This is for you.' It was an oval pendant, swinging from his hand by a slender gold chain. She hesitated, watching the sunlight trickling up and down the fine links; people so rarely gave her things that she was at a loss as to what to do or say. A little diffidently, Richard pushed his gift closer. Still she did not take it, but glanced from his face to the magic he held between his fingers in a confusion of doubt and wonder. Suddenly he leaned towards her and slipped the chain round her neck, then sat back to wait for her reaction. Anne touched the pendant with reverence; it was warm from his body. Thus encouraged she bent to examine it properly, and the uncertainty in her eyes was wholly chased away by the wonder.

Round the edge were tiny pink and white gems which blinked at her in a friendly way. There was a blue T-shaped cross on a gold ground, and in the centre a miniature golden bird's nest complete with fledgelings. It was more delicate and pretty than any piece of jewellery she had ever seen, and it was hers. Hearing her soft contented sigh, Richard released his own breath.

'Oh, Richard, it's . . . too beautiful.' He could not remember her having called him by name before, and obscurely it touched him as much as her pleasure in his gift.

After a moment he said, 'I had it made specially. This is the cross of St Anthony, and I've chosen him as my saint.'

'Then I shall pray to him for you, all the time you're away. This will remind me.'

'I hoped it might.' Now it was he who hesitated, shy of the next thing he wanted to say. But innocently Anne gave him his cue.

'All these little stones! And I do like the birds in their nest.' With her fingernail she traced round the engraving.

'Do you know what that is for?'

'The bird's nest?' She shook her head, but then something occurred to her. 'In the chapel there's a window. In the glass our Blessed Lady's mother is carrying a nest. There are four baby birds in it, and I think they must be very hungry because their mouths are open. Perhaps holy St Anne should have left it in the tree.' This was the sort of reflection that often ran through her head during mass; she would not have spoken them aloud to anyone else. On this occasion, however, her cousin was not really following her.

'That's why it's on your pendant. For St Anne.' He regarded her closely, to make sure she had understood. The blush rose slowly to her cheeks, and Richard sprang to his feet and made off down the mound, whistling a tuneless version of the French melody.

For a while Anne was so immersed in her joy that she could not imagine why she had ever been sad. So he had not betrayed her. When she had thought him totally occupied with his chosen future as the servant of his King, he had been secretly planning her solace. The ache of his leaving was filtering through again, but she knew he had done the best he could to soften the blow. She was even now not certain what he meant by binding them together in their patron saints, but the promise was there in the reality of the small enamelled pendant.

When he appeared again a few minutes later he brought a fistful of treasures which he laid in her lap – a red spotted toadstool, a pigeon's feather, a polished yellow celandine flower. It was a ritual from the early days; he had outgrown the jackdaw instinct, but he kept it up because she appreciated the offerings. A dusty corner of the nursery was piled with dead leaves and odd pebbles she had stored there. At this reminder of a dying past she wept, and he put his arm round her until she stopped.

'You're cold,' he said. 'Come on, let's walk.' And he took her by the hand round their stronghold to say goodbye.

She hardly spoke to him after that. There were the formalities of two days' routine to be carried out, and the leavetaking on the drawbridge at dawn on St Mark's Day. But despite the little private smile that Richard gave her as they embraced, his mind was back on his destiny. As he led his cavalcade of excited boys down the hill, she could tell that he had no regrets about riding out of his childhood. The red-and-gold of the labelled royal arms of England fluttered proudly above him; only at the rear of the procession did a man-at-arms carry the bear and ragged staff of Warwick. Inside a box by her bed the pendant of St Anthony and St Anne lay hidden from everyone's eyes but her own; yet in that bitter moment she knew that she had lost him to King Edward.

3

WEDDING AT CALAIS

Only one incident penetrated the barrenness of that first summer without Richard. It seemed to trouble nobody else, but it did nothing to lighten her loneliness. On a windless evening in July she overheard a remark dropped by a gentleman to one of her mother's ladies.

'You hear they've taken the old mad King?'

The lady shrugged. 'I wonder the Frenchwoman let him so far out of her sight.' That was all, and although Anne listened harder than usual to the casual gossip of the castle she could learn no more. There was no Richard to ask, and the henchmen she knew best had gone with him to London and been replaced by strangers. So she went back to the old condescending source of information.

'Why bother about him?' asked Isobel, who spent much of her time hob-nobbing with the younger attendants about the fashion in gowns.

'Please tell me what's happened,' persisted Anne, made bold by anxiety.

'King Henry has been captured, that's all.'

'And what ... what will they do to him?'

'I don't know. Shut him up or do away with him, I suppose.'

'But what harm has he done? He's – he was *kind*.' She could remember little of King Henry besides the long gentle hands soothing a frightened bird, yet she was sure that he deserved protection and not punishment.

'He's crazed in his wits and he has no throne,' said Isobel sharply. 'He's no good to anyone. Now do go away. Our father wouldn't be pleased to hear you defending a man he's been fighting for years.' With which rebuke she returned to a discussion on hennins.

There was nothing Anne could do. She considered writing to Richard to use his influence with his brother, but although he faithfully wrote once a month she had no means of communication except his messenger, who had gone two weeks ago. Taking refuge in the chapel from her first taste of politics, she gravitated towards the window where St Anne and St Joachim were rearing the Blessed Virgin. With some vague idea that King Henry and St Anne both loved birds, she prayed to her patroness to keep him safe.

The saint could not keep him from the Tower, but with some relief Anne learned that the old King had been placed in the Earl of Warwick's custody. Her father was a stern man, yet she was convinced he would not harm an innocent or helpless person. When he next visited Wensleydale she longed for the courage to ask him how King Henry fared. But Warwick had more congenial matters on his mind than the health of his nominal prisoner. His brother George, Anne's youngest uncle, had just been raised to the Archbishopric of York, and he was not one to waste the opportunity of displaying to England at large and the North in particular that the Nevilles still held the ascendant in the kingdom. There was much coming and going of Neville uncles and cousins on the business of planning a great feast during the winter in honour of the Archbishop's installation. Representatives of all the leading families were invited and it was through the question of the King's deputy that Anne found out what Isobel had been hugging to herself since that private interview with her father. They did not often talk in bed, but on this occasion Isobel could hardly wait for their attendant to snuff the candles and fumble her way into the cot across the doorway before she thumped her sister on the back and hissed, 'Are you asleep?'

Anne had been on the verge of it. 'What is it?' She moved Kat back to its proper position under her chin.

'Something very important. Not even our lady mother knows yet, but I must tell someone.' In spite of herself Anne was awake; her sister had not shared a confidence with her before. 'Can you guess who the King is sending to the Archbishop's feast?' For a wild moment Anne thought it might be the Duke of Gloucester, but the light died as she realised that Isobel would not consider him important.

'No. Who?'

'Why, the Duke of Clarence himself!' Isobel's whisper shook with emotion.

'Oh. That will be a great honour.' Anne could not imagine why her sister should be so affected.

'A great honour! Of course it is. But the main thing is – that we shall meet at last. After all these months of negotiation, our father has arranged it. Oh, Anne,' her low voice became ardent, 'they say that next to King Edward he's the handsomest man in England. And he is richer than anyone else – except for the crown and our father, of course.' Anne was beginning to understand. 'Do you think he's afire to see me?' It was a rhetorical question. 'But naturally, he must be – I dare swear it's he who persuaded the King to let him come. Any bridegroom would yearn to see a bride who is Warwick's daughter.'

So in place of the first gentleman in the land Isobel had been offered the second. She had subsided into blissful silence, but abruptly she reached out and clutched Anne's naked arm, digging in her fingernails. 'That is a deadly secret, and if you speak of it to a living soul, God will strike you down where you stand.' Anne could not suppress a frightened whimper at the unexpected violence. At once her sister released her and said, 'Forgive me, Anne, I didn't mean to hurt. But I'm under oath not to tell of my marriage, and now you're party to it as well. It's a dreadful thing to break one's word, and I had to warn you of what could happen if you did.' Caressing her smarting arm, Anne wondered why telling her sister had not broken Isobel's word; no doubt that was an adult sophistication beyond her comprehension.

Isobel's daydream remained unfulfilled. The Duke of Clarence was not coming after all; the King's representative would be Richard of Gloucester. She was too downcast to be envious of Anne, who was left to enjoy her quiet anticipation in peace. The banquet was to be given at the Archbishop's palace of Cawood, which involved a long day's journey from Middleham through torrential rain. Inevitably Anne caught a cold, and by the morning of the feast she had developed fever as well.

In the chilly chamber where they dressed she shivered and

tried to breathe through a stuffed nose, uninspired by the twittering excitement around her. She was laced into a new gown of cloth-of-silver with hanging sleeves, and the white brocade cote, cut away at sides and hem to display the kirtle, was slipped over her throbbing head. Isobel, in cloth-of-gold, was arranging her long honey-blond hair carefully over her shoulders and the gentle swelling of her low-cut bodice. As they twisted a silver filigree net round her head Anne looked down resignedly at her own flat chest. She would have preferred a high neckline, not only for its practical warmth, but because then she could have worn her pendant and nobody would have known. After a debate with herself the night before, thinking with difficulty between battles for breath, she had decided to leave the jewel in the box she had carefully brought from Middleham. The risk of being questioned and laughed at outweighed the possibility that Richard might notice her wearing his token and be pleased. So a red and silver Neville saltire hung round her neck instead. Richard did not need to be reminded. Although she had thought of little but his return since leaving Wensleydale, now she was not looking forward to seeing him at all. Wretchedly aware that her feverish flush was accentuated by the white purity of her gown, she wanted only to go to bed. At any other time she would probably have been encouraged to do so, but she knew better than to ask to be excused. This was an occasion when the entire family must stand together, presenting a mighty and united front to the world. Even an insignificant gap in the ranks would be deplored today. Wiping her eyes on a crumpled square of linen, Anne prepared to do battle for the family name.

The tables which ran the length of the great hall were overflowing with dishes. Every possible variety of fish, flesh and fowl jostled for pride of place, and rising above them were the fantastic towers and pinnacles of the subtleties, which Anne normally loved for their sugary ingenuity. Round the tables, packed as tightly, were rows and rows of people, as diverse as the food, the head-dresses as elaborate as the subtleties. Torches and beeswax candles flickered everywhere, and in the hearths at each end of the hall huge fires were blazing. After the unheated passages the wave of hot air, strong with sweat and roast meat and smoke, was like a physical blow. The sight of the vast assembly and the assault on Anne's aching head almost overwhelmed her; she knew nothing of her progress to the high table. They were the last to take their places, after a reverence to their host on the way.

Anne had seen her uncle George before, though not in such splendour; she took in little beyond the remembered impression of smoothness: smooth fair hair under the jewelled mitre, a long face with smooth cheeks and a smooth smile. And beside him, almost hidden behind a confection of the keys of St Peter cunningly superimposed upon the Neville arms, was the Duke of Gloucester. Her eyes fastened on the familiar figure as a rock in the swaying sea of strange colours and shapes. Yet not quite familiar. This Richard was not the Earl of Warwick's henchman; he was the King's brother and deputy, and he sat at the Archbishop's right hand in all the authority of a guest of honour. Although she fancied that a gleam of recognition lightened his grave expression as he saw her, her momentary pleasure was gone. Wedged between her other uncle and a cousin, Anne resumed her struggle for breath. A succession of silver platters heaped with expensive delicacies were placed before her and removed untouched; she was concerned only with the tide of suffocating heat which beat continually in her face, and the insidious draught that slid down the back of her gown. The chatter and clatter of the distinguished multitude came to her as a muffled roar, at once far away and unbearably loud. One voice detached itself from the surrounding din; her uncle John, the new Earl of Northumberland, was addressing her.

'You're not eating, niece. Is something troubling you?' There was a deep crease between his brows; he was a rough-cut version of his brother the Archbishop, and Anne was less nervous with him than with most members of her family.

'No, thank you, my lord.' Her own voice echoed from a great distance. 'I'm not hungry.'

'A pity, with such bounty to choose from,' he observed without censure, and returned to the shin of pork he was gnawing. Somewhere beyond him, Richard was dining, at his ease among his peers. By a strenuous effort Anne resisted the inclination to lay her head down among the crumbs and spilt sauce and give way to her misery. When at length the tables were cleared and stacked away, the interminable feast was followed by an interminable entertainment. Singers, tumblers, jugglers, mouthed and performed their antics, while a stream of grand personages mounted the dais to pay homage to Archbishop Neville. A few paid homage to his niece also, and she kept her back stiff and gave her hand to everyone who stooped before her, although their faces were only shimmering ovals of white swathed in swirling draperies. But one hand that grasped hers was different, and did not let go. Through the miasma she distinguished a pair of brown eyes peering at her.

'I'm sorry you're not well, Anne,' he said. She tried to rub away the mist with her free fist.

'I can't see you properly,' she admitted dolefully.

'You shouldn't be here. You ought to be in bed. I'll tell your mother.'

'No ... no, Richard.' She clung to him, forgetting the respect due to the King's deputy. 'I must be here. It's very important. Don't worry about me.'

'Very well, if you're sure. But I hoped you might enjoy the jugglers. You liked the ones in York last Christmas.' For a moment she saw him clearly, leaning towards her with the solicitude she remembered so well; an older Richard, whose voice had broken, but who had not forgotten her, or the strolling mountebanks who had diverted them in the priory in Lendel. She did not see him go, and nobody near had noticed anything but his grace of Gloucester saluting his cousin.

After the feast she was ill for a week, and was carried back to Middleham in a horse-litter. Apart from her own poor showing, however, the great event seemed to have been a success. It was still being discussed with complacency when summer came. The Earl of Warwick had stood sponsor at the font to the King's first child – a daughter, unfortunately, they said, and Anne felt sorry for poor little Princess Elizabeth. It was evident that, in peace or war, Edward could not do without his mightiest subject.

About midsummer the household was uprooted from Wensleydale and transported in a slow cumbersome caravan south to Warwick. It was for Anne a sickening re-enactment of that half-recollected journey northwards, but her sister scarcely complained at all. For once Anne knew the reason for her high spirits. Now that she had revealed the secret of her projected marriage, Isobel talked of it to her incessantly, presumably because there was nobody else in whom she could confide. They were moving closer to London, she explained, so that it would be easier for the Duke of Clarence to visit her.

'I expect there'll be a civic reception for him, and a procession through the town. And the King may well be with him. After all, I shall be his sister-in-law, and it's a long time since my lord our father entertained him.' Anne did not like the sound of it. But as it happened she had no cause to worry.

There was no procession, no civic reception, and certainly no King. The Duke came upon them unexpectedly and almost unannounced, one afternoon as the girls sat under the trees down by the Avon reading Boethius with their confessor. An attendant, wading through the long grass with difficulty in her voluminous kirtle, gasped out the news minutes before he appeared.

'Oh, my lady, his grace of Clarence is here, and my lord Earl, and he says we are not to incommode ourselves but to behave as if his grace were a private gentleman.' From the way the woman was behaving, hennin askew and cheeks scarlet, hands fluttering distractedly, she did not seem to have taken Warwick's advice to heart. Neither did Isobel. Springing to her feet with a small scream she began to revolve wildly, her fingers twisting before her.

'What shall I do, what shall I do? I'm not prepared to receive him. Anne, help me! Do I look terrible? I'm wearing no jewels, only my pearl brooch. What will he think of me, with my hair unbound?' Anne thought that her sister looked rather pretty in her confusion, the loose strands of blond hair floating in the breeze, but with hands as unsteady as the other two girls' she helped to brush the grass seed from Isobel's gown and to smooth her hair. The priest was on his feet too, standing irresolutely with the place still kept in *The Consolations of Philosophy*, no less perturbed than his pupils. They were still standing there, in an awkward tableau, when the Earl came into sight and strolled down the slope towards them, his guest beside him and no more than three gentlemen, who remained at a discreet distance, in attendance.

To Anne, George of Clarence had become as unreal, if not quite as menacing, as Queen Margaret. And so this tall apparition, advancing on them with long casual strides, had about him something of a walking nightmare. The illusion was heightened by what he carried: a great hunched bird-shape which rode easily on his fist. Although Anne knew perfectly well that it was a goshawk, such as she had seen countless times in the mews and flown by her father, her foreboding persisted. Her eyes lowered as she made her courtesy, she saw the pair of green-clad legs hasten their lazy pace and genuflect beside her.

'No, no, cousin. No kneeling, I implore you. It is I who have come to do homage.' Looking through her lashes Anne watched the Duke raise Isobel and press her hand to his lips. Her murmured reply was lost in a musical flurry of wings as the goshawk bated, disturbed by its master's sudden movement. 'Peace, Ganymede!' The Duke gentled the ruffled feathers of the falcon's breast, until it subsided into a faint jingling of the bells on its jesses. 'He's jealous of you, Lady Isobel. No doubt his namesake disliked Jupiter's attentions to the nymph Callisto so.'

'You must not flatter my daughter, your grace,' said Warwick indulgently, 'or I shall have to remind her of Callisto's fate.'

'If I recall, she was turned into a bear.' Clarence made a gesture of touching her cheek. 'That would be a most unlikely end for one as slender as my cousin.'

'Your grace is very kind,' said Isobel. Her self-possession was restored, and although her hair modestly concealed her face Anne could hear a little smugness in her voice.

Belatedly the Earl remembered his younger daughter, who was still kneeling in the grass. 'Your cousin the Lady Anne.'

'Ah, yes.' The Duke withdrew his attention from Isobel and came towards her. There was in him, she had quickly noticed, the likeness to King Edward that was so blessedly lacking in their youngest brother. She steeled herself for the embarrassing mockery she had endured from the King. But as she kissed his gloved hand his eyes, lighter blue than Edward's, flickered over her without interest. 'Lady, I am enchanted.' A polite smile touched his mouth as he brought her to her feet, and then he returned to Isobel. 'I was flying Ganymede in the Forest of

Arden, and found myself near your father's estates. Since I had heard that you were removed here, and have long cherished a desire to meet the illustrious Lady Isobel, I rode over on the chance that you were in residence.'

'A happy impulse, your grace,' remarked Warwick. 'We are most honoured by your presence. And the Lady Isobel, I suspect, more than honoured. I believe your wish to meet was not one-sided, eh, my child?' Isobel simpered. 'But if your grace would deign to excuse me, I have a pressing matter to attend to. May I leave my daughters to entertain you for a while?'

'Without any disrespect, my lord, I was wondering how I might contrive that very situation.' The Duke bowed towards the confessor. 'After all, we have Holy Church as our chaperon.' Holy Church, which had been wavering between disapproval of the improper classical allusions and deference to the distinguished visitor, came down on the side of the profane and beamed at the King's brother. With a gracious nod the Earl left them, taking in tow two of the loitering gentlemen. Clarence assisted both girls to settle back on to their tapestry cushions facing the river. Then, asking the priest for the loan of his book, he reclined on the grass in front of Isobel and proffered it to her. 'You would make me very happy, cousin, if you would read to me. I find great comfort in the pages of Boethius, and your voice would add to their inspiration.' Isobel demurred that she was a poor reader, but without much persuasion she yielded and took up the book.

It had not been false modesty. She pronounced the Latin without much regard for sense, stumbling several times over long words. The Duke, however, appeared to be listening with rapt attention, and the confessor followed his lead, apart from an involuntary grimace now and again at a particular mangling of the text. Having no need to please either her sister or her cousin, Anne did not feign interest. Idly she watched the great goshawk, crowned with the ludicrous tuft of feathers on its hood, turning its blind head sharply from side to side. Occasionally its master stroked its plumage or spoke a word to it; which was more than anyone did to her. She should have been grateful to be left in peace, especially after her fear that the Duke would take too much notice of her. Perversely she was not. The spectacle of his absorbed profile and Isobel's head bent demurely over her book left Anne outside and disconsolate. There was a pair of swans on the river with their family of half-grown cygnets. She followed their progress downstream, and forlornly compared the smooth Avon with the shallow rumpled waters of the Ure.

The tête-à-tête did not last long. A messenger from the Earl begged his grace to take some private refreshment with him before leaving, and Clarence leapt to his feet exclaiming at how late it was. Hastily, but with perfect courtesy, he took his leave of Isobel, promising to send her a copy of the *Canterbury Tales* of Chaucer, which she did not know. 'All the ladies at court have read them,' he had declared with a sidelong glance at the confessor. As an afterthought he kissed Anne as well, 'For she's my cousin too, cousin,' he said roguishly to Isobel. Then he strode away towards the castle, Ganymede bating excitedly at prospect of fresh sport.

Isobel slept little that night, and consequently so did Anne. Every word of the interview had to be rehearsed and commented on and Anne, her eyelids leaden with drowsiness, was called upon for a full contribution. Despite her own lack of enthusiasm for the Duke of Clarence she was glad for her sister's happiness, and had to admit that not only was he uncommonly handsome, but also already a most ardent suitor. But when Isobel had fallen at last into beatific slumbers, Anne lay staring into the darkness, the distant rush of the weir in her ears, and could not recall Clarence's face at all, but only the high curved beak of the goshawk, and the long talons gripping the leather gauntlet.

He came again several times, casually and without ceremony; Isobel was convinced that it was because he could not wait for formal meetings to be arranged. Under the influence of Chaucer's tales she was beginning to see herself as a heroine of courtly love, instead of the subject of a marriage alliance. She played and sang to him, and they went out riding on the Warwick estates. Anne was always with them, not so much tolerated as totally disregarded. But she became used to it, and as Isobel invariably recounted their conversation in full she did not miss much. The confidences were a burden, but rather a flattering one. Whenever she felt especially left out she crept into the bedchamber and pored over her pendant and Richard's latest letter.

And before long she had her compensation. The Earl and his family paid a visit to their kinsman the Archbishop at his manor of The Moor in Hertfordshire. This was within a short day's ride of London, and Isobel nursed high hopes of presentation at Westminster. Instead, Clarence came for a day's hunting, and brought Gloucester with him. As usual they had no notice of his coming, but were just walking their horses from the stable yard when a small party rode up at great speed to join them. There was much flourishing of caps and exclamations of surprise and the milling of people and horses; Anne had hardly time to register Richard's presence before he was alongside. Away ahead Warwick and his brother and elder daughter were listening raptly to the brilliant discourse of the Duke of Clarence; the leashed hounds were yelping and scrabbling in their impatience; Richard smiled and Anne smiled back, and they set off together.

When the view-halloo was given and the dogs streamed away down the hill they made little attempt to keep up with the pack. It was growing too hot for exertion, and by mutual consent they slowed their pace, dropping back from the other riders until, apart from a couple of attendants, they were alone. As the noise of the hunt faded, the peace of the high summer day flowed over them. The valleys of the Chilterns rippled with the gold of ripening crops and the sun drained the colour from the sky with its heat, so that the still green band of the beechwoods was a relief to the eye. They ate their dinner, produced from the saddlebag of Richard's unobtrusive squire, at the edge of a copse, sitting on a carpet of last year's leaves and looking down on the thatched roofs of a hamlet far below them in the hollow. The strips of cultivated land ran neatly in all directions, making an intricate pattern of varying shades from the cream of oats to the honey of wheat.

'It's like an arras,' said Anne. 'And the village is part of the design.'

'Look.' Richard pointed to two grazing cattle, tiny and motionless on their patch of green. 'On the common land beyond the church – tapestry cows!' Their game was spoiled by a man and his dog, crawling blackly along a chalky track to the village. 'Did you ever finish sewing your popinjay, by the by?'

'Yes, I gave it to one of my ladies as a wedding gift.' Brushing the crumbs of an eel pie from his thighs, Richard lay back on the dry leaves and crossed his arms behind his head.

'Frank is going to be married soon.'

'Is he?' She would have liked to ask his wife's name and when it was to be, for she was interested in Francis Lovel's welfare. But it did not seem the right time to talk of marriage, and she did not pursue it.

Her companion was squinting up at the filigree ceiling of beech leaves and azure sky through half-closed eyes. She returned to her contemplation of the somnolent valley. Out of earshot their attendants chatted quietly until, taking advantage of the inactivity, they fell asleep. The sun burned an arc across the sky and the shadows of the miniature cottages sidled lazily across the fields. Once or twice they spoke to each other, but it was unnecessary. They were complete without speech, as much here in the rolling farmland of the Chilterns as on the sparse dales of Yorkshire. When the sun began to turn to evening copper they rode leisurely back, falling in with the hunting party at the junction of two dusty bridle paths. Hounds, horses and riders were wilting from their exercise, and they had little to show for it, but the Duke of Clarence, fanning himself with his embroidered cap, was still talking. Nobody made any comment as the two truants joined them; Anne thought that perhaps their absence had not even been remarked.

A lavish supper awaited them. The Archbishop apologised for its simplicity, pleading lack of time for preparation; nevertheless there were ten courses, and cool gallons of wine from his cellars. Afterwards the two dukes disappeared with Warwick and his brother, and although both girls hoped that they would re-emerge they were still closeted at bedtime. Lying naked on their bed with the coverlet thrown back, Isobel languorously scratched her gnat bites and described the day's adventures. Tonight Anne was not listening. Her closed eyes were full of the sun, and her heart full of happiness.

Throughout the autumn Clarence continued to visit Warwick, and he was accompanied more than once by his younger brother. There was, however, no repetition of the day in the Chilterns, and the young Nevilles met the young Plantagenets only in company. Anne could not be quite easy with Richard in George's presence. He never ignored her, as Isobel did, but his allegiance was divided. Like her sister, he could not resist the allure of Clarence's conversation, and would sit mute for an hour, drinking in the stream of light witticisms from that gifted tongue. And there was a deeper reason for her disquiet, which she did not admit even to herself: a resentment of the elder brother's beauty, which threw the younger into shadow. Richard was so thin and sallow beside him, and each time she saw them together Anne felt a distant stab of that old compassion which had first drawn her towards the boy striving with the outsized sword at Middleham. But Richard with George was infinitely better than no Richard at all, and she willed herself into gratitude to Clarence for thinking of bringing him.

But after the beginning of Advent there were no more visits. The barrage of gifts and messages for Isobel ceased also. No explanation was forthcoming, either from the Duke or from Warwick. The first two weeks Isobel endured in hopeful anticipation; during the third she began to grumble half seriously to Anne about the inconstancy of suitors. By Christmas she was thoroughly piqued. The gift of a cask of rhenish to the Earl and his family from his grace of Clarence did not mend matters: there was no special mention of her in the greeting that came with it. Her nightly plaint to her sister grew more intense and sometimes tearful. The dearth of news drove her at Epiphany to the temerity of tackling her father about it. He had remained aloof throughout the festival, perhaps because the Countess was absent with a chill, but she chose a moment when, mellow from a recital of carols by his private choir, he should have been approachable.

'My lord, why is his grace neglecting me? Has anything happened?' Her back was very straight and her head up, but her voice trembled a little.

Warwick turned to her slowly, his eyebrows raised and his expression as distant as if he had never seen her before. 'That is no concern of yours, daughter,' he said coldly. Her defiant attitude crumpled. As if suddenly focusing on her, his face relaxed. 'The Duke has many duties. He cannot spend all his time a-courting. Hold your tongue, child, and be patient.' Backing away from him to her stool, she nearly tripped over her crimson train.

She sobbed long into the night, wetting Anne's pillow as well as her own. Her father had been telling her, she insisted, that George had tired of her and was looking elsewhere for a duchess. Anne did her best to offer comfort and assurance that she was mistaken. But she was nursing a quiet sorrow of her own which inclined her to join Isobel rather than to console her. There had been no word from Richard for six weeks. The monthly letter which had never failed since his departure from Yorkshire had not arrived, and he had sent her nothing at Christmas. What made it worse was her nagging sense of self-reproach. She had not lost sight of her father's admonition in the solar at Middleham. 'Study to like him better,' he had commanded, but she had not been able to change her feelings for Richard, had not known how. She had fallen short, and first he had left Yorkshire and now he had broken off contact. In some way Isobel too must have failed in her instructions and Warwick had taken steps to punish her also. Although she would not have dared stand up to their father as her sister had done, Anne took Isobel's advice to herself. If she held her tongue in patience, the Earl might relent.

Soon afterwards they moved back to Wensleydale, which threw Isobel deeper into despair. 'So far from London – how can he come even if he would!'

Clarence certainly did not materialise, but in February the Duke of Gloucester was reported to be coming north on official business. As the Earl left to join him in York he hinted that he might bring a guest back with him. Fortunately Anne did not raise her hopes too high, because he returned alone, briefly, before setting off himself for London. He brought a letter for Isobel from Clarence.

It set a pattern for the next two years. Although they saw neither of the royal brothers, Isobel received an occasional letter or gift; Anne heard nothing. At first her heart constricted when a messenger rode through the gatehouse, just in case he should be wearing the white boar of the Duke of Gloucester, but gradually her hopes died.

In her magnanimous moods – when George had just written to her – Isobel was sympathetic. 'It's probably because you're the younger daughter,' she offered helpfully, 'and his grace has thought better of it. The King's sister Margaret is betrothed to the new Duke of Burgundy. It wouldn't be fitting for their brother to marry beneath him.'

The pendant he had given her lay in its hiding place, and whenever she thought of it a faint voice of persistent loyalty assured her that Richard would not have deserted her of his own free will, that it was not in his nature to break a pledge. It made no difference; whatever the reason, she was alone.

Larger issues also were going awry. All was not well between King Edward and his greatest subject. Since his marriage Edward had been chipping away at the foundations of the privileged position occupied by the Earl who had given him his throne. Petty slights and the promoting of the Queen's grasping relatives at the expense of the Nevilles were followed by more serious affronts. The King with his own hands had taken the Great Seal away from Archbishop Neville. High indignation was voiced by Warwick's household about the rapaciousness of the Queen, who was evidently behind the whole policy, and in more discreet tones there were whispers about the ingratitude of the King. Warwick, of course, held aloof from the gossip, and appeared unperturbed by each fresh check to his dignity. But Anne noticed what others, busily mulling scandal, had probably missed: the men-at-arms were drilling more frequently, there were mutters of a rising in the far north, and whenever the Earl was in residence there were important strangers coming and going. Something was in the air, and in the chapel at Warwick, or in whichever of the Neville castles they were living at the time, Anne prayed that it would not happen. Especially under the stained glass picture of St Anne and St Joachim in Wensleydale she prayed also for Richard.

Anne's thirteenth birthday was approaching when Isobel had a message from her father which made her excited and secretive. Lately, in one of her periodic bouts of depression, there had been gloomy bedtime monologues about unmarried maidens dying of grief at seventeen. Anne expected early enlightenment on her change of mood, but there was nothing except pregnant hints and Isobel starting at every hurried footstep. This only fed her uneasiness. Rumours of an insurgent called Robin of Redesdale were growing louder, and the fact that he was on the Scottish border and they were at Warwick did not help.

It was to Warwick that the summons came, in the burly shape of their uncle Lord Fauconberg. Within an hour of his arrival the castle was alive with activity, and Anne was disturbed to hear that they were all leaving that same evening. Her immediate guess was that they were fleeing before the rebels, but the bustle was not that of panic. It was more stealthy than frightened, and Isobel, breathing 'At last, at last!' as she was dressed, told her that this was what she had been waiting for.

The sky was still pale green when they cleared the barbican and rode through the homegoing town. It was a small cavalcade with an escort of less than twenty men-at-arms, and intended to travel fast, since there was only one light chariot in case the Countess or one of her handful of ladies should need a respite. She and her daughters were mounted behind gentlemen of the household, and well wrapped against the dangerous night air, although it was as mild as a spring afternoon. Anne was happier on horseback than shut in when she was on the road, and despite the anxiety of an unknown destination there was something exhilarating about the steady rush of the horses along roads which wound into the night, barely reflecting the thin sliver of a moon that swam between the stars. On either side shouldered the companions of all her travels, the retainers in their bear and ragged staff livery, drained now to sable and argent. There was haste about them, but still no fear, and one or two of them sang softly as they rode. Catching a glimpse of Isobel where she clung to her horseman, one cheek pressed into his back, she saw that her bottom lip was caught between her teeth, her eyes wide and dark.

On the fifth night they reached Southampton, and Anne realised with great alarm that they were going to cross the sea. She had expected, and gathered that Isobel had too, that their father would be their destination. But there was only the sullen dark hulk of a ship by the quay, its skeleton masts and rigging wallowing against an overcast sky. The ladies were dismounted and handed over to the sailors, and half the men-at-arms turned their horses and clattered back the way they had come. At the top of the companionway Isobel drew back and whispered to the Countess, 'Is this necessary, madame? Could it not be done in England?'

'No, my daughter. We must do your father's bidding.' Isobel sighed and descended.

The crossing was a repetition of that earlier voyage and, owing to Anne's extreme tiredness, scarcely more distinct. But thanks to that same fatigue she slipped at length from the nightmare into a dream of a drowsy day in the country, relaxing to the easy rhythm of an ambling horse, or was it the branch of a beech tree, rocking above the lazy swell of the summer hills? Someone stood at the foot of the trunk, she knew, though she could not see, guarding her eyrie from the world of men. But the branch lurched violently, and she clutched at it to keep herself from falling into the ocean of leaves below, and it was Isobel, shaking her and saying, 'Wake up. We're here.'

'Where?' Snatched roughly from the cool green forest, Anne's bewilderment was complete.

'In Calais. Where I'm to be married.'

It was in Calais, the assertively English little outpost on the borders of France and Flanders, that Isobel was to wed her Duke. He was not there; the governor told them that his grace would be arriving shortly with the Earl and the Archbishop of York. Meanwhile, Isobel paced the chambers of Calais castle between fittings for her wedding dress. All the seamstresses in the town were commandeered into service in sewing thousands of pearls on to several yards of white silk, but theirs were the only busy hands. Everyone else sweltered in the flat heat from the marshes, and strained their eyes for a sail on the horizon. Anne was laid low with an ague the day after their landing.

She was out of bed, though not recovered, when two ships stood into the harbour, one flying the Neville saltire and the other the arms of England. Once the three lords were ashore there was no more idleness. A maelstrom of organisation swept the town: streets were hung with branches and strewn with straw, soldiers polished their pikes and women scuttled about with armfuls of freshly-starched linen. It was not the grand wedding in Westminster Abbey, acclaimed by court and country, that Isobel had yearned for. However much effort was put into its public trappings, it was a rushed fugitive affair. Isobel took comfort in her wedding gown and the attentiveness of her bridegroom. In her eyes the Duke of Clarence was even more beautiful and eligible now than he had been two years before. The spice of opposition which must have led to this runaway ceremony had only increased his glamour. She wept while she was being dressed, and wept again as she walked through the town to the church of St Mary Virgin and was cheered by the inhabitants who remembered the bride as a little girl in Calais a decade ago.

But the appearance of the young man who was waiting for her at the altar stopped her tears and her breath as well. George of Clarence might be taking a wife in defiance of royal will, but for this occasion he looked no less than the King's brother and heir presumptive to the throne of England. Against the candles and the thin daylight filtering through the stained glass, he was the sun among stars. His purple and gold gown was encrusted with jewels that gleamed and winked as if he were alive with light. Bareheaded, his blond hair was as burnished as a halo. The sun and the moon, thought Anne, when Isobel in her pearly white silk took her place beside him. He made his responses in confident tones which rang boldly beyond the small congregation into the dark places of the church; hers were murmured so that even her uncle the Archbishop, who was officiating, had to incline towards her to catch them. Just as they were pronounced man and wife Isobel glanced up shyly for the first time at her husband, but he did not look down.

Then there was the nuptial mass, and Anne became less and less sure of what was happening around her. She was not yet well, and long standing and the heat were taking their toll. Although there was a pillar next to her which she used surreptitiously for support, she sensed that her father was casting a stony eye on her and cursing the daughter who was always a broken reed at the most inconvenient moments. The Earl grew progressively less substantial, while over her head she was more and more conscious of a brooding threat. What it was she did not dare to know, but above the pageantry and the screen of candles it was surely there. The pillar was clammy beneath her fingers; that too disappeared up into the realms of darkness, and suddenly it all flooded back upon her, the hovering dead-eyed demons of her childhood. Wanting nothing more than to cower to the ground and hide herself from them, she clamped herself more firmly to her support and tried to repeat the words of the litany. Somewhere far away – in heaven, probably – a choir of cherubim were singing the amen.

'O Blessed Mary and Holy Anne and Holy Anthony save me,' she was gabbling in her head. There was a movement beside her and the Countess of Warwick was receding in the wake of a glittering procession. Bravely Anne let go of the pillar and plunged after her. Fresh air was blowing from the open door, the warm moist air of a July morning. The demons retreated, whimpering soundlessly, and she could see in front of her the tall mitre of the Archbishop and the back of her father's close-cropped dark head. As she passed through the west door a last claw of the terror struck at her from above, but so feebly that she was able defiantly to raise her eyes. It was there, gaping at her grotesquely from the parapet: a weathered old gargoyle with moss growing out of its mouth. Anne grinned back.

The feasting went on for the rest of the day, and although the company was comparatively small for a Neville celebration they made up for it with abundant victuals and a great deal of noise. Anne managed to miss a little of it by slipping away on the pretext of relieving herself and taking refuge in the chapel. She looked at the angels painted on the walls, remembering them now as old allies against the devils in the church roof. They were not really very beautiful, and the gold of their wings was flaking away in some places. The Duke of Clarence was far more splendid, but she decided that she would be easier in heaven in the company of these shabby angels than with the magnificence of seraphs like her brother-in-law. For a blessed twenty minutes she watched the pools of multi-coloured sunlight slide peacefully across the floor, and then she went back.

The presiding archangel was on his feet, proposing the

fiftieth health of the day to his father-in-law the great Earl of
Warwick. It was not as coherent as the first had been; his face
was flushed, the smooth crown of hair disordered, and the rich
chain of suns and roses hung crooked around his shoulders.
Although she had been reared on them, Anne was frightened
and repelled by the latter end of these banquets. Usually the
ladies withdrew before they became too rowdy, but since this
was a wedding breakfast the bride and her mother and sister
were expected to sit it out. Isobel, indeed, seemed to have no
objection to the conviviality which was after all for her benefit;
she was giggling and nearly as scarlet as her husband. The
pearl-strewn bodice of her gown was now speckled also with
gravy and wine. Returning from the tranquillity of the chapel,
seeing it as an outsider, Anne felt that it was all wrong. The
courtly summer wooing by the Avon should not have led to
this.

It finished late in the evening, and she was too weary to form
any opinions, negative or positive, about the wild bedding
ceremony that was its culmination. Her own bed, which
throughout her life she had shared with Isobel, should have
been a haven. But the young lady-in-waiting who was
supplying Isobel's place was a restless sleeper, and Anne spent
most of the remainder of the night fighting off the prodigal
limbs of her new bedfellow.

Despite her sister's elevation to the coveted state of
matrimony Anne expected a full account of it at an early hour.
But there was no message from Isobel when she rose, late and
queasy, and no sign of her in their mother's chamber where
they generally spent their mornings. The Countess was
working placidly at her embroidery, and her attendants sat
about on their cushions, taciturn and rather the worse for last
night's wear. When Anne had saluted her mother and taken
the stool at her side she ventured to ask where Isobel was.
Several of the ladies tittered, and their mistress turned a cool
disapproving glance upon them before saying, 'Her grace your
sister is keeping her chamber today.'

'Is she sick, madame?' It was an innocent question, but
there were more titters, and this time the censorious glance was
for her too.

'She is no longer your equal, Anne. You must not question

what she does.' The rebuke brought the sting of tears to Anne's eyes; the Countess so rarely reproved her, yet she had not meant to pry. And there was also something else: a premonition of rejection. As soon as courtesy allowed she went to look for Isobel. Mounting the stairs towards her sister's new chamber as Duchess of Clarence, she told her anxious heart that even if she were married and a duchess, she would still want someone to boast to about the felicities of a dream come true. But the attendant in the ante-room said that her grace was receiving nobody today.

'If his grace is with her I will come back later.' Anne blushed a little at her indelicacy and made to retreat.

'His grace went out some hours ago.'

'Then I'm sure my sister would want to see me.'

'Her grace is resting, lady. She gave strict instructions that she was not to be disturbed on any account.' This was Ankarette Twynyho, a woman who had been with them at Middleham, who had slept on the truckle bed across their door while Isobel whispered secrets in the dark. Her face was blank and unyielding. Anne went up to her.

'Ankarette, is my sister well?'

The expression softened at her appeal. 'You'd best go away, lady,' she answered more kindly. 'She's not who she was.' With a heavy heart Anne took her advice.

The lady-in-waiting was right. When Isobel appeared in public the next day she was far from the emotional bride who had wept and giggled her way through her wedding. Serious, distant, she applied herself to her needlework with uncommon diligence, and took no part in the gossip which had been the mainspring of her day. The Countess was visibly pleased by the change in her daughter; this, evidently, was how a sober and godly matron should behave – as she did herself. But Anne was unhappy about it, and not only because the bond of confidence between the sisters was clearly severed. Isobel should have been bubbling with high spirits; she was not one to hide her feelings. Whether flying into a temper, sulking or purring with pleasure, except in her father's presence when she was as subdued as all his womenfolk, her moods had always been indulged. She must indeed have taken her marriage vows to heart so to suppress her inclinations.

Her husband was not there to animate her. He had not been seen in the fortress since the morning after the wedding. Probably he had ridden off with Warwick to inspect the outlying fort of Guisnes. They returned together at any rate, towards evening, the Earl's armoured train enlivened by the bright trappings of the Duke's followers. Anne was on her way to the great hall for supper when she encountered a man in the passage, who pressed back against the wall to let her pass. He must have known who she was, since he bowed to her. She would scarcely have noticed him, but for the way in which he placed his fingers to his heart as he did so, which vibrated a chord softly in her mind. Not liking to look back, she went on her way, wondering where she had seen him before.

At table Clarence was already seated next to his wife. He leaned towards her, talking behind his hand in the intimate way which Anne recognised from his wooing days. But Isobel's response was subtly different. Instead of openly drinking in his conversation she seemed to be holding herself back, as if fascinated against her will; there was no more coquetry. Of course, reflected Anne, she does not need it now; the prize is won. All the same, she wished that Isobel would talk to her.

The musicians began to play in the gallery, and at once she remembered the identity of the man in the passage. A spring evening at Middleham, French troubadours putting away their instruments with delicate care, and her father's voice saying, 'Know Bertrand de Josselin again, my lord. He is worth the acquaintance.' And then that strange sidelong courtesy and the flick of the viol bow to his chest. Richard had been standing beside him, she recalled with a pang, dwarfed by the angular Frenchman. It had been his last week in Wensleydale. She had always foolishly blamed de Josselin for taking him away. Anne came back to the cramped hall of Calais Castle, where the Duke of Clarence gestured and joked between mouthfuls, and gulped down her homesickness. De Josselin was not playing tonight. His image plucked at the edge of her thoughts for a while, and then let go.

Warwick and Clarence were in Calais for only three more days. Within a fortnight of their arrival they were embarking again. The garrison and citizens were down at the harbour to give them godspeed. It was no secret, in Calais at any rate, that their small fleet carried what was virtually an invasion force. King Edward had abused the sacred trust bestowed upon him by the Earl of Warwick. He gave too much ear to the evil counsellors who had led him out of the paths of virtue. It was the mission of the great Earl, and of his son-in-law the Duke of Clarence, to remove the corrupting influences and bring the King back to his duty. That was what they said in Calais, which had remained independent under the protection of Warwick for more than a decade.

The wind was blowing auspiciously from the south-east, tossing the sea into little waves beyond the harbour wall. It was a fine day, and everything was broken up into glittering flecks of light, dancing on the waves and the sails and pennants, the helmets and lances of the soldiers. The leavetakings were rapid and then the leaders of the expedition mounted the gangplank to scattered cheering from the quay and the deck. At once the sailors cast off and the flagship was drifting away before the sails were fully hoisted. Warwick and Clarence stood side by side for a moment at the stern, an ill-assorted couple, acknowledging their send-off. The Earl went forward, leaving his son-in-law to blow kisses at the group of ladies on the quay with their skirts and head-dresses flapping unruly about them. He shouted something which the wind blew playfully towards them before tearing it to shreds. It sounded like, 'I'll bring you back a crown.'

Then the ships were out of the haven and prancing over the choppy sea towards a distant line of blue which was the English coast. The crowd was dispersing, with minds already on dinner. Warwick's family stood for a little longer, while the fleet became part of the shifting pattern of sunlight and ocean. The Countess's attitude, hands clasped limply before her, as usual gave nothing away. And Isobel, though one hand was keeping her veil from following her husband out to sea, was almost as impassive as her mother. There had been no tears, not even refined demonstrations of grief at the parting, only a sort of suppressed eagerness.

Anne had spared a puzzled thought for her sister at the time, but now she too was gazing after the ships, with a little ache of worry at her heart. It was obvious even to one as uninformed as she that Warwick had turned against his erstwhile pupil.

She looked over his head at the dim shape of Portland Bill, hunched in the sea fret, the oily water lapping between hull and quay, the squat cottages creeping up the cliff. These could be no less real than her father. If they still existed, then so did he. She knew the news was not true.

4

ORDEAL BY WATER

The news was good. The rebel Robin of Redesdale turned out to be loyal to Warwick; he won a battle on his behalf which helped persuade the King that he would be more secure in the great Earl's custody. Soon afterwards Warwick succeeded in lopping off two branches of the Queen's prolific family tree: her father and one of her brothers were beheaded outside Coventry. It was reported that England was restless, but no doubt the country would settle down contentedly as soon as the Earl and the King had firmly re-established their alliance. Anne sat over her embroidery, willing someone to say that the Duke of Gloucester had been instrumental in bringing his two kinsmen together. But he was not mentioned. With things going so well, the refugees in Calais were expecting daily a summons home. August turned into September, and nobody came to fetch them.

They were bored. Their quarters in the fortress were cramped, and with their hurried departure from Warwick there had been no time to bring the usual comforts which softened an itinerant life. Calais offered no diversions; it was a garrison town full of soldiers and wool merchants, and the little community was thrown back on its own company. Backbiting, squabbling and agues proliferated as news from England decreased. Anne was not involved. No one bothered to quarrel with her, and besides she had another preoccupation to keep her from boredom.

To her surprise, after a few weeks of sleeping in solitary state, Isobel had come back to share her bed. She offered no explanation; her possessions appeared one evening and she followed them, with a glance at her sister which challenged her to ask the reason. Of course she did not, and for several nights

Isobel addressed hardly a word to her. Her restraint, however, was showing signs of cracking. In public she was the Duchess of Clarence, but in private a light of superiority was beginning to gleam in her eye. It meant that confidences were in the offing, and Anne's spirits lifted a little. Although she was not excessively curious about her sister's innermost secrets, it was a comfort to be needed again after her time in the wilderness. At first it was only sighs and broken remarks which she could not fathom at all, hinting at something momentous growing out of past trial. Then evasive promises to tell, 'When I'm sure – if you swear not to utter a word until I give you leave.' Anne swore, and was patient – despite a suspicion that Isobel would really love to have the information coaxed out of her.

Towards the end of August she could contain herself no longer. Dismissing Ankarette, who was her personal attendant, she gave Anne a private audience.

'I've decided to tell you before it's announced to our lady mother. The person who should properly know first isn't here, and so I've chosen you,' she said magnanimously. Anne murmured her thanks. 'It's a great blessing, and proves how right my lord our father was to make the alliance. Now we must pray to the Holy Virgin to bring me safely through the months of waiting and do my duty to his grace my husband and our people.' Her speech was intended to whip up her audience's anticipation to a frenzy, but Anne was staring at her solemnly, quite at sea among the allusions and pious sentiments. 'Can't you guess?' Isobel abandoned her attitude and nudged her sister's arm impatiently.

'No, madame.'

'Oh, you're so *stupid*! Don't you notice anything?' Anne shook her head. 'I felt very dizzy the other morning and I'm sure Ankarette nearly guessed. I suppose I shall start being sick soon and it will be most unpleasant, but with many women it doesn't last long and anyway it's better than.... Oh, Anne, I'm with child. The Duke of Clarence's son. The King's nephew and perhaps one day the King himself.'

She was talking too much to see that Anne had paled, more taken aback by the news than Isobel could have expected. Indeed she had had no inkling, because it had never occurred to her that it might happen. Mothers were other people, occasional ladies-in-waiting whose gowns bulged more and more grotesquely over the months and who would disappear for a time, to reappear perhaps plump, but a more normal shape, and resume their cushions and their embroidery. Once or twice a lady had not returned, and the remaining attendants crossed themselves and muttered, 'God rest her soul,' and Anne knew that she was dead. She did not want that to happen to Isobel. She looked at her fearfully, seeing with sudden clarity the slim curve of her sister's body as she reclined on the bed, the grey eyes bright with satisfaction.

'But, Isobel, it's dangerous,' she whispered. 'You might die.' Isobel frowned. It was not a reaction she expected or liked.

'I might. It's in God's hands,' she responded sharply. 'But He won't let me. Isn't it obvious that heaven favours me? It's very rare for a woman to conceive in only four nights of marriage. My lord will be overwhelmed when he hears.' Her voice was turning querulous and Anne was ashamed of her lack of enthusiasm.

'Of course he will. I'm very glad for you, and I'm sure it will be safe really.' Trying to make amends, Anne put her arms round her in an unpractised gesture of affection, and kissed her cheek. 'It's bound to be a son.' That was what women always said to each other, and it pleased Isobel too. Yet as she repeated it Anne wondered whether people had said it to their mother the Countess while she was carrying them.

Quite mollified, Isobel yawned, and leaned towards her sister confidentially. 'It's a blessing in more ways than one,' she said darkly. 'Being a wife is not as easy as you imagine.' Anne did not intend to dispute it, but Isobel went on, 'Oh, I couldn't possibly tell you why. You're too young to understand.' And she called Ankarette back to make her ready for bed.

All the same, she did tell her, and Anne learned by degrees what had changed the Lady Isobel into the Duchess of Clarence. The painful and messy business of the wedding night, with a husband half drunk and not over-gentle; the assault on her modesty which had not improved on repetition. She had been totally unprepared for it, and even at a distance of two months her physical revulsion remained. Her pregnancy was a reprieve. For nearly a year she would be free from the demands of the Duke who, she had discovered, was not only beautiful and rich and heir presumptive to the throne, but also a man.

Confused and distressed, Anne listened to her. She was no longer reassured by sharing the elder girl's secrets. The nightly revelations were giving her glimpses of a world which was strange and disturbing to her. Ankarette had been right when she said that Isobel was not what she had been. The old terms of intimacy in which they had discussed George's courtship were impossible; there was a barrier between them, the barrier erected by experience.

Isobel refrained from revealing her condition for as long as she could, hoping that Warwick and Clarence would return in time to join their triumph with hers. But by the third month the signs were unmistakable, and she told her mother. One of the consequences was that she was removed from Anne's chamber and sent back to her own. The taboos and rituals surrounding pregnancy took her over, and once more her way of life separated her from her sister.

Something had gone wrong in England. There were no definite tidings, certainly no reports of resounding victory for the Earl's cause. In November they were sent for and crossed the Channel, fortunately in a flat calm. Southern England, as they travelled to Warwick, appeared to be quiet; the King was back in London and the Queen with him. Nothing seemed to be different. It was cold at Warwick; the great chambers, unoccupied since summer, were unaired and dank. Fingers and toes frozen during the journey thawed out very slowly as the servants humped logs up the narrow stairs to feed the freshly lighted fires.

There was still a dearth of news. When the Earl arrived, he was not in the best of tempers. It was never his custom to shout or make any demonstrations of a bad humour, yet from his silence at table, and the long hours he spent closeted with his captains, the household knew and trembled. Isobel's announcement fell on rather stony ground. She was recompensed, however, when Clarence joined them some days later. His reaction was everything she had wished for, and in public too. For a while, blushing and glancing at him sidelong through her lashes, Isobel reverted to the coquetry of their wooing days.

It was from him, via his wife, that they learned what had happened during the past four months. Despite being at one stage completely in Warwick's and Clarence's power, King Edward had somehow succeeded in outmanœuvring them and had now basely, George declared, gone back on all his pledges and concessions; the Woodvilles were rampant again, and the country groaned anew beneath their tyranny. The relationship between Clarence and Warwick was under stress. The deference shown by the Earl to his son-in-law was noticeably less, and Clarence did not pay so many fulsome compliments to the Earl. Once the Duke's voice was heard raised behind closed doors in the great chamber, and on another occasion he stormed out of the castle and was not seen again until the next day. It was, however, with some show of unity that they set off together in December for London.

Isobel had wept this time, as her husband kissed her and bade her take good care of their son. Under the privilege of her condition she had tried to wheedle George into taking her to court; her perennial dream of taking her place among the greatest ladies in the land would have had an especially rich fulfilment when she was carrying a child so close to the throne in blood. Clarence had refused, reminding her that the Woodville queen had not yet given Edward an heir, saying bluntly that this was no time to flaunt her fruitfulness. So she had to flaunt it at Warwick, which was not nearly so satisfactory. The flowing loose robe of pale green edged with ermine which she wore at Christmas was in fact more than adequate for her barely-thickened figure. She had taken the inconveniences of early pregnancy well, over-dramatising only a little, and as her bulk increased, so did her prettiness. Her sister, who had been apprehensive about the alteration of her shape, dismissed her fears and admitted to herself that Isobel had found her vocation in motherhood.

Unfortunately, her contentment was not mirrored in the country. Its quietness on their return from abroad had been deceptive; unrest was more widespread than they had imagined. So travellers reported, stopping at the castle and exchanging gossip for a night's lodging. And wherever trouble broke out, there was the Earl of Warwick, with or without the Duke of Clarence.

'If only the King would give rightful honour to our father and his grace my husband,' sighed Isobel, shaking her head and patting her belly, 'there would be peace again.' Her ladies murmured agreement over their tapestry work. Once more the castle drawbridge was up, and the portcullis down, all day as well as at night. Very occasionally, as winter dragged to a close and Isobel grew, one or other of the lords would come for a brief stay and be off again, leaving uncertainty in his wake. The situation flared into open warfare when, on St Gregory's Day, King Edward defeated one insurgent so decisively that all the leather jacks of the rebels were abandoned in the flight, giving the battle the derisory name of 'Lose-coat Field'. Not that the household at Warwick were derisive; rather to Anne's puzzlement they deplored the victory and lamented the King's execution of the leader. Clarence and Warwick were in arms; that much was certain. But whom they meant to fight, whether the rebels or the King, was not clear. Somewhere to the north at least three armies manœuvred, and perhaps not even their generals knew what they intended to do.

Anne was experiencing again the constant queasiness which had darkened her first year at Warwick, when she was only four and Edward was fighting for his throne. She dreaded going to bed, because the rush of the Avon in spate could have been the hoofbeats of a thousand armed men. Her dreams were made hideous by a huge figure in golden armour and a crowned helm who strode through the closed door of her chamber and stood above her, mailed fists on his hips, roaring with silent laughter at her terror. Behind him were others, terribly familiar, who rocked with echoing laughter and beyond them was someone else. She could hardly distinguish him, motionless and dark in the hateful brightness, yet if she could make him hear she would be safe. But her efforts to cry out were drowned by the soundless mirth, and he faded away, unheeding. Then she was awake, bolt upright in a clammy cold bed, with the weir thundering under the window.

Only in the chapel did she feel at all secure. She had learned the rules of sanctuary, and was reasonably confident that if the King's troops did take the castle, they would not dare actually to drag her out of her refuge. So she spent a good deal of her time there, kneeling at her prie-dieu, calmed by the red glow of the lamp before the Host and the lingering sweetness of incense. The saints, too, in their niches and windows, she recognised from Middleham: St Jerome with his lion, St Barbara with her book, St Agnes with her lamb. They gave her welcome and a sense of belonging. Her confessor was impressed by her piety. Finding her there once, he remarked that she might prove to have a vocation, and it was a pity that my lord Earl would not consider it.

Rude hands reached into the depths of her sleep and dragged her into wakefulness. A steely dawn was edging between the shutters, and the chamber was full of candlelight and agitated women. They hustled her out of bed and into her warm travelling clothes, their fingers clumsy with haste.

'What is it? What's happened?' Dazed and passive, Anne submitted to their ministrations, her questions lost in the muffled chaos of beds being stripped and things being thrown into chests, and women milling about aimlessly and getting in the way of others. She could smell disaster on the cold air, and flight. In their haste and her bemusement, they were outside the door before she remembered her pendant. 'I must go back. I've forgotten something.'

'There's no time, lady. My lord said half an hour.'

'I must.' Anne turned and slipped past her escort before they could stop her. The thought of leaving her treasure behind to the mercy of whatever menace was descending on the castle brought her heart lurching to life. She seized the small box, stowed it under her cloak, and returned to her ladies, who were standing irresolutely where she had left them.

The inner bailey was pandemonium. Soldiers carrying weapons and pieces of armour were everywhere, colliding with servants staggering under chests and bundles. Packhorses tossed their heads nervously as destriers were led, sidling and whinnying, in all directions. In the leaden half-light, streaked here and there with fading torch flames, it was as if someone had disturbed a giant antheap. With relief Anne saw her father, stationed at the top of the steps to the great hall. He was directing operations with the cool authority which he always showed at times of crisis. His riding boots were spattered to the thigh with foam and mud. Anne gravitated towards him, the

83

only fixed point in a seething world, and waited behind him for orders, hugging the rescued box to her stomach. In between shouting instructions for a fresh horse to a groom and despatching a page on an errand to the kitchens, the Earl caught sight of her.

'Ah, you're first. Are you well?'

'Yes, my lord.'

'Good. You shall ride with one of the gentlemen.' Then he turned away and went back to more important business.

Before long the Countess appeared, followed by Isobel and her husband. Clarence, who was as travel-stained as his father-in-law, was arguing with Isobel. 'It would be madness for you to stay here. Edward's troops are on our heels.'

'And what of travelling in my condition? That would be madness too. I would rather trust myself to the King. He is my brother-in-law.'

'And I am his brother – and see how he has used me!'

'He wouldn't harm a lady. If he were to protect me until the child is born—'

'*My* child, Isobel. Do you think he would spare a possible heir to his throne?'

'What are you saying?' Isobel's cry of alarm was reinforced by a shocked exclamation from her mother.

'Enough!' Warwick rounded sharply on his divided family. 'What's the matter?' Before his stern enquiry Isobel dropped her head, fingers twisting before her distended belly; Clarence met his gaze with a faint sneer.

'Her grace declines to accompany us,' he said sarcastically.

'I'll not have that tone of speech,' said the Earl, and Clarence swung away, scowling at the reproof. 'Isobel, don't be foolish. Your place is with your husband. You'll be quite secure in a litter.' Leaving her on the verge of tears, Warwick strode off energetically to check the loading of a baggage wagon, and muttered as he passed the Countess, 'Those girls have no stamina.' Clarence went after him with a black look at his wife, and the women watched them go in chastened silence.

As he had whipped his family into line, so Warwick tackled the organisation of a household on the edge of panic flight into an orderly retreat. It was not yet full day when the cavalcade was ready to leave. There was none of the ceremony which usually attended the departure of the Earl of Warwick from his principal seat; only a group of the attendants who were being left behind clustering anxiously outside the great hall, and the grating of the portcullis being lowered as the last horse crossed the drawbridge. No cheering crowds lined the streets of the town to hold up babies for a glimpse of the great Earl; a few citizens, abroad early, turned curiously to stare at their lord clattering by in haste beneath the dead March sky.

During their wait in the bailey Anne had contrived to transfer her pendant to her neck, abandoning the box which she could not carry on horseback. Now it hung where Richard had first placed it, moving against her chest with the rhythm of the horse. The irony of the situation had not escaped her: the donor of this gift so lovingly preserved was even now at their backs with the King and an army, pursuing them as declared traitors. This did not upset her as much as the realisation, a few miles south of Warwick, that she had not brought Kat with her. It was the first thing that he had given her, the first symbol of the pact between them which had been sealed with the blessings of St Anthony and St Anne three years later on the slopes of the old castle. She had given up cuddling it at night a few years ago, but had always kept it under her pillow, to touch whenever she was lonely or miserable. In the confusion of their sudden migration it must have been shaken out with the tumbled bedclothes, and fallen into an obscure corner. She would not see Kat again. As they rode on her loss and guilt weighed more and more on her mind, tugging it back to Warwick.

There was little to distract her in the company and surroundings. The hills of Warwickshire and Gloucestershire crawled past, brown and grey and barren. Skeleton trees stood rigid against the overcast sky, as if spring would never happen again. Oppressed by the weather and their danger, nobody was inclined to conversation, much less to the singing which had serenaded their flight to Calais last summer for Isobel's wedding. The Duchess of Clarence herself lay fearfully in her litter, clutching at the curtains or her stomach, moaning constantly that she was sure she would fall into labour at any moment with the roads so bad.

They headed south-west, and on the fourth evening they

skirted Bristol to stop at an inn nearby. While someone enquired for a ship the travellers snatched what sleep they could; outriders had reported the royal army to be less than three days' march behind them, and they were hindered by the slow-moving litter, so they dared not take long rests. No ship was forthcoming, and about midnight they set off again into an unseen drizzle. The rain did not cease. Clouds were rolling low over the Mendips when dawn came, and the tor of Glastonbury was shrouded from sight. The roads turned to a morass, and the riders were soaked as much from mud thrown up by the horses' hoofs as by the downpour. Anne was so tired and chilled that she no longer had any interest in the journey. When Isobel whispered seditiously that it would be a good thing if the King did catch up with them, she silently agreed.

Warwick and Clarence, however, were of opposite mind, ever urging on their less involved followers. As they progressed the Duke's temper frayed. He rode restlessly from one end of the cavalcade to the other, snapping at the men in charge of the litter that their sloth was holding everyone up, and his solicitude for his wife was rapidly exhausted. Once, in Anne's hearing, he told her to hold her peace and think of the child's welfare instead of her own. Warwick's spirits though were proof against the weather, their peril, and the bad roads. With that familiar light of determination in his eye, he remarked that the roads would hold up the King too, and Anne marvelled at the strange quirk in his nature which improved his morale when other men's failed.

And indeed there was still no sign of pursuit when they entered Exeter in the sodden afternoon of the tenth day. Dozing uneasily behind her riding-companion, Anne was roused by a ragged shout of 'A Warwick! A Warwick!' It was not an attack from the rear, but only a few citizens who, sharp enough to recognise the pennants of the great Earl, had not yet heard that the King had turned against him. Grateful for a little encouragement, the fugitives took heart. There was no difficulty here about a ship, since Warwick's messengers had preceded him, and not long after dark they were embarking. Only half conscious, Anne was helped on board, and as soon as she was deposited in the cabin, she curled up on some canvas and fell asleep.

When she awoke the ship was rolling and she was shivering violently. Someone had laid her on a pallet and covered her with a dry cloak, but underneath her clothes were clinging damply to her skin. The creaking of a ship under sail filled the close air, and beyond that the slap of water. There was no sound of other human occupation, and Anne thought she was alone in the cabin. As she sat up, huddling the cloak round her shoulders, she was appalled by what she saw. The hanging lanthorn was lighted, but a feeble glimmer from the companionway indicated that it was day outside. There was a bucket on the floor, which spilled its ordure with every motion of the ship, and four other pallets, each with a recumbent figure. In that moment's semi-somnolent panic, Anne fancied that she had been abandoned with four corpses. She had once read an Italian tale about a girl sealed alive into a vault who had run mad at the horror of it. Leaning towards the nearest body she found it was Isobel; in the swaying flame of the lanthorn her pink-and-white complexion was drained to a deathly green. Anne tottered to her feet, with an idea of escaping from this charnel-house at all costs, and recognised the other bodies as her mother the Countess and two ladies-in-waiting.

Then, poised for flight, she was checked. Across her path Ankarette, her sister's attendant, flung an arm above her head and groaned. Simultaneously Anne identified the acrid stench of seasickness. So they were not dead, merely spent by vomiting. The discovery did not alter her instinct to escape. She stepped over Ankarette, unsteady on the heaving boards, and clinging to the steps above she climbed towards the light. A drop of moisture hit her in the eye and made it sting, and when her head rose above deck level she realised that it was not rain, but sea-spray. The wind sprang at her, whipping her loose hair around her face so that it was difficult to see anything. Holding it back with one ill-spared hand, she drank in the sharp salty gusts with some relief, and looked about her.

All around and almost above her as the ship ploughed from side to side, the sea was lashed into angry grey peaks. Between them it was just possible to glimpse a low uncertain coastline away to the left, but otherwise there was nothing in sight but waves and the turbulent sky, and the thunderous canvas of the sail. Her first exhilaration was quickly overtaken by loneliness at these expanses of emptiness, and the wind was beginning to hurt her ears.

But as she considered whether it was better to drown or to die of suffocation, a large individual loomed up on deck, with blue snakes curled round his hairy arms. He stood gazing down at her, hands on hips, and from her vantage point his bare feet were enormous and he dwindled away to a disproportionately small head smothered in beard and an old green scarf.

'Go below, little maid,' he said, addressing her with the sort of roughness she had never heard before, but which surprisingly did not frighten her. 'Deck's no place for a wisp like you this weather – you'd be blown to Biscay if gale got hold of you.'

Anne was quite willing to obey, but something prompted her to ask him, 'Where are we going?'

'Earl's making for Southampton, but it's a hard pull against this nor'-easter. We're close-hauled as it is, and if wind veers we'll have to put in afore that.' Understanding little of the nautical jargon, she grasped that at least she was in the right ship.

'Where is my lord?'

The sailor chuckled. 'Sleeping it off for'ard. Even the great conqueror of the Dons isn't proof against the Channel in a gale.'

'They're all the same down there.' Anne nodded below.

'What about you?' her friend asked.

'I woke up and wanted some air. It's very ... close in the cabin.' He laughed, what would have been a guffaw if the wind had not scattered its force.

'Ah, I can see you're as right as rain. They may be great ones, but their stomachs are as delicate as their manners, eh?'

She tumbled to the fact that he had taken her for an attendant, and she laughed too and agreed. Laughing reminded her of the hollow state of her own stomach. 'I'm very hungry,' she remarked, without thinking of the impropriety of mentioning such a weakness to a mere sailor. He stared at her with humorous admiration.

'By the mass, you are, are you? Fine ladies and gentlemen and the famous Earl of Warwick himself flat on their backs, and this little wench says she's hungry!' The man felt in his pocket and then squatted beside her, proffering a wrinkled yellow apple. 'It's not much, but I had it from an apple-loft in Plymouth only yesterday. You're welcome to it.' At closer quarters he smelled very strongly despite the gale, yet Anne was so touched by his gesture that she took the apple and, sitting on the steps, munched it. It was soft, and the flesh was creamy and crumbly, but it tasted of the country and autumn.

While she ate the sailor chatted to her, mostly about incomprehensible naval things like quarters and bells, but she also gleaned the information that their party was not all in this ship. Several smaller craft had been commandeered, and must have fallen astern during the night. On one of them was the Duke of Clarence. Much as she relished the novelty of her new acquaintance's company, Anne was beginning to shiver again. Thanking him politely for the apple, she said that she would have to change into some dry clothes, if he would excuse her.

'Of course! And I expect that one o' *them* will wake up soon, wailing for another bucket.' He wriggled his bushy eyebrows at her slyly, and stood up. 'Both back to duty, eh? I to take the helm and you to hold heads.' Winking at her, he vanished, bare feet sure on the uneasy deck. Warmed by the irreverent wink, and by the knowledge that there were several miles of ocean between her and the Duke of Clarence, Anne clambered back down the ladder to forage for some fresh clothing.

It took the best part of three more days to make Southampton Water. Warwick hovered off the Needles for some time, in the lee of the Isle of Wight, waiting for the rest of his small fleet to come up with him, and then they made down the strait together towards the port. Although his family, save Anne, were still laid low, the Earl had recovered his sea-legs and was directing operations again. Anne would have preferred to be on deck, rather than below watching the other women vomiting, but it was made clear to her that she was in the way. Much of the time she slept, or sat on the companionway and craned her neck to see the coast slipping by, and the incredible white cliffs of the island.

When Southampton was sighted she was glad enough to be under cover. Her father might have hoped to sneak back into the country while Edward's attention was elsewhere, but the

King's vigilance was too quick for him. The haven was manned against him, and gun-stones splashed into the water uncomfortably near the foremost ship. If the use of cannon did not surprise the Earl, it unnerved the sailors, and the fleet was about and running for the open sea before he could do anything to stop it. Down in the cabin the women were screaming, convinced that the ship was about to break up and sink under the impact of thunderbolts from heaven. Anne, who had caught a glimpse of the distant engines of war, and the missiles hurtling through the air towards them, was too shaken to scream. While the harbour was still visible she remained frozen to her perch; afterwards she slid down the steps and, for the first and last time on the voyage, was sick into the bucket.

Out of the shelter of the island, they headed once more into the wind. The fleet had been battling eastwards for some hours when Warwick paid one of his perfunctory visits to his family. Since Anne was the only person capable of understanding he addressed himself to her, his head bent to avoid the roof of the cabin which was in fact only metaphorically too low to contain him.

'The gale shows signs of abating; we should reach Calais without difficulty. You can lie there until Isobel is delivered.'

'Calais. Thank God!' It was Isobel who spoke, but a whisper of relief rustled through the cabin. All their lives Calais had stood for a refuge from the ingratitude of foolish Englishmen. Now it would be a haven also from the hostile elements. In Calais they would be safe.

But the Earl's hopes were too sanguine. The wind did not drop, but veered easterly, which made their progress once beyond the protection of the coast even slower. They had been at sea for eleven days, imprisoned by sickness and weather in the stinking little cell below decks, when the wharves and roofs of Calais detached themselves from the flying spume. Anne had not been happy there, but she greeted the tower of St Mary Virgin with something like affection. At least it was solid and did not toss up and down. At the risk of a chiding she stood at the head of the companionway, keeping a tight hold on the rail and gazing hungrily towards the port. Suddenly through the buffeting wind she heard a cry from beneath her feet. Isobel was propped shakily on one elbow, staring in dismay through her tangled hair.

'I think the pains have started. Oh Anne, what shall I do?'

'Don't fret. We'll be in Calais very soon. I'll tell them to hurry.' Giving her a drink out of a pitcher of stale water, Anne mounted the steps again. She had grown used to performing small menial tasks for her incapacitated fellows, and she was not especially worried. This stage of childbirth, she had heard, could last for hours, and by the time Isobel really needed help they would be secure in the fortress, with midwives and doctors in attendance. There was a sailor close by, apparently idle, and she called him, thinking as he approached that there was something familiar about his bush of a black beard.

'Run and tell my lord Earl that her grace is in labour,' she said. 'She must be taken ashore as soon as possible.'

'Yes, mistress.' As he pulled his forelock ironically she remembered the apple he had given her, and realised that he had not yet any notion of who she was. She sat beside her sister and reassured her as best she could, while Isobel lay taut and waited for the next contraction. It was long in coming, and when it had come and gone there was still no sound of any docking manœuvres, only the roar of the wind and pounding of the sea. Indeed, the ship seemed to be making no way at all. As she was beginning to wonder about it, the Earl entered the cabin. His mouth was tight with anger.

'The quay is defended against us,' he said. 'Wenlock has run up the royal standard and will not let us land. He has betrayed me.' Anne was engulfed by a wave of shame momentarily even stronger than her shock. Such treachery to her father tainted the whole of mankind. But Isobel had caught the more practical implication.

'I can't stay here! Oh, what will become of me?' She rolled on to her side and began to sob.

'How far gone is she?' Warwick demanded of Anne.

'I don't know. The pains are still far apart.'

'Stay with her. Try to rouse your mother and the women. I'll send a message to Wenlock.' His tone was brusque. The prospect of suing for favours from his former lieutenant was bitter gall to him, and the glance he threw at his elder daughter as he left was scarcely forgiving. Yet Anne did not doubt that he would obtain the concession he wanted; at least the governor would allow the ladies to go ashore: that basic courtesy to a woman in childbed even an infidel would extend, especially when asked to do so by the Earl of Warwick.

She set about doing her father's bidding. It was impossible; for nearly two weeks the women had taken no solid food, the wind still tossed the ship like a walnut shell, and they were incapable of coherent thought, let alone action. Ankarette did try to rise at her urging, but a lurch of the ship sent her sprawling and retching again. The Countess lay with her eyes closed, murmuring, 'I can do nothing! Nothing!' while the other attendant would neither move nor speak. Giving up, Anne went over to Isobel and held her hand as she watched her back arch in another contraction. If the callous Lord Wenlock would not let them land, at least he would send a midwife, she consoled her sister and herself.

'After all,' she said, 'I can hardly deliver the baby alone.' For a moment, surveying the grown women, all mothers, who lay helplessly around, leaving a thirteen-year-old girl the only possible nurse, she saw the funny side, and smiled.

By nightfall she was past smiling. Some men had brought a brazier down and a second lanthorn; no other help had arrived. Isobel's cries were becoming anguished when Anne faced the truth that none would come. There was a moment of blind panic, a return to the insane instinct of her first awakening in the ship, to rush up on deck and trust herself to the ocean rather than this living nightmare. But a glance at her sister brought back her senses, and she sat down to consider what to do. What she needed most was advice. She shrank from disturbing her mother; a lifetime's habit of not troubling her was ingrained. It would have to be Ankarette. She had borne three children, and could at least tell her what to expect. Before rousing her Anne remembered another source of strength, and with a hand pressed to her hidden pendant she muttered a supplication to St Anne, who had given birth to the Blessed Virgin.

The night passed, timelessly, punctuated by Isobel's suffering. The wind seemed to have dropped a little, or perhaps the shipmaster had found a more sheltered anchorage. Ankarette had succeeded in keeping down a morsel of the food brought to Anne by a young gentleman who afterwards fled as from the plague; between them they had made Isobel more comfortable, and prepared her pallet for the birth. After midnight, when Anne's head was swimming with weariness and the fetid atmosphere, the only sign of the Governor of Calais' humanity appeared, with a message expressing his humble service: a cask of wine. One cupful made her so cheerful that she would eagerly have drunk several more, but Ankarette pointed out feebly that it was meant to render the Duchess of Clarence insensible, not her nurse. Removing the rag that Isobel was biting on, Anne managed after several attempts to make her swallow some without throwing up again, and on an empty stomach this had immediate effect. Between pangs she started to chatter and sing, telling her absent husband what a fine heir she had given him, complaining of his roughness, chanting fragments of love songs. It was worse than her former anguish, and Anne wanted to shut her ears against the indecent levity of her sister's babbling. But no, said Ankarette, let her keep her oblivion.

'If you'd been through it as I have, lady, you'd know what it is she's missing, and bless the kindness of my lord Wenlock.' She fell into a doze, leaving Anne, drowsy herself, to administer wine and listen to its results.

There were trickles of blood, but no sign of the sudden gush of fluid which her adviser had told her would herald the baby's emergence. But there was plenty of time for that, she assured herself, with some muddled idea that aid would come before she actually had to do anything. She was close to sleep herself when Ankarette awoke and asked suddenly if the waters had broken. After examination Anne said she thought not.

'How long has she been in labour?' With some taxing of her tired brain, Anne calculated. 'That's a long time. They should have broken by now. Still, it is her first. I was two days labouring with my first child,' Ankarette remarked proudly. A new morning crept tentatively down the companionway. The watchers broke their fast, and sent their negative news in answer to the Earl's enquiry. Despite the wine, Isobel was clearly close to exhaustion. Days of illness and twenty hours of physical exertion were taking a severe toll. When Anne sponged her face clean of sweat and winestains, she could hardly bear to look at it. Her attendant, rising gingerly from her pallet to inspect her, retired again very troubled.

'I'm afraid, lady. She'll die if the child doesn't come soon.'

'What can we do?' Anne fought down the coldness in her limbs.

'Nothing. A midwife would know . . . but we can only wait.' It was what she had feared, all those months ago in summer, in the town just over the water where salvation lay out of reach. This must have been why she was stirred by premonition on first seeing the Duke of Clarence stepping across the grass towards them with the goshawk on his fist. It was her sister's murderer that she had seen. She knelt beside her and took her hand.

'Isobel, Isobel, you must *try*.'

'Tell her to push. The baby needs help.' Anne conveyed Ankarette's order, but Isobel rolled her head wearily from side to side in defeat.

'I can't.' Her voice was slurred and faint. 'Take the pain away and let me sleep.'

'You must do something yourself, and then the pain will go. Grip my hand and push.' The attempt was pathetic, but it brought the veins out on her neck, and sweat started on her temples. And, minutes later, even through the fumes of alcohol she was yelling with agony.

'Is it coming?' In her anxiety the attendant struggled once more from her pallet and peered beneath Isobel's blanket. 'Again – tell her to do it again.' With all the will she had, Anne urged her sister on, and although she was sobbing and trembling with stress, she responded. 'Look! It's coming. Praise be to Our Lady!' Sick with anticipation, Anne joined the woman on the floor at the foot of the pallet, and there was an oval swelling like some horrible growth between Isobel's thighs. She gulped and hid her eyes against Ankarette's shoulder. 'Go and tell her,' said the attendant. 'Only a little more effort and he will be born.' Somehow Anne crawled back to her sister's side and spoke to her.

'Is it a boy? Oh Anne, is it a boy?'

'We don't know yet. . . . In a little while.'

In the last stages, she needed the support of Isobel's grip almost as much as Isobel needed hers. And when Ankarette called on her to take the child, she could not stand up. Its head was enormous, poised unsteadily above the wrinkled body and puny limbs. The eyes and mouth were only screwed little folds of flesh, and there was froth around the chin. Under the slimy streaks of blood and water the skin was tinged with blue, and so was the cord that still attached it to its mother. It was a boy. Torn between repulsion and wonder, Anne held the little thing at arm's length, while Ankarette collapsed on to her bed and Isobel lay spent and still. Suddenly, after all the striving, there was no sound but the creaking of the shipboards. Anne crouched there, frozen into an attitude of display, her body empty of sensation, until Ankarette spoke, her voice rough with fatigue.

'You must tie the cord, and cut it. There are scissors.' Dumbly Anne obeyed, fumbling with tired and slippery fingers. The child did not stir where she had laid him beside his mother and Isobel made no move towards him. Then Ankarette said sharply, 'It isn't crying.' Anne stared at her sister's baby, wondering stupidly why the attendant should begrudge them all a little peace. But as she stared, the meaning filtered through the haze of her weary mind. No crying. No movement. She advanced her hand reluctantly towards the tiny chest. No heartbeat.

'No. He isn't breathing.' She could hardly breathe herself.

'Shake it. Turn it upside down and shake it.' They tried, gently, vigorously, desperately, to shake some breath into the small empty body. It was no good. Anne hauled herself up the ladder, into the blue of a brilliant April afternoon. On the larboard bow the cliffs of Cap Gris Nez sparkled in the sun. A gentleman who was leaning on the rail, enjoying the change in the weather, detached himself and came towards her expectantly, hastily disguising his distaste at the wretched appearance of his mistress.

'Her grace is delivered. But the child is dead.' Losing her foothold, she slithered painfully back into the cabin. They were all still there, laid out neatly on their four pallets as she had seen them on first waking, four apparent corpses, only now there were five. The tears of despair blotted them out, and she groped her way to her own bed. Before they had even dampened the straw pillow, sleep claimed her.

'You evil trollop! You killed my son!' The harsh accusation

cut cruelly into her oblivion. George of Clarence was standing over her sister, his head nearly touching the rafters. Even in the poor light she could see the hysterical rage that distorted his face. Involuntarily she recoiled, and to her terror he turned on her, swaying over her pallet until the fur edge of his robe brushed her hair. 'And you connived at it. Oh, I know what you two were up to, alone down here. She smothered him and you let him die.' Choked with horror, she watched speechlessly as he returned to his wife and took her by the shoulders. 'Admit it. You could be burned for this. Admit it, you witch!' He was shaking her while he abused her, and in dreadful parody of his child that they had tried to save she did not resist, but let him toss her about like a rag doll, mouth slack in an ashen face. It was too much; beyond, the Countess was trying to rise with broken whimpers of distress, and the two gentlemen with the Duke started forward to stop him.

A thin voice cried, 'It isn't true. She nearly died herself. She wanted him so much.' Anne could not believe that it was she who had protested. But a more commanding voice was raised against the outrage, and as Warwick entered Clarence let Isobel fall back on to her bed and wheeled to confront the Earl.

'I gave you leave to board my ship so that you might visit your wife,' Warwick said, and there was no trace of the old deference to the King's brother. 'I did not expect you to treat her like one of your whores.'

'She killed my son—'

'Rubbish.' His father-in-law silenced him incisively. 'She's proved she can bear sons. As soon as she has recovered her health you can get more.' Driven on to the defensive, the Duke flung back his head and looked down his nose at the shorter man. His anger had changed to sneering scorn.

'Lie with *her* again? That's a pleasure I've willingly denied myself these past nine months. She's as cold as a nun once she's bedded – in spite of all the hot glances outside her chamber. She's like her father – promises all and gives nothing.' Warwick's hand was at his dagger, and if he had been a lesser man he would have used it then. As it was, his stillness was suddenly far more dangerous than all Clarence's raving.

'Leave my ship, my lord Duke.' It would have taken greater courage than Clarence possessed to outface that contemptuous authority. Without another word he left the cabin. The women's two attendants were weeping, and the Countess had hidden her head in her hands. For a moment the Earl remained rigid; then he shrugged and announced calmly to the company at large, 'We sail for Normandy in an hour. At the first French port we shall put in and engage a leech and a nurse.' His gaze swept over the sorry bunch of women, pausing on his elder daughter who, breathing heavily, had lapsed into unconsciousness, and coming to rest on Anne. He stepped towards her and said quietly, 'How is it with you, child?'

'Tired, my lord. That's all.'

'Don't fret about the lord Duke. He was grieving and angry. He means no harm.' Because he so seldom used kind words to her, Anne's eyes filled with tears. He turned away from her weakness with an impatient tut, and was gone.

The Countess was supported up to the deck by her two equally feeble women for the burial of her first grandson. With the shortened rites permitted to an unchristened child they committed the small heathen corpse to the ocean. The cries of the gulls as they flashed white about the mast were a mournful requiem. Anne wept softly, as she did most of her waking hours. Under the supervision of a French midwife, Isobel lay below, fighting a slow battle against childbed fever.

Despite a now following wind, it was not until May Day that the Earl's fleet dropped anchor in the harbour of Honfleur. Here at last the reception was friendly. The bear and ragged staff flew below the fleur-de-lis on the lighthouse, and boats were thrusting out from the quay before the sails were furled. Anne did not see them, nor the effusive greeting given to Warwick by the port officials when they came aboard his flagship. The energy to climb up the companionway and take an interest in proceedings had left her. She was curled on her pallet in a maudlin state between sleeping and weeping; Ankarette, who was almost well, and shrill with the relief of dry land's being so near, had to dress her like a helpless child.

It was the stout lady-in-waiting who propelled her up the ladder to join her father and the welcoming deputation. She was pushed forward to have her hand kissed, but after so long a confinement she could not take in such a welter of strange people, flickering hands and swirling fur robes. Only two faces meant anything to her. Holding the painter of one of the little dinghies which lay alongside was a sailor with a black beard. He was staring at her with a startled concentration that told her he had finally discovered her identity. But when she caught his eye, he looked away with chagrin, as if she had deliberately deceived him.

The other was among the Frenchmen, although standing so close to the Earl as to be almost by his side. He was talking rapidly, bringing one after another of the dignitaries to the attention of Warwick, who listened smiling with his head slightly bowed as though in respect. Soberly but sumptuously dressed with a great collar of silver lilies about his neck, the man gesticulated with the grace and confidence of a prince. And Anne was afraid. It was Bertrand de Josselin.

PART II
Wife

VALOGNES

Anne crossed herself and rose from her knees. Picking up her missal, she left the cool shadow of the church, where a lay sister was leisurely washing the flagstones, and passed into the cloisters. The arches were etched sharply in jade velvet on the brilliant emerald of the grass, and where the sunlight spilled on to the stone floor a pied cat lay on its back, absorbing the heat ecstatically into the white fur of its belly. It was meant to catch mice in the pantry, but took as much time off as its appetite and the Sister Cellarer would let it, especially when the weather was fine. Anne stole towards it and squatted beside the spreadeagled body. The cat opened one alert golden eye, tensing to streak away if it was Sœur Agnès. Recognising a friend it stretched in sensuous anticipation and began to purr. One of the things Anne liked most about cats was the unabashed pleasure they took in life. As the creature pushed its nose eagerly into her caressing hand, she recalled her sympathy with Sœur Louise, a young postulant from Brittany, who had been caught stroking the cat by the Mistress of Postulants, and given a penance on the spot for carnal indulgence: a harsh judgement for such mutual satisfaction.

Not that she often pitied the nuns. The Mistress of Postulants had been plagued by gout that morning; generally she was more of a nurse than an instructor to her charges. Since she came to Valognes over two months ago, Anne had found more reason to envy than to pity them. Saying goodbye to the cat, who blinked in reply, she crossed the grass towards the guest-house. The passages and chambers were deserted, so she relinquished the missal and her heavy head-dress and made her way to the Abbess's garden. Under an apple tree her mother was sewing: the same frame, the same design, so it seemed, that she had worked upon all through Anne's life. She lifted her eyes as Anne came through the gate, but made no other sign. No one else took any notice of her; the ladies were dozing, and Isobel stared listlessly before her, a book lying unopened on her lap.

It was in any case only a courtesy visit. Anne spent a great deal of her time apart from her family, either at devotion or talking to the nuns. Indeed, she had asked and obtained permission to pray in the abbey church, instead of the guest chapel, whenever the sisters were not themselves saying their offices there. The Abbess, in granting it, smiled and commented that in the past a number of English ladies had taken their vows here. The seed had fallen into fertile ground. With as much speed as decorum would allow Anne escaped from the Abbess's garden and went to find Sœur Madeleine, whom she knew would at this time of the morning be tending her herb beds. She had something important to tell her.

The sister was waist-deep in lavender bushes, plucking the misty blue flower heads and dropping them into the plaited rush basket on her arm. Anne took up an empty basket and pushed in among the fragrant shrubs to join her. Having smiled a greeting at each other they worked in silence for a while, with the scent and the bees and the sun thrumming all around them. At length Sœur Madeleine said, without pausing in her task, 'Well, Anne, what is it?'

Anne paused, glancing shyly at her friend. 'How do you always know?'

'One grows used to reading moods, living in contemplation. Now tell me.'

'I think . . . *ma sœur*, I think Our Lord has spoken to me.'

'What has happened?' Despite the emotion trembling in the younger girl's voice, the nun's tone was serene.

'It was a dream – no, more of a vision. Last night. I've been praying at St Anne's shrine for two hours, and I believe she's with me.'

'Perhaps. Can you describe the dream?'

Anne hesitated, closing her eyes against the golden radiance of the morning to summon up the tremendous presence which had come to her in the night.

'I was lying in darkness – not just the darkness of my bed, but somewhere much colder and wider and more lonely. And then I was ... lifted up ... and embraced. I was afraid at first, but I could feel Him willing me to trust Him. His arms were round me, folding me close. ...' Groping for the words to define the indefinable, an echo of the sweetness which had possessed her rippled again through her body. 'Oh, Sœur Madeleine, it was so wonderful, I can't describe ... but when it happened I was so secure and full of love that in return I wanted to give myself. ...' She faltered into exalted silence. Sœur Madeleine was regarding her with grave sympathy. 'I wish I could explain.' Anne was a little dashed by her friend's lack of response. 'Surely it was a sign from God?'

'It may be. You must wait.'

'What for?'

'To be sure. The Devil can speak to us too through dreams ... and our own longings.'

'But my longing is for God. You must believe me, *ma sœur*.'

'I do, Anne. But you mustn't be proud.'

'Proud?'

'Yes, and think that you know best. People change – grow up – what is right today may be wrong next year. There was a girl who came here, burning to serve Our Lord. The Mother took her without a dowry beçause she was so much in earnest. Yet before she was through her novitiate she left us ... for a young man from the town.'

'I wouldn't do that!' Anne was shocked by the implication.

'Of course not. It is simply to warn you against being too hasty. Giving your life to God must be a decision of your reason as well as your heart.'

'But if I *know* that He came to me—' She was interrupted by the bell for Sexte, tolling from the abbey church. Sœur Madeleine placed her basket on a stone bench by the path and took Anne's hand.

'Go on praying, and I shall do the same. Ask your confessor's advice. And be patient. If God needs you, He will not let you escape Him.'

She went away, threading briskly through the beds of rue and rosemary, and a cloud of white butterflies rose in the shimmering air and wavered about her white figure. Anne sat down on the bench and crushed a flower head in her palm.

Burying her nose in its fragrance, she tried to shake off her disappointment. When she had arrived at the convent, she had been in a state of collapse scarcely better than her sister's, and of all the nuns who had tenderly nursed them Sœur Madeleine had been the most devoted. As she recovered Anne came to rely on her for spiritual as well as material comfort. She had found it easy to talk to the girl from Poitou, who was only six years her senior, and who seemed to understand the half-articulate aspirations she had never confided to anyone else. To find a place where she would be useful and not in the way: it had grown on her, living in this peaceful and ordered community, that her place might be here.

And her overwhelming experience of last night, when God had possessed her utterly, had convinced her of it. She had hoped that her friend would be as moved as she, that she would agree this was what they had prayed for, and that she would approach the Mother Superior on her behalf. Instead she had almost snubbed her, almost disbelieved her. But then Sœur Madeleine was no mystic; she had often admitted as much – Anne hastily lighted on the excuse. The youngest of seven daughters of a nobleman ruined in the French civil wars, there had been no marriage portion for her, and that was why she had taken her vows. She was practical and prosaic, and she had to work to find her vocation. A Martha rather than a Mary, she called herself wryly, and now Anne began to see what it was that her admired friend was lacking. Direct contact with God was not given to everyone. With a thrill that was half fear and half pride, she wondered whether she was one of the elect.

Should it be so, there was no time to be lost. She knew instinctively that steps had to be taken urgently. First she must win her confessor to her side – although she did not intend to entrust him with an account of her vision – and then if Sœur Madeleine did not respond to her appeals she would have to approach the Mother herself. Anne quailed a little at the prospect of another interview with the benign yet awe-inspiring Abbess, but the courage would come to her. Together her two allies would speak to her father as soon as he returned. This part of her plan was the most vague in her mind. She could picture herself receiving the Abbess's blessing as a novice in her house; the wedding ceremony when crowned with flowers she became the bride of Christ; the eternal stillness of her cell as she knelt at her offices; but not the reaction of the Earl of Warwick to his daughter's request. She dismissed the shadow of doubt. As the sister had said, if God needed her, He would not let her escape.

But in any case the Earl would probably be glad to be rid of the burden of his youngest daughter, since she had never been anything but an encumbrance to him. He had been occupied in matters of high state ever since their landing in Normandy, as the honoured guest of the King of France. His family, settled in the guest-house of the convent, had seen nothing of him, and little, until lately, of the Duke of Clarence who had gone with him; his absence had contributed largely to the tranquillity of their existence. In the past two weeks, however, the Duke had reappeared in the district. Fortunately he spent most of his time in Valognes, where Warwick's men-at-arms were quartered. He was in an evil humour, and every visit he made to the convent was an unwelcome violation of its atmosphere. No one dared to ask why he had left the French court.

Anne stood up and wandered through the herb garden, scattering the powdered lavender on the perfumed air and thinking about the day when the door of her cell would shut out the anger and cruelty of the world and leave her alone with God.

That evening she and her mother were hearing Vespers when there was a disturbance at the door and someone came in late. From the corner of her eye Anne saw Clarence sketching a genuflexion and the sign of the cross before kneeling beside the Countess. Once or twice during the service she fancied uneasily that he was looking her way. Always disturbed by any sign of interest from the Duke, his behaviour on the ship had turned her disturbance to apprehension. She resolved to remain in the chapel after Vespers, and trust that he would have gone by the time she emerged. After the Blessing she kept her eyes fixed on her missal, but even so she sensed, as those beside her rose to go, another baleful glance directed at her.

Her fingers slid over the beads, rehearsing the Five Sorrowful Mysteries, and gradually the familiar pattern of Aves and Pater Nosters calmed her mind again. The beauty of last night's vision came back and warmed her anew; it was fruitless to worry about Clarence: soon she would be beyond his reach. The sun was sinking in a clear primrose sky by the time she judged it safe to go back to her apartments. Intending to say goodnight to her mother and then retire, she went to the Countess's room. He was still there, leaning against the table and nursing a flagon of wine. His fair complexion had a high colour, and Anne remembered the stories whispered by the ladies of his nightly drinking-bouts in the town. If she had any hope now of escaping unobserved, it was quickly dispelled.

'You're a pious little creature, aren't you, sister?' he said as soon as she entered. 'You should have kept your lady mother with you in chapel. She's rather in need of spiritual consolation at present.' Anne looked at the Countess. Her hands were unusually idle and clenched in her lap, and even the rosy light of the sunset did not disguise her pallor.

'Madame, are you unwell? I'll call your ladies.' She hurried to her mother's side, noticing that the only other occupants of the chamber were two of the Duke's gentlemen. Isobel had gone to bed before Vespers, which was fortunate, since her husband could scarcely endure speaking to her. Had he been bullying the Countess? Glancing at him, she decided that he was quite capable of it in his present mood.

He held her accusing eyes and drawled, 'Don't spend too much sympathy on her; keep some for yourself.' Her apprehension hardened into cold certainty. It was she he had come to see. She gripped her rosary in one hand and the back of the Countess's chair with the other, and thus sustained she confronted Clarence. He had not missed the surreptitious movement towards her beads. 'Which saint is it you pray to, sister? I doubt if one will be enough in future. You'll need St Michael and all his angels to protect you where you're going.'

'Where ... am I going?' It was a question he had manœuvred her into asking. He did not hide his malicious eagerness to reply, and yet in dread she had to ask.

'To Angers. To meet your husband.'

'Husband?' Her voice was so faint that it hardly reached him across the room. But the Countess leaned forward, driven for once out of her passivity to defend her daughter.

'My lord – is it necessary to tell her now?' The Duke opened his eyes wide in exaggerated innocence.

'I'm trying to prepare her gently. She must know soon, my dear madame.'

'Could it not wait until my lord returns?'

He laughed shortly. 'I doubt if he will break it to her gently.' And he returned to his prey, who was standing like a statue at her mother's elbow. 'A very illustrious husband . . . some would say. The Nevilles always marry their children well – heiresses, earls, dukes, are small fry. Even royal dukes are dispensable when something better comes along. A Prince of Wales wandering unattached round Europe – now that is a windfall for a marriageable daughter. Though there is some doubt as to who his father is.' His elaborate sarcasm was lost on Anne. She gazed at him blankly, her mind telling her only that there was no Prince of Wales. 'Oh, but there is.' She must have spoken aloud, for he was answering her thought. 'If your memory is long enough. And your father's memory is very long – when it suits his policy.' A sudden venom shot through his words as he mentioned Warwick. Throwing away innuendo, he flung her fate brutally into her face. 'He's making friends with Margaret the Frenchwoman, and he's going to marry you to her son as a seal to the treaty.' The phrases cut a jagged pattern into her brain, but they meant nothing. Clarence refilled his cup and took a long draught. Outside a blackbird began his bold salute to the evening and beyond his song the bell called the sisters to Compline.

'Oh no, he can't,' Anne said reasonably. 'I'm going to be a nun.'

'Are you indeed?' The sneer was back. 'I doubt if the Earl would let a few vows stand in the way of his plans – even if they had already been taken. Which they haven't.' Bland and menacing, his face was a barrier between her and the future.

'Madame, I cannot marry. Tell him it's impossible.'

'I may say nothing without the consent of your lord father. It is he who will make the decision. You must wait until he returns, my child, and submit to his will.' Distressed but too weak to defy her son-in-law, the Countess had retreated into her customary neutrality. There was no help here. Quietly Anne knelt for her mother's nightly blessing and made a courtesy to the Duke, in whose expression she surprised a furtive trace of irritation at her apparent capitulation.

Once outside the door, however, she did not go towards her own apartment but turned purposefully in the opposite direction. A waxing moon floated in the limpid sky as she passed across the cloisters. She did not look up, intent as she was upon the sombre mass of the abbey church. Slipping through back ways which she knew well enough to negotiate in the dark, she avoided the chancel where the nuns were at service and reached the steps which led up to the dorter. There was no light here apart from a faint sliver of grey in a high lancet window, but she did not need light. She was not afraid; within these precincts she was under the protection of Our Lady and all the saints, and the ancient laws of sanctuary. The soft tones of women's voices intoning the final Hour of the day came to her through the warm night. She pressed her back against the wall, feeling through her gown the solid roughness of the Caen stone, and waited.

In a haze of torchlight the nuns approached, the susurration of their robes rustling through the silent reaches of the church. Their heads were bowed and their hands, save for those who carried torches, were folded beneath their scapulars: modest, humble, holy. To the casual eye they would have been indistinguishable one from another, but Anne had learned to recognise Sœur Madeleine from weeks of wistful observation. Just as her friend came abreast, Anne stepped out of the darkness and plucked at the nun's sleeve. Startled out of her contemplation, Sœur Madeleine turned her head sharply. Anne could see her eyes gleaming wide in the shadow of her wimple.

'Sanctuary, I claim sanctuary,' she whispered hastily. With a bare hesitation the nun allowed Anne to draw her out of the procession, which flowed on undisturbed. The light which accompanied the sisters dwindled, and night closed softly about the two left behind. Sœur Madeleine's hands sought for the younger girl's, and held them in a cool clasp which at once began to steady her whirling thoughts.

'You shouldn't be here.' The reproach was delivered without severity.

'I know. But I'm in sore trouble, and I had to come to you.'

'You spoke of sanctuary. What did you mean? What has

happened?'

'I must take sanctuary. I need protection until Reverend Mother is ready to accept me. She will, won't she, *ma sœur*? You will speak for me?'

'Be calm, Anne.' Sœur Madeleine gentled the trembling girl, and frowned into the darkness over her state of near-hysteria. 'Tell me quietly what is the matter. Is it your brother-in-law the Duke?'

'Yes, but it's the others as well. They are all against me – against God. They will force me to marry, when I'm promised to God.'

'You are to marry. I see.'

'You're not surprised....' A disloyal suspicion rose in Anne's mind. 'You didn't know, did you?'

'No. But I could have guessed. And so could you.' The nun restrained her friend's violent start of protest. 'If you had not been so wrapped up in your dreams. Your father is a powerful man, and one of the richest in Christendom, I've heard. You are a great lady, and his only unmarried daughter.'

'You never warned me—'

'I didn't think you needed a warning. After all, it's only girls with impoverished fathers and too many sisters whose destiny leads straight to the nearest convent.' Her voice held a humorous resignation to her own fate. But Anne's refuge was beginning to crumble about her.

'You *encouraged* me.'

'To be more devout, yes. To increase your love for Our Lord and His Blessed Mother. They are not benefits reserved for those in holy orders. I tried to minister to the health of your soul – the rest of your life is not mine to meddle in.'

There was a long silence. Anne's fevered trembling had stopped, and her hands had turned cold. At length she said, steadily and very quietly, 'Then you won't help.'

'I can't, Anne. I would speak to Reverend Mother, if I thought it would do any good. But even if she were convinced of your vocation, she could not go against your father's authority, any more than I could. You are guests in our house, and to abuse the rules of hospitality would be odious to God.'

There was no further response from Anne. Had Sœur Madeleine not been holding her hands, she would have thought herself alone on the dorter steps, talking to the empty darkness. She drew the slight still body into her arms. 'It would have given me great joy to see you enter our order and live by our side. Perhaps you do have a vocation. If so, be patient. God will reveal His purpose in His own time. Submit yourself to His will, my dear Anne, and all will be well.'

Suddenly Anne's body grew rigid, and flung away from her. 'It is not the will of God,' she cried, with a despair that shattered the slumbering calm of the great church. 'It is the will of my father!' And she walked away rapidly, her footfalls receding through the deserted aisles until nothing was left but the soundless echo of her cry. Sick with impotence, Sœur Madeleine listened for some time, then returned to the chancel and prostrated herself below the tiny red glow which burned before the Host.

It was the longest night that Anne had ever endured. The night of her sister's confinement had been harrowing, but time had seemed to cease. Not like this sluggish crawl of seconds that were minutes, and minutes that were hours, and all of them keeping her from sleep and a release in oblivion. She did not dare to toss and turn, for fear of waking Isobel, and so she bore the agony without moving, except for the occasional squalls of sobs which shook her helplessly. Her mind ran endlessly in the same dark circles of desolation. Everything had failed her; she was alone without comfort in a hostile world. About the time that the birds began to wake to their summer dawn chorus, she remembered the pendant which had so often brought her solace before. But when it was in her hands, the well-loved smooth oval encircled with the miniscule roughness of pink gems did not cast its sure spell. Her separation from Richard had not occurred to her consciously for months; now it struck her with dull panic that she could not even recall his face. He too was absent, miles and years beyond her reach. The sheer misery of the discovery almost sent her to sleep, when the bell for Prime mocked her awake again with bright regular strokes.

Morning brought at least the relief of routine. Everything was as usual. No one made any untoward comments or noticed that she did not go to the abbey church. It would have been easy to delude herself into believing that last night had been an evil dream, but she had had enough of self-deception. In any case the following day Clarence was back, and it was impossible to misread the glances, mingled spite and contempt, that he sent her way. In the afternoon she undertook to read to Isobel, which was a frustrating task as her sister was apt to tire quickly and ask for a different story every paragraph. But since Anne could bear her own company even less than she could bear that of others, she opened the translation of Boccaccio's tales with some hope of forgetting herself for a while.

The weather had turned dull, and Isobel had been placed on a day-bed in the Countess's room by the gentleman who had since their arrival in France carried her everywhere. She was restless, and although her sister chose the shortest tales she would not hear any to the end. As Anne began to lose patience the door was flung open and the Duke stalked in. Waving his hand at the attendants, he said, 'Go away. I wish to speak to these ladies in private.' They shuffled out, and Clarence stationed himself before the hearth. He did not bother to dress himself carefully for the sake of his womenfolk and a conventful of nuns. A full-length silk gown of shot scarlet and russet was wrapped casually round him and fastened with a jewelled filigree belt. He surveyed the three women under drooping eyelids. 'You need not look so apprehensive,' he said. 'I bring you good news. And especially happy for you, my dearest sister.' He bowed ironically to Anne. 'Our lord Earl is to honour us with his presence before the month is out. I believe he is the bearer of a joyful message.' Anne was staring down at the open book: letters jumbled together to make nonsensical words, black smudges on a white page.

'I doubt if he will have any message for me worth the hearing, so I'm going hunting. As far as Brittany, possibly. Oh, please don't distress yourself, madame.' He took a few paces towards his wife, who like the other two women was listening to his diatribe with eyes averted, masking distaste with indifference. 'I shall not be gone for long. If your health permitted, I would willingly take you with me. However, I leave you behind as valiant defender of my good name. Your husband's good name, my lady.' Isobel did not look at him, but her fingers were plucking nervously at her girdle. There was not only savagery in his voice, but also the pain of deeply wounded pride. He turned his back on them and scowled down into the fireplace.

The heavy silence was mercifully broken by a servant announcing Mistress Evershed of London. A young woman followed him in, clad in dusty travelling clothes, incongruously cradling a bolt of soft saffron cloth. There was a smear of dirt across her forehead and on the edge of her coif and she looked very tired. As she sank to her knees the Duke moved towards her and offered her his hand, suddenly assuming the charming manner which Warwick's family now saw so seldom.

'It's good to see someone I can trust,' he said as he raised her, and she registered embarrassment at the insult to his kinswomen. Accepting the gift of kersey gracefully, he continued to speak to her, although there was no doubt that it was meant for them. 'I hope England is prepared for invasion. We do intend to invade, you know, if my good father-in-law can spare the time from revelling with the French king.' At that, with the same gesture that he had used to the servants earlier, he dismissed them. While she waited for her sister to be carried out, Anne glanced covertly at Mistress Evershed and thought she read a glimmer of shocked sympathy in her eyes.

'Who is she?' asked Isobel as she was laid in the bed they shared.

'John Wrangwysh's sister,' Anne answered absently. Isobel's curiosity had begun lately to revive as she grew stronger.

'How do you know?' Her sister's surprise was matched by her own. How had she known? Searching her mind, she was at first only aware that that intelligent face with comprehending grey eyes was connected with some warm place in her memory. Then she remembered.

'We met her once. At Middleham.' The day when John carved Kat for her. A winter day when the log fire burned in the centre of the hall and a friendship had been forged.

'I don't remember. What has she come for?'

'Who knows?' Floundering in a lonely sea of loss Anne could hardly speak.

'I think my husband knows,' said the Duchess of Clarence, and there was a note of foreboding in her voice.

Anne came to her decision very late in the night, knowing

that she would not sleep until it was made. She rose at first light and said her prayers to St Anne at the prie-dieu in her bedchamber before seeking from a drowsy and grumbling Ankarette the information she needed. Janet Evershed had been given an apartment in another wing of the guest-house. Loitering outside her door, Anne saw nobody but her red-haired journeyman, who did not notice her as he hurried past on some errand. It was past Tierce before the young woman emerged, folding back her linen cuffs. Anne went forward quickly.

'Will you be seeing the Duke of Gloucester, Mistress Evershed?' Surprise as well as courtesy had arrested Janet's brisk progress. Now it turned to puzzlement as she answered cautiously that she was not sure.

'You must have some way of reaching him – through your brother, perhaps? There is something I must return to him – if you would take it for me. There's no one else I can ask.' John's sister hesitated, slow to commit herself, nonplussed by the unexpected request and the fervour with which it was made. The pendant was burning in Anne's palm, searing her with a brand of guilt and betrayal. If it was not taken from her soon all her courage would trickle away and she would not be able to part with it. Janet's gaze met her own, searching, and softened.

'I'll take it for you, my lady.' One swift movement and it was out of her hands; she was rid of it.

'Just give it to him – he will understand.' A loop of gold chain was still visible, gleaming faintly. It was too much. She turned and ran from it, anywhere, nowhere. Where she went no longer mattered, since every way was away from him.

Warwick rode in a week later, Bertrand de Josselin at his side in all the panoply of a special envoy of the King of France. The clatter and chatter of English soldiers and French gentlemen transformed the old buildings into a court in miniature where the ordered tolling of the service bells was quite out of place. For half a day the Earl left Anne alone, but after supper she was called to the chamber which had been put at his disposal. De Josselin was there, resting his arm negligently along the overmantel; Anne had never known anyone, even the Duke of Clarence, to behave with such disrespect in her father's presence. But he did not seem offended.

He waved her to a stool by the window, although she was accustomed to standing before him. She was about to take her seat when she realised that de Josselin had not moved. With a surge of indignation she drew herself up and stared in mute defiance at the foppish Frenchman. If her life sentence was to be pronounced it would not be to the cynical ears of this musician-diplomat-spy. He glanced at Warwick, and lifting his shoulders and eyebrows slightly he walked without haste from the room. There was, to Anne's chagrin, more amusement and approval than annoyance in the glance. She sat down.

Her father took a few turns about the chamber without speaking. Had he been anyone else, she would have suspected that he did not know how to begin. At length he threw up his head and announced, 'My daughter, you belong to a great family.' She murmured the required response. 'The name of Neville is respected and feared not only in England but far beyond our shores. It is the duty of every member of the family to add to its lustre. How old are you?'

'Fourteen, my lord.'

'If you were my son, you would by now have won your knighthood.' Anne experienced the familiar dwindling of her self-respect. 'But even a girl-child can be of use. Your lady mother brought the earldom of Warwick to me; your great-aunt became Duchess of York.' He came to stand beside her stool and placed his hand on her shoulder. His voice became less rhetorical. 'I offer you the opportunity of bringing far greater glory to the House of Neville than your ancestors have done. To be a queen, Anne. And mother of kings.'

Anne had a sudden crazy desire to giggle. There was a farcical difference between the ways in which Clarence and Warwick had broken the news that quite destroyed its solemnity. She composed her features to listen again, but her father had been watching her, and mistook the tremor of amusement for something else.

'It is a high destiny. And far from easy. I shall speak to you plainly, child, because grown as you are it may be hard for you to understand.' The inclination to laugh had vanished, superseded by the knowledge that if she did not speak now, the chance would be gone for ever.

'Father.'

'Yes?'

'I want to enter this convent and take my vows.' It was the formal statement of a lost cause, and from his answer she doubted if he had even heard her.

'Yes, yes. I daresay.' He patted her shoulder. 'Now, the reasons for this alliance are too complex to explain to you. Let it suffice that we intend to right a great wrong, and that you are to be the pledge of our good faith and the crown of our success.' He paused for her comment, but there was none. 'Have you not guessed?' She would not say it. Until she said it there would be no truth in the proposition that he was trying to thrust upon her. 'You must look upon yourself as a peace offering, as a dove bearing the olive branch of matrimony. Many a feud has been buried in the marriage bed before now, but none, I think, so hard fought and so mistaken. In your union with the Prince of Wales—'

'You all said she was a witch. A demon.' Anne's voice was so strange that for a moment Warwick faltered.

'Servants' ... women's gossip. Queen Margaret has great strength of character.' He found himself fixed with a stare of utter incredulity. The gossip in the castles of her childhood, she knew very well, took its impetus from nobody but the lord of those castles. Her father had been right to doubt that she would understand. 'I've heard that Prince Edward is a fine lad. A little older than you. He should beget sturdy sons on you. He's the apple of the Queen's eye, and for his sake she will love you too.' Although he had never expected to have to do so with his meek younger daughter, Warwick was battling strenuously against the silent intractability of her gaze. Tears he could have coped with, or protest, but not this overwhelming incomprehension. He cut his losses. 'I go to Angers next month, to meet with Queen Margaret. You will follow with your lady mother, and the betrothal will take place there.'

So soon! Only a few weeks more and she would enter her purgatory. Her father had resumed his pacing. She wondered why he did not dismiss her. He stopped and said, 'Is there anything you wish to ask me?' She had not even wanted to know what he had told her already, but out of obedience she found a question.

'Will Isobel be going with us?'

'Isobel remains here. With her husband.' That information only added extra bleakness to the world ahead – for her sister as well as herself. They did not love each other, but there was a companionship between them that outweighed the alternative attractions of Prince Edward of Lancaster and George of Clarence. Again that awkward hush, with Warwick pacing.

At last she said in a small voice, 'May I go, my lord?' She rose, and he came over to her.

'Anne. . . .' His hand hovered by her head in an uncertain half-gesture. Then he gave a quick sigh and said, as though it were second-best, 'You're a good child. God bless you.' The hand rested on her hair in benediction, but that too was not what he had intended to do. When she had gone he stood for some minutes rubbing his chin with his fingers, lost most uncharacteristically in thought.

The days which before had slipped peacefully one into the next, marked only by the ordered round of Prime, Sexte and Vespers, became a torrent, bearing her with inexorable speed towards Angers. Although, feeling herself rejected by it, she no longer went to the abbey church, her rosary was still a refuge, and in the well-worn patterns of prayer she usually managed to ward off the impending future. It was more difficult now that her father had given a focus to the darkness. He had given it a name, and that summoned up memories which were strong and alive with terror. Queen Margaret was the shadow that had overcast her childhood, the spectre which had come in the night to shake her from sleep, which had lurked constantly in the dusty alcoves of castle chambers and the unguarded corners of her mind. She had heard her called so many foul things, attributed with such unspeakable crimes, that the Frenchwoman was more of a myth than a reality. It was perhaps this that carried her through the last weeks at Valognes. She could not believe that she would ever set eyes on Margaret of Anjou, nor that her father would bring himself to deliver up his hostage.

But the day came, another day of cloudless blue and gold,

and they left the sheltering walls of the convent in a long and glittering cavalcade, quite different from the weary line of litters which had carried them from Honfleur. Drawn up formally in the courtyard of the guest-house, the escort sent by King Louis looked on while the Countess and her younger daughter took leave of the Abbess and the Duchess of Clarence. Anne did not trust herself to speak. In kneeling to kiss the Mother Superior's ring, she saw her dream of acceptance into the order twisted cruelly into an irrevocable farewell; in embracing her sister she could not forget that, unwilling though she might be, she was supplanting her in their father's ambition. From the windows of the refectory the nuns were watching, and among their bobbing heads Anne could distinguish the still face of Sœur Madeleine.

The leader of the escort approached and assisted her, with much ceremony, to mount. She wanted to shake off the long strong fingers which lifted her into the saddle the appointment of Bertrand de Josselin to conduct her into Anjou seemed like a personal insult. He gave the signal to move, and as she walked her gelding obediently after him she caught sight of the abbey dovecote, with the birds sunning themselves lazily on the roof like small unseasonable patches of snow. Such contented and complacent creatures. Anne thought of her father's comparing her to a dove of peace, and remembered what happened to these doves in the winter.

2

THE HOSTAGE

Angers was the largest town she had entered for many months. The narrow streets, the overhanging houses, the milling crowds closed in about her oppressively. On top of the long journey and the heat, the stink of the kennels made her head reel. Out of the cavern of the dark streets they emerged at the river, and beyond the bridge was the château, a great castle growing out of a sheer wall of rock. She was used to castles, but she rode under the portcullis with the sensations of a prisoner. This vast fortress with its girdle of round towers would not let an army in; it would certainly not let out any individual who tried to leave against its will.

There was no welcome for them. The French men-at-arms melted away, and with only their ladies and the few English attendants who had accompanied them, Anne and the Countess were led by their guide to a small doorway, and through deserted passageways to their apartments. The chambers were lavishly furnished, there were Turkish carpets and rich tapestries on the walls. Wine and refreshments were laid, and water and clean napkins for washing. Yet still no one greeted them. De Josselin made himself discreetly useful, as he had done throughout the journey, but as he knelt beside Anne with the bowl of water, with the deference in which she always felt a veiled mockery, she was suddenly stung into speaking sharply to him.

'Are we not to be received officially, messire?'

He smiled up at her, sidelong. 'Officially, madame, you are not yet here.'

'What do you mean? Where is my lord Earl?'

'Oh, he is here. And his grace King Louis. But her grace of England has not yet arrived.' Shrugging, as if he had explained everything, he handed her a towel. Despite the luxury of their surroundings and ample provision for all their needs, the claustrophobia which had gripped her on entering the town redoubled. A few hours later she was seized with violent griping pains, and for three days she took no further interest in her surroundings.

She was on her feet again, though unsteadily, when her presence in Angers was at last acknowledged by a visit from her father. Warwick brought with him a shabby little man with a long nose. After a few perfunctory enquiries about her health – on which subject Bertrand de Josselin had evidently kept him fully informed – he turned to his companion and asked him in French if there was anything he wished to know. The man lifted his shoulders and answered in the same language, 'She is very pale – but no doubt that is the result of her sickness.' Anne understood French quite well, but the stranger, and probably her father also, were not aware of it.

'Yes, monseigneur. The journey upset her. But she is on the mend now.' It was odd; she had never heard her father address anyone with so high a title, and yet this was such an insignificant little man. She supposed that he was some great lord from the train of the terrible Queen, come to spy incognito on her proposed daughter-in-law. Remembering the pseudo-minstrel of Middleham Castle, Anne came to the disgusted conclusion that spying was the favourite French method of diplomacy. Her opinion of the French sank still lower with the next question, which she understood before the Earl translated it for her.

'Are you old enough to bear children?' She knew what he meant: Isobel had told her about the distasteful obstacle which lay between her and womanhood. Blushing, she said, 'No, my lord.'

To her further embarrassment the Frenchman laughed suddenly, a mirthless bark. Aside to Warwick he said, 'I doubt if my cousin of England will be broken-hearted to hear that.'

Warwick was not amused, but he answered with restraint, 'It does not please me so much, monseigneur, as you may imagine. But my daughter is the right age. It may happen at any moment.'

'Of course, my dear friend. I appreciate your eagerness to

mingle your blood with royal stock to produce a little Neville princeling. I just hope for your daughter's sake that my cousin the Queen has taught her son the art of love as well as the arts of war. His father apparently had little idea what to do when the bed-curtains were drawn – although his accomplishments lay in a more holy direction than do young Edward's.'

Anne was squirming with shame, and she was only comforted by the double realisation that the Countess, standing nearby, had no inkling what was being discussed, and that her father was almost as uncomfortable as she. The stranger had noticed too. Laying his arm across the Earl's shoulders, he chuckled. 'The trouble with you is that you take life too seriously. And so does this little maid, by the looks of her.' He shuffled towards her, and patted her cheek. 'Lift up your heart, child,' he said in bad English. 'I've no doubt the boy will serve you lustily – if his mother will let him bed with you.' There were small leaden images of saints stuck into the brim of his cap; Anne recognised St Paul by the sword in his hand. The small sharp eyes had seen where hers had strayed. He took off the cap, plucked one of the images from the back and gave it to her. 'Here, take St Catherine. She hasn't been very good to me lately, but she may be more use to you.' Chuckling afresh, he went back to Warwick, and linking arms familiarly with him he took him out of the chamber.

The shabby visitor was King Louis XI of France. Since her informant was Bertrand de Josselin, Anne did not ask why he affected such unkingly garb. But in the tedious days that followed she had plenty of leisure to reflect upon it. He was the third king she had encountered, and of the three only one had any appearance of royalty: her cousin Edward.

It was not he who had suddenly assumed significance but another King of England, who had impressed himself upon her childish mind by his gentleness and his little bird. Anne had always found it hard to associate King Henry with the hated Queen Margaret, yet there was little doubt – and that expressed by his enemies – that he had fathered the boy she was destined to marry. Hitherto she had thought of Prince Edward only in terms of his mother; now she allowed herself the faint possibility that there might be in him something of the nature of his father, whom she had heard referred to as a living saint.

If Prince Edward were fond of birds, if he smiled at her shyly as King Henry had done in the throne room at Greenwich, it would be easier to face the ordeal of her life with him. What was more, if the Earl meant what he said about righting a great wrong, then surely the holy King would be released from his prison in the Tower as part of the crusade. Perhaps, with the influence of a Princess of Wales – for the first time the title articulated itself with less than dread – she could see to his freedom and comfort. With that mission to give her courage she could almost envisage approaching the Queen herself, for surely some affection for her husband must linger still in that ferocious heart which so doted upon her son.

It was of King Henry that she thought as they dressed her for the betrothal. Three days before the Earl of Warwick had met Margaret of Anjou, and the momentous reconciliation had taken place. The new-found amity had its price for Warwick: the Queen had kept him on his knees for a quarter of an hour begging her pardon before she would allow her old adversary to kiss her hand. Anne did not know this. The meeting was announced to her personally by her father, and he had not mentioned it. All he had said was that Queen Margaret had graciously accepted his homage, and that the Prince of Wales was indeed a well-grown stripling, proud and good-looking. She took the opportunity of asking whether the release of King Henry would be one of the objects of his new alliance.

'Why, of course,' he had said. 'His grace is the only true King of England. Our first purpose will be to restore him to his throne.' That long anxious face of her early memory, transfigured by liberty and wearing his rightful crown: the distant vision sustained her throughout the long preparations.

Her father led her to the altar steps. The ceremony of betrothal was almost as solemn as a wedding, and to Holy Church just as binding; Warwick had enlisted the aid of his friend King Louis to ensure that the promising of his daughter to the heir of Lancaster was nobly attended. Compared with the crush of ancient titles in the cathedral at Angers, Isobel's marriage in Calais had been a hole-in-the-corner affair. Counts and princes had been waiting for some time, cheek by jowl, in a fine array of fur and jewellery. It was a hot day, and the redolent odour of sweat convinced Anne that she would once more disgrace the family and faint or vomit before she could do her duty. Leaning heavily on her father's arm, she kept her head low and gulped down her nausea. His arm was removed and she stood for a long moment alone, quite alone as the focus of all those lordly indifferent gazes. Then a hand took hers, or rather, fingers were placed around hers. She made the expected responses and another voice, young, expressionless, also answered the priest. At the appropriate words a ring was pushed on to her finger, and it was done.

Now she knew she must look up. The saintliness of King Henry would not help her here; she had to confront the present. She raised her eyes. A priest was before her, in the crimson canonicals for a martyr saint: today was the feast of St James. The Earl was standing near, his arms folded, clad in scarlet and white, and next to him not the Countess but another woman, olive-skinned and dark-eyed. The rich blue velvet of her robes would have dimmed any personality less strong than that which was marked in the firm set of her mouth and the haughty carriage of her head. With a sudden pang of realisation Anne's eyes glanced nervously away from her and met accidentally with those of the boy whose hand held hers. Black, like his mother's, not mild and grey like his father's. And like the ricochet of a game of bowls he too dropped his gaze, and would not look at her. Their palms were clinging stickily together. In her line of vision beyond Prince Edward was the King of France, and close by him Bertrand de Josselin. The spy was whispering in his master's ear; Louis tilted his head to listen, and they sniggered silently together. Anne was certain that they were laughing at her.

The ring on her finger and the place of honour at table were not the only changes in her life. When the page lit her to bed, it was not to the apartments she had shared with her mother, but to a larger chamber in another wing of the château. Her few possessions were there, including her missal on a prie-dieu cushioned in black brocade; the attendants who undressed her however were all French, and the lady who climbed into the other side of the richly-hung bed was unknown to her. Too bewildered to protest, she said her rosary under her breath until it sent her to sleep. The new waiting-women were efficient and deferential, but they showed no signs of friendship. When de Josselin came into the chamber the following morning, she was almost glad to see him. Although she distrusted him, any familiar face was welcome.

'Where is my mother?' she demanded in English, before he had even saluted her.

'*Madame la comtesse* has not yet arisen,' he said, his eyebrows raised in that slight arc of amusement which so irritated her. 'Do you wish me to carry a message to her?'

'No. I wish to see her. And my lord father.'

'As to your lady mother, she shall be brought to your grace this morning. I regret that the lord Earl is out hawking with his grace the King.' All those titles; meant to confuse her, no doubt. So her father had gone, and left her to strangers and his smooth-smiling minion.

'Why have my apartments and my women been changed?'

'To fit your new state, madame. And to place you nearer to the suites of your lord and your royal mother. But the Earl ordered me expressly before he left to attend to your comfort in any way within my power.'

'Then ask him for an audience. As soon as he returns.'

'At your command, madame.' She dismissed him, deciding now that mute indifference from the attendants was preferable to his unctuous courtesies.

In one matter at least he did not fail her. Within two hours the Countess joined her, but Anne was rather shocked when her mother sank into a deep reverence.

'Madame, you shouldn't be kneeling to me....' She had witnessed her parents' change in attitude to Isobel when she became a duchess; she had never imagined that the rules of precedence would apply to her too. The Countess replied that it was most appropriate, and waited for her daughter's permission to sit.

De Josselin escorted them both to hear mass, said by Queen Margaret's chaplain, and afterwards Anne was dismayed to find herself led in the Queen's wake to her private chamber. She was given a stool on Margaret's right, the Countess a slightly lower one on her left. She was marooned on an island of silence. The Queen talked incessantly, in rapid French which Anne could not always follow, but it was far from the aimless gossip which she had been used to in feminine circles. Men were coming and going all the time, bringing her messages and taking orders, and the Queen's hands were busy, not plying a needle, but turning over papers and signing letters. Her ladies were clearly accustomed to the carrying on of business in this inappropriate setting. They took little notice of it, and even less of Anne.

In the afternoon Prince Edward, who had been at his lessons before dinner, spent some time with his mother. He acknowledged his fiancée on arriving and leaving with an embarrassed bow, still avoiding her eyes. Otherwise he was absorbed in conversation with the Queen. Yesterday's ceremony had not inspired Anne with any curiosity about her future husband, but for lack of anything better to occupy her she observed mother and son together. Subconsciously she searched for some resemblance between the adolescent and the man sitting uneasily in that musty hall of long ago. There was none that she could discern. Neither was there a likeness in this plump handsome matron to the fiendish monster-queen of the legends. But Anne was not much consoled. Margaret in the flesh possessed other qualities which were at close range as alarming: energy, vigour, vitality – just the qualities which brought out all the shyness and clumsiness in Anne's nature. She knew that when the Queen did inevitably come to speak to her, she would be tongue-tied and blushing and her father would be ashamed of her.

But her father was not to witness that particular humiliation. During the week in which Warwick stayed in Angers, he was hardly ever in the Queen's company, and she did not deign to pay attention to Anne at all. The Earl seemed to have passed the entire responsibility for his wife and daughter to Margaret. He had not done so, however, as he explained to Anne when he called her to his private closet. As always he looked to be on the point of departure, and in fact he was leaving the next day for Valognes.

'My army requires my presence,' he said. 'The preparations for invasion must be accelerated now. I leave you here under the protection of King Louis.'

'Am I in need of protection, sire?' faltered Anne.

Warwick smiled briefly. 'We are all in need of protection, daughter. Whether that of God, or our King, or our liege lord.

As I told you once before, you are my surety of good faith. When I hold England for Queen Margaret, your marriage will be solemnised and you will of course become subject to your husband and while he is under age to his mother – and father,' he added as an afterthought. 'Until then, you are nominally in their household but actually the guest of the King of France. Is that clear?'

'Yes, my lord.'

'I leave Messire de Josselin to watch over you. Should you have any complaints about your treatment, take them to him. He is in the King's confidence as well as mine.' Anne grimaced inwardly; she could not fathom the qualities in de Josselin which made great men place such trust in him. 'I understand that the Queen is at present affording you your correct position?'

What could she say? On her stool at Margaret's right hand she had been afforded a week's indifference and stultifying boredom. Yet she could scarcely complain that nobody had offered her a friendly word or even a smile. Her father would not consider that important. Besides, the attention of the Queen would probably prove worse than her neglect. Weakly she returned the easiest answer. 'Yes, my lord.'

He was running through a pile of letters, appending his signature, 'R. Warrewyke', and sealing them with his signet; he had evidently finished with her. The pleasant odour of hot wax came to her, and before it cut her off from him she felt some compulsion to say more, to appeal for something to sustain her through the loneliness ahead. Her father was still remote to her, a figure of awe almost as much today as in the infrequent visitations of her childhood. But even in his absence the stamp of his personality had been firm upon the routine of his ménage. Near or far, he had defended them against the worst of the outside world. Now he was giving her into the keeping of someone else and, King of France or Queen of England, she had no confidence in either.

'My lord?' she said timidly, and Warwick glanced up in mild surprise. He had indeed forgotten about her. 'Shall I ... shall I see King Henry?'

'No doubt. When you come to England.'

'And shall I be in his household?'

'At first, possibly. But the Prince of Wales will be given his own establishment, perhaps in the Welsh Marches or in the North, and you will be your own mistress.' Although he intended to be reassuring, Anne did not much like the prospect of being shut up in a distant castle with the cold young man who worshipped only his mother. 'There'll be children soon enough, and you will have the satisfaction of rearing them as heirs to the kingdom.' She knew that in his matter-of-fact way her father was trying to be kind. The inadequacy of his efforts brought tears to her eyes. Fearing that he would see them, she fell on her knees for his blessing. When he had pressed his signet on to another letter, he came over to her. 'They will be Nevilles as well as Plantagenets. Never forget it, Anne. You are a Neville and will remain so.' Once more his hand weighed on her head, and unusually he raised her. 'You must do that no more. The Princess of Wales kneels to nobody except her husband and to princes of the blood royal.'

She kept her eyes lowered, summoning the control to speak steadily. But she was saved from it by the entry of one of Warwick's captains. The Earl's thoughts were immediately deflected, and she was allowed to withdraw with her dignity intact.

He went without further farewell. Anne returned to the routine which became daily more oppressive. She had not appreciated before the amount of freedom she was allowed within her father's establishment. No one had taken much account of her doings, as long as she was in the right place at the right time for meals and other formal occasions. At Valognes particularly she had been left to herself. Gazing at the shafts of dusty sunlight that penetrated into the Queen's stifling chamber, she thought of the herb garden in the convent and the clapping of the doves' wings as they flew from the roof of the dovecote. Had God listened to her instead of to her father, she might by now be robed as a novice, subject to the daily order which meant so much more than this barren existence.

Occasionally they did go out. The Prince was fond of hunting, and when he could spare time from his studies, and his mother from business, they rode together. With Margaret went her ladies, and so perforce did Anne. Anjou in the summer was very hot. The grapes in the vineyards were swelling, but she did not enjoy the countryside lying fertile under the shimmering heat. Prince Edward took a special delight in making the kill personally, and he liked his skill to be applauded by a large audience.

It was at one of these spectacles that Margaret first spoke to her son's fiancée. Edward was laughing, smearing his hands and face with the blood of the fallen deer, while the huntsmen hacked off the antlers as his prize. As usual Anne was gripping the pommel of her saddle, her eyes closed, swallowing back the bitter taste that rose into her mouth. A horse drew alongside, and a brisk voice said in accented English, 'Retching, madame? You will need a stronger stomach if you are to be the wife of a Lancastrian king.' The Queen was staring at her with hard black eyes. There was no mercy in them. Anne was incapable of answering, even if she had known what to say. She saw Margaret's fine eyebrows flicker upwards in a subtle mixture of resignation and contempt before she hung her head and heard the Queen leave her. At least the shock of the encounter was sufficient to cure that day's sickness.

At the Queen's side, she watched the solitary successes of her betrothed at the quintain and the butts – for there were no royal henchmen to share his training. Only at such times, as the arrow with a swish and a slap struck the target, was she assailed by a sudden glimpse of the past, a memory of the practice-yard at Middleham so sweet that she forced it out of her mind hastily lest it should make the present unbearable.

The summer ripened, and news came that Warwick, with Clarence and a handful of faithful Lancastrian lords, had landed in Devon. There were covert glances at Anne as the messenger made his announcement: dove of reconciliation, pledge of faith she might be; she was also a hostage. If her father's invasion failed, she would need the protection of King Louis. But his progress was exemplary. By the end of September his army had advanced close to London, and King Edward, away in the North, seemed to be asleep to the rape of his country. Warwick's brother John, now Marquess Montagu, had joined his side, and it was said optimistically around the little exiled court that England was on the point of rising for its rightful king.

She was sitting one morning soon after the first fires had

been lighted in her usual place of chilly honour beside the Queen when Prince Edward came in. Following the other women she rose from her knees at the given signal to find that the Prince had stopped in front of her. In her surprise she was staring him full in the face. He held her gaze for the first time and smiled, but more in insolence than friendship.

'Your cousin Edward of York has fled the country,' he said loudly, and paused, waiting for a reaction that did not come. 'It is reported that he was drowned in a storm off the coast of Norfolk. With his brother the Duke of Gloucester.'

She sat down abruptly on her stool. No etiquette in the world could have kept her on her feet. Her fiancé went on talking, about Warwick's entry into the capital and the release of King Henry from the Tower, but she took in none of it. When she had recovered her faculties, the Prince was leaning on his mother's chair discussing a despatch. Mechanically she continued her embroidery, not heeding the redoubled fierceness of many meaning glances.

For several days the petty slights and isolation of her life ceased to hurt. The bewildered blankness in her heart outweighed everything else. She dreamed of weeping, and woke with wet cheeks. It was Bertrand de Josselin who brought her the truth of the matter, and such was her suspicion of him that he had to give her exhaustive details before she would believe him. King Edward and Richard of Gloucester had landed destitute but safe in Holland, and had gone to ask help of the Duke of Burgundy their brother-in-law. She sent him away and celebrated secretly the good luck of Edward of York which had embraced and saved his brother also.

This was not her only disloyalty. She could not rejoice over her father's success, because it brought perilously closer the final sealing of the contract between herself and Margaret's son. The false report of his death had brought Richard painfully back to her mind. Although she fought hard to dismiss him again, she could not help comparing him with the boy she was destined to marry. Hitherto she had regarded the Prince with wary indifference, never quite relinquishing the hope that he might possess something of his father's goodness. Now she knew otherwise. Nobody good could have taken pleasure in bringing her such tidings. From that day dislike of

Edward took firm root.

Unhappily the hardening of her heart coincided with a change of attitude towards her. She was made to take a more active part in court procedure, and when de Josselin informed her that they were moving to Amboise, she knew that that was the place chosen for her marriage. Warwick had fulfilled his side of the bargain; Queen Margaret would not fail to fulfil hers.

It was a wretched journey, through the mud and drizzle of late autumn, yet for Anne the rigours of the road were preferable to what lay at the end of it. The château of Amboise, even under the slush of melting snow, was less forbidding than Angers. It was one of King Louis' favourite residences, de Josselin volunteered as they approached, subtly reminding her that here also she was the French King's protégée. Here too her apartments were richly furnished, and everything provided for her comfort except company and friendship. They arrived at the beginning of December and at once an army of dressmakers and seamstresses appeared, armed with ells of velvet and brocade for her wedding gown. There was something sinister about the quiet efficiency with which they set about their task, as if they had waited there, scissors and pins in hand, since the beginning of time, for Anne's fate to lead her to them. She let them mould the magnificent robes about her, picturing as they did so an arch-fiend with a marked resemblance to the King of France presiding over a convocation of demons who were planning the career of Anne Neville.

The day appointed was the Feast of St Lucy, and the morning before a gift arrived from her father: a great ruby set in a gold clasp, enamelled with the red saltire of the Nevilles. His message was clear. She was to use it to fasten her mantle at her wedding, and everyone would see that she stood for her family, now holding England in the name of King Henry. Warwick also sent her several lengths of fine English woollen cloth, to make her warm gowns against the winter. Both gifts were noticeably grander than those she received from her fiancé and his mother. Anne did not particularly care, but Bertrand de Josselin was incensed.

'The Queen is insulting my lord Earl with such paltry

offerings,' he said to her in an indignant undertone. 'Of course, if she were challenged she would plead poverty, and all Europe knows she lives on the charity of our lord King Louis. But she was willing to pawn Calais to gain his help. Her credit would stretch if she wanted it to do so.' It was the first Anne had heard of Margaret's desperate gambit, and she was far more shocked by the idea of Calais being betrayed to the French than by the poor quality of her bridegifts. She wondered if her father, Captain of Calais through many stirring years, knew about his allies' bargain.

At all events, he was powerless now to prevent the fruition of his scheme. On 13 December his younger daughter married Edward of Lancaster and became Princess of Wales – discounting the fact that six weeks earlier, in sanctuary at Westminster, the wife of Edward IV had given birth to his heir, another Edward Prince of Wales. Anne's only hope of reprieve, she told herself bitterly as she took her place beside her impassive bridegroom, was that God would strike her down for perjury as she gave her consent. But she said 'Volo' and heaven was silent. In the abbey church of Valognes she had cried out to the summer night against her father's will ruling her life. Now it had bound her irrevocably to a young man who despised her, and she could do nothing.

And slowly, as the day and the wedding festivities wore tediously on, her fatalistic mood was succeeded by something far worse. The great hall at Amboise, filled with the babel of a hundred conversations and with sweating servants plying constantly to and fro, brought back to mind her sister's wedding feast, in the fortress of Calais. She thought of touching dignity submerged in tipsy coquetry, beautiful clothes spoiled, the obscene glances of her brother-in-law, and was more and more afraid. She recalled with growing clarity the aftermath of that feast: the dimming of Isobel's personality, the horrific tales told in the darkness, worst of all the stinking cabin and the dead child in her arms. After the meal there was dancing, and somehow Anne stumbled through the figures, praying that she might faint or be taken suddenly ill, and remaining obstinately on her feet.

The winter evening closed over the dutiful revels; a select company assembled to escort the bridal pair to their chamber.

Queen Margaret, the Countess of Warwick, Bertrand de Josselin, the priest who had married them ... only from her mother might she hope for sympathy, and she seemed determined to keep her head averted. Almost in silence they were disrobed and laid together in bed. The appropriate blessings and charms were muttered over them, and then they were left alone. As soon as the door closed, Edward sat up. Stricken with terror, Anne watched him reach to the shelf above their heads, and light a second candle from the single one burning there. His bedgown was open to his smooth chest, and there was a carefully darned tear in its satin revers. He leaned back against the bolster, and with a glance at Anne he suddenly raised his voice.

'Messire de Josselin!' After a brief pause, the curtains at the end of the bed twitched apart.

'Monseigneur?' enquired the Frenchman blandly.

'Which of your masters are you spying for tonight?' said the Prince, speaking in English so that Anne should understand. Clutching the sheets convulsively to her chin, she was for an instant united with her husband in abhorrence of the official eavesdropper. He smiled non-committally and did not answer. 'We do not require your assistance,' said Edward. 'Leave us, messire.'

'A thousand apologies, but I was given instructions—'

'You will take your instructions from me. Leave us.' Accepting his defeat with the slightest lifting of his shoulders, the spy bowed, wished them good night, and disappeared. Imprisoned again within the heavy bed-curtains, Anne shrank from the Prince's next movement. But it was away from and not towards her. He threw back the coverlet, swung his legs to the floor, and put on the fur-lined robe which lay beside the bed. Then he turned and looked down at Anne, his lips still curled in the disdain he had shown to de Josselin.

'You surely didn't imagine that I was going to lie with you? Let that French fox believe it if he will, and report it to whom he will. I'm not going to waste my seed on an earl's younger daughter for his benefit, or his employers'.' Anne caught her breath, and he took up one of the candlesticks. The pale light flowed over his hard young face. 'Yes, I'm going. Don't expect me to share your bed again. We have been forced to keep this bargain, but there is no guarantee that Warwick will keep faith. He's too fond of power to be trusted. When we have taken England from him, I must be free to mate according to my station.' His mother's imperious voice, instilling statecraft, echoed behind his own.

'Anyway,' he added, and now he was all arrogant young man, 'I doubt if I'd find much pleasure inside you. Or get a healthy son on you, to judge by your sister's achievement.' He stalked off to a low door in the arras, and the tapestry fell soundlessly behind him.

The wave of humiliation that engulfed her was so powerful that she thought she would die of it. Sleep was long in releasing her.

It was no secret, she was sure. The Prince had been acting on orders in leaving her, and not only de Josselin would have guessed the truth. Her waiting-women, for instance, dressing a grey-faced bride the morning after her wedding, had not needed to strip the bed to read the situation. Their attitude to her, outwardly more obsequious, was slyly charged with a sort of triumph. Throughout the court it was repeated, especially among the English ladies in Margaret's train. Some had been with her for years, living in penury and exile because their husbands or fathers had fought for Lancaster and had rejected or been refused the victorious Yorkists' pardon. Small wonder that they were hostile to the girl who had come to take the highest place among them, richly clad and provided for by the lord who was the author of their hardship. Small wonder, too,.that when she was virtually repudiated by her husband at the outset of their marriage, they should rejoice in it. And so the confirmation of her status made her life even more comfortless.

Edward no longer ignored her. He seemed in a contrary way to believe that he had asserted himself; he shed his diffidence and became quite jocular towards her. The jesting remarks he made were usually at her expense, or that of her father. Anne could not tell if these refinements of behaviour were authorised or not. Since the Queen maintained her lofty indifference, she was inclined to think that they were his own invention. Her only defence was to pretend she neither heard nor felt the pinpricks. At night she lay alone in the ceremonial bed, and its privacy was some small compensation for its shame.

Before long they were heading north-east for Paris. There was no welcome for them in the sullen winter towns on their route. The Prince, riding through streets full of citizens busily intent on their own doings, clenched his hand on his rein and muttered, 'When I am king France will be mine again, and then they shall show me some respect.' Anne caught a glimpse of the dark brows drawn together and the bitter line of his mouth, and trembled for the towns if they should ever surrender to his mercy. They paused in Paris, and then pushed on towards the north. She did not need the ubiquitous de Josselin to inform her that they were making for the coast and England. At Dieppe they halted, within sight of the dull slaty sea, and waited.

For what, nobody seemed to know. Over the Channel, the English had submitted to Warwick's rule in the name of King Henry. All Margaret had to do to regain the throne she had fought for through ten tireless years was to cross those few miles of sea and accept it. But she did not. There was no sign of their embarking, and after some weeks of busy aimlessness the whole company moved inland.

The itinerant life continued through January. Margaret paced between the towns of Normandy as a man would pace a room, impatient to be doing and yet lacking the resolution to do it. Her court trailed after her, spirits dropping and tempers rising with each depressing day. De Josselin was overtly displeased. He reported to Anne in the Queen's presence with deliberately raised voice that the Duke of Burgundy had received Edward of York and the Duke of Gloucester in Bruges, and that he had promised troops and ships to them. The fact that the Duke of York – as he was known in Lancastrian circles – might be preparing to invade England did nothing to stir his greatest rival to positive action. One person at any rate had no doubt of the reason.

'It is your father's fault.' The Prince threw it at Anne during dinner. She put down her knife, sensing unpleasantness to come. 'He should have come to meet us.' She was stung into defence of her father, who had never failed to accomplish his purposes, however extraordinary they might be.

'My lord Earl is holding London for you, sire. He can't be in two places at once.'

A little taken aback at being answered at all, Edward said defensively, 'Then he should send one of his brothers. We can't cross the Channel without an armed escort, not with the Burgundian fleet at sea. Besides, it's not right for the Queen of England and the Prince of Wales to sidle into some port without proper preparation for our welcome. We should be given a royal reception.' His eyes flashed a challenge to his wife, but she was intent upon the wine in her goblet.

'I'm sure my father knows his duty in honouring you, your grace,' she said quietly. It did not occur to her to include herself in the royal reception.

In February they came to rest at Honfleur. The ships collected again in the harbour; some stores were embarked, and even a few of the men-at-arms. But once more the Queen delayed. Officially, a contrary wind was holding up the sailing. March came, and with it news that the Duke of Burgundy was fitting up a fleet at Flushing for King Edward's return to England. Serious strife erupted at the centre of the exiled court. The Queen and the Prince were closeted for hours with their advisers. When they emerged, an aura of frustration clung heavily about them, the royal pair with their mouths set in similarly obstinate lines, the counsellors glaring at each other or at the floor. The impatience of the lords was echoed through the lower orders. Several soldiers and one gentleman were killed or wounded as they vented their overwrought feelings in street fights.

And the silent persecution of the Princess of Wales intensified. For some reason that nobody could quite fathom, the Earl of Warwick was to blame for their present detention. Because the culprit was out of reach, his daughter was a convenient scapegoat. If she had not been to some extent inured to her treatment the new wave of resentment directed at her would have been very hard to bear. Instead, she too began to long for England. Since Valognes she had not dared to look to the future; she expected little from it now. But at least her father was in England. What he could do to improve her lot she shied from considering: recognition of her marriage would only mean the worse evil of consummation. It would be enough that they stood upon the same soil. Her faith in him still survived.

Finally it was Margaret's hatred of Edward of York that drove her to the ships. While she squabbled with her advisers and rode restlessly along the quayside where the ships lay idle, the Yorkist armada sailed. Whatever her doubts, her conflicts of pride and ambition and fear, to which only her son had the key, she could not endure the thought that the usurper should return before her. On the same day that the news came to her, she ordered embarkation in a passion which swept away her vacillation. The Prince was jubilant.

'I thank the saints that we have waited till now,' he said to his mother, his dark eyes glistening. 'Please God there's a chance that I may meet the archer's bastard in battle, and kill him myself.'

'Please God it will not come to that,' retorted the Queen. 'If there is any justice in heaven, he will in truth be drowned this time.' Anne was perplexed by the exchange until she worked out that the archer's bastard must be King Edward. She had heard her husband called a bastard by the Duke of Clarence, but she had not realised that the mud of scandal was flung so liberally.

The new alacrity of its leaders was not enough to launch the expedition immediately. Some of the soldiers were scattered around the neighbourhood, pilfering, poaching, or just wandering; many of the seamen had gone home, and it took time to muster them in Honfleur. It was a week before the Lancastrian fleet left the harbour. And once they were in open water, they were struck by the full force of the excuse which had kept them so long in Normandy. The wind which had blown Edward of York from Flushing to Cromer in one day kept Queen Margaret at sea for three weeks.

They landed at last at Weymouth on Easter Day. A feeble advance guard of the Lancastrian leaders attended Confession and High Mass in the parish church. Above them, after a long delay and remonstrance with the mayor of the town, the bells were pealing a belated welcome to the Queen of England and the Prince and Princess of Wales. The weather-beaten ships were still straggling into the harbour when they learned of the reason for Weymouth's frowardness. It was news that struck hard at the morale of the storm-tossed travellers, and turned Margaret of Anjou white to the lips with fury. While they had been drifting with the wind about the English Channel there had been a revolution in the state of affairs in England. Edward of York was ranging the Midlands with a powerful army at his back; deserted by his son-in-law Clarence, the Earl of Warwick was last heard of besieged in his city of Coventry.

How this appalling situation had come about was obscure, but the Queen did not wait to find out. Quartering herself at Cerne Abbey, she threw herself into a frenzy of activity. The Prince was always at her side, or running errands for her, his normally sullen face transfigured with the desire to do her service. Yet Anne noticed that although he was turned seventeen, he never took any initiative himself. Perhaps, belying his looks, he had a little of his father in him after all. It was not likely to endear him to his wife at this late stage. No one talked of King Henry now; only of revenge upon his usurper who had so disgracefully beaten all odds to contend once more for the crown.

The Queen and her train were on the quay, supervising the unloading of a small cannon, when a horseman joined them, so travel-grimed that his livery was indistinguishable. He went straight to Margaret, urging his horse unceremoniously between her and the gentleman she was speaking to. Anne was too far away to hear what was said, but she saw the Queen start forward as the man delivered his message, clutching at his saddle-skirts as if for support. The next moment she glanced over her shoulder, swiftly, almost involuntarily, and straight at Anne; the messenger's eyes followed hers. As if she were being immersed in icy water Anne felt herself being drawn into their conference. And by some trick of the fitful breeze, a few scraps of it drifted to her ears.

'... at Barnet,' said the man, '... and his brother the Lord Montagu.' In answer to a question from Margaret he shook his head: '... no doubt ... dead.'

When Margaret had finished with him she gestured him towards her daughter-in-law. He went down on one knee before Anne where she stood stiffly beside a coil of hawser, and told her that the Earl of Warwick had been defeated and killed by Edward of York at Barnet north of London on Easter Day.

Clarence had bound himself firmly to the Earl's cause by his marriage. But the King's youngest brother must have chosen differently. Of course, the evil counsellors that people talked about so glibly were the Woodvilles, the Queen's acquisitive relatives. After they had been reduced to their proper positions all would be well again. Yet the prospect of her father and her cousin Richard being, however nominally, in opposite camps made Anne apprehensive. At the first opportunity she burned candles to both their patron saints for concord.

3

INTO LIMBO

They dressed her in black, though Warwick would have told them that it was a colour unbecoming to her complexion. Mass was said for his soul by the Queen's chaplain, and she could not take the words seriously. Prince Edward was beside her, representing his mother, who had kept her chamber. At the end he said to her, 'You're not weeping, madame. Are you not grieved for your lord father?'

She turned her head and met his eyes steadily. 'You told me a lie before. Why should I believe you now?'

His gaze wavered, uncertain of her meaning, and then his jaw tightened and he said, 'As you will. The Queen my mother has taken it ill, but for myself, I'm glad he's gone. Now we can win our own victory over the usurper, and share the glory with no one.' Anne disdained to reply, thinking of how his young bravado would soon quail before the cool regard of the Earl of Warwick.

The army marched; Anne went with it. Her interest in its progress was minimal. Along the roads the hedgerows were showing green, and at any moment her father would appear under the red and white banner of the bear and ragged staff. She did not notice the new grimness in the Queen's expression, the desperation with which she flogged her forces northwards to meet the promised Welsh reinforcements. Peasants ran away from them, the streets of the towns they entered were strangely deserted; there was no resistance and no enemy. Anne fancied that the Lancastrian fleet had sunk in the Channel – they were all in Purgatory and it was their ghosts the people fled. The Earl would wait in vain for their coming, and perhaps he would make Clarence Henry's heir, and Isobel would be Queen after all.

Anne herself might indeed have been a ghost for all the notice taken of her. The pretence that her husband slept with her was abandoned; she like the other ladies lay nightly on a pallet in whatever chamber was allotted to the Queen. By day she rode with them, somewhere in the heart of the Lancastrian army, and even the hostility was gone. They had forgotten her. She gazed at the springing countryside and reflected that if she left the column and went to seek her father nobody would be the wiser; but she felt it was too much trouble.

Insulated by her separation, she did not share the apprehension which stalked the Queen's forces. Few volunteers were joining them, and reinforcements were slow to come in. Before they reached Bristol they learned that Edward had left London with his two brothers and an army fully reconstituted after its losses at Barnet. Captains and ladies, recruits and men-at-arms, knew the legendary speed of his marches, and the pace of their own journey quickened, despite the dragging feet of the infantry and the drooping heads of the horses. Margaret and her son rode up and down the column shouting encouragement, assuring their men that all would be well once they crossed the Severn at Gloucester and joined with Lord Pembroke in Wales.

Anne too was deadly weary, but she had seen it before: the menace of the swift golden warrior over the nearby hill, the fear that spurred them along the road, the hope that safety lay round its next turning. Perhaps Warwick was waiting to take King Edward in the rear, which was why he had not made himself known to his allies before?

At Gloucester their unimpeded progress met a check. Margaret's scouts came back to report that the city had closed its gates against them. Outwardly undismayed by the foiling of her plans, the Queen addressed her demoralised men.

'The usurper thinks to prevent us from crossing Severn,' she cried, the resonance of her accented voice reaching far back into the ranks. 'He may have cowed his good people of Gloucester, but he has no power over those who serve the true King. We will go on; there is another bridge in a short march, at Tewkesbury.' Then she wheeled her horse and kicked it into a tired canter, defying her troops not to follow her lead.

It was late afternoon before the tower of Tewkesbury Abbey

was sighted. The army shuffled to a standstill again while scouts went forward and the Queen conferred with her captains. Men-at-arms dismounted and threw themselves on the grass which grew lush and damp between the two roads from Gloucester. They were too tired now to fear the enemy.

A page in the Duke of Somerset's livery was zigzagging through the scattered troops, rounding up the Queen's ladies like a sheepdog. He brought them to a house off the road; wagons were being unloaded and the baggage carried inside. In a long low upstairs room Margaret and her commanders stood round a crude map on a table. As Anne was led through they were wrangling fiercely.

'There's no time to cross with York less than ten miles away.'

'Under correction, my lord Somerset, if we begin now the army could all be over by midnight. Edward will not attack before dawn.'

'My men are weary, sire,' said the Queen. 'They must have rest.'

'My lord of Wenlock is familiar with the habits of the usurper,' Somerset broke in sarcastically, 'and in a mighty hurry to run away from him.' There was a rattle of steel as Wenlock laid his hand on his dagger, and glancing back from the far end of the room Anne saw Margaret move swiftly between the two glowering noblemen. A leather curtain dropped over the scene, but her voice still penetrated.

'None of us is afraid of the usurper. We shall face him and fight if he challenges us.'

'Yes, it's time he was taught who is master in England,' the Prince added hotly. There was a chorus of agreement, and the conference sank below hearing.

The ladies were all asleep, fully clothed on their pallets; Anne was beyond fatigue. She sat hugging her knees while the blue square of sky in the dormer window and the sounds of bivouacking faded. Next door the council of war went on and on, voices rising and ebbing in the growing dusk. Anne did not think she could rest in such proximity to a man like Lord Wenlock, the Captain of Calais who had so treacherously kept them from landing when Isobel was in labour. He had been the cause of Anne's ordeal and her sister's suffering, and he had betrayed the Earl of Warwick. What kind of success could Margaret expect when her army was led by such men?

She lay down and closed her eyes, but sleep was nowhere near. When she next turned her head towards the leather curtain, light was trickling round the edges from a candle in the room beyond. The conversation had ceased, but it was still occupied, for a board creaked regularly as if someone were pacing up and down. There was no sound of the fall of boots, and Anne suspected that it was the Queen who walked to and fro, like her daughter-in-law unable to find any repose.

The dawn chorus was no more than a quartet before there was stirring in the camp; a horse galloped through the half-light and scudded to a halt under the window. Hasty footsteps went to the door, and admittance was sought and gained. Not long afterwards, with the objects in the chamber as yet colourless, a page came in and summoned the ladies to the Queen. She was already dressed, if indeed she had undressed, and her armourer was strapping on the steel corselet she had had made when the conflict between York and Lancaster first flared into war. She gave no good morning to her attendants beyond the curt remark, 'The usurper is drawing up his men in battle order. We must fight.'

An early mist like swathes of white muslin lay across the meadows, and on all sides soldiers were wading through it knee-high to take up their positions. Margaret mounted the tall black mare held ready for her and Anne, almost crippled by stiffness from yesterday's ride, scrambled ungracefully into the saddle of a palfrey. From her new vantage point she could see the clear ground fretted with ditches where they had rested the day before, and beyond that, in the direction of Gloucester, another body of men. There too standards and lances were manœuvring, and she realised with a stab of horror that it was the Yorkist army.

The Lancastrian captains approached, gallant mounted figures in full armour and emblazoned surcoats, their helmets carried behind them by their squires. While the Prince of Wales trotted forward to embrace his mother, the other lords saluted her formally. Then, urging her horse past them, the Queen led the way to the centre of the battle line which was just forming out of the confusion. She wheeled to face her troops, and reached back to take the Prince's hand. Over her breastplate she was wearing a great purple mantle, which was spread in opulent folds over the mare's crupper; it was fastened with a gold chain, and on her wedding finger was an emerald set about with diamonds which she had kept from the pawnbroker. Her dark eyes, which had of late held only fierce determination, glowed as she surveyed her son, who was caparisoned as bravely as she. She spoke to Lord Wenlock, but her voice carried over the suddenly hushed men.

'My lord, in token of our trust, we place at your side our most precious hope, and the future of England. The Prince of Wales shall share with you the command of our centre.' As Wenlock acknowledged the honour the front ranks brandished their weapons and cheered, and the cry of 'Edward! Edward!' rolled back to the rearguard and out to the flanks of the army. When the shouting subsided, a mocking echo of it drifted to them from the south: the Yorkist army also were acclaiming their leader. The Queen, pulling in her mare's head so sharply that the animal snorted in protest, turned to Anne.

'Salute your husband, madame.' The palfrey was much smaller than Edward's grey war-horse. Anne stared up at the Prince and wondered what one said on such occasions. He had no wish to say anything and, as at their first meeting, he avoided her gaze. At length, impelled by an impatient gesture from his mother, he leaned over, touched his cheek to hers, and gratefully left her. Humiliated yet again by her husband's open antipathy, she retired into the anonymity of the Queen's ladies. The Queen and the Prince were embracing and speaking many words to each other. It was now full daylight, and southwards drums were beating insistently. With a final handclasp, Margaret drove her spurs into the mare and set a furious pace back over the meadows.

A boat was waiting for them near the confluence of the Severn and Avon. Anne and the ladies-in-waiting clambered in eagerly, but the Queen hung back. Behind them a cannonade had begun, and the boatmen stood ready to cast off. The Queen was arguing with the gentlemen who had escorted her to the river, and ever casting glances back towards the belt of trees which hid the battleground. They prevailed at last and handed her on board. The broad stream flowed swiftly as the oarsmen pulled across the current. Now that the danger was less immediate Anne was seized by impotent panic. From her seat in the stern the farther bank was impossibly distant, and the fear of pursuing Yorkists pouring on to the eastern shore prickled down her back. Not so her mother-in-law. She faced the side they had left; her lips moved, but in nothing as mechanical as prayer, and in her face was such naked yearning that Anne shrank from it. This evidence of frailty in one so indomitable utterly unnerved her.

Their refuge was a small monastery, which Margaret at once began to convert into a military outpost. She herself took over a chamber which looked towards the river, and although she could see neither the water nor the engagement which must have joined beyond it, she returned to the deep embrasure constantly. Having deployed her few men, she had come to the end of her resources. She had done her utmost, and it was left to others to conclude the business. Soon after the lay brothers had borne away the dinner platters one of the Queen's messengers came in, breathless and jubilant. He had spoken to one of Somerset's archers, who reported that the Duke had routed the left wing of the Yorkists by a cunning circling movement.

'Gloucester's men are in flight, and the fellow said the field was as good as ours already.' Margaret's eyes glittered, and she gave the courier a mark from a purse which was almost empty, but she did not speak. In her years of campaigning she had seen too many twists of fortune to believe in such an easy victory. He went back to his post and his mistress resumed her pacing.

Anne was in the corner; no one had marked her indrawn breath when Gloucester was mentioned, or the way she retreated further from the light. She told herself without conviction that it was the contingent from the city of Gloucester the messenger meant, but beneath ran the cold certainty that it was not so. Richard was there, not a mile away, giving ground before the inexorable advance of her husband. The false report of his drowning had perhaps only been to prepare her for this. In an automatic gesture she had not used for a long time she touched the place between her breasts where their talisman had hung. But it was gone. She had no claim on him, not even the right to pray for his safety. If he died, it would be without sparing a thought for her. With her hand pressed to the memory of the pendant, she sat quietly and suffered. Roaming the chamber in tigerish frustration, Margaret suffered too.

The stillness outside was uncanny. Bells rang for Tierce, and again a barren three hours later for Sexte. There was no hint that across the river thousands of men were struggling bloodily for the mastery of England. Only a knot of tense silent women in the guest-house and a few wary retainers patrolling outside. Not until the afternoon did anything else happen. There was a commotion outside the door and one of Margaret's French bodyguard shuffled in, hauling behind him the draggled caricature of an archer. He manhandled the creature before the Queen, where it collapsed in a sodden heap. More formally, the man-at-arms knelt beside it, keeping a firm grip on its collar.

'Madame, he came across the river. He was trying to desert.'

Margaret looked down at the shivering archer with distaste. 'Whom does he serve?'

'My lord of Devon, madame. I could not understand any more.' The dowager Countess of Devon started up with an inarticulate cry, and subsided.

'Well, fellow,' the Queen said in English, 'speak for yourself. I am your Queen. Why have you left the field?' He raised his head, shook it, and mumbled something unintelligible. Rivulets of water ran down his face, mixed on one temple with a streak of blood. His eyes were popping with terror. 'Speak more clearly, or you will be whipped into plain words.' Making an effort, he repeated himself. The Queen threw out a hand impatiently. 'Can anyone tell what he is saying?'

'He says, "They're coming, we must run."' It was Anne who interpreted in a small voice; there had been a groom in her father's service from Bideford.

'What does the wretch mean? Ask him!' Margaret ordered, terse with foreboding. The man rolled his eyes towards Anne like a sick dog as she came forward. His breath stank of onions. In a neutral tone she translated his dialect.

'He swam the river. The current nearly swept him away. He wants to go home.' With sudden weak urgency, he raised himself on one elbow and with the other hand clutched at

Anne's skirt. They all understood the word he gasped.

'Drink!' Anne recoiled, snatching her gown out of his muddy fist with disgust. One of the ladies proffered at arm's length a cupful of the thin ale left over from their dinner, and he grabbed it and gulped it down noisily, smacking his lips. With renewed strength he beckoned to Anne, who did not this time come so close, and told the rest of his story. There was no more fighting, only killing, and everyone was trying to run away from the Yorkists. Most had been cut down in the meadows where the Avon barred their escape, and many of those who tried to cross had not been able to swim. The Devon man had gone another way, and hidden in the rushes until he could launch himself unseen across the wider river.

'And now we must all run away, mistress. King Edward will murder us all if he catches us.' Hoisting himself on to all fours, he peered earnestly up at the Queen, dimly aware that she was the most important person present.

She was drawn up very still, staring at the wall, and a nervous tic was plucking at the corner of her mouth.

'This man is a liar,' she said quietly. 'The usurper has sent him to deceive us.' Nobody spoke, and the Frenchman shifted uneasily on his knees. She stooped abruptly and seized the archer by the wet forelock, forcing his head back. 'Where . . . is . . . the . . . Prince?' she asked with slow precision. He flinched from her intensity and gabbled a jumble of words that not even Anne could distinguish, except for the recurring phrase, 'I don't know.' Margaret let him go and he subsided to the floor again. His head-wound had reopened and thick crimson blood was oozing through his hair.

'Take him away,' she said through her teeth. Her bodyguard was about to ask for further instructions, but he thought better of it and retreated as hurriedly as he could with the exhausted fugitive.

The unnatural silence descended, and for a moment the Queen gazed down at the dark damp patch on the flagstones. Then she made for the door, and without waiting for an attendant she flung it open and strode outside. Drawn mindlessly after, the other women followed, through the gatehouse where the porter gaped at them, down the slope among the scattered trees towards the river. Margaret's men, no longer on guard, were in a huddle by an elm tree, all looking one way. The midday sun was invisible, but the willows on the far side of the grey Severn were clearly defined. Even from here no sound except the birds, but among the trees there was movement, as though the bank were swarming with insects. Transfixed, the men-at-arms and the ladies watched, until two of the insects broke into full view. Swaying for an instant on the brink of the water, there was a gleam of steel, a distant cry and a splash, and the bank was empty again. Margaret roused first, rounding sharply on her idle bodyguard.

'Why have you left your posts? Go back at once. Do you wish the Prince to find you unprepared when he comes?' She turned on her heel and went towards the gatehouse. The men, lingering together, exchanged glances and did not immediately obey her orders.

Once more they were penned up in the guest-chamber, with no sound but the fall of the Queen's restless feet. Sick and light-headed from lack of sleep, Anne dozed on the uncomfortable bench where she sat, and started awake to the Queen's bulky figure crossing and recrossing the window. Over all there was the persistent beat of horses' hoofs, the rumbling of wagons and the scuffing tread of hundreds of soldiers, all jumbled up with the present and the recent past.

A man stood in the room, although she had not seen him enter. Her sluggish memory placed him slowly. It was William Joseph, one of the Queen's secretaries, who had accompanied them to the ferry this morning. The normally sleek hair around his clerk's tonsure was dishevelled, and there was mud on the hem of his gown.

'Madame, you must fly. We are lost.' The Queen had turned from the window, her clenched fist with its great green stone resting on the embrasure, and was looking at Joseph with hostility.

'I have heard such tales before, from cowards trying to save their own face.'

'I'm no soldier, madame, so I have no face to lose,' he replied, with a spark of anger he would not formerly have dared to show. 'It is all over. King Edward is in Tewkesbury.'

'But Somerset drove the left wing from the field—'

'His grace is a prisoner. I was in the abbey with him – it was full of our men seeking sanctuary. The King arrested them all. I only escaped because I have a friend among the brothers who guided me out by a side door.'

'The King? The usurper . . . who profanes holy sanctuary to win his battles.'

'Please, madame.' The clerk fell to his knees and took her hand. 'If we go now we can be away before they begin the search for you. My lord of Pembroke is somewhere near—'

'No!' Margaret flung away from him. 'We shall wait for the Prince. With the men he has saved we can join Pembroke. . . . Why do you shake your head?' She wheeled back and glared down at her secretary. 'Where is the Prince?'

'I don't know. All your captains are killed or taken. I didn't see the lord Prince in the abbey. I fear he—'

'It is not true,' she cut trenchantly across his hesitant words. 'He will come, and I will wait for him. Save yourself if you wish, Master Joseph.' She thrust out her hand for him to kiss, but when he tried to speak again she silenced him. 'No more. Go to the refectory for refreshment before you leave.' There was a concerted cry from Margaret's ladies, all burning for tidings of their menfolk, and they rose and converged on their mistress and the secretary like a flock of dowdy birds.

Their wings flapped round Anne, shutting out the light, and their anxious babble did not reach her. She needed no further news. The Queen's defiant blindness had exposed the folly of her own. The Prince of Wales would not come to the succour of the woman who waited for him, and neither would anyone come to hers. She knew that he was dead, and so was her father. This small chamber was adrift in a world devoid of form and shelter. The mighty presence of the Earl of Warwick, which had overshadowed and ordered it since her birth, was gone, and chaos returned.

It was there that Sir William Stanley found them the following day. His armed escort was small, but the Prior made no difficulty about admitting him; he was too prudent a man to defy the officer of a king so decisively and so locally reseated on the throne. Hearing the chink of armour in the doorway, Queen Margaret whirled from her rigid posture by the window, light leaping into her haggard face.

'My son!'

'No, Madame Margaret. Not your son.' Perhaps because they had been half expecting the visitation there were one or two muffled shrieks among the attendants. But although the light was extinguished, Margaret did not flinch.

'Do as you will with me, sire. My son will avenge any wrongs I may suffer.' Stanley laughed, a short sharp bark.

'I doubt that – unless he can influence the divine judgment from Purgatory.' Seeing her stand still in wilful incomprehension, he continued with brutal relish. 'He's dead, madame. So give up your hopes and go with me to the King.'

There came a low inhuman sound between a moan and a snarl, and even the hardbitten Sir William almost gave back a pace before the wild rage that suddenly possessed the Queen. The two soldiers outside brought their lances to the ready in case their captain was attacked. But she did not move; the menace was in her hunched shoulders and out-thrust head, like a dangerous beast at bay.

'It is a foul lie,' she hissed. With the courage of the lances at his back Stanley contradicted her, a vicious levity in his voice paying her for his moment of fright.

'No lie. I saw his body myself. Stripped. Three sword wounds, two in the back. But King Edward has ordered Christian burial for him in the abbey, along with all the other traitors.' She was rocking slightly on her feet, and her eyes had glazed.

'It is a lie. I will not believe it. He is alive.'

'My word on it as a gentleman,' said Stanley curtly, tired of baiting her. 'Now surrender yourself and go with us. The King wishes you to follow him to Coventry.'

'I will not go. Take me to my son.'

'Come, madame. His grace is merciful and has commanded us to use you with courtesy, but he will be obeyed.'

'Take me to my son. I will not stir from this place until you swear to do so. Or would you commit more sacrilege by using force in a holy house?' Her voice was still quiet, but it wavered perilously close to the hysterical. Humanity was not a great virtue of Sir William Stanley, but he balked at the prospect of laying hands on this half crazy woman who had also been his Queen. Moreover, his discovery of her hiding-place would bring him enough credit to allow her a little latitude. His master King Edward did not look kindly on the ill-treatment of women.

They had laid the Prince out in the infirmary of the abbey, along with the other noble corpses that they had not yet had time to bury. The headless bodies of the Lancastrians executed by King Edward after the battle had been first interred; here the slain in action awaited the digging of their graves, with coarse grey sheets drawn over them. The rottenness of putrefaction polluted the atmosphere even at a distance, and the old Countess of Devon, whose son had been killed, staggered and could not go on. Margaret pressed forward, almost sweeping aside the Father Abbot in her impatience. A way was made too for Anne, and she was compelled to follow her mother-in-law. Beside the high cot the Queen halted, motionless, while the Abbot turned down the edge of the sheet. The Prince's skin, waxen yellow, stretched tight on the bones of the skull, had lost all semblance of youth.

For an eternity the Queen stared down at him, her face as stony as that of her son. Then with a slow terrible gesture she laid hold of the sheet and stripped it from him. Her arms outstretched as though crucified she sank to the floor, and the cry of a forsaken soul shivered on the foul air, a wordless keening that rose to a pitch of agony and sank to the whimper of a wounded animal. Anne looked on, half stupefied by the stench and the horror of what she saw: the bloodless corpse with the livid scar between the ribs; the swollen belly above the pathetically virgin manhood. It was too obscene to be anything but a mockery of life. Margaret had torn off her head-dress and her thick hair, grey streaks among the midnight, spilled over her shoulders. Swaying on her knees she cradled the Prince's head against her breast. Her hair fell over the deep sockets of his eyes, and all the while she was crooning, a strange primitive lament.

It was the Abbot who attempted to end the tragic spectacle. Approaching the Queen from his place of retreat by the door, he laid his hand gingerly on her arm.

'Be of good comfort, my daughter ...' he began, but he faltered lamely to a stop. At his touch, a violent shudder shook her and she recoiled as if from something loathsome. She flung out her hands to ward him off, and as she did so the Prince's head, unsupported, fell askew back on to the cot; one dead arm slithered over the edge and dangled.

Margaret's eyes snapped wide, seeing and understanding at last the decay that was before her. Her fingers drove deep into her hair, tugging at the roots in torment. She began to scream, not the ritual mourning wail of before, but a howl of pain and loss and outrage against the injustice of God. The body of her son lay as it had fallen, indecently sprawled, and the flying ends of her hair flicked at his cold flesh as she lurched from side to side in a paroxysm of anguish. Tears were flowing now, the tears she would not shed before, and mingling with her own blood, for she was raking her nails down her cheeks in frenzied self-mutilation.

This was too much for Sir William Stanley. Cynically unmoved as he was, he could not allow his prisoner the freedom to destroy herself. He called two of his men, who shouldered through the huddled petrified groups of monks and women at the door, and strode forward purposefully. The Abbot's voice pursued him, the feeble protest lost among the screams of the demented Queen.

'My lord, my lord. . . .'

The graceless scuffle that followed was nothing but a blur in Anne's memory, less distinct even than the preceding events. She was at one moment standing in the reek of the infirmary, at the next bumping in a chariot, at the next stationary again and being served with a bowl of broth by a brightly clad page. Her companions were still with her, and they were in a small panelled chamber with carts and hoofs rattling outside the window. The Queen was there too, but Anne avoided looking at her, and she was not making a sound. Anne drank the broth mechanically, although it made her empty stomach heave. The page took the bowls away, and it might have been hours later that the door opened again and someone else came in. He paused on the threshold and glanced slowly round the room, taking in all the occupants. Then he inclined slightly towards the chair where Margaret sat, and said, 'Madame, would you come with me? His grace will receive you, with your ladies.' Without a word the Queen rose to obey, but as the young man turned to lead the way his eyes lighted on Anne, as if by design. Her atrophied senses took in little of his appearance, but it seemed to her that his lips widened into a brief smile before he moved on.

They were taken to a high chamber full of people, and at one end on a dais were two tall noblemen. The ghost of an old fear, of two old fears, touched Anne's heart. Their guide bowed before the taller of the nobles, who held out his hand in a familiar fashion and drew the young man up beside him. Margaret, foremost among the party of women, stood with her head drooping.

'Well, madame.' The voice, deep and easy, rang through the hall and Anne knew it down the years. 'You owe our country much blood and many widows' and mothers' tears. I will speak no more of your guilt because I think you have now tasted its grief for yourself. We shall show you more mercy than you deserve.' The King's gaze swept over the woebegone figures of the ex-Queen's companions, and even Anne acknowledged that it softened. 'Ladies, we shall use you gently. You have suffered enough. The war is over.'

'Sir William?' Stanley stepped forward, square and smug. 'For your good offices, we place Dame Margaret in your custody for the present.'

As Stanley accepted his charge, the young man on the dais spoke to the King, who bent to listen, placing an arm round his neck. At his left the other spoke, and Edward took him also into the compass of his arms. One tall blond lord and one slight dark lord, linked together by the casual affection of the King. Anne saw that they were talking about her, and although the concentrated attention of King Edward and the Duke of Clarence should have frozen her, the presence of Richard of Gloucester obscurely made everything well.

She was separated from the other women and lodged in a house nearby. The mistress of the house, a comfortable soul married to a corn-chandler, fussed over her guest and talked incessantly, even when she had put her to bed and ordered her to sleep. Her stream of chatter passed meaninglessly through Anne's tired mind; she was more bewildered by the good woman's concern for her comfort than she had been by the neglect of the past months. She submitted to her ministrations and said nothing. To a monologue of gossip her hair was being combed the next morning when the Duke of Gloucester was announced. The goodwife stopped in mid-anecdote, blushed crimson, and plumped to the floor in a deep courtesy as he entered.

Anne saw his reflection in the looking-glass, standing inside the door, scarcely aware of the stout woman squeezing breathlessly past him out of the room. She stayed where she was, staring in the mirror, and his image came beside her, and the eyes met hers. Brown, as she remembered them, but their expression was strange: troubled, searching for something in her and not finding. At last he said stiltedly, 'Madame, accept my condolences on the loss of your lord husband.' She looked down at her hands and noted with dull surprise that she was still wearing a wedding ring; the mourning she had assumed for her father had not needed change.

'Yes. Thank you.' Her voice sounded oddly – perhaps it was days since she had spoken aloud. Another silence hung uneasily between them.

'They are caring for you, I hope,' said the Duke.

'Yes, your grace.' She could feel that he was asking her for some response, but she could not tell what; it was too difficult.

He moved abruptly out of her view and said in slightly muffled tones, 'We shall be leaving Coventry soon. My brother of Clarence has offered to take you under his protection until we reach London. There you will be able to go to our sister the Duchess. Later perhaps your lady mother will be permitted to join you too.'

'My mother?' Anne was shaken far enough out of her lethargy to turn and face him. The Duke was by the bed, intent on a signet on his right hand. 'My mother was drowned.' She had heard nothing of her since they had left France on separate ships.

'Why no. Did you think she was?' Glancing up in quick sympathy, he lost his diffidence for a moment. 'She came ashore at Portsmouth and took sanctuary at Beaulieu when she heard ... about Barnet Field. My brother the King is keeping her under surveillance. I'm glad that I've been the bearer of some good news. They should have told you before.'

'Messire de Josselin would have told me ... but he disappeared. I don't know when or where.'

'I'm sorry. Was he a friend?'

'No,' she said emphatically. 'But he used to attend on me and tell me things.'

Encouraged by her garrulity, Richard took a pace towards her. 'If there's anything I can tell you – any way in which I can serve you. . . .'

'Your grace is very kind.'

'No, no. Not kind at all.' He drew a breath to say more, and then stopped, unsure once again. As he hesitated, Anne caught a glimpse in the young man he was of the boy he had been, tongue-tied before the greatness of his mentor the Earl of Warwick, and she was seized with a desire to explain what had happened to Kat. How she had been hustled out of Warwick Castle at daybreak, barely awake, and how in the flurry of packing the poppet had been mislaid. She wanted him to understand how miserable she had felt, how long she had mourned. . . . But the lean jawline was freshly shaven, the furrow between the long brows was ingrained; he was grown and mature, and had forgotten the follies of his childhood and the conspiracy shared with a little girl. Anne would not shame him by recalling it. He shifted from one foot to the other. 'I mustn't keep you longer from your tiring.' It was not what he had been going to say. 'Though it is a pity to bind your hair,' he added shyly. Somewhat embarrassed by his own boldness, he muttered that he would send the goodwife back to her, and departed with as much haste as courtesy would allow.

She turned again to the glass, and pushed her fingers idly through the mass of pale hair that framed her face. No one had ever commended it before; its only virtue was its length. Although she had resolved long ago to dismiss all memories of that part of her life, they were edging back irresistibly: the grave obeisance he had made her as he took her favour to wear in the lists; the way he had noticed her new blue gown. He had always been kind to her, and even now, when she was nothing to him, he was kind still. For a moment she pondered that mute appeal he had made to her, trying to fathom his meaning. What could he want that she could give him? But the possibilities all slid away from her, and she had not the will to pursue them. The mere effort of so much thinking left her fatigued and close to tears. She wished that he had not come.

Richard was baffled. At chess that night he allowed his brother to capture his queen and checkmate him with only a token resistance.

'What's the matter, Dickon?' asked Edward. 'You're surely not too tired to make me fight for my victory?' They had spent all day preparing the army to march out of Coventry in the morning; now their dispositions were made and they sat at ease over a chessboard and a bowl of wine. But when Richard did play games, he tended to take them seriously and play well. The King surveyed him shrewdly. 'If you were any other man, I would diagnose a woman.'

Startled that Edward could divine his thoughts with such facility, Richard denied that anything was wrong.

'Why don't you go and join George at a bawdy house? That would drown your sorrows better than wine.' Edward watched with a grin as his young brother's mouth pinched into primness. 'But, jesting apart, tell me, Dickon. Is it our cousin Anne that plagues you?'

'You've been spying on me!'

'Not I, lad. I can't spare the time. Some of my loyal subjects apparently have less to do.'

'I only went to make sure that she was well.'

'And is she?'

Richard picked up one of the rooks and examined it closely. 'She is very low. I think she grieves for her husband.'

The King raised his eyebrows in disbelief. 'For her father, perhaps,' he corrected, and he was no longer bantering. 'You have little cause to fear Edward of Lancaster, Dickon. The marriage was not consummated.'

'How do you know that!'

'Spies again. It was common gossip at Margaret's court. The young bastard did everything his mother told him. But if there had been any liking between him and Anne, surely he would have defied her and lain with his wife. He never did.'

His brother was shaking his head slowly, reluctant to believe him. 'She was so distant . . . it is too soon.'

Edward reached over and covered Richard's hand with his own. 'Do you still want her?' There was no answer, but the young man's eyes were raised to his brother's, who read his heart in them. With a vigour that sent the chessman spinning into the rushes, Edward wrung his hand. 'Then to her, man!' he cried, and the gentlemen and pages in the far reaches of the room were jolted out of their own quiet occupations and turned to stare at their King. Then to Richard's relief he dropped his voice as he asked, 'Has Marja taught you nothing?'

'This is different,' Richard protested in an embarrassed undertone.

'Not altogether. This may take longer, that's all. Don't give up so easily.'

'You ... approve, then, Edward?'

'I don't oppose it. She's a poor match for a prince now, whatever her market value in the past. She'll bring precious little with her. But you know that as well as I do. At least she's no pawn any longer. If she'll take you – and she'd be a fool not to in her position – you shall have my consent.'

'Thank you.' The Duke of Gloucester bent to retrieve his rook in order to hide his emotion, and set it on its square. 'Shall we play?'

Even so, it was not until they reached the outskirts of London that he found an opportunity to visit Anne again. She had been carried along with the victorious royal army in much the same way as she had travelled with the Lancastrians. Her new custodian, the Duke of Clarence, provided lodgings and transport for her, but she never saw him, or anyone else she recognised. In her grey world where even drawing breath was a labour, nothing was of much significance. Only the thought of Richard's visit, drifting occasionally into her mind unbidden, roused her for a time to worry and aimless wondering. But wherever she was, and however uncertain her grip on reality, the words of the mass were the same, and the beads on her rosary meant the same prayers. In her overwhelming weariness she leant on the familiarity of God. Often enough on the journey to London she was lodged in a house of religion, and she would find her way instinctively to the chapel and kneel for hours, while services began and ended, and her beads slid through her fingers, and her knees grew numb. Once she forgot to go to her bed and was awoken, cramped and chilled, still at the prie-dieu, by the bell for

Prime. No one noticed her and no one missed her.

She found on this evening the energy to rise when Vespers was over and attempt to drag herself back to the quarters assigned to her for the night. At the end of the nave, motionless in the shadows by the font, someone was waiting, and she knew it was Richard. Dressed in a dark gown, bareheaded, he assumed form as she approached and when she reached him he bowed, to her or to the altar, and fell in beside her without speaking. The cloisters were already dimming into twilight, though the sky was clear blue with drifting translucent cloudlets. They walked slowly, and again, as at Coventry, Richard was searching for something to say. It was all very well for Edward to cite Marja, he thought, yet it was useless to compare her with the waif at his side, sealed into the solitary cell of her own misery. She walked with him not because she wanted to, but because obedience to another's will was bred into her. Perhaps she no longer had any power to choose, even to walk or not to walk.

'I thought you might be lonely,' he said. There was no answer. Loneliness and companionship too seemed to have lost their meaning for her. They turned a corner of the cloister and an early swallow swooped under the arch before them and up to its invisible nest. He tried a different tack. 'John was wounded at Barnet. Fighting next to me.'

'John?' Her voice was thin, listless.

'John Wrangwysh. You remember. I left him unconscious at Baynard's Castle. His sister Janet is nursing him.' She did remember. The long-legged boy who had carved her Kat. It was unfair of Richard to stir up the dead leaves of their childhood. 'Maybe you would pray for him. He is very ill.'

'If you wish it, my lord.'

Another corner rounded, and he said, 'Frank Lovel is still with me. And Robert Percy.' Almost he seemed to be deliberately invoking the buried past. She had not believed he would be so thoughtless. But he must have changed so much more than she. 'Frank plays the lute very well. And writes his own songs.'

The pain of memory halted her. 'This is ungentle in you, my lord.' Her narrow face was upturned, the remoteness gone; the eyes awake, pools of anguish reflecting the last light of the sky.

'Believe me, I had no intention. . . .' Distressed by her misunderstanding, Richard tried clumsily to explain himself. 'I only hoped that you might . . . remember them – us – with kindness. If I was mistaken, forgive me. It was all a long time ago and perhaps it's . . . best forgotten.' There was a note in his voice which hurt more than the memories. If only he would tell her in plain words what he wanted, or if she had the insight to read his riddle.

'I lost Kat,' she whispered. 'And then last year . . . it was the end.'

'Only if you will it, Anne.' For the first time he used her name, and it woke a dim response deep within her.

'I have no will.' Driftwood has no will, she thought, and no feelings, but she walked on so that Richard had to catch up with her.

'Does it trouble you to see me?'

'Yes.'

'Then . . . you do not wish me to come again?' He knew it was unsubtle, that Edward would laugh at him if he told and call him callow, but there was no other way of reaching through her unhappiness to the truth of her.

'Are you going away?'

There was a forlorn break in her voice which gave him the courage to say again, 'Only if you will it.' They paced the length of one side of the cloisters, his boots ringing hollow over the faint slithering of the hem of her gown. When they reached the door of the church, he decided, he would take her silence for dissent and leave.

'Please come again.' Richard could scarcely be sure that he had heard correctly, that his eager ears had not misconstrued a mere sigh. Glancing aside at her, he met only her bowed head and two hands clasped over her rosary and the folds of her gown, pale shapes floating motionless in the twilight. He must blunder on in his own way and risk frightening her away for ever.

'Anne?' At least she stopped once more. She could barely make out what lay in his hand, although she already guessed it. And perhaps it was this offer that she had been trying, in some contrary way, to prevent. To take it back, to take him back, would be an action too absolute for her to bear the

157

consequences. It would have been easier not to move, to keep her fingers twined in her beads and the safety of God. If he had thrust it at her, or placed it round her neck gently as he had on the old castle in Wensleydale, she would not have needed to choose. But he was hard; he was forcing choice on her with his stillness and that appeal which at last was plain. She looked up at him, darkling beneath the arch of the cloister, and stretched out her hand. Richard placed the pendant in its hollow and their palms met, enclosing the devices of St Anthony and St Anne.

4

THE COOK-MAID

She could not believe it. The pendant hung in its old place under the bodice of her gown as if it had never been away. Waking the next morning, she fancied herself back in the convent at Valognes: the whitewashed walls, the high window admitting a thin stream of sunlight, and Richard's token around her neck. In those drowsy moments the year between was no more and she was at peace. Full consciousness soon peopled the darkness where the sun did not reach with the lurking things she had briefly forgotten. Her twilight interview with the Duke of Gloucester took its place among them, no nearer and no more real than her wedding night and the infirmary of Tewkesbury Abbey. All she could be sure of was the keepsake which, somehow, had returned to her, and the nebulous hope that clung to it.

It was not the quiet alleys of the Norman sanctuary that lay outside her sleeping-cell but the City of London, in fierce holiday mood, ready to acclaim its restored King and to execrate its fallen Queen. Anne was well to the rear of the cavalcade which stretched for several miles from the Duke of Gloucester at its head to the camp-followers straggling at the end, basking in their own fag-end of the glory. Narrow streets, shouting people and pealing bells were hell to her, even with senses impaired. And yet ahead of her, some half a mile out of sight, another woman was deeper in hell: Margaret of Anjou was dragged through London in an open chariot. Had it not been for the delicacy of the King's younger brother, her widowed daughter-in-law might have been sharing her shame, instead of being concealed behind the curtains of a litter.

Anne knew nothing of that; she knew the relief of turning out of the main way into the comparative hush of a side street.

When the litter stopped she had no idea where she was, and did not care. A young squire drew the curtains and helped her down into the courtyard of a large house. With a deference that had for long been foreign to her she was met by the steward and taken within. At the door of the solar the decorum was dispersed by a plump girl who threw her arms round Anne and burst into tears. Through the smothering embrace Anne recognised with difficulty her sister Isobel.

For the rest of the day she would not leave Anne alone. Her behaviour repelled Anne, who had been ignored for so long that she had come to dislike human contact. She shrank from Isobel's incoherent outpourings of emotion, her clutchings and strokings. One thing only lit a spark of pleasure in her: Ankarette Twynyho, her old ally from the disastrous voyage to Normandy, was still in the Duchess's service and was among the attendants assigned to her.

Isobel soon tired of her sister's unresponsiveness. The meek and attentive auditor she had hoped to regain, to shore up her crumbled vanity, was so withdrawn behind her pale drained face that she seemed hardly to be conscious. Isobel had not yet admitted to herself that her figure was spoiled and her hair lack-lustre, but, deprived of the admiration she thrived on, she was taking less and less care of her appearance. Anne was thoughtless, she said to herself, neither to thank her for her hospitality nor to declare how much she had missed her sister. And she retired to bed to sulk with a bowl of sugared almonds.

That night Anne had a dream. It was so vivid that she came to herself reluctantly, trembling with an intensity which was absent from her waking life. Under its ravishing influence she strove to return and plunge again into its depths, but beyond the bed-curtains her attendants were laying out her clothes and preparing her toilet, making the humdrum little noises that destroy illusions. Resigned to its loss, she lay still and savoured the departing echo of its richness. She had not dreamed like that since before her betrothal. And as her mind roused, she began to comprehend why. Last summer, in France, God had called to her in the same way, and His purpose had been thwarted by the Earl of Warwick. But Sœur Madeleine had assured her that He would not give her up if He needed her. Now that her earthly father's commands were discharged, had not her Father in Heaven renewed His assault? So much reasoning tired her. Yet as the flat light of another purposeless day flooded through the opened shutters, she knew a wistful desire to abandon herself to the loving passionate presence of her sleep.

There was a prie-dieu in her chamber, and like a homing bird she went to it after mass and breaking her fast. Her sister, having whispered to her throughout the service, did not pursue her. If she showed God how devout she was, if she were allowed the time to call upon Him, perhaps He would give her a sure sign and tell her what to do. Crossing herself, she encountered the pendant that hung accidently outside her bodice, and for a moment she was disconcerted. But Richard would understand. She began the Credo.

Until dinner the next day she was left to her devotions. She dined with the Duchess in her solar, and Isobel chattered on without waiting for any replies, pressing food on her sister and referring endlessly to their sad bereavements and to how ill she looked. The second course was being cleared away when her conversation faltered, and a furtive fear chased away her animation. The company shuffled to its feet, licking fingers and knives surreptitiously, and offered its duty to the master of the house. Clarence strolled down the room, taking no notice of his household, and cast his cloak carelessly in the direction of an oak chest. Anne could not help being aware that he was making for her. There was a skirmish at the head of the table as people were shunted away and a chair placed to the right of the Duchess. But the Duke ignored it and leant instead over his wife's shoulder, taking a knife from his belt and stabbing it into a chunk of beef that had not yet been removed.

'Well, sister,' he said with his mouth full, 'there's another of our enemies despatched to a place where he can do no more mischief.' Some of the servants rustled, and the men-at-arms who had followed Clarence's entrance and his example with the dinner nodded knowingly at each other. The two ladies stared at their platters in ignorance. 'They're not ringing the bells, though it would seem a fitting epitaph for one so reputedly holy.' His followers sniggered. 'Your mother-in-law has already been informed – the news hadn't far to travel to her – but I don't suppose anyone has bothered to tell you. The old

King has died in the Tower. Apparently he was so disillusioned by the wickedness of this world that he gave up the ghost voluntarily to find a better one.'

Fishing a piece of gristle from between his teeth with the point of the knife, Clarence watched his sister-in-law with interest, but he gained no satisfaction. She did not flinch or cry, and she remained so unmoved that she might not have heard. Like his wife, he found that Anne was no longer a good listener. Isobel, easily affected, began to snuffle a little, but soon stopped when Clarence demanded acidly what concern it was of hers if the crazy old fool of a king had finally consented to give up breathing, which he should have done years ago. Then he sat down and ordered some more beef, beans and a stoup of wine.

'Best malmsey,' he called. 'We must celebrate the removal of a great danger to our royal brother's throne.' He would have been happier if he could have seen in Anne's mind the slow sad procession of thoughts: the gentle man with the bird who had smiled on her childhood, the saintly wanderer who had so wrongfully been shut up in prison, the aspirations to do him good that had given her strength to go through with her marriage, they were gone. For the rest of the meal, avoiding the curious glances of the Duke, she recited mentally the prayers for the faithful departed.

She could not avoid Clarence when he interrupted her afternoon's reading from her book of hours. He was accompanied by two gentlemen, almost as sumptuously dressed as himself, but wearing in their caps instead of their own cognizances the badge of the Duke of Clarence. They remained by the door, casually lounging shoulder to shoulder over the entrance. Anne stood before her brother-in-law, while the attendant who had been sewing in the window-seat scuttled away at her lord's signal.

'I trust you are satisfied with our hospitality,' said Clarence.

'Yes, my lord is most gracious.'

'It is my duty to care for a kinswoman so tragically deprived of her family. I'm sure your noble father would have approved of my assuming responsibility for you. After all, he entrusted his elder daughter to me with his own hands – even if he thought better of it later.' The irony could not fail to reach

Anne through the armour of her indifference. He saw her slight shrinking from his implication and pressed his advantage. 'But I assure you, dearest sister, that I shall not change my mind and abandon you. I intend to make sure that you are safe from all harm for the rest of your life.' Stepping up to her, he took her chin in his fingers and forced her to meet his eyes. In the depths of hers the blank grey was troubled by a shadow of dread. 'But in return for my good offices, it's only just that I should ask for co-operation. You do agree, sister?' Unable to nod, Anne mouthed consent.

'Then hear me. You are under my protection and mine alone. There's no need for any interference from anyone else, however powerful. The King himself has committed you to my custody, and he will expect that charge to be fulfilled. If you should appeal to another for assistance, in words or in writing, it would be looked upon by his grace, and of course by me also, as disloyalty to his wishes.' A cold prickle ran down her backbone. She did not yet grasp his meaning, but she read the casual cruelty in the hand that held her captive. 'For your own safety, Anne. There are those who may seek to use you for their own ends – especially in the places where you would look only for friends.' The sympathetic tone did not deceive her. When he released her she could hardly keep her balance. 'I am instructing all my people to look to you, so you need have no fears, even when I'm absent.' The two gentlemen guarding the door exchanged glances. Inclining his head graciously, Clarence left, and with equally correct courtesies and not quite hidden insolence his companions followed.

Accustomed throughout her life to sense the moods beneath words rather than to interpret the words themselves, Anne was left in no doubt as to her brother-in-law's attitude. His oblique phrases and expressions of concern amounted to one thing: she was helpless and at his mercy. She still held her book of hours, and with all the fervency she was capable of she applied to the only source of assistance which the Duke of Clarence could not forbid.

Her respite had not lasted long. Once more she was watched, by eyes either uninterested or hostile. Isobel avoided her and even Ankarette seemed embarrassed to speak to her. The Duke was seldom there, but his influence hung over the house and he was obeyed as if he were present. It did not occur to Anne to question why she was being so treated. Once, however, at mealtime, which was the only occasion on which she met her sister, she asked if their mother would be coming to London soon. The Duchess peered round her guiltily before whispering that the Countess was still at Beaulieu and it would be best not to mention the subject. Resigned to mystery, Anne said no more.

As always she took refuge in prayer, and in this direction she met no check and no disapproval.

Repentance would bring her closer to God, and He might soon issue a command which would outweigh those of the Duke of Clarence. Unexpectedly, she began to wonder if the wishes of the greater and the lesser lord were necessarily in conflict.

During one of his visitations the Duke addressed her suddenly. 'I hear you spend much time at your devotions. My wife's confessor speaks well of you.' Anne bowed her head mutely. Although his tone was pleasant enough, she could not believe that there would be no sting in the sequel. Yet all he added was, 'Your lady mother is still at Beaulieu. She is considering whether to take the veil.' Could he be edging her towards the path she was groping for herself?

Like all other complex problems, it was beyond her powers of reasoning, so she continued to earn the praise of the confessor and began to practise small deprivations: fasting throughout Fridays, waking herself to say her offices in the night. If it had been winter she would have worn thin clothes, but spring was warming into summer and that would have been no hardship. Despite the absence of ecstatic daytime visions she was rewarded by another dream. Quivering awake in a glow of perspiration, she found she was clutching, not her crucifix, but the pendant that she kept in its old hiding-place beneath her pillow. Richard, she thought for a moment. Would Richard understand? She had no means of knowing, and, exchanging St Anthony and St Anne for her Saviour, she began to repeat Prime silently, so as not to disturb the girl asleep at her side.

But doubt about Richard began to prey on her mind. There was nobody she could turn to for advice, nobody whom she could trust for a disinterested opinion about this most important decision of her life. Except for the Duke of Gloucester. A daring resolution hardened in her to write and ask him what he thought – daring because she had never before written an unsolicited letter. Ankarette looked askance when she requested writing materials, and more doubtful when given the note to be delivered where my lord of Gloucester lay. However, she took it, and Anne's heart lightened a little as it left her hands. It had been a trial for her composing even so simple a message, but now she could return to her missal and leave the issue to God and to Richard.

Clarence broke in upon her two evenings later as she prepared for bed. In sudden guilty haste Ankarette snatched up Anne's bedgown, wrapped it around her, and hurried from the room without meeting her gaze. Tall and inexorable he stood over her, and the diamond clasp at his throat winked balefully at her like a third cold eye.

'Madame, you are a treacherous ingrate!' The vicious accusation did not cut as deeply as the sight of the scrap of paper in his fingers, inscribed in her own unpractised hand, 'For the Lord Duke of Gloucester'. His reading of the few lines so laboriously penned was such violation of her privacy that she could see no further. But then he tossed the letter contemptuously into her lap and said, 'Explain yourself.' She could not explain what she did not comprehend. There was no crime in what she had written. Clarence chose to read guilt into her silence. 'So much for your faith. You swore to me that you would trust to my protection, yet here you are attempting to smuggle begging letters out to the very man I warned you against.'

To that she must reply. 'Oh, no, my lord. I wrote only to my cousin of Gloucester.'

'Only? And am I to believe that you know nothing of my brother's dangerous ambition? Would you make an alliance with one who seeks through you to lay hands on your own mother's inheritance?' Mock-concern honeyed his voice. 'No doubt he beguiled you with promises of love or some such idleness. It is easy in your position to be deceived. And just for that reason I am keeping you close. Until the self-seekers grow weary and look for other victims. But until then, you will abide by my rules and my instructions. For your own sake.' Before she could move to protect it Clarence had taken up her note again. 'Most particularly, you will not communicate with my brother of Gloucester, nor above all receive him. If you do so, you will sadly distress your sister and your lady mother.' His tone lightened. 'Besides, the Duke of Gloucester is out of town, and it is not known when he will return.' For a tormenting second he swung the little missive between thumb and forefinger; then deliberately he tore it into pieces.

The fragments fluttered lazily in the wake of his going, and settled among the rushes. Anne felt that her reason lay with them, scattered into meaningless shreds. What he had said of Richard was beyond belief, and yet it was beyond belief that he could so malign his own brother. Stupefied by that first blow, Clarence's final barbs could not yet hurt her. She was still staring down at the débris of her cry for help when Isobel came to her, patting her with anxious intruding hands.

'What did he do, Anne? Did he hurt you?'

Anne recoiled from her touch and her concern. 'Nothing. No.'

'He was with me when Ankarette brought him your letter. He fell into such a passion that I thought he would harm her for letting you write it. She was very frightened. But he let her alone, and we knew he would go to you instead. Oh, Anne, why did you do it? He can't abide to be reminded of our brother of Gloucester.'

'Why?' It was not a request for information, but Isobel took it as such and launched into involved explanations of politics that she no more than half understood herself. The busy tripping voice nagged at the edge of Anne's consciousness, but the sense did not penetrate. She wanted to be left alone in her desert. Disappointed that her sister was not crying, as she did still whenever she was the butt of her husband's disapproval, Isobel soon decided that she had done her humane duty and went back to her apartments. Anne did not move. Too ashamed of her betrayal to return, Ankarette left her unattended. Not until the untrimmed candle guttered smokily did she stir, to snuff it and stretch herself open-eyed on the bed.

The wounds that Clarence had dealt her unnoticed began to ache the next day. And for a wilderness of days after that she brooded over them, powerless to cure, unable to forget. That Richard had deceived her, that he had gone away without a word to her, was inconceivable, but ever the doubt worried at her and would not let her rest. She could not sleep and she could not pray, and no one came to distract her except a chastened Ankarette, who slunk around her shamefaced and escaped as soon as her duty was done. Anne's fifteenth birthday passed unmarked, and she sat and did nothing. Life was not interested in her, and she had little interest in life either.

The door opened on her one morning, and the fall of riding boots roused her to the one strong emotion that was still hers: fear of the Duke of Clarence. She half rose in a mist of panic as he advanced, and then her vision cleared. Her knees gave beneath her and she sank to the floor before Richard's concerned frown. His hands reached for hers and remotely, as if she held them before a distant blaze, she felt the warmth transferring slowly into her fingers. He said something about not kneeling, calling her by her name, and as his life spread upwards into her arms she stood facing him.

'I prayed for you to come,' she said, although the prayer had been made by her heart and not her lips. Miraculously he was restoring her power of thought. There were none of Clarence's gentlemen leaning negligently against the door like jailors. 'But how did you get in? He said he would not let you see me.'

Anxiety was joined by puzzlement in his sallow face. 'He?'

'Our brother the Duke.'

'Why ever not?'

How could he know nothing of her confinement, of the slurs which George had cast upon his conduct? She had not listened to Isobel's explanation and her brain could formulate only a crude summary. 'I don't know, but Isobel says it is something to do with my mother's property. It belongs to him and he thinks you want it.' She so needed him to deny the allegation with vigour that she hardly heard what he said next. Nothing to do with George and Isobel, he said. Only with you and me. His grasp strengthened, and through that as much as through her ears she understood the purpose of his visit.

'I have the King's good will and I've come to ask you to marry me.'

It could not be true. The brown eyes looking into hers were so earnest that he could not be mocking. The pattern of words was repeating itself all round the room and inside her head, cutting her off from him in a surge of sound. Then his arm was round her shoulders, the warm flesh pressing through her sleeve and driving away the faintness. Her ringing head was supported against his breast and she knew that there she could sleep.

'Will you, Anne?' Her name again, spoken in the gentle intimate way which no one else had ever matched.

'Oh, my lord, it is the only hope I have left.' His heart was beating steadily beneath her temple, restoring her senses with every stroke. She saw with sudden wonder how the sun flooding into the room from the window behind them defined their mingled shadows on the floor as delicately as an artist. The downtrodden rushes were given a glossy distinction by its generosity. A gleam of white among them caught her eye. It was a corner of the letter she had written to Richard. The world of her imprisonment crashed in upon their fools' paradise. She disengaged herself, and felt with anguish his reluctance to let her go. 'But I can't accept. I must ask his consent for everything I do. . . .' There was not only her own danger to consider, but his as well. Thick-tongued in her haste she tried to warn him, but there was only troubled incomprehension in his face. His sole response was to take her hand again.

Her efforts were fruitless. Clarence was there, timing his entrance with diabolical precision to destroy her newborn hope. And his anger was directed, incredibly, against his brother.

'How dare you invade my house in this manner?' The acrid scorn of his presence was appalling, and although Anne sensed that Richard was stiffening to her defence, she knew helplessly that his strength was not enough. He had no weapons against the kind of words that George was flinging at him. Her mind rejected their meaning, but their harshness tore into the softness of her heart so recently opened to Richard. When he rose to Clarence's challenge she was desperately afraid for him. He was answering evenly, his voice conciliatory, and yet he could not disguise the underlying pain from either of his listeners.

'I want nothing of yours, brother. And I sent my man to inform you as soon as I arrived. Anne is my sister-in-law and I was not aware that I required permission to visit her. She is not a prisoner.' The way in which he said it seemed to clamp the fetters more securely on her wrists.

And of course it was no use reasoning with Clarence. As he had twisted Richard's concern for Anne into self-seeking, so he placed a base construction on his visiting her. Too agitated to follow their arguments, she could see too clearly how Richard was losing ground, hamstrung by sincerity and natural affection, before the ruthless onslaught of his brother. She was the battleground over which they fought, the trampled and disregarded centre of contention as she had so often been before.

But abruptly she was converted to a combatant. Richard was drawing her forward, asking her opinion. Did she want to be his wife? Her heart leapt into her throat in terror; her limbs were suddenly emptied of sensation. She had already given him her answer, but that had been safely within the circle of his arms, not under the searing glare of the Duke of Clarence's animosity. To deny him now would be despicable; she had only to stand with him and speak her heart before one witness, however hostile, and church law would have bound them indissolubly. George stood over them, reducing them to naughty children caught out in mischief. Resistance would be risible. And when Anne felt a tremor running through Richard's hand, she was lost.

'Well, Cousin Anne? Do you want to be the Duchess of Gloucester?' A brief beautiful vision of herself as Duchess of Gloucester flashed before her and was swallowed in panic.

'If it pleases you, my lord.' Her surrender was made more bitter by the immediate pleasure it brought to Clarence's expression.

'There you are, Richard. What better evidence could you want? Anne has placed herself voluntarily under my protection. Would the King force a young lady to give her hand against her expressed wishes?' Anne could not tell whether her trembling took its violence from Richard's or her own humiliation. But Richard broke out at last into anger, cutting across his brother's light insults with scarcely articulate protest. He did not continue for long, as he realised what Anne had already known. Clarence had annihilated them. What was more, he now had his own witnesses. Dimly she made out the discreet stealth of servants in the doorway, and through her link with Richard she shared his shame. Off-handedly Clarence ordered the attendants away, retaining his wife who had somehow been among them.

'Take your sister to your chamber and make her lie down. She has been unduly excited.' Isobel approached to obey him, too frightened to show any sympathy. As long as she had hold of Richard's hand, Anne had not quite given up the shreds of hope; they were not yet physically parted, and she still clung remotely to her dependence on him. But his grasp loosened, and without a word or glance he let her go. She left her remaining strength with him, and could not have moved without her sister's support.

Now it was worse than before. To have been within a breath of escape and herself to have thrown it away was sufficient sin to cut her off from God as well as Richard. She lived again and again the one moment of decision that life had offered her and which she had been too craven to accept. If she had complained against her fate before, at least she had not been to blame. Not until she brought herself to confession of her failure did she find, hardly relief, but a use for it. We are all nothing before God, the chaplain declared, and anything that brings us nearer to the knowledge of our utter insignificance is a step towards sanctity. Brooding upon his advice afterwards, Anne began to wonder if through what appeared to be such defeat God had not actually spoken at last. And she also wondered why she was not filled with exultation.

Richard took refuge in action. The Scots were making trouble on the Border and the King despatched him to deal with them. To be in the saddle again and commanding an army lifted his London despondency. Edward had insisted on a reconciliation with Clarence before he left, and with his face to the North he could believe in George's professions of good intentions. But as the distance lengthened between him and his disappointment, he began to lose his certainty. George might assure him that he was concerned only with Anne's happiness, that she was still too overwhelmed with grief for her father and husband to be fit for such a step as marriage. He had waited so long in patience, had come so near to his heart's desire, that this check was hard to take. His depression grew as he crossed into Yorkshire. Not often did he allow himself to dream, but he had in unguarded moments visualised himself coming back here with Anne, to the place where they had lived as children. During that calamitous interview he had had no chance to tell her that, together with Warwick's other Yorkshire estates, the King had given Middleham to him.

At Doncaster his captains noticed his low spirits. Several had known him since boyhood, and expected to see their lord in good heart so near to Wensleydale, and to their meeting with the Scots. Reticent as he was, he directed the billeting of his men with his customary efficiency; only tighter lips and a terser manner manifested the mood within. The sympathetic glances of his friends made Richard restive. He did not want to confide in them, and busied himself unnecessarily with routine work. It was while he was doing the rounds of the billets, going from house to house through the dark wells of Doncaster's evening streets, that he decided to ride to Pomfret. Taking half a dozen men he departed at once, leaving word that he would rejoin his troops tomorrow on the road to York.

He set a hard pace during the two hours to Pomfret, for one who had ridden all day. His companions were soon strung out behind him, which gave him the solitude to think, not of the past as he had been doing, but of the night to come. Marja was at Pomfret. She had followed him over from Flanders and he had installed her at the castle to await the birth of their child. During the amazing triumphs of the past few months he had had no time to communicate with her; he did not even know if she was yet delivered. The rhythm of the horse beneath him and the anonymous grey of the road in the light of a waning moon enclosed him in a cocoon of memories and hopes. He tried to reckon when the child was due, counting on his fingers from the proud night, so short a space after their meeting, on which she had told him that she had conceived. His first impulse had been to run to Edward and announce the success of the experiment which he had instigated, but Marja restrained him, pointing out that no doubt the lord King was engaged on business of his own and that she did deserve a little of the credit herself. So, when he had made sure carefully that it could do no harm, he made love to her instead.

The warm smoothness of her limbs clinging round his naked body, the heat they had engendered even in the chilly depths of the Flemish winter, made his flesh stir yet, fleeing though he was from the ruins of his suit to Anne. Marja had always roused his desire so easily, which must have been one of the reasons why Edward, connoisseur of women, had chosen her for him. Not only for that, but also because she was a widow, young, well-born, even-tempered. Edward had gone about his task seriously. He had been positively scandalised when he had, with much tact and some ruthlessness, rooted out his brother's shame.

'A virgin at eighteen, Dickon! You're a disgrace to the family. Why, I tumbled my first girl at twelve, and as for George....' Richard had no real excuse to offer, so the King had taken him in hand, silencing his feeble protests with the succinct statement that it was his duty to the country. If Anne had still been free, wherever she was, Richard might have held out against having a mistress foisted on him. But she was at Angers, betrothed to Edward of Lancaster, so far beyond him that the question of disloyalty hardly arose. Besides, she had returned his token. . . .

And Edward always knew best. His first sight of Marja van Soeters daunted him more than the waves of the North Sea as the Yorkists had embarked in their cockleshell boats from Lynn. So calm, so beautiful, so unassailable. Yet there had been too that fluttering in the loins which he had not felt so powerfully before towards any other woman. And when they were alone and she began to remove her clothes, quietly and without fuss, and then had come to him nude with her cool friendly smile and stripped him with the same practicality, he had realised that she was not unassailable at all. Now, Richard looked into the night ahead and smiled back at her, and forward, for he did not think that their four-month separation would make any difference to their ease. He, who had always expressed himself with difficulty, had found himself speaking to his mistress without reserve. With others his diffidence was unchanged, but privately with Marja he had spoken of things that he was scarcely aware even of thinking.

He was at Pomfret well before midnight, reassuring the alarmed gatekeeper that there was no emergency, the Scots were not invading, and he was simply on personal business. The sleepy castle exhibited the same sort of mild panic at the unheralded visitation of its new lord, but in Marja's chamber the peace was unruffled. She was in bed, suckling a very small baby, whose arms waved in vague content from the swaddling bands as it fed.

Suddenly shy at her very lack of surprise, Richard hesitated. Marja smiled, and said, 'My lord. How thoughtful to arrange for your visit to correspond with mealtime.' At that he came forward to take the hand she had freed without disturbing the nuzzling child. She had not seen or heard from him for nearly five months, but she made no demonstration beyond her usual cordiality. He looked down at her, knowing that he did not need to say anything until he was ready. Her dark red hair was braided for the night, and one plait lay between her breasts, in startling contrast to her clear skin. His eyes were drawn to them, awed by the way in which the milk had swelled their remembered contours and darkened the pink knot of her exposed nipple.

'I saw no need of a wet-nurse,' Marja answered his unformed question. 'And I am following the example of our dowager Duchess in Burgundy. His grace the Duke seems to have flourished on his mother's milk, and I think this little one likes it too.' As she talked she detached the baby from one breast and transferred it to the other. The child did not open its eyes, but clutched at the plait as it passed. Firmly anchored to its mother's hair, it resumed sucking. 'She's not very pretty, is she?' Again, she was putting into words the half-wondering, half-repelled reaction of Richard to the screwed-up scarlet face and scanty tuft of dark hair that were all he could see of his firstborn.

'She? A girl?'

'Yes. And before her time. I was riding too vigorously in the hills. But she was no trouble.'

'I didn't know. I would have sent some wine ... or ...' He felt he ought to apologise for allowing her to go through the

173

hazards of confinement without giving her a thought.

'No, my lord. I didn't expect it. You've been occupied in winning your royal brother's kingdom back for him.' She smiled again at him, sidelong, for she had understood without his explaining how strongly burned his passion to serve King Edward.

Immediately he was at ease. Sitting beside her on the bed, he touched the baby's soft head and said, 'Have you named her?'

'Katherine. I hope you approve. But I had to call her something.'

'Yes, it's a very good name. Are her eyes open yet?' he asked with the seriousness of a man who has had more dealing with hound puppies than with babies.

'Oh, yes, during the day,' Marja answered with appropriate gravity. She knew better than to laugh at him. They fell silent, and Richard watched his mistress and his daughter, trying in vain to believe in the connection between the blind springing moment of conception and this tiny, busy, somnolent creature. When she had finished, Marja called her attendant and the baby was replaced, sleeping soundly, in her crib. Sending the woman to her own bed, she settled her white wrap round her shoulders and regarded the Duke of Gloucester intently.

'What troubles you, my lord?'

He was taken aback, for he had thought himself unusually contented. 'Why do you say that?'

'There is a frown behind your eyes.' Sometimes the flaws in her fluent English improved upon the original. Disarmed by her perception, he prevaricated no further. As he had probably intended, he told her everything: the finding of Anne, the wooing, the pledge, and then the veto from that most cruelly unexpected direction. She listened quietly, and at the end she pondered a little before asking, 'Is there a reason for your lord brother's objections?' Richard shook his head hopelessly.

'None that I am aware of.'

'And – forgive me – you are sure of the Lady Anne's wishes?'

'I know her,' he said simply.

Yes, he knew Warwick's daughter as he would never know her, Marja reflected, however intimate their relations and frank their discourse. She had no illusions about her place in Richard's heart; from the way he had talked of Anne, in

Flanders and just now, it was clear that his marriage would be the end of any liaisons. And she was fond enough of her lover to view the prospect with deep regret – not because of loss of prestige or the fear that he would abandon her, but for his own strange, earnest, innocent sake. He was gazing at her now with a kind of dumb trust, as if she were an oracle who could be relied upon for a comfortable prophecy, and she hated to disappoint him.

'It is some caprice of your brother's,' she said finally. 'He must relent, if he has any love for you.'

'Oh, yes, he said as much before we parted,' agreed Richard, eager to excuse Clarence in his own eyes as well as in Marja's. 'I shouldn't be so low-spirited. It's foolish of me to fear the worst – and to burden you with my troubles, too, when I should be giving you thanks for yours.' Foolish or not, his bravery was turning to bravado. 'It was just. . . . You see, I had waited so long, and then it seemed that God had granted her to me at last . . . and to lose her. . . .' He spoke through stiff lips that were striving not to tremble.

'You haven't lost her,' Marja said gently. 'She has promised herself to you. You will come together when God pleases.' What she had meant as consolation brought forth the tears he had been trying to check. Appalled by the breakdown of a young man who had always before, even in the throes of love, retained a certain self-command, she reached out and brought his head down to her bosom. Stroking his hair and crooning endearments in Flemish, she was no longer mistress or counsellor, but a mother soothing her injured child.

Yet the child was barely six years her junior, and as his sobs subsided she became aware less of his distress than of the weight of his head where it lay. Still without calculation she found his hand and placed it under her wrap on her right breast. She felt the limp fingers tense suddenly with knowledge, and then he had moved his head and his lips were over her nipple, pulling at it with the same instinctive search for comfort as the child of their bodies. The old tenderness rose up in her and flared into desire. She put her arms round him and pressed towards him, but it was he who flung back the sheet to uncover her full nakedness.

It was a stormy night. Despite the intensity of their

lovemaking, neither could sleep and so, clasped stickily together and wanting each other too much to seek separate coolness, they caressed again and made love again. There was five months' celibacy and a nameless dread of the morning to drive them on. When at last they were dozing in exhaustion the baby woke, crying with hunger. While Marja fed her, Richard lay with his arms folded behind his head, watching her through narrowed eyes. His expression was neutral, too tired for unhappiness or lust or even interest, although as soon as the child was put down he would begin once more to rouse her. Yet she thought that one day soon he would regret this night. His odd code of morality would class it as a betrayal. Her heart moved in mingled envy and pity for the girl that he loved : envy that she should be the object of such single-minded devotion, and pity that she should need it. Marja van Soeters would always make shift for herself.

Four days after Richard's visit Anne was taken to Clarence's closet. He gave a businesslike appearance behind a table covered with scattered papers, but there was also a rosary carved in onyx tossed to one side. His manner was mild and reasonable and he let her sit down before beginning to speak.

'I hope that the distressing incident of the other morning is all forgotten?' Anne had learned by now that the only reaction that her brother-in-law noticed was fear, so she made no response. 'I do feel it deeply myself, that my noble brother should so far forget himself as to commit such an outrage. One as close to God as you, sister, will find it easier to forgive, no doubt. But it has made me consider your future very seriously. Since you have taken this great decision to give yourself to Holy Church it is unthinkable that you should be pestered again in that way. You made yourself very clear to his grace of Gloucester while he was here, but I am afraid of his persistence. He is a stubborn young man. I know him, sister, I know him.' Clarence leaned back, shaking his head sorrowfully. Anne wondered dully if the performance was for her or for the inevitable brace of gentlemen inside the door. Brisk again, he went on.

'I have come to the conclusion that there is one way to protect you from the grasping ambition which threatens you.

Of course, you will wish to take orders as soon as possible. This has already been set in motion, and when you've expressed your preference my influence will smooth the way to any house that you name. But it takes time to arrange admission, and there is the question of dowry.... There will be a delay, which could be dangerous while you're known to be under my roof. So I've found a temporary refuge for you, a place where a ... fanatical admirer ... wouldn't think of seeking you.

'Thomas?' One of the men stepped forward, with coarse badger hair and incongruously thick-set shoulders under his silken sleeves. 'Sir Thomas will take care of you. There must of course be great caution, so you must go with him, whenever he comes for you, and trust him. There may be a little ... discomfort, while you wait, but it would be best if you accepted it without complaint. Your sister and your lady mother would I'm sure expect it.' Through the smile she read the iron threat, and said nothing. 'Thomas, accompany the Lady Anne back to her chamber. So that you may become acquainted. Go with God, dear sister.' She would not have been surprised if he had made the sign of the cross over her; it was a common tale that the Devil could assume a holy shape at will.

On the walk back to her apartments Sir Thomas Burdet did not break the silence. Perhaps a jailor who looked like a noble ruffian was better than one of the effete young men who were the Duke's other companions. She did nothing to prepare for her departure. She had no possessions of her own, besides her clothes, except a missal and an hour-book and her rosary. And there was no attempt to escape from it. Anne had given up struggling. Once God's will for her had been pitted unsuccessfully against that of the Earl of Warwick; now He seemed to be allied with the power of evil to impose Himself on her. She was no longer surprised. His ways were mysterious beyond her imaginings, and He had left her without choice. The passionate yearnings of her youth, a year ago, had starved to death. It was little enough of herself that she could offer to the service of Holy Church. But it would be quiet in the convent, and the Duke of Clarence would not be there.

Burdet came for her one night after she had retired. He made her put on her plainest gown of mourning and would not let her call Ankarette. His only concession to her modesty was to leave the room while she fumbled with the laces which before had been tied for her. The great house was sleeping as he led her to the stable yard and mounted her behind him on a ready-saddled horse. Passing out of the postern it crossed Anne's mind that he meant to take her to the river and drop her in. She was not particularly disturbed. It would be a neat solution to everyone's problems. Nobody was abroad in the London streets, where the odours of a hot day were still imprisoned under the jutting eaves. Lamps flickered here and there, and gleamed startlingly in the eyes of scavenging cats. The horse's hoofs, muffled by the layer of refuse, raised no echoes. At the time, it was a hopeless journey into nowhere, but looking back on it Anne remembered the breadth of the deserted streets and the wedge of starlit sky between the gables.

They halted at a narrow gate, and as Burdet knocked softly the chimes of a church clock, close at hand, struck midnight. Anne had time to count all the strokes before the gate was unbarred and they were admitted. In the courtyard of another large house, two people were standing with shuttered lanthorns. A few words were exchanged, then Burdet lifted her off the horse, pushed her towards the strangers, and was gone. One of the figures seized her by the upper arm in an unnecessarily firm grasp and propelled her through an archway. There the lanthorn was lifted and a sudden flood of light was released on to her face. Closing her eyes tightly against the glare, Anne saw nothing of her hosts except that they were both men, and neither of an excessively villainous countenance. Clarence had evidently elected not to kill her yet.

'She doesn't look very strong,' said one in a low voice.

'She'll learn,' said the other laconically. Then shuttering the lanthorn again he addressed Anne. 'Have you eaten, lass?'

The familiarity of his tone was so foreign to her that she simply answered meekly, 'Yes, I thank you, sire.'

'There you are,' her interrogator said to his companion. 'Mild as milk. She'll learn.' He returned to Anne. 'Then you must be off to your bed. They'll wake you at first light. Do as you're told and keep your mouth shut, and no harm'll come to you.' Taking her arm again he marched her down a passage, up some steps, and into a room without a door which was full of snoring and the musty stench of sleepers. A last flash from the lanthorn lit up an empty pallet almost at her feet, and then the strangers too were swallowed by the night.

For some minutes Anne stood where she had been left, too bemused by events for any action. She could not attempt to make sense of them, and soon a deadly weight of weariness began to bear down on her, so that she could think only of the pallet below her. The last thing she was conscious of was the hard little beads of her rosary pressing into her cheek.

Her sleep did not last until dawn. There was a creeping sensation over her thigh, and she came back to awareness of the same unquiet obscurity, with an additional activity centred around her upper legs. Wanting only to sleep again before her brain awoke, she scratched and turned over. But when she was still again the irritation returned, making its slow deliberate path towards her knee. In sudden revulsion she sat up, throwing off the single blanket and chafing furiously at her thighs beneath her kirtle. A groan came from the darkness to her right and she froze, more apprehensive of disturbing her unknown neighbour than of the visitor in her bed. Although she stayed motionless for some minutes, there was no further response from either. Her head swimming with tiredness, she gingerly lay down again, but it was too late for sleep. She was no stranger to bedbugs. Even in the most well-regulated bedchambers they sometimes appeared, singly; on the terrible voyage to Normandy they had been rife. But to be attacked within hours of entering a house did not say much for its standards. Anne hoped that her proper apartments, when she was transferred there in the morning, would be cleaner.

The woman who roused the dormitory showed her scant respect. The four other occupants had sprung from their pallets at the first stentorian call, and she came to stand over Anne, arms akimbo, blotting out the feeble morning that crept through the doorway.

'And who are you, mistress, to be a slug-a-bed when your betters are already scouring pots? Up, child, at once. I'll have no laziness here.' Too stunned to wonder why, she scrambled to her feet and tried to smooth down the badly crumpled linen of her gown. 'None of those airs, now,' said the ogress. 'You'll have an apron later – and a cap to keep back all that hair' – it was straggling in a tangled mass over Anne's shoulders, not having been brushed and plaited the night before. The woman pushed Anne before her down the steps, and then took her by the arm back into the courtyard. It was a fair-sized space, now bustling with ostlers leading horses and lads on errands. In the centre, by the pump, a cluster of people in servant's garb waited to wash; Anne was placed among them. 'This is a respectable house,' declared her guide. 'We'll have washing night *and* morning, if you please.' And instead of the gentle laving of hands and face from a silver bowl held by an attendant, Anne's head was thrust under the full jet of water and so were her arms.

Soaked to the elbow, and with rat's-tails of hair dripping inside her collar, she was hauled off to the kitchen. As she tied on the apron and pushed her damp hair under a cap, both starched but threadbare with use, the woman made a speech to her and her four sleeping-companions and a skeletal boy who proved to be the turnspit.

'This is not what you're used to, I dare say. But beggars can't be choosers. Just remember that you take your orders from me, and you'll live well enough. What do they call you?'

'Anne Nev—'

'First names are enough. I want to know no more. Well, Nan, off with you to your work. Petronilla, show her where to put the ashes when she's cleaned out the grates.' The youngest of the four, a girl of about Anne's age, stayed while the woman and the others dispersed. With an air of faint boredom, she indicated the two wide hearths, carpeted with the dead embers of last night's cooking-fires.

'There's the shovel, and there's the bucket,' she said, with a strong London accent that made her almost unintelligible. 'When it's full I'll tell you where to tip it.' Anne stared down at her task, not believing yet that she was really expected to perform it. There was some mistake. She had been taken for someone else. Sir Thomas Burdet had falsely brought her to the wrong house. Since Petronilla seemed more approachable than any of the adults, she made an attempt to clarify the situation.

'When shall I see the master of the house?' she asked timidly as the girl turned to leave her.

'When shall *you* see the master?' Petronilla was heavily sarcastic. 'In two years' time, if you work well, you may be serving at table in the great hall. Until then you'll have to wait. Master Twynyho doesn't visit the kitchens very often.' And she flounced off to her own duties, which due to Anne's advent were now slightly elevated. Master Twynyho. So it was not the wrong house. He must be some relation of Ankarette's, and no doubt all would be set right as soon as he learned that his secret guest had been misplaced in his kitchens. Meanwhile there was not much she could do except as she was told. Short of making a scene, which she dreaded, she could see no way of reaching him before he reached her.

Within twenty minutes she was trembling with fatigue and half-choked from inhaling wood-ash. The white apron and her newly washed face and hands were coated with a fine grey film, and the bucket was no more than two-thirds full. When Petronilla came back, more as a foreman than a helper, Anne staggered to her feet and said, 'I don't think I can do any more.'

All the good nature in the other girl's face was replaced by contempt. 'Can't do any more? You've only just begun! And there's the pots to be scoured after that, and the floor to be scrubbed before cooking begins. I'll have to be telling Old Mary that you're still trying to play the lady if you don't get on. She doesn't like slackers.' Having effectively crushed the new girl, Petronilla went smugly away.

She finished at last, although in carrying the third full bucket out to the ash heap in the yard every muscle in her arm and back shrieked in protest, and Old Mary had some sharp words to say about the length of time it had taken her. There was a blessed interlude then, when the kitchen staff gathered round the trestle table and broke their fast with bread and ale and a generous slice of cold mutton. Nobody spoke to Anne despite the shrill babble of conversation, but she was too glad of the respite to be much concerned. If only Master Twynyho would send for her.

But he did not, and the work continued, as Petronilla had promised, scouring, scrubbing, and then, as the cooking of dinner commenced, the emptying of more buckets and their filling at the well with water. The morning was already hot, and with the two hearths ablaze, and cauldrons and joints of meat seething and sizzling, the temperature inside the kitchen was most unpleasant. Had it not been for the rising agony in her shoulders, Anne might have appreciated the few steps through the coolness of the shadows at the edge of the courtyard, and even the comparatively fresh warmth of the sunshine. The heat and the activity rose to a pitch simultaneously as dinner was served, and Anne, pushed sweating into a corner out of the way, looked on in bewilderment as she observed the ritual for the first time from the other end. By the time she was given her own portion her hunger had gone. All that was left was the conviction that soon Ankarette's kinsman would lift her out of this slavery and take her to a room where she could be alone and cool and sleep.

The washing up occupied most of the afternoon, pewter dishes and tankards, trenchers and ladles in endless piles and then the cooking pans again. She was still wading elbow-deep in grease when a small commotion behind her made her glance over her shoulder in fear that she had done something wrong. At the far end of the long chamber a group of men were standing in the doorway, and one was pointing something out to another, portly and well-dressed in a long russet gown. The old sensation of eyes on her came back to Anne and she turned round, hands dripping unnoticed down her apron. Even at a distance she identified one of the lanthorn-bearers from last night, and she knew that her hour of release was here. Starting forward in relief, her rising spirit was caught on the wing by an iron grip on her wrist.

'And where are you going?' It was the ogress they called Old Mary.

'That is Master Twynyho. I must go to him.'

'Indeed you must not. Do you think he has time to spare for chits like you?'

'But he's come to look for me.... You must tell him I'm here.... He's going away!' Having apparently seen what he came to see, the master of the house was moving slowly from the doorway. The only way to attract his attention now was to cry out, to make him come back for her and do her justice. She opened her mouth and drew a breath, and then the cry died in her. All the dreadful consequences of such a breach of the peace – the immediate reaction of the woman who held her prisoner, the inevitable wrath of the Duke of Clarence, the repercussions on Isobel and her mother – rose before her and stifled her defiance. For the second time in a month she was silent when she should have spoken, and Francis Twynyho returned to his negotiations with a dealer in Castile soap from Seville, satisfied that the Lancastrian orphan his patron had sent to him was usefully employed in his household as the Duke had requested.

Anne did not expect another chance. She finished the washing up and other labours assigned to her without consciousness of what she was doing, and when she was dismissed in the evening she found her way to the dormitory and lay on her pallet until sleep took her. Experience had not given her a great fund of optimism to draw on. The machinations of her brother-in-law were clear to her now: he had never intended to let her take holy orders, but just to shuffle her out of the way, into a place where nobody would recognise her, and nobody would think of searching for her – if indeed anyone wished to. And she would simply be forgotten. She no longer questioned George's malignancy towards her; it had been a fact of her life for too long. He had deceived God as well as her. With a kind of kindred feeling towards a fellow victim, she resolved vaguely to say her rosary . . . as soon as she was not so tired.

With the exception of Sundays and holy days, when she was herded with the servants of a dozen households at the rear of the church of St James de Garlickehithe, the beads remained untouched. In church she could not concentrate, distracted by the proximity of a mass of stinking, wriggling, alien creatures whose language she could barely comprehend, and in whose world she existed on sufferance as an interloper.

They did not like her. This came to her slowly, because for the first weeks she was so much obsessed by the sheer muscular effort needed to drive her through a day's work that there was no room to observe anything outside herself. Beyond the ashes, and the slops, and the scrubbing brush the other inhabitants of the kitchen hovered as slightly hostile presences, only materialising when she had left a task unfinished or not well enough done to please the sharp eye of Old Mary. She took her scoldings indifferently, for she could do no better than she had done; she could walk no faster, carry no heavier loads, scour the flagstones no cleaner. And it was because of her indifference that they were against her. If she had kicked against her treatment, complained loudly of the drudgery foisted on her, they would have understood; it had happened to them, even to Old Mary, who once upon a time had been young Mary. If she had wept occasionally, into the ashes, or her hard pillow, they would have sympathised; almost all they knew of her was that she was a gentleman's orphan. And they were prepared to be kind to her and take her with them to Bartholomew Fair after supper was out of the way on a sultry evening in August. But there was never a protest, never a tear, never a smile or an attempt to make friends. Only the white empty face and the dogged application to her work.

It might have been exasperation at her listlessness that made Old Mary cuff her one morning when she spilt some grease on the freshly scrubbed trestle top. For a moment shock shuddered through her body and started into her eyes. Then she went meekly to fetch a dish-clout and clean up the mess. It was taken as a signal that Nan was fair game. There was no more help for her. Petronilla was sullen or haughty and the groom and the stable lad did not offer to carry her heaviest buckets. They talked behind her back but never to her, and they tried to think of ways to 'push her off her high-and-mighty perch'. Their satisfaction was little enough. Anne scarcely noticed them or their pinpricks. She dragged through the day in a haze which was motivated by one ambition only: to be tired enough to fall asleep before the bed-bugs awoke.

There was one person who talked to her, or as near as he could come to talking, and he was below her in the whipping-order. The turnspit was called Dog, for some forgotten reason, and he might have been eight or thirteen, so underdeveloped was he. He was not good at speaking, or at anything else except turning the spit for hours at a time, which he sometimes seemed to do in his sleep. As Anne knelt washing the flags he would crawl over to her and say things, disjointed phrases that meant very little, but his goodwill was evident, because he would bring her scraps of food, lumps of meat and crusts of bread saved from the day before. He did not appear to eat anything himself. And she responded to the creature, recognising in him someone in worse case than herself and yet showing generosity in his wretchedness. She could not stop his being beaten when he fell asleep at the spit, and she could do nothing about the baiting of him that went on in the yard, barking at him, pretending to snap at him, kicking him as if he were indeed the dog of his name. But she did nudge him awake whenever she found him nodding, and once or twice she surreptitiously turned the spit for him when nobody was looking and she was briefly free. After such incidents he would sidle up to her with an air of wagging his tail, and present to her most of his day's ration of food. She did not eat his offerings, because her own appetite was diminishing, but she accepted them.

The featureless days were losing their heat, and the dawn queues at the pump becoming more reluctant, when her relationship with Dog was violently altered. She was peeling onions at the table – normally she did not touch the vegetables, but this was not a popular chore – and she was too occupied with the handicap of impaired sight to notice Dog. The first thing she knew was a hand sliding beneath her kirtle, groping upwards. Starting to her feet, she let out the scream which nothing else had been able to shock from her. She retreated blindly and drew her hand across her smarting eyes, assailed by confused memories of her sister in tears and a disdainful young man in a darned nightshirt far more terrible than the fumbling which had provoked them. People came running at her cry and converged on a figure, dimly perceived, who grovelled near her stool.

There were other shrieks now, in a highpitched childish voice that she knew, and through it Old Mary said to her, 'We saw what he did. It's not the first time. He's a lewd rascal. You should have known better than to encourage him.' Then to the mass of people, 'Take him outside. Tam will teach him.' And, still shrieking mindlessly, Dog was dragged into the courtyard. Anne could hear what happened, even the fall of the ostler's crop on the boy's back and the howl that arose with each stroke. She cowered against the table, sick with loathing. But when they brought him back, and dropped him into his usual place in the hearth, she had to look at him, and she found she did not hate him. He was so puny and forlorn, and his back was bleeding a little through his torn shirt; he was lying so still that perhaps they had killed him. Compassion had nearly overcome her fear, and she was about to go to him when she was forestalled. One of the girls came back and splashed cold water briskly over the boy's back. Then she hoisted him up by the neck of his shirt and thrust a mug of ale against his mouth. He revived at the scent of the drink and gulped some of it down. The girl left him, having made the prescribed gestures of charity, and as soon as she was gone he threw up all he had taken. Anne returned to her task, and she was not sure whether the tears she shed were induced by the onions or by pity.

He did not try to speak to her again. Indeed, although he seemed to recover from his punishment and resumed his simple duties, he scarcely ever moved from his chimney-corner, preferring to sleep away the meal breaks. Often Anne would come from her chilly morning bed to find him still lying in the same place, his head pillowed on a dry log. It was difficult to wake him, but she would usually make an effort, if only to clear the ground for her first labour. His face grew more peaked as he ate less and less.

But Anne gave little consideration to Dog's plight. Although familiarity might in time have eased her lot, the daily routine was instead becoming harder for her to sustain. Each dawn was more difficult to face. As the first frosts came with October a curtain was hung before the open doorway of the dormitory, but it did not keep out the shivers and the nip in the toes. There was much grumbling when their cockerel Old Mary crowed the girls from their pallets. Nobody, however, failed to rise at the call except Anne, who was generally so drugged with broken sleep that a great effort of will was necessary to move at all. This was looked upon as arrant laziness, and as often as not the stout arm of the old woman provided the spur to lift her from her bed. Her tiredness eventually brought the threat of a whipping if it did not stop, but even that was no incentive. On a dull damp day near Hallowmas, Old Mary took the birch to her. With her head wedged ignominiously beneath her tormentor's armpit, she endured the pain as she endured the rest, in silence. She was not aware of the expressions of the spectators – nervously self-righteous, disappointed again by her lack of feeling.

It was all merging into one for Anne. For a week after the beating she could not lie on her back, but it was no worse than the icy shock of the water on her head in the half-light of the courtyard, the stiff numbness of her hands and knees as she shuffled across the flagstones with her scrubbing-brush, the interminable journeys from sweaty kitchen to fogbound yard, the crawling chill of her pallet. They were less real than the dreams that again began to visit her, vividly shaking the depths of her exhausted sleep. Not from God – He had deserted her with everyone else – but profane dreams which she knew were sinful even as she surrendered to their delight. Nothing solid endured into the unfriendly dawn, but once or twice, just before the influence fled from the encroaching cold, she caught a glimpse of who had been sharing the dream with her. Her pendant was still with her, a last reminder of the hope she had flung away, and she touched it half-unwillingly to banish the unholy image.

If she had not been the protégée of Master Twynyho they would not have kept her. She was becoming more and more idle, more and more uncaring about the way she did her work. They would find her sometimes with her arms in a bowl of fast-cooling soapy water, staring at vacancy, and the grease congealing on the dinner platters. Had she been ill, or in love, her behaviour might have been excusable, but apart from a recurring cold and cough she seemed quite hale, and she never went to any place where she could be meeting a lover. They did not dare to whip her too much either, in case the master should capriciously decide to ask after the cook-maid he was sheltering under his roof. Surreptitious cuffs, however, left no mark, and those in authority in the kitchen used them when punishment was required, although Nan showed no signs of mending her ways.

One event did leave an impression on her failing mind. Dog was thrashed again, for his old crime of sleeping at his post, and soon afterwards he began to cough. It was no ordinary cough, but one that tore through the clatter and bustle of the kitchen for minutes at a time. He was dosed with throat-soothing syrup, to promote the general peace of the staff, but it had no effect. After several days of it he was too weak to turn the spit, and it was clear even to the indifferent eyes of his workmates that he was very ill.

As Petronilla was passing one morning she said, quick and sharp, 'He's bleeding!' He was coughing blood, which spattered his improvised straw bed. They took him away and Anne did not see him again. She thought of paying for a mass for him, but she had no money and no energy to walk as far as the church.

It was very cold, and fog writhed round the ill-fitting curtain and wandered about the dormitory, muffling the rushlights that the girls used for rising and retiring. They had pushed their pallets together and slept curled up with each other for the warmth, like a cluster of hibernating dormice. Anne was not included, and she was chilled even in her sleep, except when the flames of her dreams lent an illusory and shameful heat. There was no misery in her heart now, no regret and no hope; all her life was smothered in the fog of weariness. She was totally cut off from the people around her; even their rough contacts, to shake her out of bed or chastise her, did not really touch her. Her tasks were performed on the other side of the fog, by arms and legs which had no direct connection with her, Anne Neville who once was. Now she no longer knew what she was, or where, or anything but that she wanted to sleep.

Perhaps she was stirring the stock-pot, and it might have been for supper; she had been doing it for a long time, round and round with the ladle that scraped on the bottom, scratching against the crackle of flames and some huger noise which was behind her. Round and round, and the puffs of steam from the stew and the monotony made her eyes close and her head nod, until the clatter of a dish close by woke her again. Round and round, and then there was something different to rouse her, not a noise but a silence close beside her. With the last dregs of her will she raised her head, and he was there, on the far side of the wall of mist, but there, and his hand was reaching to her through the gloom. She was too soiled and wretched to be able to go to him. Automatically she wiped her fingers down her apron.

It was a nebulous touch, a faint and faraway clasp, but it was drawing her after him, away from the hearth and through the door she had never passed. A man was in the doorway that could have been Master Twynyho if she could have remembered what he looked like, but he was wringing his hands and ducking his head in an odd fashion. Then it was dark, and light again, and there were long tunnels and steep steps, and at last a draught of bitter night air. All the way he was ahead of her, pulling her along by the hand that was beginning to tingle slightly, and was the only part of her not to be struck by the frost. A horse loomed up, moving restlessly, and she was swung on to its back. He was behind her now; the length of his body was close enough to push away the mist. When he wrapped his cloak around her, binding her to him, they were together inside the hostile barrier of fog, like the girls in their dormouse sleep. He might have spoken to her, but she retained no memory of it, only the profound slow-kindling spark which was stirring in the ashes of her heart.

5

THE AWAKENING

He had gone when she woke, and as usual she sought to burrow back into her slumber and recapture her dream before the crude call of morning. An angelic dream, she thought hazily, wholesome and kindly, unlike the wild thrilling visions of before ... and she sank into sleep again. Consciousness drifted back with a sense of something lacking. No furtive scrabblings of insects, no rustling of straw, no shivering; and no summons. She opened her eyes on the familiar wreaths of intrusive fog, but it was daylight, and an old man was sitting there, a frill of white hair round his shaven red crown. Instead of shaking her and shouting he smiled at her. So long since anyone had smiled at her, she hardly knew what it meant. But it meant that miraculously she was left in her bed to doze. Then there was a gentle arm about her shoulders, urging her to lift her head, and a spoonful of hot broth pressed to her lips. The aroma almost made her retch after long fasting, but with kindly insistence she was made to swallow it, and two spoonfuls more. The monk said, 'Rest now, my child,' and she understood the soothing tone of the voice though not the words.

She slept and slept, waking only to take a little broth or curds from the same elderly monk. And gradually the uneasiness in her mind, the fearful waiting for a command to rise and be about her business, was lulled into restfulness. On the beams above her head, sometimes an insipid patch of sunlight would appear, and drowsily, between naps, she would mark its journey across the ceiling, humping adroitly over the rafters in its path, and disappearing just as her nurse brought her midday broth. She grew quite interested in it, and missed it on the days when the sun did not shine. Many days of sunshine, and more without, passed before she began to wonder where she was. It was far simpler to let be, not to question for fear of disturbing the miraculous peace. The old man who tended her spoke seldom, finding that he could convey more with smiles and gentleness. Even on the occasions when she could not keep down her minute food helpings, he would smile patiently, clean her up, and try to make her take more. They had exchanged barely a score of words when she summoned the strength to ask, 'What is this place?'

'You are in the sanctuary of St Martin-le-Grand, my daughter.' She had none of the hardihood necessary for the next step; if that cloudy memory proved to be part of her sleep all this goodness would be in vain; she might as well go back to her scrubbing and have done. But in his mercy the old monk anticipated her. 'His grace of Gloucester left you in our keeping. He gave very particular instructions about your care – forgetting perhaps that we would do as much for any of God's children under our rule of charity.' In her mind's eye Anne saw suddenly a clear picture of Richard, with a slight crease between his brows, gravely instructing the brothers of St Martin's in their Christian duty. With a wonderful sense of freedom she returned the monk's smile, and managed to finish the coddled eggs he had brought for her.

Richard came on a morning when the luminous light on the rafters told her snow was falling outside. There were still flakes of it lying half-melted on his sleeves and entangled in the brown hair at his temples. They looked at each other without speaking, until the snowflakes had turned into damp on the cloth. Then he bent and kissed her forehead.

'A merry Christmas, Anne.'

'Christmas? Is it Christmas?'

'Indeed it is. Three days since. Today is Childermas.' How appropriate, he thought, for this hurt innocent, and he swallowed his rising emotion. Still grey-pale in the pallid reflection from the snow, at least now there was something living in her. On that ride to the sanctuary a month ago, he had feared that she would die in his arms. 'The brothers tell me that you have been no trouble to them.' Her old monk, reading in the corner, beamed absently. Another silence fell, and Richard, wanting to say one thing above all, could keep it back no longer.

'Anne, the King has given Middleham to me.' The infirmarian had warned him not to excite her, but ever since the summer, through all adversity, he had cherished the prospect of telling her at last. Now he was rewarded by the limpid happiness that for a moment transformed her pinched face.

'Oh, Richard,' she whispered, for she knew that her dream was his too, and always had been.

'I've also been given the lordship of the North Marches towards Scotland. Will you come and help me to govern for my brother?'

'Yes. As soon as you wish it.' His joy was clouded briefly by the recollection of the uneasy situation he had left at Westminster: the persistent truculence of a George enraged by defeat, Edward's attempts to satisfy the two brothers whose objects were diametrically opposed. But there was no need to worry Anne with problems which would, the King had given his word, be smoothed out in due course.

'As soon as you're well.' Anne was a little shamefacedly relieved. She was prepared to follow Richard to the limits of her strength, but at present those limits were very close, and she could not bear to fail him. He saw the tiny relaxation, and judged that it was time to go. Yet she was loath to let him. Guessing it, Richard promised to return each week, and before he left he kissed her again. The light touch of his lips seemed to linger after him, and when she closed her eyes Anne could fancy that he was still with her.

Every week he visited her, and as her health improved she progressed from praying that he would come, to hoping, and finally to knowing that he would. He sat with her and talked to her, mainly of what he intended to do in the North, and with her growing vitality she began to join in. Only once did he refer to the past. It was to explain that the credit for discovering her whereabouts belonged not to him but to John Wrangwysh's sister Janet.

'She has suffered in our service,' he smiled. 'Waiting outside the White Tower through a foggy afternoon to give me the news gave her nothing but a bad chill.'

'We must thank her,' said Anne, and he agreed. Discussing suitable rewards, neither thought to wonder whence came

Janet Evershed's information; they never asked her.

For his part, while he was with Anne inside the walls of the greatest sanctuary in London, Richard could shake off for a few hours the depression induced by his brother's continued opposition to his marriage. The wheels were grinding slowly towards a settlement in Richard's favour, but the result was likely to embitter George for ever against him. In terms of property Clarence should have had no complaints: the richer share of Warwick's estates would go to him. Yet however much King Edward might concede to placate his second brother, he would revoke neither his gift of the Yorkshire properties to Richard, nor permission for his marrying Anne. And Clarence, who had intended to make a clean sweep of his father-in-law's possessions, was irreconcilable. To watch the life returning, day by day, to the empty shell of a girl he had salvaged from the kitchen of Francis Twynyho restored Richard's own spirit also.

On an afternoon of February, unseasonably mild, Anne was permitted to walk for a little while in the garden of the guest-house. The birds had performed their Valentine's rites and were bustling about their spring duties, and the bare trees were loud with them as Richard made his way to join her. Two ladies, lent by his mother the Duchess of York to attend Anne's convalescence, gossiped quietly, but Anne stood by an almond tree that was thrusting forth early pink buds, and stared down at the ring of crocuses that encircled the trunk. She looked at him unsmiling as he took her hand with his usual brief pressure.

'The spring last year,' she said in real distress, 'where did it go? I saw none of it. And the summer. I remember nothing. Only heat and cold.'

He kept her hand in his and said, 'I don't know. But this year, I promise, there will be spring and summer. In Wensleydale. If you are willing, we shall be married next week.' She raised her eyes from the golden flames licking from the winter earth to the pale sky between the almond twigs. Then she turned to him.

'Yes. Yes, that would mend everything.'

It was a modest wedding, celebrated in the privacy of the royal chapel at Westminster. They had sent to the Pope for a dispensation, since they were strictly within the prohibited bounds of kinship, but Richard brushed aside the formality of waiting for it. Since Anne was not yet in the best of health she was grateful for the lack of ceremony, although she shrank nervously from the information that the King would be there. She had not outgrown the dread of the golden giant of her childhood. Yet now he was to give her away as a bride. His intimidating bulk had grown no less, his costume out-glittered the burnished gold of the sacred ornaments, and he tucked her hand most familiarly under his elbow as he led her to the altar.

But he led her to Richard, and fixing her gaze on the slight figure who awaited her, his back stiff with the solemnity of the occasion, her mind was emptied of any other consideration. Now they were side by side, and she could just see his grave profile lifted to the crucifix. Although he seemed to take no notice of her coming she felt the awareness in him and was glad. Not until their hands were joined by the priest did he look at her, and then she was afraid. Such sincerity, such intensity that it was almost grief. His voice shook as he made his vows. She began to repeat her own, those words she had spoken before at Amboise in hollow mockery of their sense, and she saw in Richard's eyes what it would mean to fulfil them.

She was appalled; she was too weak, she had not the courage to follow where he would lead, to cleave to him in the teeth of destiny. Her responses faltered, and she hovered on the brink of a headlong flight back to St Martin's and the security of God. But the light clasp tightened, forcing her again to meet his eyes. They smiled at her, steadying her erratic heartbeat, and she continued with her promise to love, honour and obey until the parting of death. As the wedding ring came finally to rest on her fourth finger, she smiled back fearlessly at her husband.

Richard had used the slight irregularity of the marriage to insist upon a minimum of revelry. He had watched Anne suffering through formal banquets as a child, and had no wish to inflict any more on her on this of all days. So, much to the disappointment of King Edward, who would have delighted in lavishing merriment on his favourite brother's nuptials, there was a quiet wedding-breakfast in the Duke of Gloucester's apartments attended only by those present at the ceremony. Music in the gallery was provided by the King's singers, and only now and again were their chansons drowned by a shout of laughter from their royal master.

As soon as he decently could Richard thanked his guests and sent them, with the utmost tact, on their way. His anxious eye on Anne told him that she was already fatigued. The Duchess of York raised her daughter-in-law with cool kindness, speaking her blessing on her future like the benediction of an abbess. In her awe Anne kissed her ring as if she was indeed her mother in God instead of in law.

Edward was the last to leave, and he prevented her from kneeling and enveloped her in his scintillating embrace. As she emerged, panting a little, he said to her husband, 'You know, Dickon, she still doesn't trust me.' Moderating his voice to its most gentle, he turned back to her. 'Anne, dear maid, if you knew how much I pray for your happiness – yours and Dickon's – I think you would have to trust me.' He kissed her quickly on the cheek, and departed. For the first time, Anne's heart warmed a little towards him. Once, he had disturbed her childhood; later, she had dreaded him as a rival for Richard's devotion. She understood now, in the light of her own security, that that devotion was not one-sided; she could forgive much to anyone who loved Richard.

There were old friends among the small circle of intimates remaining in the Duke's solar, although they needed to be reintroduced. Frank Lovel, his fair boy's face lengthened into a man's, but his hair still unable to decide which way to lie down; John Wrangwysh, taller, more silent; Robert Percy, his belligerence tempered by war in earnest into rather wry restraint. In remembering and placing their boyish characteristics and tracing them through to their present personalities, Anne was absorbed without having to be involved. They did not ignore her; it would have been difficult with their lord sitting on a stool by her knee; but they included her without expecting her to exert herself in any way. It was as if she had never left their company. The years that lay between dwindled to nothing. Her tensions of the early morning were soothed away by the even flow of the conversation and her husband's nearness. Soon her eyelids were drooping, and the drift of voices was only a pleasing background. When she next looked up, they had all gone except for her two attendants and

Richard. Rising from his stool, he helped her to her feet.

'Time for bed.' Dropping a kiss on her wrist, he delivered her to the women.

They had wrapped her in the bedgown which was a wedding gift from Richard: full and fleecy-lined, of pale blue velvet trimmed with white fur. After many months of privation she had declared it to be too splendid for her, but he had reminded her of that blue gown which she had worn as a little girl, and asked her to wear this for his sake. Her hair, tangled during the day, had been brushed again, straight down her back and over her shoulders, until the ends flew and crackled; her hands and feet had been bathed in rosewater. Then they had left her, melting into the winter night. She stood by the fire, gazing dreamily into its golden heart, the sensuous comfort of warmth and safety lapping her round. The tiny crack of the flames intensified the peace. So the quiet closing of the door and the soft footfall roused her a little to wonder why one of her women had returned. But it was Richard. He came over to the hearth, and resting his elbow on the overmantel he too contemplated the fire. An inexplicable tremor of disquiet ran through her tranquillity. She knew that there was a restraint between them, and that he was searching for something to say. Finding it, he spoke stiltedly, not to her but into the fire.

'I'm glad you accepted the gown. The hue becomes you so well. I chose it on purpose, Anne.' Suddenly there was her name, in the intimate tone that never failed to move her. He had turned to her now, his brown eyes deep in the subdued light. Her restraint melting away, she went to him and he took her in his arms. This was all her desire, to be encompassed by such tenderness, to be so shielded from the rawness of life that it could never hurt her again. Through the sweet-smelling darkness of velvet and musk, his hand moved softly over her hair, caressing her as the sun had caressed the fur of the little cat in the cloisters of Valognes. He tipped up her face and kissed her brow, and then her closed eyelids, and the tip of her nose, and her lips, and with a firm gentle gesture he pressed her cheek again to his shoulder. She snuggled closer.

She could blissfully have died thus, and indeed time ceased to matter; she had no consciousness of its passing. But she became aware, at some point in her eternity, that Richard had changed. He was no longer at rest. And she caught the sense of the words he was murmuring.

'We must go to bed.' Coming back by degrees to the candlelit chamber, she found her husband holding her by the shoulders, and the fire sinking to embers. 'Will you let me be your handmaiden?' he said lightly, and unfastened the girdle of her gown. She was quite back in her bedchamber now, her feet in the fur of the rug, one of the candles guttering, the air chilly as the layers of rich stuff slipped from her. 'You're shivering,' said Richard solicitously. 'Into bed before you take a fever.' And he turned back the sheet and plumped the pillows and helped to make her comfortable, for all the world as if he were her old monk at St Martin's.

But he was not, and when he had snuffed out every candle but one, instead of leaving her to sleep he came back after a moment divested of his dark red gown and joined her in the bed. Anne lay in suspended animation; somewhere very close still was that beautiful state from which she had barely emerged, but beyond it lurked another possibility which was slowly, inexorably, possessing her. Richard drew together the heavy gold hangings on his side of the bed, and smiled across at her reassuringly. They were alone in a tiny chamber with brocade walls, lit softly by the single candle. All the security in the world should have been contained there. Yet instead there was this monstrous growth of dread, within and all about her. As Richard leaned over to put out the candle it came horribly to birth. The curtains at the foot of the bed were stirring. Anne flung herself into a sitting position.

'Is anybody there?' she called in a high strange voice. Swiftly Richard was with her, his arm round her.

'What is it, Anne? No one is there.'

'Yes,' she whispered, starting eyes fixed on the join of the curtains. '*He's* there. Watching us.'

'There's no one,' repeated Richard firmly, and with the decision of a practical man he demonstrated it. All the curtains were drawn back, each corner of the chamber illuminated in turn, and then the doors bolted. Coming back, he stood beside the bed in his nightshirt, candle held steady, and said once more quietly, 'You see, there is no one here but us.' Then he closed the bed-curtains again and returned to his place with Anne. She was scarcely less rigid against his chest than she had been before. 'Who did you think it was, dear love?' he asked very gently, and for a long while he had no more response than a slight shaking of her head.

At last, as he persisted, she murmured, 'He was sent to spy on us. De Josselin.'

'De Josselin?' Richard spoke the name as if it was completely unknown to him, but then he remembered. 'King Louis' agent? But he's not even in England, Anne. He was recalled by his master as soon as . . . your father died. I believe the King is employing him now on missions to Milan. You have no cause to fear him, of all people.' His rationality made some impression on her. She was trembling now.

'No, not this time. Before. He was there. And my . . . the Prince ordered him out.'

Richard comprehended, and swallowed down his disgust, for his wife was in a pitiable enough state without his becoming upset. 'That was last year. You don't suspect me of playing you so false, do you?'

'No. No, not you. You would never leave me, would you?'

She had gone beyond him again, but he held her more tightly and said, 'Of course not. You can trust me, Anne.'

'Yes.' She realised that she had been subject to a hallucination, but the terror of it was not all dispersed. It was not only that manifestation on her first wedding night, not only the humiliation of being abandoned in her marriage bed. . . . Without her noticing, Richard had eased her down on to the pillows, and he began almost imperceptibly to caress her. What had happened on that night when she was Prince Edward's bride was a mystery, and perhaps for his own peace of mind it should remain so. The thought of Anne's being defiled in any way was insupportable. But it had hurt her profoundly, and there was only one way to heal her: to extinguish its image for ever with his love. She was still trembling, but she had relaxed and he was encouraged to believe that the worst was over. Tenderness for her vulnerability rose in him, and he snuffed the candle with one hand without taking the other from her hair.

She was allowing herself to be gentled like a nervous horse, and the sweet oblivion was creeping over her again, obliterating ugly memories, when she became conscious of his fingers inside her shift, touching her breast. The sensation was oddly pleasurable, yet it did not soothe her as his other caresses had done. His fingers were stroking lower, beneath the coverlet, and then fumbling for the hem of her shift. She opened her eyes on darkness, and was suddenly and coldly awake. Sensing it at once, Richard stopped.

'What is it, dear heart?' he asked, but she could not tell him. He tried to go on, but there was no response. Her softness, her earlier yielding to his embrace, had disappeared, leaving her an inanimate body under his hands. It was out of his experience. He had not expected to rouse her as quickly as Marja, but he had not foreseen this, and he was at a loss. As for Anne, how could she explain that all his dear familiarity had in that instant become alien, so that they were no longer his caresses? Other people drifted near her, and they were smiling slyly down at her: Isobel, King Louis, de Josselin, and, more distinct than the others, the Duke of Clarence. Vivid little scenes from her past were re-enacted in her head, irrelevant, nonsensical, and yet each of them was more real to her than the shadowy husband who strove to reawaken her body and to reach her absent mind.

In the end, he left the bed again to fetch the flagon of wine and two goblets placed by some thoughtful attendant on the table. Pouring a cupful for Anne, he made her drink it all before he took his own, although he needed it more. Dispirited and physically weary, he had used every blandishment which Marja had taught him, and more that he had discovered himself, and to no avail. Even so, his tenderness for her remained constant. In the rekindled candleflame her face was so pallid, the hollows in her cheeks so pronounced, that he was in danger of weeping for her. They spoke very little, but once more he had submerged the lover in the nurse. And she, obediently swallowing her second cup of wine, wondered that the Richard she knew had reappeared.

So it was through a haze of alcohol that Anne lost her virginity. She remembered nothing of it afterwards except Richard showering kisses on her and muttering, 'I was first, and I shall be best, I promise you, sweetest Anne.' He also was rather drunk.

Waking in a frosty dawn, she found her husband propped on his elbow beside her, watching her anxiously.

'How is it with you this morning?'

'I have a headache,' she said.

'Is that all?' Puzzled, she answered that it was, and a brief grin flashed across his sombre features. 'Then there's hope for the future,' he said, with which cryptic remark he kissed her and rose to don his bedgown.

She did not see much of him that day. They had agreed while she was still in sanctuary that they should travel up to Yorkshire at the earliest opportunity, and there were many things for Richard to attend to. But Anne had no time to brood about the events of the night, for to her surprise she was constantly in demand. A stream of visitors asked for audience, and they bore with them wedding gifts and good wishes from the most unexpected quarters. An alderman from Warwick, her birthplace, brought the duty of his corporation and a chest of carved Arden oak; the Staple of Calais sent a self-assured merchant with a length of fine woollen cloth; and there were others, of more or less importance. She did her best to receive them courteously and with gratitude, although she was unsure of herself in the presence of so many strangers. All her life she had been surrounded by homage, yet never before had it been paid directly to her in her own right, and she did not know how to accept it. And of course it was not she that they were honouring, but the King's brother, the new lord of the North. She was acting on behalf of her husband, and the thought of even that responsibility made her quail. Anne Neville had been a cypher or a nobody. The Duchess of Gloucester was the third lady in the land. The Duke of Gloucester returned in time to take supper with his wife, and found a slightly bemused Anne, picking at her pigeon pie.

'All those people,' she said with awe. 'How they must love you.'

'Perhaps.' He signed to a page to replace the uneaten pie with honey-cakes. 'I am a craven to go abroad on business and leave you here with the diplomatic duties. Did they tire you?' She denied it, but not very emphatically, and Richard frowned.

'We could say you were unwell, that you must keep your chamber for a few days. . . .'

'No! I'm quite well. Simply unaccustomed to such things.' He must not think that she had failed him through inadequacy, on the very first day.

He was satisfied, because he nodded, and said, 'Well, I have brought a little compensation for you.' One of his henchmen came forward, and he took a box from him and laid it in Anne's lap. There were holes in the lid, and with a child's curiosity she held her breath as she opened it. The lining was blue satin, and in the soft nest of the interior was a white bundle of fur with ears. As the light fell on it the bundle uncurled, thrust out one small paw with all claws spread, and opened a rose-pink mouth in a miniature but gigantic yawn. Anne could only gasp, and at length her husband picked up the kitten and placed it, limbs sprawling, in her arms.

'Its dam came from Persia,' he explained. 'And the scoundrel who sold it to me swears on the tomb of his fathers that she was the Queen's pet cat. So you hold the child of a queen's queen.' Anne would not let it go. The miracle which had happened all those years ago, when the half-dead alley kitten had begun to purr in her hands, had happened again. The tiny pink nose pushed against her own, the violet eyes closed in ecstasy, and the triangular tail stood erect as she tickled its chin. There was no question about its name. Kat slept in its mistress's chamber and was appallingly spoiled, which being a royal kitten it took as its due.

They went early to bed, and this time there was no preamble. Richard put out all the candles, drew the curtains and gathered Anne into his arms.

'Are you very tired, Anne?' he whispered, and although she was, caution made her ask why.

'If you would prefer to sleep . . . tonight. . . .' Once more he was making allowances for her, excusing her from a duty that he did not believe she was capable of fulfilling.

Remembering her marriage vows, she said quickly, 'No, I'm not at all sleepy.' Maybe she had sounded too eager, for he needed no further prompting. Wine did not cloud the act tonight. She was offended by the intimacy of his fondling, hurt by the roughness of his entry into her, and shocked by the violence of his orgasm. Yet she forced herself to lie still, to hold him, to sigh when he did, and even to smile into the dark when he asked if all was well. He lay beside her for a long while after that without speaking, and she thought he had gone to sleep. When he broke the silence, she found that she had not deceived him entirely.

'It's new to you, dear love. Don't distress yourself if there's not much pleasure. Trust me, and that will come in time.' And then he did fall asleep, with his head tucked under her chin. She lay still, while numbness crept along her arm because she did not dare move it from beneath him, and pondered her newly acquired knowledge. Now she had some understanding of the change in Isobel after her marriage night. And she wondered what pleasure Richard could possibly be promising her.

But repetition took much of the repugnance out of her nights. Richard was unfailingly gentle, and the pain soon disappeared. She could respond to his kisses, even sometimes to his caresses, yet always there was a barrier across which she could feel nothing. The days were busy, with preparations for going north and with learning to be the Duchess of Gloucester, and so mercifully she slept soundly and had little opportunity for her old idle self-searchings. Her husband's affection for her was ever-present, and he gave her no indication that she was inadequate in any way. Only occasionally, examining in her looking-glass the poor drained complexion and immature breasts, did she question why Richard should have wanted to marry her.

Shortly before they were due to leave, they were able to pay an outstanding debt. Janet Evershed came to visit them, and brought her own hand-worked wedding gifts. They in turn gave her a gift, a token of their thanks for her part in the rescue of Anne from the city kitchen. As Janet and Richard talked like long-standing acquaintances, Anne observed her with interest. It was rumoured that she had been the King's mistress for many years, and yet she had the appearance only of what she was by profession: a well-to-do independent mercer in widow's mourning. Not at all the kind of woman Anne would have expected to attract – and keep – the flamboyant Edward. Still, she did not lie with him for material advantage, or she would be a court lady by now. Anne found herself envying a little the poise of the King's paramour, and at the same time wanting her as a friend. When her husband invited Janet to visit them at Middleham, she endorsed the invitation with sincerity.

The pace of her new public life was telling on Anne. With each strenuous day she longed more for the haven of Wensleydale, and she discovered one night that Richard was of the same mind. Waking in the darkness she found herself alone, and her anxieties of desertion revived again. But he had heard her movement of disquiet, and came back from where he had been pacing. She asked what was wrong.

'Nothing. I was restless and didn't want to disturb you. But I have, it seems.' When he was lying beside her again he added with unaccustomed vehemence, 'I shall be glad to leave this city. Outside London I can sleep easy.' He gave no reasons, and soon fell asleep, yet Anne was comforted. Sometimes she had suspected that it was only duty and the humouring of her that was driving him away from the King his brother's side.

There was no mistaking his lightheartedness as he led his train to Bishopsgate on the day of their departure. He waved gaily to the knots of citizens who always turned out for a procession, especially if their beloved King was gracing it. Anne rode between Edward and her husband – on horseback, as she had insisted despite Richard's doubts – and in her relief at turning her back on the city of her captivity she brought herself to follow his example and acknowledge the crowd. Behind them the knights of the Duke's household were behaving like excited boys. Even those who were not Yorkshire-bred were eager to face the challenge of the wide lands of the North, to win them, from their long allegiance to the Nevilles, to the loyalty of the Duke of Gloucester and King Edward. Outside Bishopsgate the formal partings took place, and Anne submitted with grace to a vigorous kiss from her brother-in-law. There was no longer any cause for her to fear him: she had won Richard.

Now she rode under the device of the white boar, and was treated as a personage instead of as part of the baggage. However, the journey was no idyll. The warm spell in February had given way to hard weather, frost, wind and sleet, as if winter were reluctant to loose its grip a second time.

Although the cavalcade covered little more than fifteen miles a day, Anne was soon regretting her gallant resolve to ride on horseback all the way. When she caught a cold near Nottingham Richard overruled her still-vocal protests and transferred her to the chariot which, piled with cushions and furs, had been shadowing her from London.

'It's like carrying my coffin with us!' she had complained, but he merely said, 'I hope not.' Indeed, she was secretly pleased to be so cosseted. Kat was let out of his basket to travel with her, and spent half his day stalking unsteadily up and down the jolting mountains of velvet and fur, and the other half cat-napping tastefully in the centre of a scarlet cushion. He was a welcome distraction for Anne between the bouts of sickness which always assailed her in litters and chariots. Richard was very concerned for her. At every stopping-place his primary consideration was a chamber for the Duchess, and he would make sure that she was suitably installed, with warming-pans in the bed, before he saw to anything else. She slept the nights through, almost as heavily as she had done at St Martin's. Often enough she was already asleep when her husband came to her, and he let her be. His desire for her would always be subordinated to her comfort. There would be the rest of their lives at Middleham, he told himself, and deferred their mutual satisfaction until later.

It was over three weeks before they left York behind them and crossed into Wensleydale. Anne was mounted again, determined that however her head might ache with weariness she would greet her home worthily. Her home: an odd word to spring so readily into her mind. She was not really sure what it meant, since she had heard nobody but attendants and the women in Twynyho's kitchen talk about it. Somewhere to return to, somewhere to rest your thoughts and yourself in peace. It was good enough for Middleham.

Dashing the rain from her eyes, Anne lifted them to the skyline, close and steep to her left, and knew that beyond that rise another hill rose, and another, on and on, with heather roots and sheep and brown bracken, unaffected by the sparse villages and castles which by their courtesy took shelter from the weather in their folds. Awesome, yet reassuring. Richard pushed his horse alongside, and she realised that in her eagerness to reach her destination she had outstripped the other riders. Exchanging a glance of perfect harmony, they spurred forward. The horses were almost blown, dropping again into a walk, when the wonder happened.

As if a curtain had been drawn aside, the squall passed. The rainclouds careered away towards the Vale of York, and before them the sky was scoured clean, the blue of a thrush's egg. Late sunshine dusted the downward slopes, and the battlements of the castle were touched with pale honey. It looked near enough to reach with an outstretched finger, as solid and as living as the broad back of the mare beneath her.

'Middleham!' It was Richard who uttered it, but they reined in with one accord and gazed, silent in the fullness of their hearts.

A boy, trudging towards them on an errand to Jervaulx Abbey, stopped short, stared at lord and lady motionless in their magnificence, then yelled ecstatically, threw up his cap, and pelted back towards the town. At the same time the gentlemen came up with them, chattering, slapping each other on the back, laughing, expressing in their different ways their own delight. But Richard and Anne rode into Middleham town the first of all their train, to the impromptu but enthusiastic greeting of every resident within earshot of their shrill harbinger. The warm North Riding tones struck familiar chords in Anne's memory, and no effort was needed here to smile and call out her thanks to the lads who splashed beside her horse in the recent puddles, a mobile guard of honour to the castle gate. The porter had not changed, she noticed with astonished joy as he pulled his forelock beyond the arch of the gatehouse; it was impossible to believe that she had left here less than five years previously.

Yet how different was this homecoming. The small garrison, drawn up smartly in the inner bailey, wore bright new surcoats adorned with the white boar, and Anne was with Richard as he paced his horse solemnly down their rank, inspecting them as her soldiers as well as his. And when he lifted her from her horse, and led her by the hand out of the sudden sunshine and up the stairs under the massive walls of the keep, the attendants and the servants who awaited them in the great hall were smiling, pleased to greet their young Duke and Duchess, murmuring with northern hospitality, 'Welcome home, lord; welcome back to Middleham, lady.'

It was too much. She hardly kept her feet to the great chamber, and then Richard saw how faint she was and supported her into his own presence chamber. The curtains had not yet been hung on the bed, and the posts stood naked above the soft green hill of the coverlet. As she was disrobed and left to rest, her wandering mind returned to the day when the bed was hung with scarlet and white, still crumpled from travelling, and her father had commanded her to study to like the Duke of Gloucester better. Her husband still hovered near, and he heard her giggle faintly. Bending over her, he said, 'What amuses you, dear love?'

'I learned that lesson well,' she answered drowsily, and fell asleep.

March had gone out like a lion before she saw any more of Middleham. Her reaction to three weeks' travelling was severe, and she paid heavily for her days of riding exposed to winter's rearguard attack. Richard would not have her moved to the lady chamber in the south curtain, keeping her in his own bed, secluded beyond the great chamber, yet close enough to sit with her in any moment spared from business. He also slept with her, but never made any advances beyond kissing her night and morning. Holding himself responsible for her collapse by hastening their departure from London and pressing on too rapidly with the journey, he would do nothing that might hinder her recovery. As always she was grateful for his forbearance and care. And then, as she improved enough to leave her bed for a while in the afternoons, she began to miss what she had merely endured at Westminster. The closeness of his embrace, the uneasy thrill as his hands touched her naked flesh. Strangest of all, she dreamed once again one of her old dreams, and there was no doubt as to who was stirring her to that torrid exultation. She woke with a start, and Richard's voice spoke sleepily.

'Anne?'

'A dream; that's all.'

'Dreams cannot hurt, they're only fancies,' he said soothingly, thinking that it was a nightmare she had suffered. Moving nearer, he put his arm round her. Anne listened until his breathing became slow and regular, wishing that her fancy had been true.

She was ashamed of her thought in the morning, but she dismissed it quickly, for today she was to move to her own chamber, and to dine in the great hall with all the household. Ceremoniously she was escorted across the wooden bridge, which was so much shorter and lower than she remembered, to the apartments which had been her mother's and now were hers. Smaller than her memory of it, the solar was gay with arras and strewn with fresh rushes which bruised under the feet into sweetness. The bed was hung with the golden brocade from her chamber in London, but the coverlet was another gift from her husband, embroidered with birds flying to and from their nests.

'I saved it until we reached Middleham,' he said diffidently, 'for the sake of St Anne in the chapel window.' It was another instance of his generosity, and of his thoughtfulness, and once more she could not thank him. Then he dismissed their attendants and took her up the spiral stair to the battlements. As she emerged into the clear air she saw how much change her time of sickness had wrought in Wensleydale. The year had budded into green and blue April, the wide dome of the sky full of hurrying birds and cloudlets, the high hills lilac with distance, the trees springing into leaf, and up there, the mounds of the old castle flecked with the sunshine of early gorse. Unthinking, her hand crept beneath her cloak to where her pendant hung, and then Richard's hand was laid over both. She leaned back against him, and they recalled together the boy and girl who had sealed a pact yonder which was at last fulfilled. At length he turned her to him and kissed her lips. Perhaps it was the warmth of the past, so strong between them, or perhaps it was the spring about them: some response moved deep within her that was new and urgent; if only she had known how to express it. But in no more than two quickened heartbeats he had released her, and it faded back into the loveliness of the countryside.

A week later they rode together up the dale to Nappa Hall at Askrigg, where Richard had business with the Recorder of the city of York. Anne had not been so far since their arrival, but the warm weather held, and she would not be left behind.

They took the way that ran below the crown of the hills; on their left the little irregular fields with their embroidery of drystone walls tumbled down to the glint of the river, and then climbed up the other side towards the far crest. Frank Lovel lifted his voice to the freshness of the day and sang, and soon the others joined in.

By the time they left Askrigg the sun had reversed its position and was poised in a golden blaze above the Pennines. It had been a visit of an informality that quite disconcerted Anne, unused as she was to the manners of the prosperous gentry. She watched the Duke of Gloucester take leave of Miles Metcalfe and his goodwife with an ease she had not seen him use among the high lords at Westminster. Sped on their way by stirrup-cups of good malmsey, they made for Aysgarth and the valley road by the river.

They came down a steep hill from the village, turned a corner, and the din of water abruptly filled their ears. Above and below the bridge the Ure thundered, great plumes and sheets of whiteness where it leaped down the huge staircase of its upper course. Cowed by this sudden manifestation of power, in a river which only a dozen miles downstream purled peacefully over the stones near the castle, Anne pushed her mare closer to Richard. He was staring out at the cataracts, preoccupied, and when he looked at her there was still something absent in his eyes, strangely wild, which disturbed her as much as the falls. They passed on over the bridge.

On each side of the road the undergrowth was starred with flowers. Reining in involuntarily, she gazed at them stretching into the distance between the tangle of budding twigs, windflowers like a fall of late snow, lit here and there to brilliance by the sun, and her throat constricted with emotion. She had never seen such beauty, and she wanted to weep. Then she found that Richard was lifting her from her horse, and as she stood for a moment irresolute, not sure what to do with the freedom he had given her, he pushed her forward.

'Go on. You may do as you wish.' And so she did as she had not been allowed before: she gave way to impulse and ran in among the trees, among the myriads of delicate blossoms. A kind of madness seized her. She fell to her knees and began to pick them feverishly, as if she would gather all their loveliness to her before it vanished. Here and there were greater treasures still – modest clumps of primroses hiding under their wrinkled leaves. Without heed of the twigs that caught in her headcloth she searched for more, uttering little inarticulate cries of triumph as she spied another plant. A drop splashed on a leaf before her and she looked up, startled that rain could come from a clear sky. But it was her own tears, and through them she saw Richard, leaning against a slender alder trunk and watching her. She stood up, and her flowers scattered.

'What is the matter with me?' she said shakily. 'You must think I'm crazed.... It was the flowers ... and the sun ... I don't know.'

All he said was, 'Look. You've dropped your flowers,' and he stooped to collect them for her. The other members of the party had dispersed, following the fortunes of those who had brought their hawks with them, and Richard and Anne were alone, near the brink of the river. Only the graceful alders stood between them and the rushing of the Ure in its shallow gorge. He gave her the fallen windflowers and primroses, and held her hands between his. She was facing the sun, and in its westering light her cheeks were flushed with warm colour, and her eyes were soft and bright. His face was dark and she could not read the expression, but the touch of his hands lit a spark somewhere which made her gasp with its fierceness. She flung herself into his arms, and the flowers tumbled again to their feet unnoticed. It was like no embrace they had shared before, like nothing in her experience. She was acutely conscious of his body pressed against her, of the flesh beneath their garments straining to be welded together. The spark grew into a sheet of flame that seemed to envelop them both and then, suddenly, they were two again and he was holding her at arms' length, and he was trembling as violently as she. Her legs were so weak that but for his grasp she would have fallen.

'Anne,' he said, in a low voice that shook, and she gazed back at him with the same dumbfounded amazement. Then he begun to pull her by the hand back towards the road, at a speed which took no account of the rough ground or the unsteadiness of her gait.

They were mounted and away before the surprised grooms had collected their wits, and it was some time before their companions, pursuing at the gallop with ruffled falcons on their wrists, came up with them, enquiring gaily if the Scots had invaded. Richard only laughed, and Anne joined in, a little hysterically. She was in such tumult that nothing much outside herself, save the figure of her husband urging his horse forward, was of any significance. Racing with him towards an unknown consummation of instincts she did not understand, she felt only the delicious upsurge of her heart as she relived those moments by the river, and the throbbing expectancy of whatever was to come. Soon after dark they were home, and as the sweating horses were being rubbed down in the stables, Anne and Richard bolted their supper in his chamber. They were oblivious of the surreptitious mirth that rippled among their attendants, as they intercepted and interpreted without difficulty the hungry glances that passed between the Duke and Duchess over the eel pie and cheese. With a tactful degree of collusion they sought their dismissal and slipped away.

She had scarcely taken her eyes from Richard since they entered the castle, clinging to him in imagination as decorum kept her from doing in fact. But when they were alone after centuries of impatience, the doors shut, there was no restraining the tingling eagerness of her body. Her modesty, his diffidence, were flung aside as they sprang to each other. Somehow they reached his bed, and then it was all desperate quivering haste, to tear away the obstacles that held them apart, to kindle again the flame that had leapt between them among the windflowers, to fan the flame into a single blaze. The possession she had tolerated was now essential, and as he took her she cried out. But that was not the end, it was the beginning of a greater conflagration, and as he moved within her a wave of light and colour swelled from the fire until it swept over her and she was engulfed in its warm flood. And together they drowned in the iridescent whirlpool of its ebbing.

She returned to her separate self with her husband gently smoothing the hair from her damp forehead. A dream, she thought bemusedly, and yet no dream had carried her to such heights before. Bathed in its radiance, she could almost believe that it was true, and she lay with her eyes still closed, trying as so often vainly before to plunge back into sleep and recapture it. Richard's hand slid to her breast, and she opened her eyes on his face, not kind, but grave, passionate, his own hair disordered and sweat gleaming on his temples in the candlelight. She saw that they were naked, their bodies intertwined on the velvet coverlet, and she understood that all her dreams had been but shadows of the reality. She caught her breath at the revelation, and he bent to kiss her with a new languor which saluted their unity. Then he smiled, and pulling over them the fur which had almost fallen from the bed, he stretched himself close against her. His heart beat against her own ribs, not yet stilled from its pounding, and she was aware of all his thin nervous frame relaxed at her side. And as she had wept for the beauty and frailty of the white flowers by the waterfalls, so she wept again with the sadness that is inseparable from joy.

6

NEWCOMERS

Anne did not learn all in one night. The weeks of celibacy that had roused her senses, and sharpened his, had brought them together with extraordinary passion, which they must discover again with patience. As Richard had once remarked to his brother, Anne was totally different from the mistress who had instructed him, and he was a pupil as much as she. But they were willing scholars, who often sacrificed their sleep for their studies and yawned happily through the day while they reflected on their progress. It was hardest for her to accept that he could find such delight in her body, which she knew well, from her own observation and from a lifetime's disapproval in others, was not beautiful. He tried to convince her with words and demonstration, but she still believed he was only being kind to her. And so it stood until she found that he thought as little of his own physique as she did of hers. They were talking of the old days, of the rigorous régime which the boys had undergone in their knightly training.

'I fear the good master of henchmen looked on me with some despair when I first arrived,' remarked Richard ruefully.

'Oh no.' Anne denied it quickly. 'He must have realised that you were more courageous than any of the others, because you were the King's brother.'

He shrugged. 'King's brothers have no monopoly on courage, dear heart. It was a hard struggle.'

'I know. I saw it.' She hesitated. Until this moment her witnessing of his solitary practising with the broadsword in the quiet courtyard had remained close in her heart, and she was not sure that he would be pleased to hear of it. But she had to go on, haltingly, and explain. 'I didn't mean to watch. It was a place I often went to be alone. And you were down below. I couldn't help myself. I think ... I think that is when I first loved you.' Industriously she traced the silken flight of a bird on the coverlet, and did not see that Richard was deeply touched by the little secret she had cherished for so long.

'Well,' he said, trying to laugh, 'I taught myself to swing a battle-axe, but it has done my shoulder no good. I'm almost a hunchback.'

'No, you're not!' With an exclamation almost of pain she turned on him, and shyly touched the knot of muscles that swelled out his right shoulder a little higher than his left. 'I'm glad it's like that. It – it is *you*. ...' And then she stopped, understanding suddenly how he also could love her for herself, and nothing more.

Her life was a constant discovery, and at first she was afraid to be too happy. That, also, had to be learned, and in the security of Middleham, in the spring of Wensleydale, the tight-closed bud of her personality, so nearly withered by the coldness of neglect, opened at last to the sun. It was not all lovemaking and May Day jaunts in search of flowering boughs of hawthorn. She was expected to be the mistress of Middleham in more than name. The steward, the cook, the chief sewer, came to her for instructions in her own right, and not as her husband's deputy. If she had thought about it, Nan the kitchen-maid of last autumn, directing the running of a great castle household, she would never have been able to face it. But there was no time to think. During the day as well as the night she must strive to please Richard in everything. If it pleased him that she should approve the cook's newest sauce, or sanction the buying of twenty ells of damask for bed-hangings, then she would do it gladly. He never criticised her, and there was nobody else of sufficient rank to dare. Instead of the snubs of the past she met with respect and obedience. Her tentative orders were translated into efficient action by a well-trained staff, her uncertain choices deferred to, and she gained confidence as she observed daily with some wonder that the business of the castle was running more and more smoothly.

While she inspected the linen-presses and pantries of her domain with an unexpected relish, her husband was tackling the wider problem of governing the North for the King. To begin with he stayed at Middleham, but soon he began to travel farther afield, to Bolton Castle, to Skipton and Richmond, and to spend nights away in York or at Sheriff Hutton. It was the first little cloud on the unshadowed surface of Anne's happiness. Foolishly she had imagined that he would never stir from the castle without her for more than twelve hours.

'Yorkshire is a great shire,' he said to her gently, pitying her distress at the prospect of sleeping alone, 'and if I had a horse with wings I would fly back to you. But one night is very short, love. And we will make merry when I return, shall we not?' So she had to smile and pretend not to care at all for the lonely hours of darkness when she would lie and worry about his safety as far as forty miles away. But the brief separations ended in reunions which almost compensated in their delight for the time apart, and soon enough she became accustomed to them. In the ideal world which she had glimpsed, they would be always together with nothing to distract them from their devotion to each other. In this world, experience had taught her to expect little; Anne knew she must offer fervent thanks for the riches she had.

Richard was away at Pickering when she was sick one morning upon rising. Her new attendant Margaret held her head, washed her, and sent her back to bed, despatching another lady for a hot posset. Anne was too preoccupied to notice the meaning glance that passed between the other two women. Before the sun had risen high enough to look in the windows of her chamber she had recovered, and she made no mention of the indisposition to her husband when he came home. Since her collapse on arrival at Middleham her health had been perfect, and she was ashamed of having spoiled her good record after only eight weeks. But Richard was with her a few days later when the same thing happened, and he carried her back to bed himself. Although he tended her with his usual solicitude, and brushed aside her apologies, there was a suppressed emotion in him which was not like anxiety. That night he made love to her with a special gentleness. Neither referred to the morning, but she could not dismiss a foreboding that she was sickening for some illness which would make her a liability to him. The third time, she waited until Richard had left her, in surprisingly high spirits, for a meeting of the newly-formed Council of the North; miserable and queasy, she summoned Margaret.

Margaret Cropper had been a ward of the Earl of Warwick, and on taking over responsibility for her, Richard had invited her to leave her sequestered estate near Skipton and to attend on his wife. Her gaiety had immediately endeared her to the Duke and Duchess, and her warmth soon drew her into a friendship with Anne closer than any since the summer with Sœur Madeleine.

'I think you must fetch the physician to me, Meg,' she said. 'He may know of some remedy to prevent my growing worse.'

'The remedy is many months away, madame,' replied Margaret cheerfully, and Anne was a little hurt.

'This is not a time for jesting. My lord would be most displeased if I were to fall ill again. There are so many things for me to do.'

'It will pass, lady, in a few weeks.' Her attendant's eyes were indecorously brighter still. 'And I doubt very much if my lord will expect you to work quite as hard when it does.'

'Meg, why are you laughing?' asked Anne quite severely; she had always hated jokes that she did not share. Margaret dropped to her knees beside the bed.

'Dear madame, you are nigh on the last person in the castle to guess.'

'Guess what?' Suspicions began to float into her mind.

'What happened to your monthly course in May?' Nothing had happened, but since they had begun in the sanctuary of St Martin's only half a year before she had thought nothing of the irregularity. Now she remembered Isobel, pale and ill in the mornings, smug in the evenings, in the fortress at Calais, and at once she understood.

'Oh no, Meg. We couldn't tell so soon. There must be other signs . . . before we can be sure.'

'Of course. We can't be certain until June is out. But my lord suspects, madame. He asked me the other day if there was any news, and I had to say none.'

The nausea was fading away, and a feeling of awe was slowly taking its place. This was a consequence of her marriage that she had not foreseen at all. That their hours of love could lead so quickly to conception, that she was a vessel capable of bearing Richard's child, had never occurred to her. To Margaret's dismay she suddenly pressed her hands over her eyes and whispered in a tremulous voice, 'I'm not strong enough. I'm not worthy.'

She did not break the news to Richard until another clear month had passed. Even then she was hustled into it by a sudden remembrance that her brother-in-law had abandoned her sister's bed as soon as she was pregnant, and had not returned to it until long after Isobel's sad deliverance. It came to her one hot night as Richard went to touch her, and she could not respond to him. When he asked what was wrong she replied, 'Perhaps we should not while I am – I think I am – oh, Richard, I believe I am with child.' And then she could say no more, for he stopped her mouth with kiss after kiss, interspersed with delighted endearments. In the confirmation of an event he had divined weeks ago, he was far more than usually exuberant. Anne was taken aback by his reception of the tidings she had received so solemnly.

'Why so grave, dear love?' he rallied her. 'It's a birth we're awaiting, not a death.'

That made her smile a little, but she said, 'It is so far ahead. What if something should happen to me? I might fall ill again.'

He drew her into the crook of his arm, and was serious again. 'In Wensleydale? With me and all of Yorkshire to watch over you? It's not possible.' He placed one hand softly on her belly. 'You are as safe in Middleham as our child in your womb.' Then he would have caressed her further, and she tensed again.

'Will it not harm him, Richard?'

'Of course not. You have thrived on our lovemaking, so why should our son not thrive too?' And gratefully she relaxed into his embrace, submitting to his judgement and never questioning the source of his certitude. Even the high honour of carrying his heir would be tedious without his comfort in bed.

By St Swithun the morning sickness had gone and they resumed the gentle tours together that they loved, visiting not only their noble and clerical neighbours in castle and abbey, but also the humbler folk in village and shepherd's cot. It was part of Richard's purpose to meet as many as possible of the people beneath his rule, to learn their needs, their hopes and their fears. Like her husband, Anne found a sort of fellowship with the undemanding people of the dales.

Richard still left her behind when he journeyed farther afield, with admonitions to take care of herself. Towards the end of July he rode in with sunset, returning from Pomfret. As usual Anne was on the steps of the keep to greet him, but he was preoccupied, kissing her with the warmth but not the joy that was customary on his homecoming. Although he behaved normally during the evening, and talked of no troubles, his wife's eyes detected a hidden tension, and she longed to be alone with him so he could unburden himself. When he came to her, instead of throwing off his robe and hastening their reunion he wandered around the chamber for a while, scuffing in the rushes. At length he sat on the side of the bed, twisting the signet ring he wore on his little finger. She broke the silence timidly.

'What's amiss, Richard?'

'Nothing, love. Nothing.' He seemed to make an effort to collect himself, and smiled at her. Anne persisted.

'Did something go ill at Pomfret?'

Ignoring her second question, he flung aside the sheet that covered her and said, with a playfulness that was slightly forced, 'How our son grows! I swear he has swelled you since Thursday night.'

She caught at his hand and said urgently, 'Richard, you can tell me. If it is bad news that concerns you, then it concerns me too. You may be eased by sharing it.' Surprisingly, hurtfully, there was no answering pressure.

'No, Anne.' He spoke quite coldly. 'I cannot share it. There is nothing that need trouble you.' The rebuff was the most bitter she had ever received from him, and she sat motionless, feeling the coldness from his voice and his grasp spread into her heart and stomach. It was the tremor in her hands that made him look into her stricken face and see how he had wounded her. At once his strangeness melted and he raised her chilled fingers to his lips. 'Truly, dear love, I cannot tell you. It is not my secret. And there must be times – only now and again – when there comes a matter which I cannot discuss with you.' His want of frankness became less important as the Richard she loved reasserted himself. She found herself indeed almost apologising as he discarded his bedgown and came back to her.

'I didn't mean to pry. But to see you unhappy—'

'Not unhappy. A little disquieted, that's all. Now, let me measure the size of this mighty child of ours. . . .' She giggled, and the hurt was forgotten in their loveplay.

Her pregnancy ripened with the corn in the little fields by the Ure. When the harvest was in, there was no longer need for Richard to jest about her size; the thin stuff of her summer gowns displayed unmistakably her increased girth. Since the early sickness she had suffered no other ailments, and Richard observed with approval the well-being which filled out her thin face with the bloom of health. The little broken creature he had salvaged from the kitchen ashes not a year ago was becoming a person. As he had scarcely dared to hope, Wensleydale and his love were restoring her, and the child would complete the cure.

So it was hard to break it to her that he must go to London for the autumn session of the Parliament. For himself, he hated the city, and he was deprived of the pleasure of watching and supporting his wife through several important months; for her, he was wretched at the thought of her loneliness. But she took it better than he expected. Once accustomed to the idea of parting for one or two nights, she was braced for longer absences. London, he pointed out, was only five days' ride away, and she should hear from him as often as he had time to write. Summer was drawing to a golden close as they woke in each other's arms on the morning of his departure. They said little, but he kissed the new curve of her body; it was a pledge that, although he would not be there, a part of him lay within her. As he rode down the steep main street at the head of his company, Anne was reminded of the boy who had ridden eagerly towards London and the service of his brother without a backward glance. Now he turned again and again to wave to her, until he was out of sight, and the ache of his going was solaced with the knowledge that he would not forget her.

The nights were the worst. During the day she still took an active part in the running of the household, and somehow the baby seemed to take up a great deal of time, in thinking, speculating and talking about it. She took Margaret to bed with her and found that she was a restless sleeper, totally different from Richard, who hardly moved from night until morning. Or perhaps it was because, exhausted from the exertions of love, she and Richard had seldom had any difficulty in sleeping together. There was some excuse for Margaret's unquiet nights: she was falling in love with John Wrangwysh. He, who from her arrival had been bewitched by her, had not yet realised what was happening, and Margaret suffered agonies of fear in the small hours that he would not requite her. From the lofty eminence of her own matrimony Anne looked on and listened with sympathetic amusement. The little romantic drama helped to pass the time. She wrote of it in one of her notes to Richard, borne by the tireless Sir James Tyrell, who spent most of that autumn riding up and down Ermine Street between his master and mistress. In November he was the welcome herald of the Duke's return, and Richard and his train materialised out of the fog of a raw afternoon near St Andrew's Day.

London was apparently as usual a hotbed of intrigue and discontent. Richard told her little of what had occurred, but she gleaned the information that her *bête noire* the Duke of Clarence was still making trouble about the division of her mother's lands. That perhaps was why the King, anxious for the Countess's safety, had kept her confined ever since the battle at Tewkesbury in Beaulieu Abbey. The subject of Richard's recalcitrant brother was a delicate one, never raised willingly between them, but because in this case it was Anne's portion that Clarence was coveting they could not entirely ignore it.

'Don't concern yourself,' said Richard. 'The King my brother will find an equable solution. And you will lose no jot of what is yours. Any legal quibble there might be about your right to inherit is fortunately nullified by my having married you. Nobody can dispute his gifts to me – and what is mine is yours.' Anne thanked him, although in fact she cared nothing for titles and possessions, as long as she was allowed to live at Middleham in peace. But something else was nagging at her conscience.

'What will become of my mother, Richard? When all the arguments are over?' He had not really considered it, assuming that, like many widowed or dispossessed ladies, she would exchange one religious retreat for another and pass the rest of her life in seclusion.

But Anne had not forgotten her brother-in-law's threat when he committed her to the household of Francis Twynyho. Isobel, permanent hostage to her own husband, was beyond help, but once the Countess of Warwick was released from the protection of the King's troops, Anne did not think that any convent wall would be thick enough to keep out the vengeance of the Duke of Clarence. Secure and beloved in Wensleydale, she was out of reach; she did not doubt that he would vent his spite where he could. She brooded upon it in spare moments, comparing all she had with the destitution and danger of her mother. Christmas approached, and she lighted on a possible remedy. It would depend entirely on Richard's charity and co-operation. For some reason inexplicable to Anne, her husband maintained a steady affection for his brother George, despite all that he had done to ruin his hopes of happiness, and the request would have to be framed carefully. Christmas would be a good time to approach him, she decided, when the combination of her imminent confinement and seasonal goodwill would work for her.

Preparations buzzed all around her; the Yule log was hauled into the great hall, and the pages swarmed up the walls to deck the torch-cressets and windows with boughs of ivy and holly and bayleaves. Her childhood Yuletides in the North had been spent as guest of the Augustinian monks in York, but the winter roads might prove too risky for her present condition, and she and Richard had agreed to brave the wilds of Wensleydale for their first Christmas as lord and lady of Middleham. So they heard midnight mass on Christmas Eve in their own chilly little chapel in the keep, and afterwards broke their fast by torchlight in the great hall, where the ruddy smiling faces round the fire almost compensated for the positive gale of draughts that swept through the chamber. Presiding with her husband over the twelve days of junketing that followed, Anne knew herself to be the happiest woman in the world – were it not for the plight of her mother plucking at her conscience.

Not until the concluding celebrations of Twelfth Night did she find the opening or the courage to broach the matter. They were watching the mummers who had travelled all the way from Leyburn to perform for the Duke and Duchess, and as the hilarity reached its height, the child kicked violently in Anne's womb. Never quite accustomed to the amazing vigour of her unborn baby, she started and gasped in surprise. Richard was immediately distracted from his enjoyment of the pantomime and gripped her hand.

'Is it coming, love?'

'No, no. But he struck me so hard.' Her husband's rare grin flashed across his face.

'He wants to see St George and the dragon, I daresay. Tell him that next year he can share Christmas with us from a better vantage-point.' Sharing Christmas next year. Anne laughed and seized her opportunity. She did not express herself very well, and half-way through they were interrupted by Martin, their new fool, who waved his inflated pig's bladder in his mistress's face and saucily demanded a fine from her.

'Why, Martin?' she asked, humouring him. 'What have I done to displease you?'

'Madame, you are setting yourself up as a rival to my bauble,' he replied, indicating the swollen lap of her green velvet gown. She could not be angry with any impertinence that referred to her proud burden, so she gave him a mark as earnest of her intention to reform before another month was out. When he had pranced away to make fun of someone else, Anne returned to her plea. Richard had been considering it during the interlude.

'Would she wish to come back to a secular life?' he queried. 'You see, her ... misfortunes ... have deprived her of any status and she will have only the income the King allows her. Would she not be demeaned by living as my dependant?'

'We should have to ask her. She has no one to protect her now, and I think she must be very lonely. And I would ... I would like to have her here, Richard. To help with the baby.' It was the right note to strike. The friendless lady in distress, the coming child, his wife's comfort: no more was needed to sway Richard's chivalrous and loving heart. Before St George had slain the dragon, he had promised to mention the matter to the King in his next letter, and to follow it up in person when he went south in the spring for the next session of Parliament.

The mummers from Leyburn found themselves no longer the chief attraction as the household of the Duke of Gloucester observed with benevolent curiosity the Duchess flinging her arms round her lord and kissing him in full public view.

Her pregnancy had been so free from trouble that she had hardly anticipated any difficulties in the birth. If she did give any thought to it, it was to assure herself that the bearing of Richard's child, like her union with him, was bound to be blessed with the same good fortune. And therefore she was unprepared for the pains that gripped her one afternoon as she stood talking to her chamberlain in the solar. Lady Lovel and Margaret Cropper, who were with her, helped her to sit on a nearby chest, and instantly recognising what their mistress did not, told the alarmed official to send a page for the midwife. Before the midwife could be fetched from the town, where she was gossiping with a cousin, Anne was in bed, with her ladies trying vainly to soothe her. She was afraid, and the arrival of her nurse did little to reassure her.

'You're early, lady,' remarked the midwife cheerfully, breathing heavily from all the stairs she had climbed. 'A good thing too, as like as not. It will make the lying-in easier.' But Anne was not listening.

'My lord. I want my lord.' Richard was over in Wharfedale at Bolton Abbey and was not expected home until after dark. So insistent was the Duchess on her need for him that a messenger was despatched to meet him on the road and hasten him.

Until he came, Anne lay in inconsolable agony. It was not the pain she feared, nor the possibility of death which had suddenly approached very close. It was the prospect of dying without Richard beside her that terrified her into believing that every pang could be her end. Her chamber was bright with candlelight, the January evening excluded with arras drawn tight over the windows, a seacoal fire in the hearth and braziers by the bed, but to her the castle was as cold as it had been in the winter after young Richard had left her to serve his brother, as cold as the cabin where she had delivered her sister's dead child amid the stench of seasickness. And to make it worse she found herself betrayed by her own people.

'Oh, no, madame. My lord cannot possibly come in here.

Not until the child is born. It's not the custom.'

'But I must see him. I must.' He was no good to her pacing the next chamber for hours, waiting for bulletins from her female jailors. She needed his hand to clutch as the pain came, his face to be there as she opened her eyes at its ebbing. They were all adamant; the idea of a man in a confinement chamber was shocking; and she began to doubt if they would even tell her when he arrived.

They were given no chance to keep it from her. Still booted and spurred, he strode into the room, and the women fell back before him with scarcely a murmur of protest. As he sat beside her and took her hands, Anne could smell the frosty air that still clung to him.

'I wish I had been here,' he said, sensing immediately her state of near-hysteria. 'Is all well?'

'Yes ... yes, now you're here. Richard—' At that moment the next contraction ripped through her, and for its duration her only anchor on life and safety was her husband's handclasp. But as she emerged, she found that he as well was perturbed, almost scared.

'Anne – you must let your women help you. They know what to do. I shall stay within earshot.'

'You're not leaving me?' .

'Yes, dear love, I must. It isn't the custom for men to be present. Besides, I would be in the way.'

'Richard!' Her frantic strength restrained him from going. There were so many things she wanted to say to him, now, when she might not see him again; she could not remember one. But he was talking to her, willing courage into her, and endurance, for the sake of their son, and soon she was ashamed of her cowardice, surrounded as she was by capable friends and well-wishers.

'And I shall come at once if you need me.' She allowed him to disengage his hands, and with a kiss and a reassuring smile he left her.

Several of his gentlemen were waiting in the antechamber, with the slightly embarrassed air of males on the fringe of a purely feminine mystery. Richard told them curtly that the Duchess was well and dismissed them, before throwing himself into a chair and passing a hand over his eyes.

A giant merciless hand was crushing her in its grasp. Sometimes it loosened its hold, but only so that the renewed constriction would be harder to withstand. Yet always in the depths of her tired mind was the sure knowledge that Richard was near, and even in the midst of her struggle it gave her strength to go on.

Long since she had lost touch with the reactions of her attendants, and she did not hear the whispers that asked if my lord should be sent for. The labour was taking too long; none of them spoke of their ultimate fear, but the strain told in their faces and the silence that fell as for the second night candles were lighted in the lying-in chamber. Through the eternity of her ordeal Anne could feel that every time the pain clutched at her body her resistance to it grew less. But she clenched her teeth upon the welling cries of terror and suffering. It was her duty to give birth to a healthy son, whatever it might cost her, and she would do it without complaint. Her tenacity amazed the women who served her. From blind instinct she continued to strive when those with far more natural vigour would have surrendered.

And at last she was triumphant. Although she felt only an intensification of the pain that had been possessing her for as long as she could remember, a babble of excitement broke out among the anxious attendants, and a flurry of activity. Then its grip relaxed far enough for her to open her eyes, and through blurred vision she made out a cluster of women bending over her, and then one lifting something up. Again she was back in the ship, a frightened girl with a small limp body in her hands, and with an agonising effort she cried out, 'Dear Mother of God, is he living?'

They were the first words she had spoken for hours, so intent had she been upon her task, and the women started guiltily. They had forgotten about the mother in their concentration upon the child. One of them – it was Margaret – came to her side and said tremulously, 'It is a boy, madame, and soon you will hear him cry.' She laved her mistress's damp face.

'Why is he not crying now? He is dead, isn't he, and you are afraid to tell me.'

'No, madame, no. Sometimes it takes minutes....' Margaret glanced over her shoulder, and there was no conviction in her voice. Anne could hear it, and with her hopes her remaining strength was draining away.

'Meg,' she murmured, 'let no one go to my lord. I must break the news myself. It is my fault.' Her eyes were closing over the hot sting of defeated tears, when a thin mewling came to her from far away. 'It must be Kat asking to be let in,' was her weary thought, but Margaret was shaking her hand and speaking in a different tone.

'There, madame, you hear?' The plaining was repeated, a small noise, but persistent, and hope flooded back into her heart.

'Let me see, oh, let me see him!' And they placed him in her arms, a tiny bundle of swaddling clothes with red wrinkled face like the monkey her mother had once kept as a pet, but its mouth was open in a little round O, crying its humanity to the circle of delighted women, and most of all to its mother. They called for the Duke and he came swiftly, hollow-eyed and unshaven. For a moment he stood silent, looking down on his wife and child, unable to find words. It was Anne who spoke.

'It is a boy, Richard.'

'Yes, of course, love. Did you doubt it?' And then he kissed her and inspected his son, pushing back the shawl with two tentative fingers. Glancing back at Anne, he found her eyes fastened on him, big, grey-shadowed eyes, yearning for his approval, and with tears in his own he said what she wanted to hear. 'He's a fine lad. Thank you, dear heart, for giving him to me.' The radiance in her face momentarily obliterated the exhaustion, but almost at once her lids drooped, and the greyness came back. Turning for help, he encountered the midwife, who had been keeping watch on her charge from a respectful distance.

'She must sleep, my lord. The lying-in would have taxed the endurance of a far lustier girl.' Obediently Richard went.

It was more than mere fatigue that oppressed Anne. Had it not been for the thoroughness of her nurse, she might have bled to death from an undiscovered haemorrhage. As it was she lost a great deal of blood before it was checked, and for days she was too feeble even to sit up without aid. Richard was not allowed to see her, and set the castle by the ears with his unusual bad humour. In a private interview with his doctor, who had examined the Duchess and her infant, he had been told that if the child had been larger, or even if it had been female, Anne would probably not have survived the birth. The baby also, some weeks premature, was very frail, and would need exceptionally careful rearing.

'He shall have it,' said Richard brusquely, and dismissed the doctor. He required no instructions from a physician on how to cherish his own son. The crease between his brows was deep as he went about his duties with punctilious efficiency, and night and morning he paid a visit to the round tower on the south-west corner of the castle curtain, where his son's nursery was established.

The wetnurse was a young woman from Middleham town who had lost her own son at birth. Jane Collins never spoke of the dream she had nourished, as her pregnancy kept pace with that of the Duchess, of suckling a baby at each breast – one the child of a tiler, one the heir to a royal prince. She gave all her attention to the delicate little boy who had to be coaxed into taking each drop of her milk. And watching her dedication, Richard's mood lightened whenever he went to the nursery, certain that Jane would not allow his son to ail.

With February, Anne was pronounced well, and Richard began to smile sometimes again and to talk to his friends. To Anne it was another return to life, like her escape from the kitchen into the haven of St Martin-le-Grand, but to a far fuller life. Her son's name, she discovered, was Edward. Richard had chosen it, and had assumed that she would agree, since it was in honour of the King. The name held no happy associations for Anne, and some unhappy, and she would naturally have preferred another Richard, for her husband and her father. But since her husband wished it, she reconciled herself quickly. After all, this Edward was, and would be, like no other.

It was even more of a wrench this time for Richard to quit Yorkshire for the south. He was expected to attend Parliament, however, and his personal feelings must not be consulted. At least he was able to leave some consoling news with Anne. The King had replied favourably to his brother's request for custody of the Countess of Warwick. Practical details would be settled when they met in London, and by the summer, Richard predicted, Anne's mother might be travelling to her new refuge.

He was true to his word. In the spring James Tyrell brought tidings that King Edward had consented to release the Countess into Richard's care. In June Tyrell returned as her escort. For over two years Anne and her mother had not met. In the early summer brightness of the inner bailey the Duchess of Gloucester embraced the Great Earl's widow and led her to the apartments made ready near her own. There was no perceptible change in the Countess; the soft features had displayed little of the beauty of youth, and they retained little mark of loss and adversity. Perhaps she was pleased to see her daughter again, no longer a humiliated princess but a happy wife and the mistress of a great castle; she showed no sign of it. Anne was disappointed for the first few hours. She realised that, once her embroidery frame was set up, her mother would fade into the background of life at Middleham just as she had done at Warwick and Calais and Amboise. And for an illuminating instant, Anne glimpsed how she might have become the same, if destiny had given her the kind of masterful lord who had shaped her mother's existence. She had been foolish to expect companionship where she had never found it before, and she must take comfort in the salving of her conscience.

Anne had perforce to be contented with the company of son and mother throughout that spring. There were murmurings of revolt in the south, stirred by that inveterate Lancastrian the Earl of Oxford, and the King needed his younger brother's presence. When he did return to Wensleydale he assured his wife, who had been beset by fears of renewed warfare, that it was not a serious alarm. The people were too weary of strife to give widespread support to Oxford. The fires he lighted would soon go out from lack of fuel. But King Edward had no intention of being caught defenceless as had happened three years before. Richard was to hold himself in readiness to raise men and march south at short notice if necessary. Meanwhile he was based at Middleham, and ready between his duties to be suitably impressed by the amazing progress of his son, as related to him with a wealth of detail by his wife.

At Lammas John Wrangwysh, who had finally realised that

he was in love with Margaret, married her. The Duke of Gloucester, as her guardian, gave her away in the castle chapel. For her dowry he had restored the lands confiscated after her brother's death at Barnet. Sharing their wedding breakfast, Anne wondered if John remembered carving the poppet for her so long ago in this same hall, and knew that he was not the kind of man to forget things. She was glad that she and Richard had been able to repay him for bringing them together. The event crowned the summer. Despite the faint threat of Richard's leaving that hung over the autumn ahead, she was serenely happy.

One evening whilst they sat at supper in the great chamber, a messenger was admitted. Drawn laughing from Margaret's witty chattering, Richard raised his eyebrows at being disturbed at table, but took the letter. As he read it the animation drained from his face, leaving it cold and dead. Without a word, he rose abruptly and, motioning the messenger to go with him, retired to his chamber. The merriment of the gathering was shattered; even Margaret attempted no more quips, and a low anxious hum of conversation replaced the usual hubbub. Eyes were constantly glancing at the door to the inner chamber, fearing at any moment the announcement of some disaster to the kingdom. But none came, save a page tendering the Duke's apologies for not rejoining them that night.

Suddenly alone amid the speculation, Anne took refuge in silence, and her mother, a few places from her, might, if she had had the perception, have seen again the still, remote figure who sat ignored at Prince Edward's left hand at Amboise. The friends who surrounded her were nothing; the cataclysm that would destroy her happiness was at hand, she was sure: it was time for payment. When the meal was finished she did not follow her husband as she was entitled, but stayed to hear – or rather to be present at – the music-making which often concluded the day at Middleham. Richard would ask for her if he needed her. She would not make the mistake of interfering again.

He did not send, but when she was in bed with the candles snuffed he came, as was his custom, lighted by a page whom he dismissed as soon as he was inside the door. He made no attempt to rekindle the candles.

'Richard?' Anne spoke into the darkness, faintly leavened by the starlight through the uncovered windows, knowing it was he, wanting reassurance.

'Yes.' At that he moved from where he had been standing motionless, and lay down beside her. After another heavy silence he began to make love to her. It was not the same. Although he did everything that usually raised them to ecstasy, with the same skill and the same gentleness, it was as if there was no heart within it. Anne could find no satisfaction, and she sensed that he had little enough himself. Yet afterwards he held her very close, stroking her hair, and there was sadness in the soft slow caress of his hand.

She could not ask him. Fearing a rebuff if she did so, fearing still more what he might reveal to her, she watched him through two barren days. Outwardly he had thrown off his distress, and only the most observant could tell that it had simply gone underground. While Margaret was brushing her hair on the second night Anne appealed to her for help.

'Meg, what ails my lord? Do you know?' Margaret usually heard things before her mistress.

'No, madame, I have no idea. John is worried about him too, and asked me the same last night. But it can't concern you, or my lord would have told you.'

That was what he had said to her the other time: 'I cannot share it. There is nothing that need trouble you.' Could he not see that it did trouble her, that this absent-minded lovemaking was worse than leaving her to sleep alone?

He could see, and the next night she realised when he entered her chamber that he had come to a decision. Greeting her with formal courtesy, he sat down in the chair by the hearth. Under his bedgown, which was generally the only garment he wore in summer, she glimpsed with surprise and vague dread shirt and hose. She braced herself. Even so he could not find the words to begin and she had to prompt him.

'What is it, Richard?'

'I heard the other day of the death of a friend who was. . .dear to me.'

Irrational relief lifted Anne's spirits.

'Oh, my love, I am sorry. I will have a mass said for him.'

'No, Anne. It was not a male friend.' His tone was hesitant, deliberately expressionless, and her relief evaporated. 'She was a noble lady of Flanders, and I have known her since I was exiled in Bruges. Since our return to England she has been living at Pomfret. A week past she was thrown from her horse as she rode in the hills, and her neck was broken.' The carefully controlled voice, speaking aloud what he had been brooding on since the messenger arrived, was full of misery, but Anne did not hear it. She was trying not to make sense of what he had said. But he stripped away the illusions she was calling up desperately to her aid. 'She was my mistress, Anne. I did not tell you because I had no wish to cause you pain over something that was past and done. I would not tell you now but that she left me a charge that you must know.' His wife's eyes, fixed on his face, were dark with disbelief and dawning anguish but he went on steadily. 'I fathered two children on her. They are only babies. I must take them under my protection. She did not need to ask – '

'No.' The trenchant monosyllable cut across his measured words and he broke off, staring at Anne, who was trembling violently, her shoulders hunched and arms wrapped round her, nails digging into her elbows. 'I won't have that whore's bastards in my household.'

'Anne! They're my children too.'

'Bastards! That makes it worse. To bring them here, to flaunt them before our friends. To shame me...'

'It is no shame to you. The shame, if there is any, is mine, and everyone will know that.'

'Yes, yours!' Immediately the strange terrifying wrath of his gentle wife was turned on him, and he quailed before it. 'How dare you! You deceived me!'

'I never deceived you...' The denial stuck in his throat, as that torrid night two summers ago came back to him with full force. Anne had promised to marry him, and he had at the first set-back gone straight to the arms of his mistress. His son had been conceived of that fevered copulation, and he had been born two months after Richard married Anne. She was right; he had deceived her. 'I would not have hurt you for the world – and nor would Marja. She never wrote to me, or asked to see me. But the children – '

'No! No! You deceived me...you lied to me...' He could not recall ever lying to her, but the cold guilt of her accusation penetrated to the depths of his being. His excuses were done. With head averted he sat on mutely, feeling the familiar intense gaze on him, charged with a shocking new hostility. At length he rose and went to her, trying the only way he knew of reaching her. But before he could touch her she stiffened and recoiled.

'Leave me! Go away!' For a second they hung there, frozen into the tableau of what he would never have believed possible – her rejection of him. Then he straightened up and quietly left the room.

She would not forgive him. She could not, for her faith in him had been shaken to its roots. As the death of her father had shattered her childhood world, so now the earthly paradise of Wensleydale was corrupted. The innocence had gone out of Eden. Rigidly governing her thoughts and behaviour, she carried on her normal routine, although she escaped more frequently to the nursery tower, where there was a new pleasure and a new distress in watching the slow progress of her son from helplessness to enterprise and discovery. It was necessary to be in Richard's company as often as he was at home, and she maintained a façade of cordiality. He did not impose himself on her in private and for a week neither referred to the incident which had divided them so disastrously. Around them their friends looked on, discussing the breach mournfully between themselves, but not daring to offer any advice or comfort. Even Martin the Fool did not use his prerogative to comment on the situation, for he was as fond of his master and mistress as anyone at Middleham.

For Richard, seven days marked the limit of endurance. It tore his heart to see Anne so unhappy, she whom he had pledged himself to protect. Respecting her resentment against him for so long, he had hoped that common sense would reassert itself and that she would relent. It did not happen, and he went to her chamber one night intending to explain more fully and gain her understanding. The coldness of his reception killed all eloquence on his lips, and he could only utter commonplaces, as if they were at table in the great hall. He longed to ask what she held so bitterly against him, to describe his relationship with Marja and how it could never endanger his love for her, to appeal on behalf of the motherless children living at Pomfret. The pale figure huddled against the pillows, wrapped in its unapproachable silence, forbade all that. Refusing to admit utter failure, he joined her in bed, but he could tell by the way she drew back from him that she would not let him compose the quarrel so easily.

They lay awake for many hours, a few feet apart, wishing occasionally that the other would reach a reconciling hand across the wilderness. For the most part, however, sleeplessness fed their rancour. He had not suspected her before of selfishness, of wanting him all to herself and ignoring the needs of his innocent son and daughter.

She brooded on his licentiousness, his weak succumbing to the vicious influence of his brother Edward, and looked back with revulsion on the amorous stratagems he had employed on her, learned no doubt from his paramour and passed off as pure gold on his unsuspecting wife. Doubtless he was expecting even now to win her back with the honey sweetness of a love-trick sullied by its use on another woman. . .

It was a pattern of torture that they had set for themselves, strangers at board and in bed, the rupture widened rather than healed by proximity and time. They had always hitherto been so much in accord that they had not needed words to communicate. As a result, they knew none with which to break the deadlock. Richard made one attempt. He found Anne sitting outside the walls on the sunny southern slopes facing the old castle; she was trying to induce little Ned to crawl towards her by shaking a rattle of gilded walnut shells before him, while Jane dozed a short way off. So charming a picture of domestic calm, but as Richard approached, the rowels of his spurs chinking faintly, Anne stopped playing with her son and her head went up warily.

'I must go to inspect some field-pieces that have arrived at Skipton,' he said, and it sounded more like a military announcement than the casual remark he had intended. She did not answer, but picked at the gilding on the shells. Dropping to his heels beside the baby he put his forefinger absently into the child's firm grip.

'Anne, the governor of Pomfret is waiting for a message from me. The matter must be settled before I march south. Katherine is two. She is old enough to miss her mother, and weep for her. And although John is younger, he needs love just as much. If it were Ned – '

'Don't speak of those – those – don't speak of them in the same breath as our son. They should never have been born.'

'Perhaps not. But it is no fault of theirs that they were. Punish me if you will. They are guiltless.' A spark of temper had entered Richard's normally equable voice. Recognising it, Anne pressed her lips together and said no more. At that moment Jane awoke from her doze and beamed in her good-natured way at the Duke and Duchess, apparently made friends again by the benign influence of her precious charge. As soon as he could Richard escaped, and the wet-nurse's fond hopes were dashed by the desperate face that Anne turned after him. If only he could forget the children. They could just as well be reared at Pomfret where they were already established. She could forgive Richard in time, if they were not forever close at hand, reminding her of his infidelity, of the woman who had reaped the first harvest of his love.

But Richard could not so turn his back on his responsibilities, even to regain his wife's affection. That time he had called at Pomfret on his way back to Middleham and a pregnant Anne, he had been profoundly disturbed to find another baby in the cradle in Marja's chamber.

'But it was only one night,' he protested, and she had said with her sidelong glance. 'And your wife with child after two months of marriage – you are very potent, my lord, that is all.' It was a short visit – although Marja had declared laughingly that she was not going to seduce him if he stayed the night – and he had never seen his mistress again. As long as she was alive his conscience could rest, knowing that the discreet household he maintained at Pomfret would ensure a secure existence for Marja and their son and daughter. Now that she was dead, he was set on removing Katherine and John to his own residence. Even were it not for her last request to him, he would have done no less.

His emotions for Anne fluctuated between deep pity and extreme exasperation. Sometimes he wished she would scream at him, attack him or throw something at him, and then he could lose his temper too and there would be a battle, which would inevitably end in each other's arms. Against this withdrawal of hers he had no weapon or defence. It was an admission of defeat that finally he had to assert his authority over her to do his will. The King's summons had come, and he must lead his little army southwards without delay. The castle was overflowing with soldiers showing off with a swagger their new liveries of *blanc sanglier*, most of them amateurs and volunteers, but all determined to do credit to their Duke. To a background of mounting bustle Richard completed his preparations and sent for his wife.

The formality of the interview in his chamber, a table with orderly piles of depatches freshly sealed, his secretary John Kendall scratching away at a further letter in the good light under the window, daunted Anne and put her on her guard before he began to speak. At first he ran over the routine matters he was leaving in her hands, as he generally did whenever he quitted Middleham for a spell. But when Kendall had finished his writing and laid it before the Duke for signature, Richard dismissed him. He scrawled his name, sanded it, folded the parchment and sealed it with his signet without saying anything more, as if the mechanical task required all his concentration. Only when it was placed on top of the pile did he look up.

'I have here instructions for the governor at Pomfret Castle. He is ordered to make arrangements for my son John and my daughter Katherine to be conveyed to Middleham with their belongings and attendants. They will be arriving possibly next month, or in early November. It is difficult to be precise, because small children cannot be expected to travel fast. But I have asked the governor to keep you informed of their progress.' He had paused at the end of each sentence, waiting for an outburst of protest. None came; Anne was sitting rigidly and there were two flaming spots high on her cheekbones. For an instant, forgetting the feud which was her reason for being here, he thought solicitously that she was running a fever and must be put to bed, before he came back to himself and realised that it was suppressed anger that coloured her. Still no reply, so he drove on, in that impersonal tone he had found himself using whenever he spoke of Marja or the children.

'There will be sufficient time to make ready for them. It is my wish that they should be given a proper welcome.' He could not be sure whether she understood what he was saying, or whether this was her ultimate defiance. One could not issue orders if they were not acknowledged. Intending to sound stern, he said, 'Will you do this, Anne?' But that use of her Christian name had so many times brought them closer, and he found himself adding, almost pleading, 'Use them kindly for my sake.' She flinched, and recovered herself.

'For your sake, Richard.' And he knew he had won no concession from her. She would do her duty as he had bidden her, because she was dedicated to obeying him. Against his natural children her mind was closed; there was no trace of compassion.

It was bitter anguish for both to part unreconciled. Yet as the orderly ranks of well-armed, well-trained men filed over the drawbridge and down into the September mist that lay still asleep in the valley, they trembled on the verge of a rapport. Their embrace was conventional, their kiss perfunctory, the roles they had played in public since the rupture. Then as they drew back, Anne saw her husband with vision unclouded. In his armour, with the labelled leopards and lilies of England bright on his surcoat, he was suddenly at a remove from the administrator, husband and father she had come to know this past twenty months. He was the henchman who had ridden at the quintain bearing her colours, the very perfect gentle knight of Chaucer's tales who had rescued her from the dread Queen Margaret, plucked her from the hearth, and made her his lady indeed. There was no flaw in him. She sought his gaze and held it, fumbling for the words that would make all well.

Time defeated her. All the men were out of the bailey, and Richard could not delay. With a slight shake of the head in which there was surely regret, he swung away and thrust his foot into the stirrup held for him by a henchman. The boy shook his hair out of his eyes and stared up at his lord in naked adoration for a second before dashing for his own pony to follow him under the gatehouse arch. It was the child's worship, as much as the straight back of the Duke on his grey stallion, riding away from her, that plunged Anne abruptly into a pit of despair.

Only a few days after his father's departure, little Edward fell ill. Jane blamed herself vociferously for bringing his cough into the nursery herself, but the damage was done and Anne did not add to the wetnurse's self-reproach. Indeed, she saw in her baby's sickness a kind of mystical judgement on her intransigence. She went straight from the sickbed to her confessor, and asked for severe penances for the breaking of her marriage vows. Her feelings for Richard had softened as soon as he was out of sight, and with this manifestation of divine wrath brooding over Middleham she yearned desperately for his forgiveness and his reassurance. Surely no harm could reach little Ned if his parents were at one. She wrote to Richard with her own hand, ostensibly to greet him on his twenty-first birthday, making light of Edward's condition, never mentioning her longing for his return, simply tendering him her humble duty. It was the only practical reparation she could offer. For her son, she could only pray and watch by him.

He had suffered small childish ailments before, colds and rashes and colic, and Jane had nursed him through them without troubling her mistress overmuch. This time the doctor had been called, for the cough was affecting his breathing. As often as she could during the day, and through many broken nights when the companionship of Jane in the nursery was preferable to her cold bed, Anne sat by his crib. He was no trouble; he had never cried very much, and now he was not fretful. There was just his tiny body, with limbs of almost a bird's slenderness, lying quite still, the wheezing breath, and the occasional cough rasping cruelly through him. Often she wanted to shed tears, but none would come past the painful knot in her throat. It was less distressing to tear herself away from his side than it was to return and face the news of his condition.

Yet Jane was the only person in the castle to see her true face. Outside the nursery she hid her anxiety and her loneliness and continued her normal duties. Because they were used to a certain reserve in their lady whenever the Duke was absent, the household were left to guess whether there had been a reconciliation before their parting or not. At any rate she was carrying out her husband's instructions. The arrangements for the reception of the children from Pomfret had been placed in the hands of the chamberlain and his wife. Since they had several small children of their own, Anne had given them *carte blanche*, and wished only to be informed when the preparations were complete. She wanted as little to do with her expected guests as possible. Her change of heart towards Richard did not embrace his bastards; they should be hidden away in a remote wing of the castle, and she would ignore their existence. Evidence that Richard was less than perfection had no place in her life.

And her preoccupation with her son did drive them from her thoughts. When on St Luke's day he took a turn for the better her heart lifted, and she was heard to sing in her chamber on a golden morning near St Crispin. The doctor had pronounced Lord Edward on the road to recovery, and Richard had replied to her letter. His grave formal phrases revealed no flood of emotion, but she believed she could read between the lines that he had forgiven her.

She was humming to herself on another morning, more dun-coloured than golden, at the beginning of November, as she crossed the bridge from the keep to her apartments. Below her there was activity in the inner bailey, and she stopped to look; it might be another messenger from Richard. But it was a horse-litter, halted a little way off, and two wagons in the process of unloading. Servants were appearing, as always on the arrival of visitors, from nowhere, to lend a hand or just to stare. Bundles were being borne past in the direction of the north curtain, but all around the litter was quiet; the passenger must have disembarked already. Even as she thought it, Anne saw that the passenger had indeed disembarked. She was standing motionless where she had been placed by some attendant, a short distance away. A little girl, nursing a wooden baby which like her was wrapped in a dark blue cloak and hood. She was showing no curiosity in her surroundings, and no fear at being left alone; simply a blank stare before her, either of resignation or tiredness.

A curious sensation was possessing Anne, a division of herself. She was still the Duchess of Gloucester, looking down on the courtyard of her castle on an autumn morning, but also she was the child by the litter, bewildered, lost, picked up and set down in strange places for reasons never explained, sick from the motion of the journey, and with only a poppet for comfort. Even as she hovered between past and present, a woman bustled round the leading horse, and the girl turned to her in sudden animation. The woman plunged within the leather curtains and emerged with another child in her arms. Speaking a word to the girl, she set off the way she had come, and her charge hitched the poppet higher in the crook of her elbow and trotted obediently after her.

So that was who she was! In nauseated revulsion Anne drew back from the rail and hurried onwards, making for the haven of the nursery. There she would be safe from dangerous illusions, and the unspeakable newcomers would be consigned to their proper oblivion. When the chamberlain reported later in the day that Dame Katherine and Master John were settled in their apartments, she thanked him shortly and ordered him to take full responsibility for their well-being.

She banished them from her mind as resolutely as if they had been still sixty miles away at Pomfret. In such a large castle there was small likelihood of their paths crossing hers, and she did not allow herself the idleness to brood about them. Edward's cough had gone, but he was listless and weak, and with the winter coming on she spent much time on considering and discussing ways to nurse him through the severe weather. Then there was Richard to think of; he wrote that the Earl of Oxford had gone to earth on St Michael's Mount off Cornwall, and he would hardly be rooted out before spring. Otherwise, however, the petty rebellion was nearly dead, and he would be home when the King could spare him. He did not mention to Anne Clarence's part in the revolt, stirred because of his discontent over the division of the Countess of Warwick's property; that was a matter which could be settled between Parliament and the three brothers. So Anne fed strengthening possets to her son and daydreamed of her husband's return, pushing aside the occasional traitorous suggestion that the presence of his two other children would for ever jar their concord.

Snow came early, clothing the world skilfully overnight in a flawless white robe. Cold though it was, she could not resist climbing to the parapet above her chamber, to gaze at the old castle up the hill clad in its winter mystery. The cloud of her breath hung on the frozen air, and written in it she seemed to see the first conversation she and Richard had shared twelve years before. She could not remember the words, but the solemn tones of their exchange were so real to her that she expected a second cloud of moisture to drift beside her own.

There was a burst of shrill laughter, and she looked about her with a start. She and Richard had not laughed like that, not then; her memory must be playing her false. No, the children were down in the meadow outside the curtain wall, and they were too young for herself and her cousin. There was white fur round the little girl's hood, and she was jumping up and down in the snow with tiny squeaks of excitement which carried clearly to the watcher on the battlements. The other child was stumping purposefully along, small booted feet and arms spread wide, and when he fell, as inevitably he did every few steps, he added a satisfied roar to his sister's piping. The same stout woman who had carried him from the litter in the courtyard pursued him and brushed him down every time he heaved himself to his feet again. Enthralled, Anne stared down at them; she had seen lambs frisk with just that wholehearted joy in living on the spring hills of Wensleydale. And it was not the reminder that they should not exist at all that turned the spectacle sour for her; it was simple envy. She cried for Richard in bed that night.

He would be coming, he wrote, in the New Year. Anne speeded her efforts to finish the cushion that she, who hated embroidery, was working painstakingly for his chamber. It was a peace-offering, and poor enough, she knew, to atone for weeks of heartache that they had endured. But a greater one was at hand, thrust upon her possibly by the merest chance, possibly by the machinations of Margaret Wrangwysh, who had secretly and disloyally been visiting the north curtain.

Margaret was, however, nowhere in sight when Anne entered the nursery that day. It was her morning routine, after mass and before receiving her steward, to spend half an hour with Jane and her son. She was surprised that Jane was talking to someone; even more surprised that her companion was a small girl. But she could not mistake that figure, even from the back. She was wearing the same fur-trimmed hood but it was thrown back, dark straight hair straying from beneath a red cap. And she was leaning over the crib, one foot kicking idly at the other ankle. Jane rose in a flurry as she saw her mistress, making a particularly deep courtesy in which Anne read guilt. The child showed no such agitation. She lifted her head and turned to Anne. Her brown eyes were wide with serious wonder.

'Baby's asleep now,' she told Anne in a confidential whisper. 'Kate wants to see blue eyes. Wake up soon?' Then she transferred her attention back to the sleeping child. Anne could not speak, but when the nurse drew breath, clearly intending to bring the little girl to due respect, she signed to her to be quiet. With a strange fluttering in the throat, she moved to the other side of the crib and sat on the stool placed there for her. Katherine was paying no heed to her now. She was absorbed in the contemplation of the magical delicate doll with fair hair and real fingers, so much smaller than she had ever imagined a baby could be; her brother John had never in her memory been either so small or so delicate – besides, his hair was red. The tip of her tongue protruded from the corner of her wide mouth in her concentration, but it was not that which had struck Anne dumb.

Her eyes were Richard's. It was with just such an expression that he had spoken of his brother Edward who had just become King of England. And the Edward that this child was worshipping silently was her own Edward. Dark Katherine and red-headed John, and blond Edward; they were all Richard's, and it did not matter who their mothers were. As they were part of Richard, so she must love them as she loved him. And while she waited with Katherine van Soeters for her baby to awake and prove that his eyes were blue, the knowledge came to her that it would not be only for Richard's sake. Blinded no longer by foolish pride, she saw that she could take these two children to her heart as naturally as she had taken the shivering kitten from beside its dead mother, and the little boy who had practised secretly with a broadsword almost too heavy for him to lift.

Passing Jervaulx Abbey, Richard did not as usual urge his horse to a faster pace for the last few miles home. He was deadly weary, and he thought more of the uphill road to Middleham than of the shortness of the distance. The months in the south had dispirited him; not only the ill-tempered contentiousness of his brother George but, more dearly, the change that was overcoming his brother Edward, the sybaritic court that was moulding his all-conquering splendour to its own triviality. George was satisfied for the present with grants of land far wider than the King had intended, the Earl of Oxford was on the point of surrender to starvation, and Edward had been as affectionate as ever, lauding Richard warmly for the work he had already accomplished in the North. Yet it was with a sense of disappointment too deep to be articulate that the Duke of Gloucester left the butterfly world of Westminster, and he had not shaken it off. For he was not sure of his reception at Middleham. He thought that Anne had forgiven him his harshness, but their meeting would be difficult with the shade of Marja between them still. His gentlemen, glad to be heading for their wives and suppers, had long ago forgotten that there was any disagreement between their lord and lady, and wondered if the Duke were ill.

It was growing twilight before they crossed the drawbridge and thankfully slid from their horses in the inner bailey. The usual commotion of homecoming was about them, and for once Richard hung back, unwilling to make haste towards the poor welcome that might await him. Torches were already flaring in cressets up the stairway to the keep, and as his reluctant eyes were raised to the top, they encountered a procession slowly descending. His wife was leading, and on one arm she carried her baby son. The other hand was given to a little boy, whose auburn hair gleamed in the torchlight as he clambered laboriously down the steps. Behind, with a stoical and condescending Kat draped over her shoulder, was his daughter Katherine. Not until they all reached the bottom could Anne look up. Immediately she met his gaze and smiled at him. Almost stumbling in his eagerness, he ran towards her.

PART III
Queen

THE PROTECTOR'S WIFE

The Earl of Salisbury was the first to shoot. Walking steadily to his mark, he inclined ceremoniously to the spectators, unslung his bow and fitted an arrow. Without haste he took his aim at the target and drew back the string to his ear. Although the bow was not full-sized, the effort needed was visible at a distance. Still he did not hurry; his arm quivering with strain, he remembered to lift the arrowhead and slew it to the right to allow for flight and the cross-breeze. The string twanged and the arrow sang to its goal. A man stationed to tell the score passed the word up: 'A good outer.'

Polite applause, and rather more than that from the Earl's mother, the Duchess of Gloucester. Maintaining his solemnity, showing neither pleasure nor exasperation, he bowed again and gave place to the next contestant. The new archer ran to the centre of the tiltyard, and grinning broadly he waved to the audience; one of the ladies blew kisses. Before making his shot he combed his auburn fringe out of his eyes with his fingers, leaving clearly visible black smudges on his forehead.

'Oh, look, madame, John is dirty already,' said the dark girl next to the Duchess in vexation.

'Hush, Kate,' retorted the Duchess mildly. 'A black face won't spoil his aim.' Apparently she was wrong, for John's shot was wild and missed the target altogether. There were half a dozen in the contest; the eldest was twelve, the youngest was Richard Wrangwysh, aged only eight and a half but determined to keep up with the best of his companions. Each boy was greeted with acclamation, especially loud from the corner of the yard where his friends or family stood, and each shot applauded, whether or not the arrow reached its mark. There was a fine trophy at stake, a silver-mounted mazer presented by the Duke, and the event possessed all the grandeur and seriousness of a great occasion: the master and mistress of Middleham in special seats with pennons flying above them, their gentlemen and ladies grouped about them, off-duty servants and men-at-arms held back from the butts by ropes, an enclosure for the townsfolk, and the April sun shining to boot. Even John of Pomfret, after his first muffed shot, restrained his wayward spirits and played in earnest.

But although he came in the third round within a hair's breadth of the gold, it was Lord Edward of Salisbury who loosed the winning shaft. Circumspect, with only a flush along the cheekbones to betray his feelings, he approached the Duke and Duchess and knelt before their chairs. Richard handed the trophy to his wife and it was she who presented it to the young Earl. No words passed between them, but she kissed him on both cheeks and his flush deepened. Everyone was cheering the victor, the vanquished the most lustily of all. Before he rose, Lord Edward looked shyly up at the Duke.

'My son,' said Richard quietly, and at last the boy smiled.

Although he bore himself proudly as they left the butts, both his parents were aware of his fatigue, and Richard laid an arm lightly round his shoulders. The weeks of intensive practice, the determination to acquit himself well, had told on his strength; there was unnatural tension in his tired muscles. They would not speak of it, but Anne and Richard lived with the dilemma of fiercely wanting their son to succeed in the normal exercises of knightly training, and the constant fear that he would overtax himself.

'He is so like you,' Anne said often to her husband, and behind the conventional remark of a mother to a father was the memory of the dogged little Duke of Gloucester fighting his way from delicacy to resilient manhood. They had bred no more children, yet what was to Anne a secret sorrow was to Richard a private relief; his doctor had warned him soon after Edward's birth of the danger to her life of further conception. We have no need of more, Richard would have said if they had discussed it, Ned has passed his tenth birthday and he grows stronger every year.

Deep in technicalities, father and son were criticising the latter's performance at the butts today. Anne, judging herself unqualified, did not join in, but she was touched to hear that Edward was harder on himself than his father was. The boys had drifted away to make the most of the free hours before supper, but Richard's daughter Katherine walked at her side, hands clasped and head slightly bowed in contemplation as was her habit. Anne had suggested to him that perhaps she would take happily to a convent life, but he thought that she would do better to make a good marriage, unless her objection was very strong. Whether to a cloister or to a husband, Anne would be sorry to lose her. Serene and gentle, even in her twelfth year she had reached a maturity which Anne leaned on in times of stress. And they shared a common devotion to the Duke of Gloucester and the Earl of Salisbury.

As they entered the inner bailey through the postern in the east curtain a cloud swept across the sun and dimmed its radiance for a moment like a great bird's wing. It passed, and a horseman rode in at the gatehouse. The cloud was an omen which drew darkness also across Anne's heart. Through the tranquil years in Wensleydale bad news had ridden often enough under the gatehouse to justify her premonition. The death of her sister Isobel six winters ago; the murder of poor Ankarette Twynyho by the maddened widower on a wild charge of having poisoned her mistress and her infant son; the retribution on Clarence's act which had taken Richard in haste to London to plead his cause with the King. Anne had not argued with his decision to go. That her old persecutor lay in the Tower on a charge of high treason did not exactly delight her – in the contentment of Middleham she had let her hatred for him slide into oblivion – but she could not sympathise with her husband's profound distress. When he returned he had not needed to tell her that George was dead, but several months of extreme tact and much love had been necessary to restore him.

From London the news was always bad. Even this year, coming home from his Christmas at Westminster, Richard had brought tidings of a disaster to King Edward's diplomacy: Louis of France had deserted his English alliance and made treaty with his old adversaries the Burgundians. Anne recalled her meeting with the man they called the Spider King, who had been her father's friend and ultimately his destroyer, at the time of her betrothal to Prince Edward. Despite the shabbiness of his appearance, she had known instinctively that Louis would never be the loser.

'He's wearing the livery of Hastings, madame!' her son's voice broke in on her troubled thought. 'Look. Or, a maunch gules.'

'Is it, Ned?' she said absently, although normally she would have been impressed by the boy's erudition. The rider had dismounted and Richard quickened his pace to meet him.

'I've never seen it before,' Edward continued eagerly, 'but I have it in my manual.' It was indeed an unknown sight in Wensleydale, the livery of the King's chamberlain, Lord Hastings. Richard was talking to the courier now, and even at a distance of twenty yards Anne saw the way in which her husband was suddenly still. The messenger went on speaking and Richard remained rigid with his back to her until, apparently in the middle of a sentence, he turned on his heel and walked rapidly towards the steps of the keep. Hastings' man remained irresolute, watching the Duke until he disappeared within the keep, and then decided to follow him. There were few people about to witness the incident. A groom came forward to take charge of the hard-ridden horse which stood trembling with its head low where its owner had left it. Anne met Katherine's eyes and was dismayed to find in them the same dread that was in hers. At a slow pace which pretended that there was nothing amiss, they went after the Duke. He stood by the ring of stones in the centre of the great hall where the firewood lay ready for kindling in the evening; a page was leaving him at a run, but Richard did not move. Although his face was only a blur, Anne had no need to go closer to read it. She had seen him look so before.

People were beginning to congregate in the hall, scenting news, and they stationed themselves in clusters around the walls, as if for protection, hardly speaking, their eyes only turning in enquiry from their fellows to their silent lord. Gentlemen, pages, cooks, scullions; they waited for the announcement, and none of them had the courage to ask for it. Only one of the hounds, distracted from its private business by the tension, trotted up to the Duke, looked up at his unresponsive master, curled up at his feet with a bored sigh and closed its eyes.

Anne was pinned to the spot like the others by the swollen silence, her hand in her foster-daughter's, and perhaps they might have remained there in ignorance until dark if her son had not stepped forward, still carrying his silver-mounted mazer. He looked up at his father, much as the hound had done, and asked, 'What has happened, sire?'

Starting at the clear treble, so carefully controlled that there was no anxiety in it, Richard met the boy's eyes and then his gaze travelled beyond him, round the apprehensive ranks of his household.

'The King is dead,' he said. A shocked murmur like a cold wind ran through the hall. 'His son the Prince of Wales is now our sovereign lord. My royal brother was pleased to appoint me by his will as the new King's protector during his minority.' The wind rose again, confused, agitated, uncertain, and once more Richard's voice cut across it decisively. 'There will be a mass sung after Vespers for the health of King Edward's soul.' Immediately he made for the door of the great chamber, and certain of his gentlemen detached themselves from the crowd as at a given signal and made after him.

Those with no task to perform were left with their bewilderment, aimless movements and half-finished phrases, not knowing what to think or what to do, only that something of more moment even than the passing of a great king was come upon them. Anne did not speak or move, except to draw Katherine closer to her side. Her understanding of the cataclysm was no more than the attendants' and menials' who milled unhappily around her, but her knowledge was far deeper. Edward came back to them, his fair face troubled.

'My royal uncle was so strong . . . I thought he would live for ever. Why should God take him now?' He had seen the King his namesake only once five years ago, but that glimpse, fed by Richard's devotion, had created a hero in the boy's mind to stand beside his father in the ranks of greatness.

'God's purpose is beyond our reasoning, my lord,' said Katherine piously.

'Beyond reason . . .' Anne's heart repeated, and longed with fruitless intensity for the idyllic ignorance of an hour before, the butts and the sunshine and her son's winning arrow, and for that to be made eternal.

It was too terrible to be thought of, and with her old childish habit she pushed it all away into the future and disregarded it. Even the mass for the dead King was to her a memorial of a man who had always unsettled her, yet whom she had learned to respect and trust for her husband's sake; nothing to do with Richard and Ned and their life together at Middleham. But the thing thrust itself on her at length, when Richard came to her chamber very late from a council meeting hastily called. Expecting to find her asleep he had not brought a light. For a time he paced to and fro in the sinking glow of the fire, stopping occasionally with his foot on the hearth-stone to gaze searchingly into the embers.

Through the drawn-back curtains on that side of the bed Anne lay and watched him. At length she said quietly, 'You will be leaving soon?'

He looked across at her in the darkness and answered with the same neutrality, 'Within the week, if affairs can be arranged in the time. I must be in London to receive the new King when he comes from Ludlow. And no doubt everything will be at sixes and sevens. I shall be needed.'

Needed ... through the night her silence cried out to him, And we need you too. All she said was, 'Strange that my lord of Hastings should send you word.'

He came to sit on the bed, seeking and covering with his own the clenched hand that lay on the coverlet. 'Not really. He must regard himself as temporarily responsible for the administration – and the Queen Mother would not waste a messenger on me.' That was very true; the rapacious Elizabeth Woodville, backed by her tribe of grasping kinsfolk, had no love for the Duke of Gloucester, especially since he had accused her openly of poisoning King Edward's mind against his brother Clarence.

'Will she make mischief, Richard?'

'She will have no means. Edward did not mention her in his will.' The name of the dead King killed their stilted efforts at conversation. A long dragging while they remained still, contemplating or not contemplating the doom that had fallen on them. When Anne spoke again, it was to take refuge in the past.

'I am glad that Ned won his mazer. He has practised so hard.'

'Yes, he has a flair for archery. But he must learn to loose more swiftly; at present he's wasting his energy in the aiming.'

'He will learn.' There was no safety in words, for this topic also led towards the prospect which sooner or later they would be forced to face – the tearing apart, in one direction or another, of their little family. In the renewed silence, loneliness greater than she had known since before her marriage weighed upon her, and only the contact with Richard, and his barely visible outline, kept it from crushing her. The need for his closeness, for the physical pressure of his arms about her and his body upon hers, rose into desperation; it was the one thing that would blot out what had happened and what would happen. Unable to contain herself longer, she whispered, 'Richard, please ...' His grip tightened and he leaned forward as if to read her face in the dark. 'Make love to me.' He said nothing, but gathered her to him, wrapping her inside his bedgown. They laboured hard to expel from that night the demons of the past and future, and in the harmony of two hearts and bodies long attuned they achieved it. Afterwards, when it was nearly dawn, it was he who lay in the shelter of her arms, as if she were protecting him.

There followed the most wretched week of her life – the most wretched because, with the clarity of eleven years' happiness at Middleham, she could see exactly what was being shattered. To lose what she now enjoyed was ten times worse, she felt, than the miseries she had suffered in France and London. With his usual efficiency Richard set about preparing for the journey south. The activities which had as far back as memory reached caused Anne's heart to sink set the castle thrumming. John Kendall was often closeted with the Duke, and the resultant letters were borne towards all corners of Yorkshire summoning the lord of the North's retainers and friends to the rendezvous at York, and farther also to the young King's governor Lord Rivers at Ludlow. Messengers came the other way too, and one arrived wearing the same red sleeve on a gold ground that had begun it all. There was no noticeable stepping-up of the preparations, but Richard looked more withdrawn at dinner and Kendall was with him for three hours in the afternoon.

Anne's suspicions were apparently well founded, he told her that evening, pacing restlessly as he was apt to do these days when they were alone. Queen Elizabeth was showing signs of trying to seize the regency for herself.

'My lord Hastings urges me to come quickly,' Richard said, 'but I have no means of telling whether he sends the plain truth, or whether he distorts it from jealousy of the Queen. If only word would come from the council.'

'If there's danger, Richard, should you not muster an army to go with you?'

'An army? There's no need for one. There was bound to be confusion with my brother dying so suddenly – the factions at court would waste no time in springing at each other's throats.' The unaccustomed cynicism of his tone held the knowledge that soon he would be among them, and responsible for reconciling them. Then, returning to his normal decisiveness, he went on, 'They will respect my authority when I arrive. I have written to the Queen, and to the council expresssing my readiness to perform my brother's will. And I warned them to maintain the peace and the law of the land in the interim.' There seemed to be no doubt in his mind that, two hundred miles away as he was, the Queen and the royal council would obey him. He bent to trim a smoking candle, and in its sudden light Anne saw confidence in his face beneath the strain of still-fresh grief. It came to her, with a new awareness that was frightening in its disloyalty, that he was being naïve. He had been too long away from the deadly duplicities of Westminster, and perhaps his natural optimism had underestimated them. She, who had not set foot in London since her marriage, had not forgotten, and she was no optimist.

Yet the next day another courier brought an offer of aid which apparently reinforced Richard's confidence. A power-ful ally, placing himself and an armed band of followers at the Protector's disposal: the Duke of Buckingham. Anne had scarcely heard of him, never met him; he had shown no earlier signs of friendship to the Duke of Gloucester. Richard sent a grateful acceptance, and said that his support was a straw in the wind.

Robert Percy remarked drily, 'I would that all straws were as mighty!' and everyone laughed. But in Anne the chill sense of danger continued to grow.

When all was ready for departure Richard had still received no formal summons to assume the Protectorship, and he determined to leave without it, sure of its meeting him on the road. Anne had said nothing to hold him back, and neither had mentioned the place of herself and their son in his plans. With a lesser trust in him she would have thought he had forgotten them. Even so, not until their last night did he speak, suddenly, out of the darkness of their quiet bed, and she knew that their separation had been one of the hardest decisions weighing on him, this past endless, pitifully brief week.

'Anne. Will you come to me, when I send for you?'

'Yes, Richard,' she said, but after a pause, 'What of Ned?'

Although he did not answer at once, it was not because he had not considered it before. 'It will soon be summer. If he's well enough, and you judge he can stand the journey, then bring him too. But his health must be the main consideration.'

It was unfair of him, to pass the choice to her. She almost protested, and acknowledged as she drew breath that he could do no other, so she merely said, 'Of course.'

'I shall send as soon as the situation is clear. We can live at Crosby's Place. It's a beautiful house. I hoped I might show it to you one day ... although not in such circumstances.' He groped for her hand and, finding it, crushed it in his. 'I shall need you, dear heart.'

So he rode away, and she found herself, bewildered, surrounded at his departure by a jubilant throng. Wrapped in her own forebodings, she had lost touch with the temper of the household. Mourning for their late King had been sincere, and it was still manifest in the absence of gay pennants, the black garb of Richard's train. But now they had put off their sorrow, and sent their lord on his way with shouts of goodwill that pursued him along the road through the sweet spring air. What to Anne was a journey of peril and dread was to them a journey of triumph. The Duke of Gloucester, friend and benefactor to all the North Country, conqueror of the audacious Scots, was given his rightful place as defender of the new young King and ruler of England in his name. The henchmen, who had been left behind, were the shrillest in their delight, and as soon as the twist of the hilly road took the Duke out of sight, they must rush with a tattoo of flat feet for the battlements to watch him further. Edward, caught up in their enthusiasm, would not be left behind, but as he sped away he threw over his shoulder, 'Mother – Kate – you must come.'

Wishing he would not run, wondering why they were all so merry at such a sad farewell, she followed, with the more energetic of her ladies. In small heaving knots, the boys jostled for places in the embrasures, except that they made way without complaining for Lord Edward, although he had gained the parapet last. Yet even when Anne joined them, minutes later, she could tell from the heaving of his shoulders how the climb had tired him. Sick at heart she stood behind them, hearing their comments and the yells they still sent uselessly after the distant cavalcade through dulled ears, until a soft furtive sound beside her took her attention. Obedient as always to her half-brother, Katherine had come too, but she was far from joining in his sentiments, or those of her full brother John, who was leaning perilously far over the battlements in his excitement, and having to be restrained by his companions. She was crying quietly. To find her own mood echoed in another stirred Anne's misgivings more deeply.

'What's the matter, Kate?' she asked in an undertone, barely audible above the din before them. The girl brushed her cheeks with the back of her hand in a swift guilty gesture, and shook her head.

'Nothing, madame.'

'Then why are you weeping when everyone else is so ... joyful?' Anne did not really want the answer, but Katherine was an honest child.

'I'm afraid ... that he won't come back.' The same fear, spoken aloud, stabbed deep into Anne's belly.

'That's nonsense. Of course he'll come back.'

'Oh, for visits. But he will never live here again. It will never be the same.' Pierced by her truth, Anne bitterly regretted making her utter it.

The henchmen returned after dinner to their training, their vaulting and archery and Latin, and the castle fell into the routine which had never been disturbed for more than half a day at a time. Yet an ear was kept cocked for news, anyone riding in through the gatehouse was regarded with more than common interest. Anne's spare time hung heavy on her hands; she divided it between watching her son at his exercises and kneeling in her stall in the chapel. The old refuge of the rosary helped to fix her mind on the higher good of Richard's soul, but then as she had no real fears for his right conduct, her prayers would slip into asking instead for his deliverance from enemies and false friends, and his safe return to her in Wensleydale. She knew the petitions were in the wrong spirit, but she had long ago despaired of influencing God with her puny supplications.

Often she would share the chapel with her mother, who never stayed less than an hour, and sometimes for as long as three. At first, finding the drab figure motionless in a corner, except for the busy fingers on the beads, she imagined the Countess had also come to pray for Richard. But that was foolish. Upon reflection, she realised that ever since her arrival at Middleham nearly ten years before, when she had not been at her embroidery frame she had been here, solitary and unobserved except by the chaplain. Interceding, perhaps, for her husband, and lately for her elder daughter – or simply thinking the thoughts which no one had ever fathomed, or indeed tried to. With a rush of pitying revulsion, Anne wondered if the Earl had ever really had need of his wife, except as the bearer of his children. And with another little flood of emotion – of love, of pride, of uneasiness – she recalled Richard's words to her the night before his departure, 'I shall need you, dear heart.'

The news which filtered up from the south was contradictory. Northampton had been the meeting point for Richard, Buckingham, and the new King's train, and apparently young Edward was peacefully on his way to London escorted by the two dukes. Then a few days later a gentleman on a mission to Pomfret for Richard came on to Middleham with surprising tidings. His task had been to deliver to Pomfret under guard Lord Rivers, his nephew Lord Grey, and the Prince of Wales' chamberlain from Ludlow, Sir Thomas Vaughan. No, there had been no fighting, no bloodshed, he replied to Anne's anxious enquiries. He could not tell her what justification the Duke of Gloucester had had for committing such powerful men to prison, but my lord of Buckingham had been in agreement. That was all he knew. Buckingham! From the obscurity of his stronghold in the Welsh mountains, he seemed to have leapt in one skilful bound into the heart of Richard's counsel. Her instinct was to distrust him, and she prayed that until his intentions were clear her husband would do so too.

A note written at St Albans on Holy Rood Day by John Kendall with Richard's sprawling signature told her merely that King Edward V would enter his capital on the morrow, yet the messenger spoke of rumours that the Dowager Queen was fortifying the city against them, that she had seized all the late King's treasure, and that her brother Sir Edward Woodville was in possession of the fleet. It seemed impossible that Richard should assume the Protectorship without opposition, and Anne lay sleepless night after night, revolving endlessly the various hazards that he might even now be confronting. When he went to France with Edward IV's great army, to revive his ancestors' claim to the throne of King Louis, when he invaded Scotland and took Edinburgh, she had suffered far less. It was because as a soldier he faced dangers that he understood, the straightforward trial of strength and skill in deployment of forces and conditions. In London he had to deal with the tactics of men, and of a woman in particular, which would be utterly inscrutable to him. Had she been with him in France or in Scotland, Anne would have been useless, a liability, but in London she felt that she could at least warn him not to trust too much, if he would only send for her.

Yet he seemed to do well enough without her. The next definite news came from Crosby's Place in Bishopsgate Street in his own hand; he had been confirmed as Protector, Parliament was to be summoned, and the coronation of his nephew would take place at midsummer. All was quiet, and he asked that Anne should leave with convenient speed to join him. She had not expected the summons so soon, and all her longing to be at his side evaporated. London, with its strident narrow streets, its mobs of uncouth apprentices and kennels choked with refuse. She remembered the winter fogs that poisoned the lungs, the humid stench of the summer. And Westminster, which was worse – the elegance, the smiling, the opulence, the treachery. She had spent so short a time there, so long ago, but she had forgotten nothing.

And then abruptly she came to herself. The messenger was still kneeling before her, a page was lighting the candles, Kat curled asleep in her lap, portly and pampered, and at her feet Katherine sat on a cushion, the *Romance of the Rose* open where she had broken off reading, her brown eyes fixed apprehensively upon her. All the ladies, arrested in their work as if some magician had turned them to statues, were gazing at her with the same expression. Why, she wondered, what is wrong? and simultaneously she saw that the letter from Richard, with his red boar seal broken, was crumpled up in her clenched fist. Her own fears must not be allowed thus to spread despondency through her household, and so she attempted a smile and addressed Katherine, although she made sure that everyone could hear.

'My lord is well, and he has been confirmed as Protector.' Her attendants relaxed, echoed her smile, and began to chatter over the resumed needlework. Kate only did not move, but continued to stare at her.

'What else did my lord father write, madame?' she asked. Anne began mechanically to caress the cat. Sometimes her foster daughter was too perceptive.

'He has asked me to go south and join him.'

'And will you go?'

'Of course. He is my husband.'

'What about ... us?' The shadow of Katherine's question fell over Anne's mind, and forced her to acknowledge the real reason for her dread of going to London.

'I don't know, Kate. I haven't decided.' Richard had not mentioned their son in the letter; that issue he had made over to her before leaving Middleham. And it would have to be settled in the space of the next few days. Suddenly she rose, tipping Kat to the floor with an indignant little yowl.

'Ladies, I must go to the chapel. You are released from any further duties this evening.' At all costs she must escape from the accusing gaze of that pair of eyes which so reminded her of Richard's. She wanted silence and solitude about her, but more than anything she wanted his presence, and his voice to tell her what to do.

As usual she had dismissed the matter from her mind, hoping vaguely that some miracle would render the decision unnecessary. Yet it had lain beneath the surface, influencing all her prayers, colouring all the hours in which she watched Edward, and talked with him, and thought about him. Except when he was displaced by his father, he had never been far from her thoughts since the day when she knew she was carrying a child. His rearing, his health and his welfare had been her personal care, not delegated to nurses and attendants; Richard had supervised his education instead of appointing a governor. There had been no question of his being sent away for training. The Prince of Wales, who had become King, had had his own establishment at Ludlow since the age of three; the vast majority of the sons of noblemen and gentlemen were transplanted to another household for their growing years. Their Edward was different. He should remain under his parents' eyes, protected but not pampered, until he was old enough to fend for himself. And strong enough, was the unspoken phrase that hung over every discussion about his future. Meanwhile he had been on careful journeys to Pomfret, to York and Sheriff Hutton, but not for more than a week beyond his mother's sight. To take him as far as London, or to leave him behind where she could not see him for maybe many months, was both ways an evil. Struggling to channel her thoughts into a logical progression, she could not envisage ever making up her mind.

Two days later she was still vacillating, and in danger of making herself ill from constant fruitless worry. Edward had ridden hawking up into Coverdale with his companions, and she happened to be by when they came back. A biting wind had been blowing from the east all morning, sweeping away the softness of spring. Anne clutched her cloak to her against another gust, and watched the boys dismounting. To be accurate she watched Edward dismounting. He handed his falcon to Peacocke, the groom who held his mare, and slid to the ground with the ease of a born horseman. But Anne observed what none of the others, grooms or henchmen, could see. As he touched the ground he pressed his hand to his side, hunching a little over the pain. Her heart lurched, and she restrained herself from running to him. In a moment he had recovered, straightening himself with a slight shake of the shoulders, and was taking his falcon from Peacocke in order to return it to the mews himself. He passed his mother, noticed her for the first time, ducked his head courteously and smiled at her. She tried to return the smile, although she was sure she could read in his expression the lingering of that brief pang.

Turning from the errand she was bound on, she went instead up to the chapel and stood for a long time staring at the stained glass St Anne who carried so carefully and so incongruously the nest of fledglings. A squall of rain was flung rattling against the east window like a shower of pebbles. Even in her cloak she was cold. Her decision was taken, and she sensed that it was really Richard's decision, that he had left it to her only because he was sure of what she would do. If Edward suffered so from an expedition of a mere few hours, it would be madness to subject him to a journey of two hundred and fifty miles, especially in the wild weather that was paying for a calm beautiful April. And how would he fare in the plagues and bad airs of London? He would be upset, of course, at being left behind, but she would explain to him, and in the company of his friends, and the absorption of his strenuous routine, he would not grieve too much.

She must act at once before her resolution wavered. Genuflecting to the jewelled crucifix which she and Richard had presented, she left the chapel and traversed the short passage into the great hall. A few of her ladies were huddled round the unseasonal fire, although the smoke was blowing back from the roof-vent and rimming their eyes with red. Despatching one of them to summon Edward, she returned to her chamber. The women trailed after her, speculating in low voices on what was making their mistress behave in this strange abrupt way, when my lord's fortune was made and she would soon be with him in London and the first lady in the land. When Edward came in, Anne had been sitting there for some time, nervously rehearsing the words she would use to break it to him. His hair had been tossed into disorder by the wind and gave him, with his sharp little nose, a faint likeness to a ruffled chick. Anne's hand ached with the longing to reach out and smooth the soft fair down into place. She had done it so often when he was a baby, but to caress him now would be a breach of the rules she imposed upon herself. He was no longer a little boy, and must not be petted in public. So she asked, rather quickly, whether the hawking had gone well. Edward explained that the gale had prevented the falcons from stooping on their prey accurately, so they had not taken much.

'But Yseult will come to my fist now without a lure,' he added eagerly. The little falcon was his first hawk and he was very proud of her. 'She rouses whenever I come into the mews, and she'll take meat from my hand.' Anne had always been a little wary of falcons, and did not really comprehend the close relationship that men built up with their favourite birds, but she knew what perseverance and nerve went into the breaking process, and praised her son as warmly as she could.

After that she could find no way to lead gently into her subject, so she said bluntly, 'Ned, you have heard that your lord father has summoned me to London?'

'Yes, madame.'

'We do not consider it wise to take you away from Middleham at present ... with your training as it is ...' She wished she had the facility of words to make it sound less bald and formal. The boy was returning her worried gaze with his great grey eyes clear and calm; perhaps he had not yet understood. 'It will only be for a time, until something ... better can be arranged. Meanwhile, all your friends are here, and the servants. And Kate is staying with you.' That she said on impulse, realising as she spoke that she had counted on Katherine's companionship for herself in London.

'Yes, madame. Thank you,' Edward replied cheerfully, and with scarcely a pause, 'Do you suppose my lord father will remember that he promised me a puppy to train for hunting when his bitch Diana whelps? William says she'll drop the pups any day now.' Anne could not believe it. At first she thought he was putting a heroically brave face on his disappointment, and waited for the long mouth above the childish chin to tremble. Then he went on, more soberly, 'I think Diana's pining for Father. Will you tell him, madame, and remind him about the pup? When you've given him my humble duty, of course.' It was several seconds before she could answer him, and promise to give his message to his father. Then she sent him away with an abruptness which she had never used to Edward before, and which afterwards troubled her conscience. For the present, she was hurt. By his careless acceptance of the decision that had cost her such heart-searching, he was rejecting her. He was concerned only with the acquisition of a dog, and unreasonably she blamed him for not taking the news harder.

The balance was redressed and tipped the other way when she asked Katherine to stay at Middleham and watch over her half-brother while she was away. The girl was upset both by the imminent parting from her adopted mother, and the idea of Edward's being left at all. Although she agreed very willingly to Anne's request, the older woman sensed that she disapproved of her abandoning her son. Katherine had grown up with a very firm set of principles; one was that the strong should always sacrifice themselves for the weak. And Anne could not begin to explain that the strong were sometimes not as strong as they seemed, that Richard's need for her in London possibly surpassed her son's need for her in Wensleydale. All the same, her wretchedness increased.

Soon after these two unhappy interviews, John Wrangwysh arrived at the castle, sent by Richard as an escort for the Duchess and incidentally for his own wife, who would be travelling with her. Anne was a little comforted, not only by the evidence of Richard's care for her safety, but also by the closeness of the saturnine Yorkshireman's friendship with him. From John at last she could hear the truth of the situation in London and its effect on her husband.

He was not a voluble talker, and even with Margaret's experienced coaxing to help she elicited scarcely more information than she already possessed: the Duke of Gloucester worked from Crosby's Place to set in smooth motion the wheels of goverment which had been snarled by his brother's sudden death; the Duke of Buckingham and Lord Hastings worked with him; there was much coming and going about the coronation. Was my lord well? Yes, his health was very good. Where was the Dowager Queen? In sanctuary at Westminster, together with her daughters and her younger son. And the young King? In the royal apartments in the Tower. Were there any disturbances in London? No, everyone was going about their normal business. All satisfactory answers, and yet – perhaps it was sheer imagination on Anne's part – he was more reticent than he should have been. Her real questions remained unanswered. Torn between compulsion to reach Richard's side as quickly as horse would carrry her, and a heavy reluctance to leave her son and the blessed security of Middleham, she found herself at one moment urging on the preparations by sweeping aside petty complications, and at another inventing a hitch to slow them down.

But, inevitably, the day of departure was upon her. The packhorses, wagons, and other paraphernalia of a long journey were clogging the courtyard early on a May morning without promise of sun. Already tired from a broken night and rising at dawn, Anne did not feel at all prepared for the miles before her. The small escort of men-at-arms was mounted, the wagoners waited for the signal to move, and at the foot of the staircase to the keep the ceremony of farewell was taking place. So often before Anne had been the stay-at-home; it was strange and uneasy to be leaving herself. In order of precedence the castle officials, all known to her by name, wished her godspeed, then the attendants who were remaining, and then the henchmen and Katherine, who was taking her position of trust seriously and behaving with dignified restraint; the convulsive hug she had given Anne in her chamber this morning had not been for public eyes. Last, the Earl of Salisbury, who knelt to receive his mother's blessing before embracing her, as he had the right to do. She could not think of what to say to him, except silly things like, Wrap up well in the evenings, don't overtax yourself, don't forget me. Before anything sensible came to her lips he had stepped back a little and was fumbling in his pouch. He handed her a small package, his cheeks dyed suddenly scarlet. Inside was a miniature crucifix, beautifully carved from rose quartz.

'Master Bernall bought it in York. I wanted to give you a relic of St Anne, or one of your other saints, but there wasn't time to find one. I hope you like it.' He was talking fast, breathlessly, as if trying to postpone his mother's comment on the gift. But all her comment was to take him again in her arms, the tears she had promised herself not to shed spilling over. Undemonstrative as he generally was, Edward responded fervently.

She could not remember afterwards whether she ever thanked him; only that he requested her to pray for his father while she was on the road, and to pray for him when she reached London, and at the last as she was helped on to her mare, 'And, madame, you will ask my lord father about the pup?' That only increased her tears, although she wanted to laugh as well, and there was the embarrassment of riding through the ranks of her servants and followers to the gatehouse, the mistress of Middleham and first lady of England, weeping like a foolish girl.

Her social commitments were an ordeal of endurance and memory. So many lords and ladies, all dressed in the latest fashions, which made them almost indistinguishable one from the other. Two she could not mistake, however, were Richard's associates in the triumvirate of government. Lord Hastings she had encountered before, at the time of her wedding; now he was a vastly corpulent gentleman, his face a network of the little purple veins that are the mark of good living. Genial and gallant, he appeared far too frank for any subterfuge, simply the good fellow that everyone called him. Buckingham was of a different mettle. His urbane smiling expression might conceal any kind of thoughts, and the slight figure clothed in exquisite taste drew all eyes as if by right. Anne was captivated straight away by his perfect courtesy and beautifully modulated voice, as she was repelled by the aura of slight dissipation which hung about Hastings. Yet her earlier suspicions of the Duke were resurrected unaccountably when she noticed how Richard looked at him. She had seen before that unguarded admiration, and although she could not remember when, it spelt danger. And there was no doubt that there were tensions between the three, despite the efforts to present a united front. Her hypersensitive eye discerned a veiled malice between Hastings and Buckingham, and on Richard's part, who was so much less experienced at dissembling, a wariness of his brother's old boon companion.

He did not talk to her of them in their rare moments alone. Undoubtedly he was pleased to have her with him, but all the help and good advice she had planned to give him dwindled to sharing a hasty supper with him before his evening session of letter-writing with Kendall, and making love whenever they both had the energy. There was much on his mind, and she did not even like to ask him what it was. Her fears of inadequacy, long banished in the orderly routine of Wensleydale, returned to her.

One night the crease between his brows was deeper than before. He had not supped with her, but in private with the Bishop of Bath and Wells. Greeting her kindly, he asked how she had spent the day, but did not really listen to her answer. After a poor attempt at conversation he said he was going to bed. Anne could see that he was preoccupied, and although the anticipation of their evenings together sustained her through the gruelling days, she accepted his goodnight kiss and tried not to be disappointed that he went no further. She woke several times during the night, and could tell from his imperceptible breathing and stillness that he was lying open-eyed beside her. At last she said, 'Richard, why can't you sleep?'

'There's too much to think about. It is only at night that I have the leisure.'

'Is it . . . my lord Hastings that troubles you?' His head made a tiny sharp movement on the pillow.

'No. Not Hastings.' She thought he would say no more, but after a long pause he continued. 'I must work it out in my own mind first, Anne. Will you bear with me? And try to sleep.'

'Yes, my love, I'll try.' Obediently she turned over, but she found only uneasy dozes, drifting a short way into oblivion, and always returning to the unnaturally quiet body beside her staring at the invisible tester of the bed. From one of these dozes she was roused by a hand on her shoulder and a light in her eyes.

'Anne.' Richard had lit the tallow dip on the shelf above them, and was raised on his elbow. 'I must talk to you. I have considered very deeply, and I believe you have the right to know. It is your concern as much as anyone else's.' She dragged herself into a sitting position, and shivered in the before-dawn chill of the summer night. Her husband rose naked, and fetched her Indian silk wrap which he placed round her shoulders before finding his own bedgown. Anne noticed anew how thin he was – too thin, she thought, since leaving Middleham – and all the time she was calm and quiet in spite of the monstrous dread that clawed at her. As if all his stillness had been used up he roamed the chamber, noiselessly on bare feet, and she lay and listened to him.

'Bishop Stillington came today to reveal a secret to me. He has long kept it close because of the damage it could do if known. But now he is convinced that it is more dangerous to be silent than to speak. Queen Elizabeth was not my brother's legal wife. The bishop affirms that he officiated at a troth-plight between King Edward and . . . another lady some years before his marriage to Dame Elizabeth. The lady is now dead, but it makes no difference to the status of the children – of Edward and the Duke of York and the girls. They were all born out of wedlock. Illegitimate.'

For an age he went on walking to and fro, before Anne could ask levelly, 'You don't believe him?'

'He is a man of God. There seems no reason why he should invent the tale.'

To curry favour? A mouthpiece of Buckingham or Hastings or someone wanting to provoke Richard into treason? A muddleheaded churchman who had confused his canon laws? Her mind darted about, seeking to evade the conclusion which was rolling towards her and Richard to crush them with its mighty weight.

'I think he told George,' remarked Richard in that dry precise voice that was terribly familiar to her, 'and that was why Edward killed him.' George had always wanted to be a king. And perhaps his elder brother's guilty secret, blabbed to him injudiciously by the Bishop of Bath and Wells, had revived his hopes to a flowering when he was already rotten with their decay. A deadly flower. And what was kingship but a deadly flower? Holy Henry VI, murdered only because he was a king; Edward IV, cut off exhausted at forty years old; Edward V, title shaken to the roots after only two months of reigning. And . . . what next? She would let herself think no further. But Richard was saying it, gently.

'I am the next heir, Anne.'

'No, you're not. What about Clarence's children – the Earl of Warwick and Lady Margaret?' He had stopped pacing and stood looking down on her, his hands thrust into the sleeves of his gown. Slowly he shook his head.

'The attainder on their father debars them from the succession. There is only me.' With the rushlight between them she could see far into his eyes, and they were full of abhorrence.

Drawing from him some kind of reassurance she dared to ask, 'What will you do?'

'I don't know. It is not a thing to be decided hastily. I must weigh it with great care, consult the council, take advice—'

'You'll tell them?'

'I can't keep it entirely to myself; it's too important. One or two at first, that I trust most. Buckingham, of course.'

Hot words formed themselves. Why Buckingham? Who is he to arbitrate on your destiny, and England's? But she only said, 'And my lord Hastings?'

'No.' Short, clipped. 'No, I shall not inform him yet.' As though to shake off the thought, he went to the window and opened the shutters. A watery light flowed into the room, as yet too feeble to awake any colour in the chamber. The framed square of sky was grey as a pigeon's breast; a single bird winged black across it. Richard gazed out at the haphazard roofs and chimneys of the city; Anne, suddenly overcome with weariness, closed her eyes. Some time later, she felt him removing the shawl and easing her beneath the bedclothes. The growing day found glints of peacock in his gown as he threw it off and lay beside her.

'Be sure, dear heart,' he said, 'that I shall be prudent. And I shall do nothing against my conscience.'

Nothing against his conscience. Perhaps ironical demons, lurking outside the window, had laughed at his certainty. In the next few days, the inflammable secret of Bishop Stillington was pushed aside by a more explosive occurrence. On 13 June London was shaken out of its complacency by a sudden flurry of rumours. Messengers galloped full-tilt through the streets, knots of goodwives and apprentices gathered at their doors, men made sure that their swords and pikes were near at hand. At Baynard's Castle, waiting on her mother-in-law the old Duchess of York, Anne sensed the unrest in the air.

Soon it was over, the wild tales of armed risings and murders quashed, the citizens going about their work again, and all that was left was the *fait accompli*. A treasonous plot against the government had been disclosed to the Protector, in which the prime mover was William, Lord Hastings. He had been arrested at a council meeting in the White Tower, and beheaded shortly afterwards.

When Richard returned that evening he was cold and unapproachable. As if a wall stood between them Anne could make no contact with him. Although she was appalled, as much by the precipitancy of his action as by its brutality, she could not condemn him for it. By the thin line of his mouth and his mask-like face she knew how profoundly he was shaken. Hastings had been the pattern of loyalty to the Yorkist cause, and now without warning he had betrayed it. Richard's violence was a measure of anguish. The gentlemen of his household did not engage in their usual after-supper pastimes – gossiping, music, card-games. They sat separate, silent, avoiding each other's eyes. Several, those with homes to go to in London, had excused themselves. Fleeing to her chamber, Anne found the same unease among her women. Richard did not come to her.

For some reason that he did not explain, he decided to go and stay with his mother at Baynard's Castle. She let him go without protest, consoling herself with the certainty that he would have taken her were it not for an imminent arrival at Crosby's Place. Isobel's son, the Earl of Warwick, was coming from the country to live under her care. Pitying the orphaned boy, she had suggested it herself. 'He will be company for Ned when he is in London,' she had said. But the prospect of another child's presence brought back to her sharply the absence of her own son. Richard needed her so little that he was sleeping over the other side of the city. What right had she to be fostering her sister's child when hers was abandoned in Yorkshire? Perhaps she would ask Richard if she could go home soon ... just for a visit. Her head ached so much in London ... and she was sure that now the days were long Ned would be practising too late at the butts.

The young Earl was another Edward, and of an age with his cousin, but that was about all they had in common. Wiry and sudden, Warwick seemed to have imbibed no idea of discipline from his tutors in the country. He never walked when he could run, and he never attended a Latin lesson if he could truant from it. Yet in authorising whippings for him, which she had to do several times within the first few days, she found no resentment in him. Like a dog, he cowered and whimpered at the punishment, and ten minutes after he was frisking again. At first he puzzled, then he charmed her. He was a diversion, even when he shocked her by rushing unannounced through the audience she was giving to Lady Howard; her spirits were refreshed when she saw him from a window playing football with the pages in the courtyard. Yet she suspected that Richard would not approve of his nephew's wildness. Perhaps the best place for him was at Middleham with their Ned, where he could learn manners and still be a boy. Richard might let her escort him there. Yet she would miss the clatter of his feet and the sudden stream of questions he would direct at her so unselfconsciously.

'When shall I see my cousin the King?' he asked often. 'I should like to know if I can shoot farther than him.' She thought of the eldest of the three cousin Edwards, whom she had visited in the Tower, wrapped in cold and suspicious dignity, and doubted if he would approve either of Warwick's levity.

One morning Edward of Warwick asked, 'At the coronation, shall I bear the King's train? Will he make me a duke like my father?' Anne answered at random, for it had come to her that talk of the coronation had diminished since Richard went to Baynard's Castle. Preparations were still going forward, she had assumed, in other places, but it was strange that they should be spoken of less as the event drew nearer, and not more. The eager young face before her blurred into insignificance, and soon Warwick gave up, and went away to wheedle some strawberries from the pantry.

The next day Richard sent for her. It was bright and warm, there was no excuse for a litter, and so she rode through the busy streets to Baynard's Castle. The people, pressed back by her escort, pressed forward again after her to stare, and sometimes to cheer, for by the white boar liveries they knew her as the Protector's wife. There was no comfort for her in their acclaim; the shouts made her feel more exposed, more of a fraud. Some among them must surely remember, especially here by the waterside, the degraded girl called Nan who had been herded to mass at St James de Garlickehithe every

Sunday with the other menials of Francis Twynyho the grocer. She averted her eyes from the house façades of the Vintry, with a superstitious dread that a glimpse of one particular house would prove a terrible omen.

There was no need for omens. The moment that Richard met her in a room overlooking the river and took her hands she knew what he would say.

'I have decided, I must take the throne.' Such naked words, but he was gripping her tightly, as if to sustain her against their effect. She did not move or reply. 'It is my duty. The country will never accept a bastard king – not while he is a minor.' His explanations sounded in the ears of both more like an excuse.

'What will become of him?' Her thoughts rested for a moment on the proud and lonely boy in the royal apartments of the Tower.

'Nothing. What should happen to him? He and his brother and sisters shall be treated with all courtesy.'

Anne recognised the faintly pedantic style that Richard adopted when he was unsure of himself, and she said, unable to prevent herself, 'Is there no other way?'

'None.' He lifted his chin, and his face was calm and resolved again. Leading her to a window seat, he made her sit down. Now she understood why he had moved here to his mother's house: in order to wrestle with his conscience uninfluenced by Anne's presence. But her opinion carried no weight with him, nor ever had on matters of any consequence.

'Tomorrow the Lord Mayor's brother Friar Ralph will preach a sermon at Paul's Cross in which he will set forth my claim to the crown.' Richard was standing before her, awkwardly agitating the ring on his little finger. 'I shall be there to witness it, with Harry and Howard and the rest.' Remotely bitter, Anne wondered if he had isolated himself from Buckingham's influence during his time of decision. In the past week he had progressed from 'Buckingham' to 'Harry'. 'There will be a large concourse of people also, and by their reaction we shall proceed.'

'And if they reject the claim . . . ?'

'I shall go no farther. But our agents report that the citizens will be favourable.' It was like a speech to the Parliament House, by a public Richard whom she had hardly known in

Wensleydale, only occasionally in York, but whom she saw far too often in London.

'What does your lady mother say?'

'Nothing.' Richard relaxed into a smile and put his foot on the window seat. 'She's a woman of few words unless she is in a rage – so I suppose we must be thankful for her silence. Will you stay to dinner, love? And tonight?' In spite of everything, she answered his smile.

The citizens offered no objection, and four days later Anne became a queen.

2

A NORTHERN TRIUMPH

The heavy mass of cloth-of-gold engulfed her for a moment, and as it slid into place, guided by the tirers' hands, its rustling was augmented by a murmur of admiration from her attendants. For the first time in more than a century the Queen would share the King's coronation, and Peter Curteys the Keeper of the Wardrobe had risen to the occasion. But while the women stooped about her to adjust the shimmering stuff and pin the hem, the Queen remained conscious that the admiration was not universal. There was a gaze on her which did not waver or change. Anne was exposed now to many eyes, unfamiliar stares in public and private of curiosity, wonder, envy, but none as disturbing as this. She knew whence it came, and she could rarely escape from it.

Baroness Stanley stood shadowed by the hearth, slightly apart from the other attendants; she did not encourage contact with the ladies of the new court to which her husband had brought her. She affected to despise them all, and more than any other she despised the Queen. Her still, white features, drawn ascetically, expressed none of this, but Anne, so quick to scent disapproval, had read it soon enough. Why, she thought at first, I never did her wrong? I never saw her until a few weeks ago. And she asked Richard, who told her that Margaret Beaufort believed Anne to be usurping her place by virtue of her descent from John of Gaunt.

'Her son by her first husband, Henry Tydder, waits over in Brittany for a chance to press their claim. The Lancastrians and the Woodvilles are rallying to him.' Richard said it lightly, as if he thought it a faint threat.

His unconcern did nothing to diminish the malevolence of the Baroness's eyes. Clad in the magnificence of her coronation robes, Anne felt it beat upon her more strongly than ever, nullifying the warm voices of her friends, dimming the sunshine from the wide window. And the injustice of it leapt up in her throat. She did not want to be a queen. With glad tears she would have surrendered her cloth-of-gold and her diamonds and pomp to the woman who coveted them. If Margaret Beaufort could only guess how little her rival was worthy of the throne, how much she yearned to run away from London, back to Yorkshire and her son and her past with Richard, then surely she would pity and not hate her.

Master Curteys was holding a full-length mirror before her, begging her with a hint of pride in his old-young face to look at his creation. She looked, and she fancied that the basilisk stare of the Baroness had turned her to stone. By a trick of the sun on the polished steel there was no colour in her reflection. A pale face and pale hair, pale robes and pale hands clasped at her breast. No, she was not a statue, but an effigy in alabaster. A white queen who lay motionless and unfeeling on her tomb. And the whispers around her said, 'They should never have made her Queen, she was not strong enough; she abandoned her son and she failed her husband, and when she died he wept for her.' Then the whispers grew to shouts and there was an arm around her waist, a hand anxiously pulling at her collar of pearls. The mirror had turned and the gold and silver glittered again, and beside her she saw Margaret Wrangwysh.

'Dear madame, is it too heavy for you? Are you faint?'

'A little. It's nothing, Meg. The room is hot.' But by the hearth the room was cold and darkness gathered still. She shivered as they disrobed her, but when the gown was borne away she would not rest as they urged her. She must tell Richard.

He was dictating to Kendall in his closet, and although she broke in upon him halfway through a letter, he glanced at her once and said quietly, 'Thank you, John. I shall call you.' The secretary gathered his quills and went without a word. Richard brought his chair for her, but she would not sit down.

'You cannot be King, Richard.' She was still shivering, but her voice was steady. 'It will destroy us.'

'Why should it, love? If we do our duty there's no reason why we shouldn't rule for many years.' Hiding his anxiety about her, he answered her equably.

'No. It will change you. You're changed already. And I am too weak.'

'I don't believe it. You've never failed me yet.'

'Not yet. But I shall. Find someone else, let someone else be King. Even Henry Tydder. Let him and his mother see how it is, but not you.' She was losing her semblance of reasonable argument, and he took hold of her shoulders.

'Anne, that's impossible, and you know it. I've taken up this thing now and I can't just abandon my obligations.'

'And what of your obligations to me? And to our son?' It was her trump card, and she threw the challenge before him of the terrible destiny he was thrusting upon the delicate child at Middleham.

'I think of Ned constantly. If it were not for him I should have hesitated longer. He is our future, and England's security. When I've made the country strong and peaceful again, as it was in my brother's day, it will be Ned's task to keep it so. Think, Anne. We shall rear him as ruler of the North, as I was. He'll learn his kingship there, where everyone knows and loves him. And in time's fullness he'll take my place.' She knew then that she was lost. Their son was to be another sacrifice to the insatiable crown of England. In the loneliness of discovering how far divided from hers was Richard's vision of the future, she began to cry.

Always, on the rare occasions when she had done so before it had brought Richard to her, penitent for causing her grief, eager to offer consolation. But not this time. He was staring at her coldly, almost with distaste.

'Control yourself, madame. This is no time for hysterics.' Shocked out of her tears she stared back at him, seeing what London and the struggle for power was doing to him. 'I realise you are under strain. This has been a precarious month for both of us. But, God willing, the worst is over. The mischief-makers have been removed, England knows its allegiance. And I know mine.' At last he moved to her and his expression softened. 'You must remember yours too. To me, as always, and now to the country also.' With a sob she put her hands over her eyes but he forced them away, speaking on quietly and inflexibly. 'You can do it, Anne, as you recovered your health

273

for me at St Martin's, and gave me a son, and learned to be a Duchess. You can be a Queen. All it needs is the will.' Not her will, but his. She would obey him, not with gladness, but because there was no other way but with him. She bowed her head and he kissed her brow.

'Now, dear heart, go and rest before supper. You must save all your strength for the coronation. It will be a hard day.' Leading her to the door he stopped.

'There's one more thing I must ask you to do for me. Lady Stanley – I know you must feel that she dislikes you, but it is probably no more than her manner. It is necessary to conciliate her, and any other potential hostile factions. I am making her your train-bearer.'

Anne stiffened, gasped, and subsided. 'If you wish it, my lord.' So she would have answered her father. Reasons of state must prevail, and a sop to the pride of Margaret Beaufort was inevitably a wound in her own.

The colours hurt her head. Scarlet and saffron, azure and cloth-of-gold, they shifted and jigged around her, conspiring with the bray of trumpets, the bay of sackbuts, the jangling of bells, the roaring of crowds, and the all-pervading heat of the day, clashing and grinding against the pain in her skull. Early as it was, the sweat slithered down her body inside the heavy robes and her bare feet left wet patches on the ceremonial carpet. She knew that, and that somewhere near Richard was walking, also barefoot, also weighed down with too many clothes, and she remembered the long sleepless reaches of last night, but everything else was confusion. By the sudden coolness and dimness, the change in the quality of the cacophony, she sensed they had entered the Abbey, and that before her lay a ritual of such complexity and solemnity that her remaining self-mastery would crumble beneath the first invocation.

It was perhaps only her early training as a Neville that pulled her through it, those tedious occasions when the small daughter of the Earl of Warwick must stand up straight, conceal her cold, or her cough, or her headache, and be a credit to the greatest family in the land. Now she was crowned Queen of England; Warwick the Kingmaker might rest contented in his tomb, yet she wanted nothing else in the world but to be in bed and asleep. With scarcely a respite the ceremonies went on, chanting and genuflexion and processions and changes of clothes, and then an endless banquet amid the same loud multicoloured hordes. As evening drew on the sultry heat was aggravated by thousands of candles and torches.

Sometimes it seemed to Anne that she was at another banquet, many miles and many years away, and instead of being too hot it was too cold, and her uncle George was the new Archbishop of York and she had a fever. A little girl out of her depth; she felt the same here. One incident only had made her feel real on that winter day at Cawood: the concern of her cousin Richard. Where was he now? King Richard III sat at her side, crowned, robed, served as she was on bended knee, and as remote as the stars in heaven. He was one of the monarchs in the old tapestries, and so she supposed was she, raised so high above common mortals by God's chrism that they did not even breathe common air. Sanctified, and inhuman. He would not ask her how she did, or touch her hand, or give her one of those slow smiles which had reassured her across the board at Middleham. Her chest felt tight, and she was suddenly certain that she could not survive up here, in the rarefied atmosphere where love must die.

It was no surprise to anyone who knew her when the Queen did not emerge from her chamber the following morning, and remained invisible to all but her closest friends for several days. Richard came, of course, although he had not slept with her for some nights, and showed his customary kindness. In it, however, Anne's heightened sensitivity found a lingering remoteness which she saw as a reproach for her lack of stamina. The heat continued, and intensified the stifling atmosphere of London. As soon as she was fit Richard moved with her and his advisers to Greenwich.

Set in wide meadows by the broadening Thames, the palace recalled no trace of memory of the only other time she had visited it. Then it had been a vast echoing place, damp and empty from neglect, and she had met King Henry with his goldfinch. King Edward had renovated it to the standard of almost continental splendour which he loved to bring to his residences. The air was fresher here, the crowds farther away, and Anne began to mend. But she was not well enough to leave with the King on his first royal progress to the west. She tried to insist, but had not the energy even to carry her point.

'You shall join me later,' Richard decided, 'at Warwick before I go north. I cannot do without you in Yorkshire.' And, to avoid making her feel useless, he assured her that there were many duties in the capital which only she could do in his absence. The haste to leave was not entirely necessary, but Richard also had had enough of London. He did not tell his wife that one of his stops would be at Tewkesbury Abbey, where were buried her first husband, her sister, and his brother George.

They travelled together to Windsor and there he left her, only two weeks after their coronation. Such duties as were allotted to her were light, and she spent much time riding and walking gently among the great summer trees of Windsor Forest. The prospect of seeing Richard again within a short time, and beyond that of returning to Yorkshire and her son, encouraged her recuperation.

Among the visitors she had to receive was one whom, short though his stay was, she could not welcome wholeheartedly. It was the Duke of Buckingham, who for some reason had not left London with the King, but passed through Windsor in his wake a few days later, intending to catch him up around Gloucester. Naturally he would pay his respects to the Queen and eat dinner with her before going on. It was difficult for Anne to be more than barely civil to him: for one thing she saw him as the successful rival in the battle for control of Richard's will and blamed him, however irrationally, for his accepting the throne; for another, he was one of those easy charming men who had always filled her with disquiet. So puffed up with his new power, with self-congratulation for having thrown his weight on to the right side in an uncertain situation – she could not conceive how Richard could trust or like him, although he did both in great measure. That she could in fact be a better judge of his character than her husband did not enter her head.

Buckingham asked if he could bear any message to the King, but she had none she cared to send by such a courier. As he took his leave he said sympathetically, 'It must be a sorrow to you, that you were unable to pay your respects with his grace at your sister's tomb.' Then he bent over her hand, not seeing her reaction to the news which Richard had withheld from her to spare her feelings. For she knew well that it was not Isobel's grave that he would be honouring in Tewkesbury Abbey but that of Isobel's husband, who despite all his crimes had never fallen entirely from his throne in Richard's heart. Whether Buckingham was even aware of the persecution Anne had suffered was doubtful, but as he rode away amid his red-and-gold retainers his parting remark had not endeared him to his Queen.

They set off for Warwick a few days after Buckingham's visit; the baggage and personnel in this caravan were much greater than in the train Richard had taken with him, and would take several days to reach the rendezvous. Anne's spirits rose as they neared Warwick, because a harbinger had met them on the road and informed them that the King would already be in residence by the time they arrived. Another of the travellers showed his excitement by spurring his pony to the head of the column, pursued by a scolding groom, and there making it dance on its hind legs, to the amusement of all but the groom. This was the young Earl of Warwick, enthralled to be on the move after a boring month in London and approaching his titular fortress, which his uncle Richard had promised to restore to him when he was grown up. Until then he would be reared with Prince Edward and other cousins in Yorkshire, and no doubt be introduced to the discipline which up to now he had managed to avoid.

The public meeting with her husband at the castle barbican was perforce formal, but she could tell from the brightness of his eyes how glad he was to see her. They had been physically parted for only two weeks, yet it seemed much longer, and perhaps it was. For out of London Richard had shed much of the burden of sovereignty which had visibly borne on him there. Always happy in the saddle, encouraged by the warmth of reception given to him in every town on his route, he was recognisable again to the wife who had feared him estranged from her. Alone at last, in the chamber that had been her father's, his love confirmed it.

They reached Pomfret towards the end of August, after the

least disagreeable journey that Anne had ever made. Here they were to wait until their son joined them from Middleham. To be sure, the official functions continued unabated, the stream of people flowed undiminished, as throughout their slow progress north at every stopping-place; but here the accents were right, and, with the foothills of the Pennines, lying low along the western horizon, told her that she was in Yorkshire. Her heart lifted. Day by day she sat beside Richard, settling disputes, receiving gifts and homage and petitions, and all the time beneath the restrained courtesy which they showed to everybody their thoughts sprang in half-terrified, half-joyous unison towards the moment when the messenger would announce the approach of Prince Edward.

When word came, they went out a little way on the Tadcaster road to meet him, miscalculated in their eagerness, and had to sit their horses in a high wind for a good half hour before his outriders appeared. Among the advancing cavalcade there were many familiar faces; even the men-at-arms were old acquaintances from Wensleydale; but there was one face only for which two pairs of eyes were searching feverishly, and it was not there. A terrible pang of fear tore through two hearts, and they were afraid to look at each other, their hands frozen on the reins, their breathing arrested. Sir John Wrangwysh, who had escorted the procession from York, remained before the King and Queen, unnoticed, with his hat in his hand for several minutes before they turned their stricken gaze on to him. Quickly and with pity for their vulnerability he answered their unspoken question.

'My lord the Prince has been travelling by chariot. Here he is.' And the clumsy vehicle, gay with new coats of red and gold paint, rolled to a halt opposite the three horses. After a moment the door was opened and a slight figure descended, leaning on the proffered arm of his groom Metcalfe. He was not very steady on his feet, and kept hold of his prop as he found his balance and looked up at his parents. His soft fair hair whipped across his cheeks under the scarlet cap, but the wind brought no colour to his complexion. It was quite grey, and there were green stains beneath his eyes. With a conscious effort he drew himself erect and walked forward alone to the head of the King's horse. There he took off his cap and knelt carefully on one knee among the stones at the roadside.

Richard moved at last, stretching out a hand which trembled slightly towards the kneeling boy. Edward clasped it and would have kissed it but he was raised and pulled almost roughly to his father's side. Wanting to embrace him, unable to do so without dismounting, Richard was stiffly still for an instant while he blinked away the tears which would be excused by the wind; then he disengaged his hand and pressed it on the boy's head. Recalled to duty, Edward repeated his obeisance to his mother.

Dry-eyed with dread, she yet had the strength to whisper as he rose, 'How is it with you, Ned?' As the first words broke the web of silence the watchers, on foot or mounted, fidgeted and remembered themselves, and began their own reunions, so that only Richard and Anne heard his answer.

'Tired, madame, that's all, I regret I'm not such an experienced traveller as you and my lord fa— . . . the King.' He smiled sidelong at his father, and the smile was full of courageous pride. They could not help but smile back, at him and at each other, and the minutes of anxiety were deliberately submerged in the joy of the meeting.

It was in the evening, after supper in their private solar, that they learned why they had been kept waiting so long outside Pomfret. Edward had been sent early to bed, despite brave protests of perfect recovery that almost reached the point of defying his father's authority. After a public day Richard and Anne were closeted with a few intimates, mostly from their Middleham days, and among them was Katherine van Soeters. Unlike her young brother John, she had not thrust herself forward to greet her father and adopted mother, but she had been none the less affectionately welcomed. And she had something to explain to them which now overcame her reticence.

Kneeling at Anne's side she said softly, 'I could tell how distressed you were when you first saw Lord Edward today. He was not really ill, you know.' Anne touched Richard's arm to draw his attention, and Katherine continued, 'He has been much better these past few weeks, but they thought it was still too far for him to ride. Oh, he hated the idea of a chariot, but he had to obey. Maybe it was the excitement of meeting you again that brought it on ...' She blushed a little, and they nodded to urge her on. 'He was sick from the travelling after leaving Tadcaster, and we had to stop at a house on the road to clean him up and change his clothes.' Such a common malady! And one from which Anne herself had suffered since childhood. Seeing their glad relief, Katherine dropped her voice even lower. 'Please don't let my lord know that I told you. He was so ashamed – and he would be very angry with me.'

They reassured her, and then Anne called for a cushion to be brought, so they could hear from her what had passed in Wensleydale since their departure – things which were at once too trivial and too important to be mentioned in despatches.

Among the many matters that encumbered the mind of the new King, Katherine too had her place, as Anne discovered one night on retiring. Richard remarked thoughtfully, 'Kate has grown since April.' She certainly had grown in some directions, and he had noticed with appreciation that the developing curves of her body would soon possess something of her mother's voluptuousness. Marja had haunted him a little here at Pomfret, where she had lived and died, and in contemplating the copper locks of his son, the gentle femininity of his daughter, he remembered, with melancholy gratitude, what she had done for him. He must repay her, now that he had the means, although he knew better than to put it thus to Anne, whose love for the children did not embrace the mother. 'It is time we did something about her future.'

'Richard, she is only twelve!'

'Yes, but I've seen wenches of sixteen not so mature as she is.' He grinned mockingly at his wife, who had never had any claim to opulence of figure. 'And I think I've found her a husband.'

'She's far too young! And I'm sure her ambition is to take holy orders ... Who is he?'

'Will Herbert.'

'The Earl of Huntingdon?' He was with them at Pomfret, a man a little younger than Anne, not conspicuous in a crowd, but a faithful supporter of the Yorkist régime since assuming offices in Wales resigned to him by Richard after Tewkesbury.

'Yes. He needs a wife. And by the way he was looking at

Kate today he would not require much urging to take her.'

'But you wouldn't—'

'I wouldn't force her. Of course not. And I haven't broached the matter to him yet. If he is agreeable, she must be given the choice, and then the chance to know him better.'

'Would that mean her leaving Middleham?'

'That she must do soon. And you would be pleased to have her with you, wouldn't you?'

'Yes, I have missed her. But Edward . . .'

'He is surrounded by people that love and care for him, and will be at Sheriff Hutton. And he's reaching an age when men must rule him, not women. It's time Kate began to think of her own life. Oh, she is very pious, but don't you think she is too fond of people to give them all up for God? She should lavish that care on her own children, instead of those of others.' Anne allowed herself to be persuaded. They agreed that Richard would speak to Huntingdon and should he consent, Anne would break the news to Katherine. In any case, the marriage would not take place until after the girl's thirteenth birthday next year.

Later, while Richard slept, Anne's thoughts returned to a passing observation he had made about their son's growing out of the need for women's care. If this were so, what further role did she play in his life? And was it so? She had no doubt of her need for him – he and Richard were thirds of her self, as essential to her wholeness as limbs – but did he really not need her? Then she remembered the Duchess of York, who had surrendered her sons to the guardianship of the Earl of Warwick when still small boys. Yet she could hardly be said to count for nothing in their adult lives. Anne had heard tell how even her fearless son King Edward cowered before her rages. And Richard had gone to stay with her while pondering on his momentous dilemma of whether to take the throne from his nephew. The Duchess possessed great strength of character, but unlike Queen Margaret with her smothering devotion to her only son, her influence over her children was surely for the good. Anne tried to imagine how Ned would come to her for moral support, for the unspoken comfort which only a woman could give, and she could not do it. She could make no picture in her mind of herself, old and stately, and Edward a man.

Beside her Richard sighed and stirred. Since leaving Middleham he had not been the quiet sleeper of their years in Yorkshire. And fear of the future once more rose through her meditations and told her it was foolish to look ahead. She was in the county that was her home, where she was accepted and perhaps even held in affection; she was with her husband and her son and their friends, and soon they would be entering York for a ceremony which would be the climax of Richard's, and therefore of her own, life. It was more than foolish, it was insane, to conjure clouds into such a cloudless sky.

And almost cloudless was the late summer day as their great cavalcade halted outside the city to be received by the Mayor and Aldermen and other dignitaries, resplendent in scarlet and red. The formality of the occasion was tempered by the broad smiles on many a face, and the real warmth beneath the conventional words of the speeches. From a distance the resonance of bells wafted fitfully between the cheers of the people, but as the royal party passed through the black shadow of the barbican and flashed into the sunlight of Micklegate the peals from every belfry in the sixty churches of the city drowned the human noises and made the air quiver. The shouting, the bells, the narrow street packed with excited humanity – these were the very things which had beaten Anne into misery two months ago at the coronation, which she had always hated from the depths of her shy and private soul.

Yet now what was happening to her? Instead of being crushed beneath the tumult she was borne up by it, filled not with fear but with exultation. Her eyes were sharpened and not dimmed, and she noticed tiny details that before she had been too afraid to see – a stout housewife in tears as she waved a home-embroidered pennon with a white boar on it, a gaping hole in the shoulder of a blue velvet gown where a too-hastily stitched seam had given way, a row of rosy children's faces at an upper window with mouths as wide as fledglings in the nest, while their hands pointed and waved frantically. She followed the line of their gazes and found that this welcome was not only for the King and Queen and Prince of Wales. John Wrangwysh was laughing back at the children and blowing kisses – of course, the Wrangwysh family lived in Micklegate, and those must be his nephews and nieces. Unusual to see the sombre John laughing . . . and she returned to her own family, Edward riding a piebald pony between her and Richard, and their sallow faces too were lit with smiles of pure pleasure.

They were, the three of them, all lonely people, too absorbed in the struggle to keep hold of life and duty for the easy contacts and exchanges of casual friendship. Away from the tight circle of devoted followers who had learned to love them through the years they were bereft, as solitary as a ship cast on a rock in the empty ocean. But the warm-hearted people of York, for long the beneficiaries of Richard's good works, had recognised in them his good will and had gone more than half way in returning his affection to him and his family in the hour of their triumph. And surrounded by this demonstration, so generous and frank, the walls of their loneliness were breached for a short time and they were not separate any more.

The idea of a ceremony to show his gratitude to York, which Richard had conceived at Warwick and gestated at Pomfret, was expounded to his councillors the following day. Edward, created Prince of Wales and Earl of Chester officially a week since, would be solemnly invested with his titles in York Minster; the splendour of the occasion should be Richard's thanks to the citizens who had always supported him so loyally and now had received him so royally. London, because it was the capital, had had its coronation. York, because he loved it, should have this unique triumph.

In the interim, the city continued to entertain the King and his train with exhausting inventiveness, and for the first and only time of her life Anne enjoyed it all. On the day before the investiture there was a special performance of the Creed Play by the Corpus Christi Guild in the Guildhall. As many as possible of the royal party were crammed into the building, but at the front on a chair piled with cushions to give him a good view was the Prince of Wales with his tutor Master Bernall beside him. Tomorrow he would be the central figure of the great ritual; today, enthralled by the play, he had forgotten his reserve and his precocious dignity, leaning forward with flushed cheeks and wide eyes, one foot kicking happily at a leg of the chair. He too was enjoying himself. But despite his apparent recovery from the travel-sickness, Anne worried a little about his ability to endure such a long and heavy day. Richard had discounted her barely expressed fears and said that Ned was quite strong enough.

'Besides,' he added, 'he's becoming a great stoic. He would rather die on his feet, I believe, than admit fatigue.' Because that was rather what she feared, she said no more; Edward was certainly his father's son in that respect.

And indeed he played his part perfectly. It was the Feast of the Blessed Virgin, a morning soft with mist and sharp with the imminence of autumn, and when he was crowned with a golden wreath and presented with a golden rod of office, the sun slid gently through the ancient stained glass of the Minster and touched the wreath and the fair hair beneath with radiance. As he stood small and upright in the shaft of light among the soaring lines of pillars, it seemed to shine through him, making of him an insubstantial creature hardly of the earth at all. Watching him, Anne was stabbed with a love and terror so great that the ground seemed to dissolve beneath her feet. She half expected to see him ascending that ladder of sunshine, caught out of her sight and up into heaven as Galahad had been of old. And then the sun faded, Edward put up a hand to adjust his chaplet, and the momentary panic was gone. Stealing a glance at Richard, she saw that his face was full of happy pride, and as the ceremony continued she regained the sense of security which had come to her as they rode under Micklegate Bar. Nothing could harm her family here in York.

The Prince of Wales knelt before his father the King to receive the accolade; as the sword smote gently on his shoulders he closed his eyes, the better to concentrate on the dedication of himself to the service of his sovereign and his God. He was, thought Anne, taking this as seriously as Richard had taken his coronation, but whereas in Westminster Abbey she had been left outside the consecration, here in York Minster she was part of it.

Such pageantry had surely never been seen before within the ancient walls of York. As the procession emerged from the great west door of the Minster, a forest of banners and pennants unfurled and flaunted beneath the misty sun. Their tinctures and devices were reflected in the coats of the heralds, and the livery of the men-at-arms who held back the admiring and ecstatic crowd. Fresh exclamations greeted each group which passed and rose to a roar as three royal standards, leopards and lilies beaten in pure gold, preceded the King and Queen, crowned, and the Prince of Wales. Richard was wearing the long gown of purple cloth-of-gold which was Anne's coronation gift, embroidered with insignias of the Garter and the white rose of the House of York. Anne's robe was deep blue and edged with white ermine, her pale hair flowing to her waist as was permitted only to virgins and to queens. Between them their son, still bearing his rod of authority, was in crimson velvet, for the red dragon of his principality, and his head was held very high.

As they walked between the tight-packed ranks of citizens they turned from side to side, smiling, and it seemed to each member of the crowd that the smile was for themselves. This, after all, was their King, as no king had been before since the Roman emperor Constantine was proclaimed there, a thousand years before. They had known him and his Queen since they were children, riding in to spend Christmas with the monks in Lendel Priory, joining their merrymaking at Corpus Christi, making friends among them, listening to their grievances and settling their disputes, great and small. Why, the frail Prince Edward, who was really more of York than of Wales, had been born and bred in their county and would, it was promised, take over his father's responsibility for the North Country when he was grown to manhood in the castle of Sheriff Hutton. They had acclaimed other men in the past, faintly and loudly, and would in the future, but none with such full throats and glad hearts.

Young Edward's immaculate bearing during his installation was not without its price. In a disturbing echo of his mother's collapse after her coronation he developed a temperature the next day and had to be kept in bed. It was not serious – no more than a nervous reaction, said the physician – and two days later he was back to normal. But it cast something of a shadow over their hitherto joyous sojourn.

The merrymaking went on, yet Anne began to notice small signs that Richard was no longer fully at ease: he took to pacing at night when they retired to their chamber, and to twisting his signet ring as he had done in former times of stress. The truth was that Richard's puritanical conscience was being pricked by too much happiness. Now that he had given his most loyal subjects the handsome thanks they deserved, he could find less and less justification for remaining relaxed in their hospitable company. His unpredictable capital, which would, he felt instinctively, never give him the love that was his in York, had lacked him for too long. Rumours of unrest in the south and east came to him with the regular posts who plied, by the system he and King Edward had set up during the Scots war, between London and the north. And he was the very antithesis of his brother, whose capacity for relaxing and enjoying himself had sometimes had serious effects, and once nearly lost him his throne.

Recognising in him this force which would always drive him on and make life uncomfortable for those who lived with him, Anne knew that their time together as a family was limited. He would return to London, and Edward must go, first back to Middleham to complete his book education with Master Bernall, then to Sheriff Hutton to join his cousins the Earls of Lincoln and Warwick. And Anne, as before, would be rent in two. When at last Richard spoke of it, he had already perceived and considered her dilemma.

'It will be a hard parting from Ned when we leave York,' he said. 'I wonder if perhaps you should go with him.'

'To Middleham . . . ' Her voice was full of longing.

'Yes. I know you've been wanting to go back. To make sure that Dick is not causing chaos there.' Lord Richard Fitzhugh, Steward of Middleham Castle, was a highly efficient administrator.

'If I could . . . just for a while . . . to see that Ned has settled down again. But then . . . ' The other horn of the dilemma presented itself, 'I should be with you. They will think it strange that the Queen is not with the King.'

'Let them,' said Richard tersely. 'London is not all England.' That he did not immediately agree that she should be with him, because he needed her, unreasonably hurt her. 'Go with Ned. Rest for a while in Wensleydale. But I make one condition.' Anne braced herself, but Richard smiled. 'You must be back in London for Christmas. I can only do without

286

you for so long.'

So her mind was made up for her, and she had to be content. Their time in York raced to an end, and there was a last banquet, given for them by Master Thomas Wrangwysh in his house in Micklegate. Looking around the laden table, between the pheasants and hams and sucking pigs, everyone present was known to Anne, and most of them were dear to her. Acquaintances, relatives, friends, from the small eager Earl of Warwick to the genial corpulence of their host; and as the canary and burgundy went round with comfits and sugared almonds and figs, she knew they were gathered for the last time. Some, of course, would meet again, but in the nature of things this company of good will and trust was for now, and nevermore. The thought saddened her, but there was about it a sweetness too which would make a happy memory. When they were bidding farewell to Thomas Wrangwysh, Anne suddenly recalled the first time she had seen him.

'Do you know, Master Thomas,' she said, 'once you frightened me very much.'

'I, madame? God forbid! What did I do?'

'You came into the hall at Middleham to collect John for Christmas. I was very small, and you were very large.' Thomas shook his head slowly, seeing the little scrap she had been then, seeking reassurance, and how she stood now with her hand in her husband's, Queen of England to be sure, but still in need of the same reassurance.

'And are you still afeared of me, your grace?' he said, with the gentleness he reserved only for women.

'Now, I count you among my dearest friends,' Anne replied with unaccustomed frankness. The Yorkshireman seized her hand and kissed it with the freedom from obsequiousness which was characteristic of him.

'And you among mine,' he said. 'Your graces both know that you have no subject more ready to serve you, now and always.' They knew, as he kissed the King's hand also, that he spoke no more than plain truth.

Richard was the first to go, and then the contingent for Sheriff Hutton set out from Bootham Bar. Anne was praying for a dry road up into Wensleydale, since an excess of mud would hold up the wagons and force an overnight stop. But the weather had finished being kind to them, and it was two days after leaving a still-cheering York that the Queen and the Prince of Wales, damp and weary, were carried across the drawbridge of Middleham in a chariot which was leaking at every joint. The better was their homecoming. Hot baths and towels and braziers were brought before any formalities, and within an hour of their arrival mother and son were seated comfortably in dry clothes in Anne's solar with mugs of mulled ale at their elbows and bowls of steaming broth in their hands. Kat was weaving ecstatically between the legs of their chairs, and Katherine was in her old place on a cushion at Anne's feet. It was as if they had been caught in a shower riding from Nappa Hall, and that nothing had changed.

Very little had changed, except that the place was quieter without the lads who had gone to Sheriff Hutton. The same orderly routine prevailed as had been established for many years, and Anne fell back into her role of mistress of the castle with the ease of long practice. Lord Fitzhugh had grown up there as she had, so there was immediate accord between her and her steward on the management of the household. Edward did not take cold from his soaking, and although the equinoctial storms raged outside, and the swollen waterfalls thundered at Aysgarth up the dale, the community at Middleham suffered no more than draughts, and were content.

But the peace that Anne had found again so quickly was deceptive, and by the middle of October she learned that the elements were the true reflectors of the country's state. A letter from Richard at Lincoln announced baldly that armed insurrection had broken out in the south and west, and that its head and chief mover was the Duke of Buckingham. Anne's shock contained no surprise; she had sensed from the first that Buckingham was a false friend, a man of great pride who would care not what was under his feet as he climbed to the heights. But her anguish was greater at the beginning for his betrayal of Richard's love than for the physical danger in which her husband stood. For love it had been, a dazzled worshipping kind of love which since the death of King Edward had been idle for want of an object. His judgement of men was generally so sound, yet there was this one blind spot, where reason ceased to function and the heart was given without question. She had seen it in him at an early age with George of Clarence, but her awareness had never helped him. Now his crown and perhaps his life were at hazard because of it, and still she could do nothing. Her immediate instinct was to rush to his side, but that would be foolish. If he had to move fast a wife and her train would only hamper; as for his hurt, the damage was done and all he could do was hope to salve it with action, unless it was already too late.

She was waiting, wandering aimlessly around the inner bailey after early mass on a rare dry morning, when Katherine came to look for her.

'Madame, will you come? I think something has happened.' The girl's eyes were huge and afraid.

'Is it Ned?' The immediate question.

'No, not Ned. But please come.' Anne took her hand and followed. At the door of the solar Katherine stopped.

'I brought him his breakfast – as usual – scraps of chicken from last night, and you know how he loves chicken. I put the bowl beside his cushion and he was still asleep.' It was Kat she was talking about, so much was evident. 'But he has been sleeping more lately. So I tried to wake him, and he wouldn't move. And, madame, I think he's dead.' She stood aside then to let Anne into the room. Kat was lying on his green velvet cushion, the latest in a long line of beds which had been patiently replaced as his claws tore the previous one to shreds. He was curled into his attitude of sleep, a sliver of pink tongue visible, and he was quite still. Anne knelt and placed her hand gently on his furry flank. There was a faint warmth, but no movement.

'Yes, dearest, I fear he is.' At once a flood of tears spilled from Katherine's eyes, and she went into the older woman's arms. 'You mustn't grieve. He died peacefully in his sleep. And he was very old for a cat, almost twelve years old.' But she found she was crying too. Only for a cat, a pampered animal which had never given more than a condescending affection in exchange for a life of utter luxury. But Anne recalled with absolute clarity her first sight of Richard's wedding gift to her, the tiny bundle of startlingly white fluff which had gone as trustingly into her arms as Kate had just done. She had often wondered how Richard had divined her feeling for cats, and especially for small kittens, but Kat had remained, all through the years of their marriage, as a symbol of that secret understanding which had first flowered over a beloved wooden billet in this very castle.

A page was hesitating in the doorway, uncertain whether to intrude upon this scene of sorrow or to withdraw unnoticed. But Anne had seen him and, pressing Katherine's bowed head closer to her, she asked what he wanted.

'My lord Prince, madame, begs leave to wait upon your grace.' His childish face was red with embarrassment at having come upon the Queen herself weeping. And since he was as aware as anyone in the castle that the King was facing a rebellion away in the south, he had to restrain himself from begging her to tell him what had happened. Keeping her voice as steady as she was able, Anne said she would go to the Prince's apartments herself, in a few minutes. The page departed with thankful speed, and since he was a discreet child he did not tell more than his closest friend about how the Queen and Dame Katherine had been crying in each other's arms.

The Queen prepared to visit her son. It was customary for him to present himself, after his morning devotions and before his morning lessons, but today Anne did not want him in here. He would care little about the cat's death. He had always preferred dogs, and lately he had borne a particular resentment against Kat because of a fight in which the old sybarite had worsted Edward's new hound puppy, Arrow. Although the dog had ended up shivering and whining between his master's feet, with Kat arched and triumphant on the cushion, Arrow was the one who was banished from the Queen's solar on pain of whipping. Whether the whipping would be administered to boy or pup was not made plain, but Edward was an obedient child. He bore no malice against his mother for severity, because he knew well her dislike of dogs and the place Kat held in her affections; also if Arrow had been more than half-trained he would have stayed to heel and never provoked the conflict. But he could scarcely be blamed for not loving the cat, and Anne determined at once not to mention what had happened.

She sent for Lady Lovel and handed the still-sobbing Katherine over to her. Her brother was Lord Fitzhugh, and between them they would know what to do about the mourning girl and fitting obsequies for Kat. Outside her chamber she met more delay: a messenger, dark with the renewed rain, and at once Kat's death seemed to be a presage of disaster. But he wore no livery, and the seal on his letter was a merchant's mark. Thomas Wrangwysh sent word that he was that day setting forth with three hundred men to join the King's muster at Leicester. Anne silently blessed him; he would not have written if he had not guessed that any declaration of loyalty at such a time would cheer her.

In fact she was not long without news. Richard found time to scribble her a note, or dictate one to John Kendall, every few days. If he referred to Buckingham, it was as 'the great rebel' – never by name. A sizable army was rapidly assembled, and 'with good hopes' the King announced he was leading it to Coventry. There was no need for it to strike a blow. The foulness of the weather fought for King Richard instead. With the mobile assistance of local bands of loyalists, Buckingham's reluctant pressed forces melted away in the chaos caused by floods as he crossed the English border from Wales. His mighty menace collapsed as quickly as it had arisen, and he himself disappeared, no doubt a desperate fugitive. Anne ordered masses to be sung in the castle chapel and the collegiate church of Middleham, but her private prayers were not only of thanksgiving. She was praying that Buckingham would not be found alive. Only too well she remembered the effect on Richard of Hastings' treachery and execution, and he had meant less to him than Harry Stafford.

Nothing more came from him until into the second week of November, and then the courier was not a man-at-arms, but Frank Lovel. Knowing it must be serious, Anne received him alone in her solar after allowing him only the time to greet his wife and change his muddy garments. There was no need for ceremony between them.

'Buckingham is dead,' he said.

'How?'

'Beheaded. In Salisbury, on All Souls' Day.'

Anne suppressed a shudder. 'Tell me.'

'He had taken refuge with a servant, and in fitting fashion the servant betrayed him for the reward. A thousand pounds or lands worth a hundred a year. He was tried by a commission under the Vice-Constable and condemned as a traitor. There was no room for clemency.'

'No.' A silence fell. Lovel ducked his head to drink some of the broth they had brought him. Some dried mud had clotted a lock of his fair hair. 'Did Richard see him?'

'He would not. Buckingham asked for an audience ... no, I must speak truth, madame, he begged and pleaded for it. You would not have known him. They gave him some decent clothes to replace the rags he had escaped in, but all his pride was gone, broken.' She thought of the immaculate and supercilious nobleman who had kissed her hand at Windsor.

'Even so, he wanted to speak to the King.'

'Yes. Although what he hoped to say the saints alone know. He resigned himself in the end and made a good enough death.' Silence again, dragging. He finished his broth.

'And ... my husband?'

'He sent no letter.'

'He sent you instead.'

'No. I offered to come. Madame, he needs you with him.'

'Did he tell you?'

'There was no need for him to tell me. Often since we left York he has spoken of you and Lord Edward ... the Prince. Especially lately – when he has spoken at all.'

'Is he well, Frank?'

'In body, yes. But I think you should join him as soon as he returns to London.' Anne looked down at the hands clenched in her lap. It was her dilemma again, and it was insoluble. She could not be happy with Richard while Edward was in Yorkshire under anybody's care but her own; she could not be happy in Wensleydale while Richard was suffering apart from her. But in this case there was no decision to make. Lord Lovel was a high-ranking minister of the crown, and he would not have taken this long journey, at a time of crisis, had he not thought it very necessary. He knew Richard as well as any man alive, and if it was his opinion that Anne should go to her husband, then she would go. She had anyway promised to be in London for Christmas.

'You are right,' she said. 'I will arrange to leave as soon as may be.' Then she attempted to push her depression aside.

'But I have kept you too long from your wife, Frank. She has not said a word about you – no chattering like Meg about John – but I know she has missed you the more. I will see that you and Ann have your old chamber, for as long as you stay. And some music for us tonight, I hope?'

There was no rest; a little over two months after she had returned to Middleham, she left it again. Fitzhugh would stay, of course, as steward, and the Prince's household, but after the departure of the Queen's entourage the castle would be less populated than at any time in Anne's memory. She was taking Katherine with her. The girl had been pining since their pet died, spending longer than usual in the chapel with her beads, and coming out of her lassitude only for a furious argument with the chaplain about the soullessness of animals, which she fiercely denied. Anne had offered her a new kitten, but that was no consolation; Kat had been at Middleham longer than she had, he was part of the family, and no mere cat could replace him. So her foster-mother broached again the subject of the Earl of Huntingdon, who had agreed to accept the King's natural daughter as his wife, provided she was willing. And Anne was not yet sure whether she was. When the issue was first raised in York Katherine had said little except that she would consider it. Since then, nothing. She asked her point-blank, one evening after supper. After a moment Katherine said, 'I shall do as the King my father wishes.'

'And what of your wishes, Kate? Your father has left the decision to you.'

'What would he do with me if I refused?'

'I think,' said Anne gently, 'he would look for another husband more to your taste. It would disappoint him, of course.'

'He would not let me ... I had thought of entering St Clement's Convent in York.' It was as Anne had suspected, and it put her in a quandary. She saw herself at Katherine's age, or a little older, and felt the echo of that yearning for peace and order, for obedience and discipline, which had been so strong in her too, and had been brutally crushed by a forced marriage. Crushed but not destroyed. Only after a second marriage to a man she loved had she realised that another motive than piety lay behind the desire to become a nun, and that was the instinct to run away and hide from responsibility. How much of that was there in this earnest retiring girl?

On an impulse she said, 'That was my ambition, once.' And she found herself telling Katherine what she had told no one, not even Richard. The tranquil summer in the Norman convent, her friendship with Sœur Madeleine, the night when she had learned of her impending betrothal and attempted to defy her father. She told her too, as clearly as she could remember it, what Sœur Madeleine had said: 'Don't be proud, and think that only you know what is right. Your mind may change. And if God needs you, He will not let you escape.'

Katherine gazed at her foster-mother, the ready tears coming to her eyes. 'I never knew how you suffered,' she murmured.

Thanking God that she never really would know, Anne replied, 'But, you see, if my prayers had been answered as I wished then, I would not have married your father, nor become Ned's mother. There are more ways than one of serving God; in the world as well as out of it.' The girl nodded slowly, considering. 'So, Kate, if you will come to London with me, as your father asks, we shall see what happens. If in the end you find you cannot marry, that it is against your conscience and your reason as well as your heart, I think he will not force you.'

She gained her consent, and it was both of them this time who said their farewells to Edward in the Queen's apartments. He had recently thrown off a cold, but a nagging cough had persisted, and Anne gave way to her maternal instincts in making him promise to practise no outdoor pursuits until it had disappeared.

'You will be moving to Sheriff Hutton as soon as spring comes, and for that you'll need all your health.' Katherine showed no such restraint, and wept profusely as she embraced him. Edward accepted her demonstration patiently, for he was fond of her. When she had done he took her hand and regarded her seriously.

'Kate,' he said, 'it would be best, I think, if you married Lord Huntingdon. He's a good man, and my father the King trusts him. And he likes you.' Surprised, Anne asked how he knew.

'Because of the way he looked at her,' he answered, as if it was a stupid question. Katherine was struck quite dumb by the boy's perspicacity, and to hide her suddenly scarlet cheeks she embraced him again. It had evidently not occurred to her that any man might look at her in that kind of way. Anne recalled that Richard had said much the same to her at Pomfret, and wondered if her son's revelation would help or hinder his scheme.

There was the usual formal parting by the gatehouse: Edward and his tutor, Lord Fitzhugh and all the officers of the castle assembled in force. Diana's whelp Arrow was sitting quietly beside his master, and to please her son Anne forced herself to stoop and pat the hound's head. Arrow took no notice, but Edward's reaction was unexpected. He flung his arms round his mother and held her against him in a convulsive grip. She heard the sob in his voice as he whispered close to her ear, 'Take care of Kate, Mother, and come back soon.' Then he released her and took his place by Master Bernall again, hanging his head as though ashamed of his loss of control. Anne mounted, and as she turned the steep corner into the road opposite the market cross she looked back: Edward was coughing, and trying not to; Master Bernall's hand was on his shoulder. Never yet had she managed to leave Middleham without crying, and today was no exception.

3

THE AXE FALLS

She reached London only shortly after Richard, who had come in from the south. A mopping-up of the last rebels had turned into a royal progress as the people expressed their relief at the quick suppression of further fighting. A handful of the ringleaders besides Buckingham had been executed, the rest given light punishment or pardoned. But the King was less untouched by the revolt than the capital and the country appeared to be. His face was more of a mask and his lips pressed more tightly together than before. The wall of reserve was higher, and even for Anne harder to breach. Once again she was depressed with a feeling of impotence. Despite Frank Lovel's assurance, she doubted whether her presence or absence meant very much to her husband.

Even so, he was determined to keep a lavish Christmas. Part of the business of ruling, as he had learned from his brother and from his visit to the court of Burgundy in his youth, was a generous display of pomp and opulence. There were many guests to be received and entertained, precedence and etiquette to be observed, no room for the wild and slightly silly festivities that had characterised Yuletide in Yorkshire. But among the watching and surely critical new court there were old and trusted friends. Their very familiarity made Edward's absence the more noticeable, at this time when the family had so often been together. Richard was missing his son badly, for he continuously asked questions about him when alone with Anne. He was one of the few topics on which they still talked with any freedom.

Another mutual interest showed promising development over the twelve days of Christmas. Anne had told her husband of Katherine's reluctance to leave Middleham, and he had shown her special kindness. He had also made sure that

William Huntingdon was often of the same company, and in this he had the active connivance of the Earl himself. It was true, as the Prince of Wales had remarked so acutely, that he was smitten with the girl. Virtually twice her age and a widower, his eyes followed her with schoolboy enthusiasm, and she was no longer in ignorance of it. A stranger to coquetry, she would not meet his eyes and became tongue-tied when he spoke to her. On the other hand, among the daunting spaces and luxuries of Westminster Palace, and the young courtiers left over from King Edward's time who eyed her bosom under its high neckline and speculated only just out of hearing on who her mother had been, he had at least the advantage of being an acquaintance. So she allowed him to escort her, to sit by her at mealtimes and entertainments and to dance with her, but gave him no further encouragement.

In fact she was suffering an acute attack of homesickness, although she kept her secret so well that even Anne did not find out until the evening of Childermas, when Katherine was helping to dress her and for once could not restrain her tears. Since she was herself particularly reminded of her son on this feast it did not take long to divine the girl's malaise. But when she asked to be excused from the night's banquet and dancing, Anne hardened her heart and told her she must attend. Moping in a darkened room would not help her, while a few goblets of wine probably would.

The wine that evening was especially good, a canary from King Edward's cellars that his widow had not succeeded in rifling. Anne had had a quiet word with Lord Huntingdon before the meal began, but it was not until the trestles were removed and the dancing commenced that she saw how successful he had been. The King and Queen led the first dance and afterwards there was much socialising to be done. The welfare of her foster-daughter had slipped from Anne's mind until Richard touched her arm and nodded towards the couples who were treading the intricate figures of a basse dance. Katherine was partnered by Huntingdon. Her dark hair flowed straight and shining down her back under a red cap. Her gown was also of crimson velvet, trimmed with white fur round the deep V of the neck, over a white satin kirtle. It was a present from her father which she had not worn before.

Richard had chosen the colour, and to Anne's demur that perhaps she was too young for it he had said decisively, 'I think not.' Now she saw that he was right. The Katherine who was gazing boldly into her partner's eyes with a slight smile on her parted lips, whose hand slid into his clasp with evident delight in the contact, was no child. She had always danced well, when obliged to do so, but never with this conscious pride in her own movements. Anne could hardly credit her own eyes, but Richard was smiling nostalgically. Katherine had inherited her mother's sensual nature, and tonight it had awakened. He remembered the quick fire that had flashed between him and Marja on their first meeting in Flanders, and now he saw the same mysterious alchemy at work between their daughter and his friend. Watching his wife's puzzled expression, he thought tenderly that she had been as mistaken about Katherine's vocation for chastity as about her own.

It was the canary which had accomplished the transformation. Still a little drunk, Katherine claimed the task of brushing the Queen's hair before bed so she could talk to her. Her reflection in the real glass mirror showed pink cheeks and wine-bright eyes.

'It was so strange, madame,' she whispered feverishly, and Anne tried not to flinch as her trembling hands wielded the brush with less than her usual care. 'I didn't mind his looking at me . . . I liked it. And I wanted him to . . . to touch me.' The brush was still and her gaze met Anne's in the looking-glass, uncertain and yet exhilarated. 'Should I be ashamed? I don't feel wicked. But perhaps I should confess it tomorrow. Do you think I should?' Anne turned and put her hands on the young shoulders, quivering under the first experience of eroticism.

'Did Lord Huntingdon share these feelings?'

'Oh, yes. It was . . . both of us,' Katherine said lamely. 'He kissed my cheek when he said goodnight.'

'In that case, my dear, go and sleep, if you can. In the morning, if you still don't believe you are wicked, then there will be no need for confession.'

'Truly, madame?'

'Truly, Kate. After all, Lord Huntingdon has asked to marry you. There can be nothing sinful in wishing to be his wife.' Katherine said no more, completed her task none so ill, and went to bed. Waiting for Richard to come to her, Anne rejoiced that at least his daughter would not enter into marriage blindfold, as she herself had done.

With morning and sobriety Katherine became shy again, shyer than before for a while, until she found that her suitor did not think any the less of her for her display of the night of Childermas, which was rather hazy in her own mind. But she did not forget what she had learned about herself, and she wore her crimson gown several more times, until Twelfth Night put an end to the festivities. And the Earl of Huntingdon had not yet played his trump card, which he did not even realise he held. It was quite by accident, in one of the conversations which were beginning to flower between them, that he mentioned his daughter. Katherine's eyes kindled. She knew that his first wife Mary had been Elizabeth Woodville's sister, and that she had died several years since, but the information had not come from Huntingdon, and he had certainly not talked of any children.

'You have a daughter?' she asked eagerly.

'Yes. Elizabeth.' The Earl spoke defensively; it occurred to him that there might be jealousy, with so few years between the two girls.

'How old is she?'

'I think – just past her ninth birthday.'

'And she has no mother.'

'No. My wife died when Bess was still small.' He could talk of Mary Woodville without emotion, since she had never aroused very much. It was partly for that reason that he had not brought her into his exchanges with Katherine; the other reason was delicacy. And the same delicacy could not yet understand her interest in his only child, whom he scarcely ever saw.

'Just like my mother,' breathed Katherine.

They were interrupted then, but Katherine lost little time in returning to the subject when they were next together.

'Where is your daughter now?' she asked without preamble.

'In Wales, living on one of my manors.'

'Will she be coming to London soon?'

'There are no plans for it,' Huntingdon said vaguely. Encouraged as he was to have her questioning him with such avidity, he still did not catch her drift.

'How she must miss you!' That the Earl doubted; he was awkward in the company of little girls, until of course they became as nubile as the one sitting beside him at dinner, and he and Elizabeth had never found much to say to each other on his rare visits. Katherine cut up a piece of roast beef thoughtfully, and then said with diffidence, 'Would you perhaps be able to arrange for her to come here? Just for a little time? I am sure she would be pleased to see you again. And . . . I should like to meet her.' It was the first request she had ever made of him, and he was touched. He was beginning to realise that her concern for his child was that of one motherless daughter for another.

And of course she had been reared in an unusual ménage: the Duke of Gloucester had lived for much of his married life in only one of his castles, together with his entire family – wife, son, mother-in-law, and illegitimate children. Huntingdon supposed that the common practice of offspring living separately from their parents must be as odd to her as her upbringing was to him. She was looking down at her platter, pushing a slice of bread nervously through the gravy, trying to say something else.

'She might be . . . If I were to marry you,' she said at last, very low, hardly audible above the chatter of the rest of the table, 'she would be my daughter too.'

Before January was out Elizabeth Herbert arrived in London, a pretty child who had inherited her Woodville mother's gilt-fair hair. When Katherine first called on her she was also a tired and frightened child, uprooted from her secluded Border valley at a few days' notice and transported to the greatest and busiest city in the land. She could not have gone more directly to Katherine's heart. What the elder girl had experienced so recently herself was to be especially pitied in the younger. And she set to work to put Elizabeth, who was at first bewildered by her attentions, at her ease in these new surroundings. No one had thought to let Huntingdon's daughter know that he was thinking of marrying Dame Katherine Plantagenet, so she tended to shy away from this unaccustomed kindness and affection. It was to win her over that Katherine confided to her before anyone else the decision she had reached, not realising until the statement was made that she had actually decided.

Richard and Anne were overjoyed, and among the pressing business of his first Parliament the King made the time to draw up a covenant ensuring a generous portion for the Countess of Huntingdon.

Anne hardly saw Richard, who was working harder than ever to push as much as possible of his reforming legislation through Parliament before the end of the session. He was straining every nerve in the process, as if everything must be accomplished at one stroke, as if he had no time to take things at an easier pace. Once she ventured to ask him what the hurry was, and his frown deepened before he answered simply that there was so much to be done. What he had been able to do for the citizens of York in a small way, he was attempting to spread over the whole country by parliamentary act.

More unexpectedly he achieved another of his objects, only days after the members of lords and commons had dispersed. Elizabeth Woodville, snug in sanctuary in Westminster Abbey with her daughters since Richard had turned the tables on her the previous summer, capitulated. In return for the King's promise that he would maintain and care for his nieces, and a bare competency for herself, she gave up the five former princesses into his keeping, a gesture of trust which London found difficult to believe. It was no secret that bad blood had existed between King Edward's widow and youngest brother for many years, and during his *coup d'état* two of the very few heads to fall had been those of her own brother and second son by her first marriage, Rivers and Grey. And what of her two bastard boys by Edward in their Tower lodgings? There was never a shortage of rumour-spreaders in London, whether from malice or idleness.

But it was not only to the scandal-mongers that Elizabeth's surrender was a mystery. Even in royal circles it was not known how the King had brought about such a change of heart. On the surface he had done nothing; neither blackmail, bribes nor threats had been used. It was suspected that the crux of the matter must lie with the nephews that Richard had supplanted. But they had not been mentioned officially for months. Aware that the King was not entirely easy in his conscience about the way he had assumed power, his friends did not speak of them in his presence. It was not a subject on which Anne herself felt safe to approach her husband, but she took comfort from the fact that Robert Brakenbury, Constable of the Tower and a friend from their Yorkshire days, still frequented their intimate gatherings with no sign of uneasiness. The boys were directly in his charge, and he was surely too honest a man to have connived at any foul play and continued to brazen it out at court. She thought of questioning him, but that would have been going behind Richard's back.

At length, on the day when in a public ceremony the King swore to abide by the terms set forth in his declaration concerning Elizabeth and her daughters, she resolved to speak. As usual he was late to bed, but she stayed awake until he came. It was extremely seldom that he retired to his own chamber and did not sleep with his wife for the few hours he allowed himself to rest. After some remark about the ceremony it was easy to ask where Elizabeth and Edward's five daughters would be living after they left sanctuary.

'Here in the palace, I expect,' Richard answered readily enough, 'if their mother is agreeable. We shall have left London by the time they take up residence, but when we return they will, with your permission, be attached to your household. Later, perhaps, Sheriff Hutton, for the younger ones at any rate.'

'And will their brothers join them?'

He looked up warily, but after a moment he said, 'In Yorkshire, maybe. Not at Westminster.' She knew by his defensiveness that she was on dangerous ground, but she must go on.

'I'm sure they would be glad to mix with other children again. They must have been lonely, these past months.'

'They have been given every consideration,' Richard said sharply.

'Of course. But they are only boys. And there cannot be much space for sports and recreation . . . in the Tower.' Now he stood up from where he was sitting on the bed and faced her – at bay, she thought.

'Are you implying that I have not done my duty by my

nephews?'

'No, dear heart, how could I doubt that?' She held out a hand to him, placatingly, but he drew away.

'Then why the inquisition, Anne?'

Subtlety of speech had never been her strong point, and she abandoned it. 'So little has been heard of them since ... since you became King. I believe that some fear all is not well with them.'

'And do you fear it too?'

'I don't know. But I do know that if harm has, or did, come to them it would not be through you.'

'No, not through me,' Richard agreed emphatically, and fell silent. Then he said coldly, 'And if ... harm, as you put it, had come to these boys who have been in my care, and in my power, for the past nine months, do you believe that their mother would therefore have consented to place her daughters also in my sole care and power?' It was the question which all London was asking vainly, which all England and perhaps all Europe would soon be seeking fruitlessly to answer. Anne could only shake her head wordlessly, and then wait for so long that she wondered if the question would remain rhetorical.

At length he said, with apparent inconsequence, 'Henry Tydder has sworn a sacred oath to take Elizabeth Plantagenet to wife—'

'—to which the Queen – Dame Elizabeth I mean – has agreed.'

'She had. Now she has thought better of it. Hence her consent to place her daughters at my disposal instead of that of the Tydder.'

'But why?'

Richard laughed bitterly. 'Isn't it obvious? Dame Elizabeth was persuaded that her sons were dead. She knows now that they are not.'

He began to pace the room, while Anne tried to fit together the pieces of the conundrum. What struck most forcibly to her mother's heart was the cruelty of the deception practised on the ex-queen. A pang of the anguish which she must surely have felt on receiving such terrible tidings touched Anne, and she murmured, 'She must have been overwhelmed with joy when she found the tale was untrue.'

'No more than a chess-queen is overwhelmed on finding that two pawns she thought lost to her game are still on the board and not far from being crowned.' He saw how he had shocked his wife, and said less cynically, 'She is not a woman of sentiment, Anne. Ambition is her ruling spirit, still, although all may seem lost. I know that, and have made her no concessions. Dame Elizabeth has called a truce, but it is an armed truce.'

'And her sons?'

His face closed again. 'That is my concern,' he said shortly, and went purposefully to trim a smoky candle. At last he came back to sit beside her.

'You will of course speak to no one of this, Anne?'

No, she would speak to no one – as he would not have spoken to her if she had not forced it from him. He kissed the palms of her hands, carefully, while she strove to suppress her hurt that it took so much to wring a confidence out of him. Then as her husband's arms closed round her another thought arose: how little was her isolation beside that of the two solitary boys in their comfortable imprisonment, whose mother wanted them only for what they could gain for her. Two little pawns; and two queens, herself one of them. Richard was kissing her again, less carefully. Her king at least was still in the game, she told herself confusedly, and he had won the last move. He was not the king to let himself be mated; not as long as his consort was watching over him. She closed her eyes and gave herself up to love.

They were on the road again. March was heralding spring, and having salved his conscience with three fruitful months' stay in London, the King was itching to be away from it. The eventual goal was Nottingham, a strategic point in the very centre of the kingdom from which to observe any attempt at invasion by Henry Tydder. On the way, however, the royal couple would visit Cambridge; Richard had been to Oxford the previous summer and did not wish to antagonise the touchy schoolmen of the younger university. Tact was not the only reason: for one thing, there was the building of King's College Chapel, which he had endowed, to oversee; for another, the atmosphere of ancient learning was very congenial, especially after the brash modernity of London.

They came there when crocuses and the first daffodils were brightening the grass by the River Cam, under the biting wind that swept across the fens from the North Sea. It was colder than Wensleydale in winter, Anne declared, shivering in their college lodgings while the smoke from the sea-coal fire blew back down the chimney. But the warmth of their reception made up for the chilly wind. The House of York had been generous to the University of Cambridge: Edward IV had made possible the resumption of work on the chapel of King's College, and his queen had founded a college. Poor Henry VI had done the same thing, but his money had run out when it was half-constructed. Picking her way through the builders' débris surrounding the chapel, Anne spared a thought for the man who had been her father-in-law, and who, it was said, was now being prayed to as a saint in some parts of the country. Saint or no, he had been a good man, that was sure, although a failure in the eyes of the world. And like her husband and herself, he would have been at home in this island of scholarship among the East Anglian marshes. If his college was ever completed, she hoped that it would still bear his name.

Its chapel, at any rate, was already roofed. The master mason, John Wolrich, appeared for his presentation to the King and Queen surrounded by an entourage of his own. Richard received him with due respect, and Anne saw that the mask of worry he wore in London was beginning to animate. Architecture had been an absorbing interest of his ever since he owned any property to improve. He loved to turn the dark draughty strongholds which had been constructed for defence into comfortable residences, with wall fireplaces and, above all, large windows.

'Why waste money on tallow and oil when the day will light the place for us?' he had said many times. He had even had his boar carved into the ceiling of a fine oriel window overlooking the Tees at Barnard Castle, so that posterity should know who had provided the splendid vista. So it was with particular delight that he learned that the east window was about to be glazed, and asked eagerly to see the cartoon. The side-chapels to right and left of the altar were already complete, glazed and vaulted. Richard stood in each, examining each boss and groin. In the second, he caught hold of Anne's hand and pressed it in a rare public gesture of affection.

'This is what will last,' he murmured, to himself perhaps, and she placed her other hand on the cool white stone of the wall. 'A chantry or a tower or a window – that's what I'd like to be remembered for. Like Julius Caesar's Tower in London. All the citizens know that, but how many could name one of his battles?' Anne always felt very close to him when he was borne up by one of his enthusiasms. And when they emerged from the hopeful shell and she looked up among the scaffolding at the buttresses and the pinnacles piercing that vivid sky, she was grateful that they had come here.

They lingered several days longer. A man in search of knowledge among those devoted to its pursuit, a lover of beauty in a city full of it, Richard was displaying in Cambridge that curious reverse side of a character which was also happy in the saddle, in constant purposeful movement in the open air. Anne found her husband restored to her almost as he had been before Hastings' messenger arrived at Middleham. There was business, always, to attend to, but he smiled more freely, and at night he slept soundly beside her. With regret they took their departure, Anne no less than her husband feeling the tug of the sequestered academic life, kin to her long-abandoned dream of the cloister. The daffodils beside the Cam bowed a farewell, as graceful and self-contained as the trained minds of the scholars. To be attached to nothing but learning and God might indeed be a simpler way to pass one's days. But she had chosen, years ago, or rather Richard had chosen for her. Ahead lay Nottingham, affairs of state, and an impending invasion by Henry Tydder.

They had been installed in the castle there, on its red rock high above the town, for nearly a month and there was no stirring from Brittany. Already the court was more of a reflection of Richard's character than the ready-made one he had inherited at Westminster: more work, less ostentation, and a great deal of music. There were other ways in which the austerity of Richard's régime was lightened, for he was well aware of the necessity to impress observers both English and foreign with shows of royal bounty. It was an unseasonably hot April that suggested an entertainment in Sherwood Forest for the benefit of a group of merchants from Ghent and Bruges, guests of the King at Nottingham while they discussed trade treaties between England and the Archduke Maximilian. First there would be a hunt, and then if the weather held, as it surely would, an alfresco meal with accompanying pageantry. As always, Anne declined the hunting, with the excuse that her foster-daughter was due to arrive from London, but she would join the party for the gentler pursuits after the kill. Katherine had been nursing little Elizabeth Herbert through a bout of measles, but now was happy to greet Anne again, accompanied by an unspotty Bess. Despite a long journey she waited only to despatch her charge to the nursery before preparing to set out for the forest with the Queen's entourage. Anne kept her at her side as they left the town; since Richard's elevation Katherine was perhaps her closest confidante. And there was one thing in particular that she wanted to learn from her, in the comparative privacy of their pacing mares.

'Have the Lady Elizabeth and her sisters come from sanctuary yet?'

Katherine thought she understood her anxiety: even if their mother was not permitted to come to court, the girls were quite old enough to have been primed as her instruments, and especially with the King absent they would have endless opportunity to stir trouble.

'Yes, madame, they are at the palace. There were wagons and wagons of their possessions – it took a whole morning to unload them. I don't think their living in sanctuary could have been so hard,' she added ingenuously.

'Indeed not,' said Anne a little tartly. 'It was said that a wall had to be broken down when they arrived there, to admit all the chattels that had been stolen from King Edward's apartments. Have you seen them?'

'The Lady Elizabeth sent for me – I don't know why.' To herself Anne reflected that perhaps it was a case of royal bastards making common cause, but she said nothing so unkind; however much she might have disapproved of Richard's mistress, she had certainly died too soon to inculcate any grandiose ambitions in her children. Not so Elizabeth Woodville.

'Was she proud?'

'A little proud, yes. But that was to be expected, wasn't it? She was kind too, and asked after your health, and my lord father's. And my brother John's. I didn't think she would be so ... grown. She is very tall and elegant, and although not beautiful she has ... something. I don't know. Not cold. Rather shy. As if she wanted one to help her.'

Well, Anne thought, if she had the skill to appeal to Kate's maternal instinct in their first meeting, this girl was formidable indeed. Unless it was genuine. She remembered Richard saying that the breaking off of her betrothal to the Dauphin, the winter before King Edward died, had been a terrible blow to her as well as to her father. Give her the benefit of the doubt. Perhaps she really was in need of friends.

'I think she's good,' concluded Katherine positively, 'although the Lady Cecily is prettier.'

They were out of the town now, approaching the eaves of the forest, and they turned to easier topics. Among them was a projected visit to Middleham, if all remained quiet for another month. The King was to superintend the fitting of his fleet at Scarborough, and it was hoped that on the way the royal parents would at last be able to escort their son from his birthplace to Sheriff Hutton. Katherine talked with animation of how she was longing to tell Ned that he had been right about the Earl of Huntingdon.

'He'll make a good king, won't he, madame, if he can see so easily into people's hearts?' With various reservations, Anne agreed. She had caught her foster-daughter's high spirits, abetted by the delicious freshness of the spring noon, the new grass fretted with the shadows of the half-fledged branches. The hollow thud of the mares' hoofs on the turf was balm to the hearing after the hard ring of city cobbles. She found herself humming the tune of a ballad of Robin Hood, in anticipation perhaps of the revelry to come, and Margaret Wrangwysh and then others of her ladies joined in with the words.

With singing they came to the clearing where the rendezvous was appointed. The huntsmen were there already, while servants bustled about the long trestle tables and camp fires and strained every nerve to set before the King and his guests an immaculate miracle of a dinner. Richard was apart beside an oak tree, his foot resting on an upthrust root, deep in conversation with one of the Flemings, not about the hunt but about wool. He broke off to greet his wife, and to summon Katherine for a kiss. There was a long scratch across his forehead and he explained laughing that a low branch had found out his lack of practice in hard riding.

'For the honour of England I had to keep up with our friends from Flanders,' he said, 'but you see it was not without punishment that I accomplished it.'

'His grace speaks with great modesty.' The merchant bowed, smiling. 'A lesser horseman would have been swept to the ground; I was witness to it.'

Richard, at his most relaxed, made a deprecatory gesture. If all his diplomacy could be conducted from horseback, his wife was thinking, the state need have no fear for the future. Out here beneath the trees, in his own setting as it were, he lost the over-careful striving for effect which he could not help under the critical eyes at Westminster Palace. The colour in his normally sallow cheeks was that of healthy physical exertion. With admirable promptitude the meal was announced, and Richard himself conducted his guest to the table, strolling across the glade with his wife and daughter on one side and the Fleming on the other.

When appetite had slackened its hold the promised masque of Robin Hood began. The townsfolk of Nottingham had been busy for several weeks, in guildhall and private house, fortified by much ale, to prepare their show. All clad correctly in Lincoln green, longbows in hand, they leapt with enthusiasm into action. To the foreign visitors it was no doubt mostly incomprehensible, but with the sun warming their backs and their host's wine warming their bellies they had no need of a translation, and roared and applauded with the rest. Being unfamiliar with the legends of the beloved English outlaw, they were probably ignorant of the climax which was to every English subject present a foregone conclusion. Sure enough, at length the band of very merry men congregated, discussed, and advanced *en masse* to the head of the table, where King Richard himself, most appropriately named, would be asked to forgive bold Robin, and no doubt reward him to boot.

Two horsemen cantered into the clearing and were greeted with a cheer, as a surprise addition to the pageant. The players took no notice and ranged themselves before the King, as one of the riders dismounted and began to push his way slowly through the milling greenery. With almost one accord they dropped to their knees, hands clasped in supplication. The newcomer remained standing for a moment, and then he too knelt. A familiar figure; far more so than the excited laughing faces of the masqueraders. And he was not laughing.

Fingers had closed on Anne's arm, and were gripping tighter and tighter until pain began to shrill through her nerves. She knew him too, as Richard had recognised him already. Metcalfe, Ned's groom, who with Peacocke hardly ever left his side. He had met their eyes only once and now, head bowed, proffered a sealed packet across the scrap-strewn table. It was unnecessary. The pain was not in her arm but everywhere, and the infernal echoing racket of the bird-song was rising inside her head to an unbearable shattering single scream. Somewhere, not near enough to affect her, were the soft wide frightened eyes of her foster-daughter and voices, but all that was real to her was that numbing, comforting grip on her arm and a continuous low groaning that counterpointed her own wordless keening.

There was no need for Metcalfe to speak; no need for the carefully penned letter from Lord Fitzhugh. Awed and shaken, court and commons present in that clearing of Sherwood Forest watched while their normally restrained King and Queen gave way to their grief. The axe which had been poised over the neck of their son, from the hour of his uncertain entry into the world, which they had half-expected to fall every day of his delicate life, had fallen, and their preparedness did nothing to allay the agony of it. The cowed band of merry men were packed off hastily back to Nottingham with their bows, although the next day they were sent the purses which the tragic arrival had prevented them from receiving. Robert Percy and John Wrangwysh persuaded the King to mount his horse, but the Queen, in silent shock since she had stopped screaming, would not leave him and in the end he took her up before him. It was the only time they had ridden thus since he carried her from Francis Twynyho's kitchen to St Martin's sanctuary. At the castle they were escorted to the King's private solar and left there. John Kendall dealt with Metcalfe the messenger, who had also broken down; Prince Edward had been in his charge since the age of five years old.

It was possible, of course, for the government to carry on without the presence of its head. Richard had chosen efficient administrators and they did their work – decrees, commissions of array and despatches continued to issue from Nottingham under the Royal Seal – although there were few who did their duty in those latter days of April with more than half a heart. A gloom hung over the castle and the town until even the children and the dogs were subdued by it. The bereaved parents remained out of sight. But the right of sorrow to privacy can only extend so far. Uneasiness began to disturb the unnatural hush of the castle passages. The privy council met, privately, and Lord Lovel was proposed to represent their anxiety to the absent King. Reminding them that the King had, in fact, signed a number of letters and transacted several pieces of business through Kendall's agency, since the secretary's presence was so familiar as not to be an intrusion, Lovel agreed. He was forestalled. While he was still revolving the best form of words to use, Richard emerged, and announced crisply that he would be receiving public petitions in the great hall the following morning.

His minister's relief was not only that of human sympathy; it was also an acknowledgement of their need for him. In less than a year he had wrenched the administration away from the road to chaos where King Edward's sudden death and Queen Elizabeth's irresponsibility had driven it; it was practical, functional, well-staffed. Yet its weakness was its dependence on the very man who had created it. Richard was its direction. After five days of self-indulgence, the lifelong habit of subjection to duty had reasserted itself, and he took up his abandoned position as head of state, to all intents and purposes as if nothing had happened, because he had to. But now, as discerning eyes soon perceived, beneath the closing in upon himself which was his response to the series of blows struck at him these past twelve months, he had lost his own direction.

Like the inhabitants of an anthill when it is kicked over, he was very busy to no purpose. And like the ants, perhaps mercifully, he was not yet aware of it.

For his wife there was no such compulsion to duty. She remained secluded in the royal apartments, and only her foster-daughter was admitted to attend her. On the fourth day after Richard had resumed his public life, Katherine sought an interview with him. Her eyes were circled with the dark evidence of the tears she had saved for the privacy of her own bed. Her sorrow had seemed subordinate to the matter of helping Anne to bear hers.

'Father, you must talk to her,' she said at once. 'She just lies there, not weeping, not eating, not speaking. I'm afraid ...' Richard walked up and down the chamber once, and returned to face his daughter. The line between his brows was deeper than usual.

'I know.' He spent each moment he could spare with his wife, as well as every night. 'I would have feared to have left her at all, had I not been able to trust her to you. But what can I say, Kate? What words of comfort are there?' His rigidly governed voice was shaking, and only the determination which Katherine had inherited stopped her from flinging her arms round him.

'It's not comfort she needs, sire. She must be forced back into living, or she won't even try. And you are the only person she'll listen to.'

'Will she? I wonder.' All she had done, these past nine days, was to cling to him, exerting a frightening strength when he had to leave her. It seemed to him as if human speech made no kind of impact on her stricken brain.

'You must make her. Or do you want to lose her too?' There was the rise of hysteria behind the girl's voice, and in a movement of panic, for that and for what she had suggested, Richard caught her to him. Holding her smooth dark head against his chest, he controlled himself.

'You are right, Kate. I will go to her now.' Tipping her face up towards him he kissed her forehead. 'God bless your care of us,' he said, and went.

Anne was lying, as she had lain for so long, prone on her bed, her face turned into the crook of her arm. Her hair, which had been combed solicitously by Katherine, was arranged with unnatural sleekness down her back. Fear cold in his stomach, Richard knelt at her side. Her eyes were open. But as he repeated her name several times there was barely a flicker of recognition in them. He lifted a handful of hair and watched its fineness slip through his fingers. At least before today she had found some kind of solace in his presence, but now even that seemed to have gone. Seized anew with the panic his daughter had roused in him, he raised the inert body and shifted it awkwardly until she was sitting beside him on the bed, leaning against his shoulder. In the process her loose sleeve had fallen back, uncovering the bluish remains of the great bruise Richard's grasp had inflicted upon her in the first paroxysm of his knowledge. Only now realising its origin, he was stabbed with remorse. What other injuries had he done her since he took charge of her life, less obvious but more lasting? What right had he ever had to order her destiny? She had wanted to be a nun. Instead he had taken her from the care of the brothers of St Martin's and subjected her to a hard public career and a dangerous childbirth; he had made her assume a crown she expressly rejected, parted her from her son and neglected her for his royal duties. And at last this cataclysm. She lay in his arm like a rag doll, the little resilience she had crushed out of her.

But he loved her, and selfish and guilty though he might be, he could not spare her. This past year her mere presence had kept him human in the superhuman task he had set himself; and now, more than ever before, he needed her in his loneliness. He had fought for her before. Unwillingly the picture came into his mind of George shouting at him, and he pushed it away, as he always did. Then he saw her as she had been amid the clatter of the kitchen, stirring the stewpot. The girl he had led to freedom from that kitchen had had scarcely more animation in her than this woman whose heartbeat was faint beneath his palm. But twelve years ago the future had been bright with promise, which today was only a hopeless struggle. What could he say, indeed? He gathered her limp hands in one of his, and was rewarded by a response. Like a baby's instinctive grip, her fingers curled around his, and he knew that at least she was aware of him.

Quietly he began to speak. He spoke of the things that bound them together, the past which uniquely they shared: of Kat's various manifestations as wooden billet, doll and kitten; of the buried forgotten castle at Middleham whose grave had been their sanctuary; of St Anne and St Anthony and mummers in the priory in York. He touched too upon incidents which perhaps had never before been put into words between them: his distress at her returning the pendant which was the pledge of his faith; his joy when she had taken it back in the darkening abbey cloisters. In an eloquence which appeared out of nowhere he told her of the sweetness she had brought to his life, omitting the subject of their son. Carried away by the flood of his own memories, he came to that one which for him marked the crowning felicity of their early marriage: the sunset among the flowers by the Falls of Aysgarth, when their love had become passion.

As he recalled their mutual eagerness for consummation he felt that his fingers were wet. Faltering to a stop he looked at his wife. Tears were sliding from her open eyes, flooding down her still face and falling unchecked to her lap. Hope lifted Richard's heart even as she murmured, almost inaudibly, 'It's no good. It's gone.' Words of despair, but the first she had uttered for many days. He braced himself to snatch at the slender advantage he had been given.

'No, it's not all gone. We are still here. Have you forgotten what odds we defeated to come together? Because we were blessed with such happiness is no reason to expect it to continue for ever. We have no right to that. Love is not easy. But as long as it is still here, nothing is impossible. And it is still here, isn't it, Anne?' It was a challenge, an appeal, no rhetorical question. Never before had he asked her if she loved him, and now it was necessary for her life, for his peace, that she should answer it. There was only the weary turn of her head against his shoulder.

'I don't know.'

'You *must* know!' Richard tightened his clasp; Katherine had warned him that gentleness would not be enough. 'Why then did you marry me? Was it as they said, for position and security and wealth you'd lost the chance of any other way?' She moaned and her body tensed. 'And why did I take you?

For charity?' It was cruel, flinging at her when she was defenceless the rumours he had kept from her when she was a happy bride. But she had to defend herself.

'You don't believe that,' she whispered, and there was a spark of protest somewhere.

'What should I believe? That your love was not strong enough to survive adversity?'

'Not my love. How could you doubt it? But myself. I'm too weak; I always told you so.' She, who with his help had dragged herself from the scrapheap of society and fitted herself to order the efficient running of a great castle within a few months; she had the strength, if she could be persuaded to use it.

'Then it's a poor kind of love,' he said harshly, 'and you have failed me.'

'No, no! I haven't!' She was sitting up now, her hands trembling in his.

'Prove it!'

'How can I? I'm no use to you, only a burden. Any purpose I had in your life has gone now. Even in that I failed.'

That way lay despair; he pulled her back. 'I need you today. A dispute between two broiderers from the town about a girl prentice who ran away, from one to the other. I believe she was ill-treated. It wants a woman's judgement and compassion. Yours.' It was a shrewd stroke, from a fortuitous circumstance. He knew her fellow-feeling towards the persecuted and helpless.

After a moment Anne asked, 'How old is she?'

Concealing his relief Richard said, 'About Kate's age, I should judge.'

'Kate. Poor Kate—'

That had been a miscalculation; he broke in, 'Will you come?'

Again a pause, and then, 'If you wish it.'

'No – I ask it.' Bowing her head, she rose to her feet in token of assent. Immediately she tottered backwards into Richard's arms, and he was struck with conscience at his severity towards her. He knew well that he alone could have stimulated her fading will to survive, but this time perhaps his demands on her physical resources had been too great. Then he recalled that she must have fasted for days, and laying her back on the bed he went hastily to call for food and wine before her impulse was dissipated.

An hour later, with the aid of Kate's tremulously hopeful ministrations and Richard's constant presence, the Queen was prepared to take up her role. She would have to lean heavily on her husband's arm, and there were great smudges of grief and fatigue beneath her eyes, but together they had won the fight. For the time being, at least, she would have part with the living and not with the dead. There was however one thing more that Richard had to inflict upon her, and he nerved himself to do it now, for fear of a worse relapse later. Just before they passed out of the bedchamber he turned her to him and said, 'There is something else I have to ask of you, love.'

She raised her eyes to his, and he almost stammered over his next words at the sad trust in them. 'You must go to Middleham with me.' She flung her head up as violently as if he had hit her.

'No! I can't! Not that, Richard – have mercy on me!'

Her anguish was his, and this time his voice showed it. 'I beg you, Anne. To go alone ... would be unbearable.' The prospect of his breaking down accomplished what more sternness could not have done. Shaken from her self-woven cocoon of suffering, she saw that it was his loss too. She touched his face with a soothing gesture.

'Then I will come with you.'

Spring was in full flood through Wensleydale. The beeches by Jervaulx Abbey were clothed in their delicate silk-fringed leaves, and the may was in bloom. The weather had been abnormally warm since leaving Nottingham, almost too hot for travelling, if either of the principal travellers had been in the state to heed external conditions. A few days' stop in York was a relief to their retinue, if not to Richard and Anne. There had been no cheering from the massed crowds in the streets of the northern capital, as the royal couple rode through them stony-faced. The people of York understood; they were one with their King and Queen in loss as they had been a pitifully short eight months before in their triumph. Miles Metcalfe, Thomas Wrangwysh and other friends received them, and suffered with them. If the ordeal wàs hard in York, it was doubly so at Middleham. But, by a combination of will-power and numbness, they had found a way to face it. Both Richard and Anne had in the past possessed a certain ability to withdraw into themselves when the world was too much for them; at this most severe test they seemed to take refuge in and draw strength from each other. Outwardly they were unmoved by returning to the home that was tragically deprived of the main reason which had made it home to them for the past eleven years. Their agony was expressed privately and in silence.

One incident only almost broke Anne's composure and threw her back into the state of collapse from which her husband had with such difficulty raised her. She went to the castle chapel, an old habit of hers when she wished to lose herself in familiar prayer beneath the benevolent eye of St Anne. But under the glass saint with her nest of fledglings a coffin was standing on a bier, draped with the royal arms of England and the Prince of Wales' feathers. It was not this, for which she should have been prepared, nor the faint stench of corruption which was trapped in the hot little room with the morning sun, that struck at her most cruelly. Within the altar rails, chin on paws and still as a grey stone sentinel, was Edward's hound, Arrow. By some curious instinct the animal recognised her step. It rolled a lack-lustre eye towards her and thumped its tail once. Anne began to shake uncontrollably and Katherine, as usual close behind her, ran for Richard. He was in the great hall, not far away, and came at once. With his arms round her, at a distance from the bier and its solitary mourner, she was able to speak.

'Ned loved him and I was unkind to him. I threatened to whip him, and I meant it. Yet the dog was with him when he died and I was a hundred miles away. And even now he won't leave him. What a wretched mother I am when a hound can show more devotion!' Again Richard had to suppress his own emotions to summon up rational argument: dogs were simple creatures whose lives followed simple rules; it was his nature to stay with the master he had learned to obey.

'You must not take the behaviour of a brute as a reproach to you. As well blame a falcon for killing pigeons.'

'It's not that. You don't understand.'

He did not. The hound was a reproach to Anne in a way he could not know. But Katherine was still within earshot and she knew. Slipping to her knees beside her foster-mother she said quietly, 'Ned bore no grudge, madame. Don't you remember how pleased he was when you made friends with Arrow?' She did remember suddenly how by the gatehouse last autumn she had overcome her repugnance for dogs and patted Arrow on the head; and how Edward had thanked her for it. Her conscience would never quite clear her of the severity she had used to him in a moment of anger, or of leaving him to die, but Katherine had said the right words. The wound still bled, but a grain of poison had been drawn from it. She wept.

Later, her thought returned to Arrow's vigil.

'What will happen to the hound, Richard? He could pine away. I've heard of such things.'

'I'll take him,' said Richard, who had already resolved on it. 'I hope he'll run with his dam. It's not so long since he was weaned, and Diana should remember him.' Anne thanked him, feeling that some reparation had been made for her dislike of Ned's dog.

It was from this occurrence that Richard realised he would have to bury his son alone. He had inflicted enough on Anne in bringing her to this place of vanished happiness; he would have to be hardy to take the last step without her. It was not a very long journey. To go to London was out of the question. Richard had neither the time nor the inclination for a state funeral in Westminster Abbey. Besides, the hot weather had made interment necessary. York Minster seemed the most appropriate spot, but he had hesitated over it in the considerations he had shared with no one. The generous sympathy of his people of York he had received once. He did not think he could stand it again, with the added ritual which was inevitable, and an awful reversal of that ceremony half a year ago. To his council he announced shortly, and without explanation, that the Prince of Wales would be interred in the parish church of Sheriff Hutton. They looked at each other in silence, but offered no comment. However desirable for propaganda reasons a public show of pomp and grief, the councillors respected their King's wish for privacy. Some may also have understood why he had chosen Sheriff Hutton, where the Prince was to have grown to manhood and responsibility, for the boy's final rest. Anne might have wanted him to stay at Middleham, in the collegiate church they had founded together, but she too accepted his decision without a word.

After her outburst over the dog she had lapsed into silence again, performing her duties with the remoteness of a sleep-walker. But she performed them, although Richard and her attendants watched her closely, aware of how thin were her defences. The time for the departure of the cortège arrived, and it was suggested to her delicately that she should keep her chamber that day. She shook her head, and was in her place by the gatehouse at the appointed hour.

When the small coffin was borne down the steps of the keep, by Metcalfe and Peacocke, faithfully attending the Prince as they had done in life, the only two people apparently unmoved were the dead boy's parents. The King followed slowly, in deep black riding clothes, and stood by while the coffin was secured on its open chariot. The horses drawing it tossed their heads uneasily, scenting decay, as he crossed to the Queen. He took her hand, kissed her cheek, and said for her alone, 'Pray for us.'

The cavalcade was mounted and moving from the bailey to the street over the drawbridge; inside, the royal household, outside, the population of Middleham, and most it seemed were audibly weeping. Lifting over the eastern curtain the sun shone in a cloudless sky, as it had done so often these past few weeks. Beyond the walls the busy birds of late spring were singing as the clatter and rumble faded. It was traditional to climb to the battlements for a final farewell, and they climbed. If any memories of past farewells were haunting Anne, she did not show it. The sad procession was winding away through the trees, towards Masham and the Vale of York. One royal coat of arms only fluttered over them. Perhaps she did not see any of it. What was real to her was the touch of Richard's lips upon her cheek, and she was already carrying out his injunction, praying as she knew he meant for the two that had gone and for herself who remained: peace for the dead and endurance for the living.

4

SPRING

She had spent several weeks making friends with her five
nieces. By inviting them to her apartments, talking to them,
giving them small thoughtful presents, she made every effort to
gain their confidence. With the four younger girls it was easy.
Cecily, the most beautiful, was an open and friendly soul, as
ready to laugh at the admiration of young lords and pages as to
flirt with the zest of a nubile fifteen-year-old. Her junior by
nearly seven years, Nan was quiet and biddable, and the two
little ones, Cat and Bridget, were both adorable. All possessed
the sweet nature which Anne had come to recognise in their
father King Edward.

Elizabeth presented more problems. For one thing, she was
already a woman; for another she did not so readily show her
feelings. Since she displayed the tall smooth blondeness of her
mother, Anne feared at first that she had taken after her in
other respects as well. But what appeared coldness and
haughtiness, she was learning, hid the uncertainty which Kate
had read at once, back in the spring. More than her sisters,
Elizabeth had been dominated by the ex-queen's ambition;
removed from her influence she found it difficult to stand on
her own feet. Sympathising, her aunt handled her gently. She
dreaded the prospect of Elizabeth as her enemy, but more than
the dread she wanted her as a friend. It was something she
could do for Richard while he was away from London, and it
might help to fill the gap left by Kate's marriage in the
summer. So on many evenings, whenever she was not too tired,
the tapestries were drawn over the windows against the early-
fading light, and the five girls were summoned to share the
Queen's privacy. Anne was often tired, these days. Since
returning to Westminster in early autumn it had been an effort

to give her full attention to all the audiences and receptions expected of her. The journey of course had been fatiguing, as always. The rest she set down to the debilitating atmosphere of London, and the time of year. She was determined, however, to do her best for her nieces.

At Soulmas, Nan celebrated her ninth birthday. On her own initiative and from her own purse Anne hired a troupe of tumblers and jugglers for the occasion. It was the kind of entertainment she had enjoyed herself at the same age. After the performers had gathered up their brightly coloured clubs and hoops and balls and gone, she was rewarded. On rising from a well-trained thank-you courtesy, four-year-old Bridget flung her warm fat arms round her aunt's knees. Following the child's impulse, Anne picked her up and hugged her close. Giddy with the sudden emotion, she just had time to set Bridget on her feet before sitting down rather abruptly in her chair. And she was further surprised when the tall figure of Elizabeth stooped before her, to say that she hoped her grace's kindness had not indisposed her. The long, rather severe lines of her face softened with real concern. Anne smiled a little tremulously and shook her head. The shouts of the entertainers, the cries and applause of the entertained had, it was true, been rather wearing, but they had been worthwhile. She had concrete proof of a small foothold in the affections of at least two of Edward's daughters.

On a quieter afternoon a few days later, the girls were again the Queen's guests. She had discovered that Elizabeth used to play chess with her father and had challenged her to a game. It was soon clear that her niece was a quick and skilful opponent, but Richard, a pupil of the same teacher, had taught Anne to play seriously and she played on, losing her pieces, as well as she was able. There was little to disturb their concentration: Cecily embroidered and watched the moves good-humouredly; Nan's head was bent with Margaret Wrangwysh's over the illustrations in the Queen's own book of hours. The only sounds were the low voices of Cat and Bridget, playing mothers with a poppet, and the dry shifting of charred logs in the fireplace. But Elizabeth kept her advantage and Anne's queen was threatened. Trying to visualise a series of alternative moves in her head, Anne found the atmosphere soporific instead of stimulating. Her eyes would keep closing, and the logical sequences would keep drifting into chaos.

It was some time before she realised that the lulling small sounds had changed, and she raised her head to encounter her ladies and nieces on their knees, and before her was her husband. There was something in his face that dispersed her drowsiness instantly, the end of an emotion which he was endeavouring to hide, and which suddenly frightened her. She would have risen to go to him but he stepped quickly forward, his boots making no sound on the fur rug, and pressed her back into her chair with his hands on her shoulders, kissing her.

'Forgive me for disturbing you,' he said rapidly, as if merely for something to say. 'I should have waited until the game – the games –' his smile included the two children and their poppet – 'were over. Please be easy, all of you.' He replaced Elizabeth on her stool and sat between the two players.

The rest of the company complied with his request but Anne said, trying to sound natural, 'I'm afraid our niece is too good for me. See what desperate straits I'm in.' Richard enquired whose move it was and studied the board.

'Not entirely,' he said. 'If you move your remaining knight there ...' Anne did so, and her opponent immediately followed, taking an unconsidered step not at all like her previous game. Glancing at her, Anne saw an unexpected flush in her pale cheeks. It was unlike her to show embarrassment. But the match had evidently lost its interest for both of them, and they muddled through to a victory for Elizabeth without any expertise. For her part, Anne's initial alarm was swallowed up in the joy of seeing her husband again after several months apart; for nothing could be very ill provided that he was well, and here with her. And another feeling, sharper and more urgent, increased with every moment he sat beside her and was polite to his eldest niece. Tonight he would make love to her. She shifted in her chair as the intensity of her anticipation caught her unawares. Surely he must sense it too. But he went on explaining to Elizabeth how she could have mated her opponent in four moves less.

Going to his wife's chamber late that night after a customary session with his secretary, Richard trod softly to avoid waking her. Almost the last thing he expected was to find her out of bed and flinging herself into his arms before he had safely set the candle down.

'Gently, gently! Or you will have us alight.' Already as he gathered her into his embrace she was scrabbling at the girdle of his bedgown.

'Oh, Richard, I've missed you so! And I thought that wretched John Kendall would be writing all night. Do come to bed.'

His body was eager enough to respond to her haste as her hands slid inside his robe, but there was something strange about it which gave him pause. Never before had he known her to take so much of an initiative. Although she could be as passionate as he, she had always followed his lead, and to caress him as she was doing now she generally needed hours of intimacy. Could she have been drinking too much wine while waiting for him? After her appearance this afternoon he could hardly believe in any other explanation. He drew back, and said a little breathlessly, 'Would you take me by force, love?'

And for a moment she remembered, and said, 'Then there is something wrong. The Tydder has invaded,' and her avid hands were still.

Cursing himself Richard answered, 'No, not a sign of him. Nothing is wrong. But as you say, we must go to bed. It's scarcely the time of year for nakedness.' There was no wine on her breath as he kissed her and drew the fur coverlet over them, but his misgivings dissolved in the heat of their renewed contact. He caught her ardour, and their coupling was as fierce as any in the twelve years of their marriage. But when his breathing had returned to normal, and he lay in a bemused and blissful indolence, drifting into sleep, he became conscious slowly that under his arm her breasts still rose and fell rapidly, and her heartbeat pounded against him. She was drenched with sweat. Dragging himself back into wakefulness he listened for a while with growing anxiety, and then whispered, 'Is all well with you, dear love?' The voice that came to him out of the darkness was faint, but vibrant with happiness.

'Perfectly, beautifully well.' There was nothing he could say after that, and a few minutes later he heard her giggle. 'Was I very wanton, Richard? Did I shock you?'

'Of course not,' he said unconvincingly.

'The dreams came back, you see.'

'Dreams?' By now he was a very puzzled man.

'Yes. You remember, before I married you. And after . . . until that time at Aysgarth. Dreams about . . . about lovemaking. Only I didn't know it was you then. It's strange, isn't it? We've been separated for longer than this, but they've only returned recently.' Her heart was steadier now, and Richard was beginning to feel rather foolish. If that was indeed all . . . His brother Edward had twitted him several times with prudishness, and who was he to deny Anne her pleasure? She had little enough, God knew, in her life these days. So did he, for that matter. Desire stirred him again, but when he touched her he found she was suddenly and deeply asleep.

They met circumspectly enough the next day, when the Queen was called into conference with those of Richard's council left in charge of the administration in London, and she slept the night through. The craving came and went. Sometimes she could barely keep her eyes open until her ladies were out of the bedchamber; at others she awoke from torrid dreams gasping for satisfaction, or restrained herself with difficulty during daily hours of waiting until bedtime. Burying his misgivings, Richard gave what she demanded and took what she offered.

It was possible in such moments to forget that two traitors were on trial for sedition, that the staunch old Lancastrian Earl of Oxford had escaped from custody and joined the Tydder; to forget the poisonous odour of invasion which crept beneath everything. Anne was no longer kept in ignorance of her husband's difficulties and fears. He had learned the lesson of Nottingham well, and took her into his confidence at all times; she was free to attend privy council meetings. At one of these he thanked her officially for her care of the Lady Elizabeth and her sisters, and encouraged by this she ventured in private to ask a favour on their behalf.

'Could we not provide them with new gowns, Richard? Whatever their mother did with the treasure she stole from King Edward, she didn't use it to clothe her daughters. All they possess are out of fashion.' Richard thought that the privy purse might stretch to five Christmas gifts. They were already in Advent, somewhat to Anne's surprise, for time slipped by her with unusual speed nowadays. She suggested employing Janet Evershed, who had among other services supplied garments and embroidery for their coronation.

'You will have to use her journeyman,' Richard answered shortly. 'Mistress Evershed is out of the country.'

'Oh? Maybe she will return before Christmas.'

'I don't think so.'

His tone was oddly dismissive. In a silence Anne looked at him, before saying quietly, 'Then I shall send for her journeyman. If she has trained him he will be more than competent.'

In the event she did not interview Master Kit Cely herself, since that day she was confined to her bed. But the gowns were ordered and the work begun. Richard told her so later, bringing a bowl of frumenty to her chamber with his own hands. She refused it.

'But you must eat, Anne. I hear you have taken nothing today.'

'Nor last night, neither,' Margaret, who was sitting nearby, interposed severely.

'I'm not hungry,' her mistress insisted. 'I've been so idle, what need have I for sustenance?'

'It is because you eat so little that you lack strength,' said Margaret, who was a plain speaker. 'You will never be well, madame, if you starve yourself.'

'I'm not ill, truly. Just tired.' Her friend and her husband exchanged glances, in which the King was given permission to exert his authority. Still protesting, the Queen ate a little of the mess of wheat and milk.

With a stern eye on her eating, Richard said, 'Now you shall have the good news I brought.'

'What is it?'

'Kate will be with us for Yule.'

Anne brightened and took another spoonful. 'Oh, that is good news indeed. Does Will come too?'

'No, he has duties elsewhere. But there are certain errands in London which he has asked Kate to run for him.' And he exchanged another glance with Margaret Wrangwysh, which Anne could not read, and that raised a distant unease, although she was not able to summmon the energy to analyse

325

it. Richard's expressions were usually so transparent to her.

There were other faces she could not read during the next month, even Katherine's, briefly, when she arrived half-way through Advent from her husband's estates in Monmouthshire. Anne suspected from time to time that there were grave tidings of some kind which they were keeping from her, but no one enlightened her, and she could not cope with much reasoned speculation. Besides, there was one face at court which she could read only too well, and that presented a more immediate problem than other nebulous imaginings.

Her niece Elizabeth was falling in love with her husband. The Queen of England had not lost Lady Anne Neville's childhood gift, if gift it was, of sensing the truth of things before they were put into words. At first, from Elizabeth's behaviour when Richard was present, it seemed that she disliked him, resentful of the man who had usurped the throne from her brother and taken away her own high status. But beneath the stiffness, the reluctance to speak, Anne began to see an opposite explanation. The eyes that dropped when they encountered his, yet sought him at all other times; the avoidance of his touch, and the blush when he did take her hand or kiss her with an uncle's solicitude. For a time she angled for his company, and then sat mute when she obtained it, but with Christmas a few days off she started to seek excuses to keep away from any informal meetings with him. Elizabeth was eighteen, a young woman of sharp intelligence and over-ripe for marriage. It was perhaps inevitable that her father's daughter should fall in love; it was more than unfortunate that she should fall where she had, and Elizabeth knew it. The King himself had no inkling of her plight, and continued to offer small kindnesses to her and her sisters quite indiscriminately. And Anne, who for some reason had few official duties lately and therefore much leisure, watched and wondered what to do.

The plainest solution was a husband. Had King Edward's diplomatic schemes gone aright, Elizabeth would have been Queen of France. But Louis XI, who long ago had made the mighty Earl of Warwick dance to his tune and give his daughter into the hands of Edward of Lancaster, had played fast and loose also with his Yorkist alliance. Even from his grave, whither within half a year he had followed Edward IV, he meddled with the happiness of his English cousins. There had been no time to betroth Elizabeth anew when she was a royal princess; as a bastard living on the King's charity she was a poor match. Richard had undertaken to arrange marriages for all the sisters, yet he seemed in no hurry to do so, ignoring even the oath which Henry Tydder had sworn a year ago to gain support in England, to take Elizabeth to wife as soon as he was able. Once Anne brought herself to ask, as idly as possible, whether any plans were afoot for their niece. Richard was non-committal, and when she mentioned the name of Tydder he said he was not going to be browbeaten into haste by the insolence of a rebel. Why the impatience, Richard asked; was the girl not content and well cared for at Westminster? Marvelling at his blindness, it was Anne's turn to be non-committal.

Christmas came with nothing resolved. For all the money and planning poured into it, to make the feast more magnificent than the last, there was a pall of indefinable melancholy over all the festivities. Two latecomers did what they could to leaven the heaviness: John of Lincoln and John of Pomfret, as the King's son was often called, arrived in the dusk of Christmas Day. Richard's nephew, the Earl of Lincoln, was now his heir presumptive, appointed back in the summer, which was perhaps a good enough reason for him to be summoned from Sheriff Hutton to pass a week at court. His younger namesake would soon be entering his teens, and Richard had an office in mind for him also, more humble certainly, and nominal too at first, but enough to give him a standing as honourable as his sister had attained in matrimony. Captain of Calais he was to be, the post that the Earl of Warwick had filled with such panache in the Queen's infancy. John's qualities as a sailor were as yet unproven, but as Anne said to her husband on approving the choice, he already had the dash and the daring. Yet even his kindling red hair and sturdy figure seemed a little subdued that winter at Westminster. Maybe it was the effect of his first exposure to the full rigours of court procedure, on so much vaster a scale than the domestic régimes he had known.

And indeed for the eye alone there was a rich harvest to be reaped around the King's high table as he kept the feast. The

King and Queen were in new robes, sewn with pearls, trimmed with soft bogey shanks, but any impartial observer would have awarded the palm not to them but to the Lady Elizabeth and her sisters. Even in the absence of its mistress, the Evershed workshop had completed its commission magnificently. Over the white velvet kirtle, Elizabeth's cloth-of-gold sleeves and gown matched exactly the gilt hair which lay like silk over her shoulders. Cecily's corn-yellow beauty was complemented by rich russet. Nan and Cat were in saffron and murrey, and small Bridget's auburn curls bobbed over a green garment which she kept stroking with reverent hands. The reinstatement of Edward's daughters, visually at least, was complete, and if the eldest of them looked more often at her platter than at her neighbours, the others could not help preening themselves. Not far below them, the Countess of Huntingdon was wearing again the crimson gown which had helped to capture a husband the previous Christmas, although now her hair was bound. She too seemed thrown into shadow this year by her cousins' fine feathers. Anne, too far away to talk to her, thought that much as she loved her family in London, Katherine must have left part of her heart with Will and her stepdaughter in Monmouthshire.

Trying to catch her eye, Anne was assailed by a fit of the coughing which had troubled her for some time and particularly when it was foggy. As she emerged from it she found she had succeeded in attracting not only Kate's attention, but also Richard's and that of almost every other person at the top table. She carried out her intention and smiled at Kate; the girl returned only a travesty of a smile and looked away. Richard was holding out her wine goblet and telling her to drink; he too would not meet her eyes. Conversation had died so that each note played by the consort of viols in the gallery fell clearly into the vacuum. Uneasily Anne glanced round the brilliant assembly, seeing the way in which they bent too eagerly to their platters or drank too deeply from their cups. Above their heads intrusive drifts of fog blurred the painted hammer-beams of the roof, at odds with the brightness below. Why was she also condemned to obscurity, cut off from some conspiracy which everyone shared but she?

So often in her life she had felt isolated, never more so than on these formal occasions when she should have been a focal point of the great gathering. A child at Cawood, a young woman on her first wedding day, a queen at her coronation, she was alone, forsaken by God and man. In the midst of her solitude, there was a hand on her arm.

'Do you wish to retire, dear heart?' said Richard's voice. This time his gaze did meet hers, full of a compassion which made her bless him for sensing her mood. Full too of a pain he could not hide.

'What is wrong, Richard?' she whispered to him. 'What is it that you all know and keep from me?' He would have replied but she shook her head emphatically. 'Don't deny it. Only a block could have failed to notice.' A page moved between them to remove her untouched meat and offer on his knee a dish of salted almonds.

She refused them with a gesture and as he passed on Richard muttered, 'If only you would eat—'

Scenting an evasion, she said curtly, 'You know I have no appetite for these banquets,' and returned to the point. 'I will ask Kate. She wouldn't lie to me.'

'Would I?' The pain had crept into his voice. She knew she was hurting him, and what was more in public, but she did not stop.

'Perhaps you would, in this case. But I have as much right to the truth as anyone, Richard. You must share it with me.' The King rubbed nervous fingers across his forehead, surreptitiously wiping away beads of perspiration.

'You may be right. But don't mention it to Kate, I beg you.'

'Then you will tell me?'

'I'll think on it.'

'Swear that you'll tell me.'

Their exchange was drawing attention, even among those who most feigned to be otherwise engaged. Even so, Richard was slow to give the promise she demanded. Absently he ate several almonds and washed them down with burgundy before saying with a leaden tongue, 'Very well.' And as he turned to repair his discourtesy to his other neighbour, he added quietly as if to himself, 'You will have to know eventually.'

It was the late morning of Childermas, and the Queen's ladies were robing her for yet another dinner. She had overslept, and since nobody had seen fit to wake her, to her shame she had missed the Mass of the Holy Innocents, which was of particular significance this year with her own innocent to remember. On rising she promised herself an hour of prayer in penance, sometime today. They were having trouble with the girdle of her gown, which had been made last winter and seemed to hang far too loosely now. Anne supposed she had lost a considerable amount of weight lately, and stood patiently while they pleated and pinned. Before they were through the Countess of Huntingdon was announced, and the women moved aside as Anne clasped Katherine's hands and raised her.

'Madame, may I speak with you?' At her tone, and at her expression, the others exchanged glances and began to leave the room. Margaret went hastily, but not before her mistress had seen the tears starting.

'What is it, Kate? The King – he is –' She had not seen Richard last night; indeed she recalled nothing after dark yesterday except being very hot.

'In good health, madame.'

'Then why are you so pale? You must be ill ...' Thrusting aside the forebodings which rose so rapidly, Anne continued quickly, 'or are you with child? The early months are wretched, but they will pass.'

Katherine still held her hands, and more and more she was bearing the Queen's weight. 'You must sit down.'

The nearest seat was the stool before the looking-glass, where she would soon have sat to have her hair dressed. She sank down, saying breathlessly, 'Yes, I sometimes feel a little faint early in the morning. But it's not early, is it? It's disgracefully late, and I've been such a slug-a-bed. On the first sunny day for weeks, too.'

Startled, Katherine looked up and saw that it was true. Although at its midwinter nadir and barely above the window-sill, the sun was valiantly picking out tiny rainbows in the border of the Venetian looking-glass. But the light reflected into the Queen's face was merciless. She averted her own, and silence pressed down on them both. Anne said suddenly, 'Will you brush my hair, Kate? No one has a touch like yours; I've missed it.'

Still mute, Katherine took up the silver brush and began to tease out the elf-locks of a restless night. The other saw mirrored behind her the downcast eyes and teeth that caught nervously at her lip, and recalled the sweet eagerness of that same face in the same glass a year before. Quite calmly, she said, 'What have you to tell me, my dear, I know it has nothing to do with a baby.' At that moment a paroxysm of coughing shook her. Katherine flung an arm helplessly round her shoulders until it was over, and Anne could gasp, 'Go on brushing ... Perhaps it will go now the fog has cleared. It's easier than it was.'

'No, madame – it's worse. That is what I have to tell you.' Expressionlessly the girl began to speak at last. 'Father would have told you last night, but you were in a fever, and then you slept and he wouldn't wake you. The physicians have said that we cannot hope for recovery. You are in a consumption. If you take great care, you may live to the summer.' The brush swept on through the lustreless hair. Anne could see now the hollowed cheeks and the wasted breasts beneath the rich brocade.

'And if I do not ... take care?'

'Until spring, perhaps.'

'And everybody knows.'

'All but you, madame.'

With a dry laugh Anne said, 'It was the same when I was carrying Ned. I was the last to find out. Strange, when I can read others so quickly.' There was a strangled sob and then Katherine was on her knees, her head in her foster-mother's lap, weeping uncontrollably. Anne soothed her wordlessly, stroking her hair and holding her gently, until she lay quiet.

'What a weakling I am,' the girl said at length, muffled by the folds of the Queen's gown. 'You should not be comforting me.'

'No, it must have taken courage to accept this errand. How was it that your father let you come?'

Katherine raised her head and said, almost defiantly, 'He doesn't know. I came without his permission. This morning at mass he looked so weary, and afterwards Father Doget was speaking to him. I'm sure he was trying to persuade my lord to give him the task. But my lord kept shaking his head. And I thought of how it must have been ... last night ... and that perhaps I could spare him a little. Oh, Mother, he's been in agony between the cruelty of keeping it from you, and the finality of telling you.'

'As if to leave it unsaid might make it untrue,' Anne murmured slowly. She was thinking of her husband lying through the night at her oblivious side, sleepless and heavy with that unshed burden. 'I expect he'll be angry with you, Kate. He doesn't take kindly to a sharing of his responsibilities. But I thank you, and I'll tell him so. Now I shall have time to prepare.'

'But how shall we do without you?' Katherine's cry was again close to tears.

'You will, my dear. You'll have to. And for you there's Will, and soon children of your own.'

'Not for Father. He has nothing but you.'

She had no easy answer to that. Instead she said, 'Will you leave me now, Kate? And would you keep my women from me for a few minutes. I believe there is time before dinner.' Incapable of another word, Katherine went into her arms, and after a quick violent embrace she departed.

Alone, Anne rose, and as she did so a city clock outside began to strike the hour of ten. She stood watching the motes in the shaft of sunlight, listening to the chiming of the bell, and wondered why she was so calm when with each stroke her time was trickling away. But time had done that all her life. Her rosary hung on its hook above her prie-dieu. Taking it down she crossed herself and knelt. What she possessed at this moment, as perhaps never before, was the quiet of certainty.

The presence of another person in the room made itself known slowly, for she had travelled far in a short while. One of her ladies-in-waiting, she supposed, with her eyes still closed, proffering misplaced sympathy. But she sensed urgency and reluctantly returned to mundane duty. It was Elizabeth who waited behind her, and dropped into a deep courtesy as the Queen turned to her.

'Your grace, forgive me for breaking in on your devotions, but there was no other time when I could find you alone. I must speak with you.' She was too wrapped in her own

332

troubles to see the ironic twist in her aunt's smile as she compared this demand for audience with that she had granted half an hour before.

'If there is anything I can do . . .' Anne replaced the rosary and went to her armchair; Elizabeth followed and again fell to her knees.

'First of all you must forgive me.'

'Oh, my prayers can wait,' said Anne mildly.

'No, for a much greater sin than that.'

'Should you not go to your confessor, niece?' From her new detachment she could not help being faintly amused by the young woman's intensity.

'I've been to him; but I haven't the strength of will to follow his advice. That's why I have come to you.' The problem of Elizabeth belonged to another age in another world, but its reality was returning to Anne little by little. More than ever, knowing what she now knew, it was imperative to face and solve her niece's difficulty. She bade her continue.

'Above all I wish to avoid causing pain to you and . . . and his grace the King. You have shown me so much kindness and I am a wretched ingrate to repay you like this. Yet I can't help myself. I must go away – as far as possible – out of harm's way. Harm to my soul and to your peace.'

'Why, Elizabeth?'

It must come out, and Elizabeth hardly blenched before saying simply, 'I love him.'

'I know.'

'How can you? I've been so careful, tried so hard to hide it.'

'Yes, but I love him too. It wasn't difficult for me to guess.'

'But he . . .' There was a sudden note of wild alarm. 'He doesn't suspect?'

'No,' Anne reassured her gently, 'I'm certain of that.'

After a moment Elizabeth said shyly, 'And you don't despise me?'

'It's no fault of yours. One cannot help loving. It's how one acts upon it that makes one base or praiseworthy. Once, when I was younger than you, I almost threw away my love because I lacked the courage to confess it openly. I always wanted to run away and it was wrong of me. But I believe in your case you are right. It has been very hard for you these past few weeks and you've endured them with honour. I shall speak to the King again.'

'Then you already have?' Elizabeth's fair complexion flushed, picturing rather belatedly how her control of her emotions had been so transparent to her aunt.

'Yes, about your marriage ... Do be comfortable, niece. Here, sit on this stool. My ladies will be back soon and we don't want them to find you as a petitioner at my feet.'

'My marriage?' asked Elizabeth guardedly.

'The King is pledged to find you a husband – you and all your sisters. Are you content?'

'Oh, yes, indeed. I'd willingly submit to his choice, because I know he would choose wisely. The sooner the better ... so I can legitimately stay away from court ... and so that I am safe from Henry Tydder,' she added in a bitter undertone. Anne had often speculated on Elizabeth's reactions to Tydder's oath.

'He seems to be very eager to marry you,' she commented.

'Of course he is. Even a bastard daughter of King Edward would be a step up for him. He's an adventurer and a cheat.' The flush had turned to anger.

'A cheat?'

'Yes, he swore to my mother last autumn that my brothers were dead, to gain her support. It was a foul lie.'

This was dangerous ground, the ground of state secrets, and Anne almost asked her to lower her voice. Yet she could not resist asking, 'How do you know?'

'His grace proved it to my mother. She never told me how, but afterwards she was far more hostile to the Tydder than she ever was to my lord the King. One of the reasons why she let us out of sanctuary was so that we could find husbands quickly and be out of the Tydder's reach.' Elizabeth spoke of her mother a little satirically, and with no sentiment whatsoever. Anne was convinced that she would never have unburdened herself so unreservedly to Dame Elizabeth Woodville as she had to her aunt. That cold spell was well broken. The Queen longed to see this girl who had all her life been a political pawn securely and happily married, so that in the warmth of mutual affection her personality could open to the sun, as her own had done during those idyllic years at Middleham. But, if it happened, it would be beyond her span. She must merely do the little that was in her power to help bring it about.

'I shall speak to the King,' she repeated. And Elizabeth, who was not insensitive, heard the change in her tone and began to feel superfluous. The Queen's eyes were suddenly luminous in her peaked face, and she was not seeing her niece at all.

Anne was contemplating what speaking to her husband would mean, tonight when at all costs she must keep herself awake. For everything between them was changed. No longer was she the questor, groping in the dark for a meaning and a purpose. Because of what Katherine had courageously undertaken to tell her – and despite his anger Anne could imagine the bleak relief which would flicker through his eyes at her assumption of his duty – because of it her way was clear. He was the one who would be left behind. For the first time in their lives together, she could offer him strength and compassion. In the weeks or months remaining to her she must teach him not to be afraid, as she was not afraid, and give him enough love to sustain him throughout his loss of her. She must share with him her serenity of acceptance.

Thereafter her health declined rapidly. One of the royal physicians who had attended the Queen's sister the Duchess of Clarence in her last consumption had observed the same phenomenon in the Duchess's case: from the time when the news of fatality was broken, a rapid sinking, as though in eagerness to embrace the promised end. But there was a great difference, the doctor remarked to his colleague, shaking a sage head; the Duchess Isobel had gone in terror of her husband, especially since the loss of her newborn son, and death could scarcely have been more dreadful than facing his wrath. Queen Anne, on the other hand, could not have been more beloved, or more cherished, by her husband.

Indeed, Richard exercised a considerable amount of his royal power to ensure his wife's comfort. He had of course sent for Katherine, and then for his son, because she was fond of them. Several others – Lord Lovel, Robert Percy, John Wrangwysh – were found business which would keep them in London for the rest of the winter, and so in constant attendance on the King and Queen. He offered also to send for the dowager Countess of Warwick, but this Anne would not allow. Her mother was an ageing woman, who should not be dislodged from her comfortable apartments at Middleham to make a long midwinter journey, especially for a purpose which would distress her. Besides, she had never been anything of a companion to Anne, who kept to herself the fact that since leaving Yorkshire she had scarcely noticed her mother's absence. All the friends whose presence she did need were gathered together at Westminster, and in other ways too Richard tried to recreate, far away, the home where they had been happy. London, that still-alien city, was not the setting either of them would have chosen for such a time, but Wensleydale was beyond their reach, and in any case a place full of ghosts, living and dead; and soon Anne was too ill to be moved even to the comparative proximity of Windsor or Greenwich.

So the crowded rooftops of London were blotted out by tapestries conveyed from the solar at Middleham; the altar cross and monstrance presented to the chapel of Middleham Castle by the Earl of Warwick took their places in the Chapel Royal of Westminster Palace; and the coverlet embroidered with birds from the Duchess of Gloucester's bed, now threadbare and fading, appeared in the Queen's sickroom. Richard attempted again to give Anne a kitten, but still perhaps with a curious loyalty to the memory of Kat, she refused. Artfully he compromised, and gave one to his daughter instead, who always happened to bring it with her when she attended the Queen. Less aristocratic than Kat, the tiny creature was consequently less dignified and more playful. Anne never laughed so freely as when the black and white scrap of fur, neatly arranged on her pillow, suddenly took mock-fright at nothing and charged haphazardly about her bed until, alarm over, it dropped just as abruptly into deep slumber. Sometimes it was still asleep when Katherine left, and since she said it was a pity to disturb it, the kitten remained.

As January passed, Anne's expeditions from her chamber became more and more restricted. Even to go as far as the chapel for mass induced fatigue and sometimes a fever; a short walk left her gasping for breath, and every effort might bring on the endless, debilitating cough. So her world narrowed, and

Richard's lovingly constructed fiction took on verisimilitude. Surrounded by the people and objects of another existence, her imagination was at liberty to dwell in it. Although her appearances in public were at an end, she was not isolated from events. Understanding that as much as ever she needed to be in his confidence, Richard continued to discuss with her his dilemmas and decisions, to ask her advice and opinions. Since there was a certain tendency, even among the best-intentioned, to treat her because she was ill as if she was losing her wits, she was gratified, and gathered up her weary faculties to do him justice. She learned that the Tydder had made a definite commitment to invade when the campaigning season began, and asked her husband if he should not be in Nottingham. There was no danger yet, he said, and in any case all was prepared; the Welshman was under surveillance. And in the spring?

'I will not leave you,' he said definitely, 'until the Tydder is at sea. Only England's extremity would take me away.' And Anne prayed to God that he would not have to choose between them.

Then there were the visitors. Her doctors disapproved and told her she should be resting in quietness, but when she asked why they shuffled and mumbled Latin. To put them back in countenance, she kindly assured them that she would send everyone away as soon as she was tired, and received her guests as long as she had the strength to talk or listen. It was mostly listening, particularly when Frank brought his lute and Katherine her guitar. Frank protested that his fingers had stiffened from signing too many official documents, but he had not lost his old skill, and with Margaret and John harmonising folk-songs, the old home-made musical gatherings returned. Whenever he could, Richard sat on a footstool by Anne's chair, or on her bed, and listened too. Despite the excellence of the royal choristers and musicians, reputed to be the finest in Europe, she declared that to her ears my Lord Lovel's consort was the sweetest by far. Frank ran his fingers through his blond hair, and smiled deprecatingly.

At such times her closely-knit circle of friends was able to forget its reason for being there, and to take pleasure in the make-believe. Anne was changed greatly since Christmas, and not only by the emaciation which almost daily seemed to suck flesh from her bones. In the kind candlelight of winter afternoons they saw also her calm and relaxation, her willingness to enjoy what they brought her. The tension which had dogged her since Richard became Protector, the sheer effort of the past nine months since her son's death, had dropped from her. In surrendering to the force that struck her down, she had found a purpose: to make a good end. And while they were with her it was difficult to be depressed by it.

It was not she who needed their help, but the King, and he could not be helped. In her presence he caught a reflection of her tranquillity and managed to live briefly in her certitude. Apart, he was already a broken man, although one who would soldier on nervelessly in his job of ruling and defending his country to his last breath. Henry Tydder would find it no easier to take England because King Richard was losing his wife.

Once only did he betray himself, when he came to her in the fading light of an early February day. She was drowsing under the eye of an attendant, who quickly scuttled away at the irruption of the King, and she struggled to her elbows to find him at her bedside. Through the dusk she could not distinguish his expression, but his hands were trembling.

'What ails you, my love?' she whispered, and at her voice he slipped to the floor and covered his face.

She reached out to touch his hair, and when he could speak he said, 'They are taking you away from me.'

'Away?'

'Those hell-spawned doctors, may God curse them.' It was so unlike him that she could only wait, brushed with the dread which only came to her now in connection with him. He pressed his fingertips into his eyes, trying to dull mental with physical pain, and collected himself a little. 'You are coughing blood,' he stated flatly. Yes; it had happened several times lately. 'They say your illness is contagious and that I have a duty to avoid infection. A duty!' He gave a wild bark of laughter. 'What else will duty take from me before it's done?'

'So you must not see me again?' Anne asked steadily, keeping her own hand on his head from trembling.

'No. That far they would not go. But – oh, God, God! – they've forbidden me your bed.' Before she had taken in what he said, he was weeping, with great rending sobs that shook the bed, and she could say nothing and do nothing to help him. For in the instant of his collapse her own serenity crumbled like a dream in waking, and she recognised the bitter reality. Here was their true parting. Whatever differences and misunderstandings had come between them, their physical accord had been complete, and it was indispensable. In every sense they had become one flesh, and to destroy that link would maim them both. Without it, the little time remaining to them would be immeasurably harder to bear. Foolishly, she had thought herself free of her wretched body, all spirit, half in heaven already, and yet the chains were still about her, dragging her back to earth, and she loved them too much to want to break from them.

With a single cry of pure loss she twisted her fingers in her husband's hair, and as convulsively he snatched her into his arms. For a long moment they clung, in blind terror at the forces that were driving them apart, but then she felt him change. When he spoke his voice was under control.

'Anne. Are you very tired today?'

'No. I've been sleeping most of the time.'

'Would it please you to defy these physicians who can't cure you, and heap useless tyrannies upon you to conceal their incompetence?' Under control, but with an edge of danger and excitement which Anne, who had never seen him on a battlefield, had not heard before. But she understood him.

'Might it not be dangerous for you, nevertheless? As they said?' she asked without conviction.

'As dangerous as last night, or the night before. And I don't care. They shall not deprive us of our farewell. Do you want me, Anne?'

'More than ever.' He released her and went to the door, groping in the near-darkness for the key. When he had locked it he crossed to the hearth and threw on more fuel before coming back, shedding clothes as he came. A spurt of flame from the stirred embers lit his body as he lifted the coverlet, and she caught a glimpse of his profile, jutting nose and long chin, before he was with her, closing down upon her like the night. There was no hesitation, no fumbling. For thirteen years they had made love, with love, and they were perfect. In her enfeebled state she was no longer active, but his hands knew how to rouse her without striving, how to prolong and how to quicken, and how to raise them both to a height which was above sickness, duty and mortality, and beyond time.

She took a pitifully long time to recover, these days, and as Richard gently wiped away the sweat, and held her gasping and shaking against him, he wondered briefly if it had been wise. But that was ridiculous. Of course it was not wise, it was reckless and shocking, and she had wanted it as much as he.

'Forgive me?' he murmured, and felt the tremor of laughter in her as she replied faintly, 'With all my heart.'

For a space they lay almost in silence. Once or twice she coughed and he was on the point of calling someone, but she stopped him. It was useless, she pointed out, she had a good supply of clean clouts, and anything else was just sympathy or hot air. Richard felt a humble admiration for the practical way, utterly lacking in self-pity, in which she faced what she had to face. Hers was the quiet courage that is seldom noticed, simply because it demands no attention. Heroic ballads are not sung about people dying of a slow and creeping disease. He drew her close again. In his hurry he had left the bed-curtains and the shutters open, and now that the fire had sunk a queer luminosity was filtering into the chamber.

'I think it's snowing,' he remarked. 'It was cold enough when I came from the Tower earlier.'

'So it is. I remember that light from ... when?' She pondered, and then said, 'Of course. St Martin-le-Grand. There were some heavy falls that winter, and I always knew, from my bed in the infirmary.' Anne had hardly ever mentioned that convalescence, and he did not know how much of it she recollected. 'It was snowing when you first came to visit me,' she went on. 'There were flakes on your hair and your clothes, and you told me it was Christmas.' That he had forgotten. 'If you had not come, I would have died. And when Ned was born. Then at Nottingham. How many times you've saved me!'

'Saved you? Don't say it, Anne. More often I've condemned you.' She moved her head in denial, and her faint voice was emphatic.

'That's quite untrue. You gave me life as surely as my

340

mother and father gave me existence.'

'And now?'

He spoke with naked anguish, and she pressed her cheek to his shoulder before saying, almost lightly, 'I think perhaps God is jealous of my love for you, and He is punishing me. Especially as I pretended once that I longed to serve only Him. There must be some saints in heaven who loved on earth. I will ask them to intercede.' He could not answer that, so instead he rose and mended the fire. That is all, she thought, now he will leave me. But he returned and lay beside her again. For the present, nothing else in the world mattered to him. As long as Anne needed him he would stay.

'Richard, when I'm dead you must marry again, soon.' His revulsion from the idea was a physical shudder, but she persisted. 'You must get sons. The country needs an undisputed heir. And it would be good for you.' She was right of course, but he could do no more than say through stiff lips that he would think about it.

'There is ... someone who might do,' she said experimentally. 'She's very popular with the people and that would be a good thing. And she loves you.'

'What? Who can you mean?' He was upset, she could tell, at what he considered her bad taste, but now she could not go back.

'Your niece, Elizabeth.'

'Elizabeth? Nonsense.' He did not believe her. In her representations to him for the girl to be moved away from London, she had spoken vaguely of a hopeless love for an ineligible nobleman. Yet it had occurred to Anne, in her hours of lonely musing, that this solution might be perfect. It was impossible for her to feel jealous of where Richard's affections would be directed when she was not there. What was important was that he should not brood over her loss.

'Yes, she does. She told me several weeks ago, but I had already guessed. The poor girl was very distressed, and was particularly anxious that you should not know it. And then I thought ... You are fond of her, aren't you, Richard?'

'Fond of her, yes. But she's my niece, Anne! My brother's daughter. A kinship far too close for marriage.'

'Yes, I knew there might be a problem about that. But the

341

Pope could give you a dispensation. He did for us, and you didn't even wait for it – remember?' There was a long pause, and Anne's hopes ebbed; she could sense that he was framing an answer which would make the refusal less harsh for her. 'Tell me, dear heart. I shan't be offended. Sick people are subject to strange fancies.'

'Of course I am fond of her, and of her sisters.' He was picking each word carefully. 'And I have done all I could for them, because they are blameless. But their parents – or at least my brother – were not. They are all illegitimate, and if I should take it into my head to marry one of them it would make nonsense of my setting them aside in the first place. It would compromise my integrity and jeopardise my legal position. Do you see that, love? Neither my personal feelings, nor hers, must enter into it.' He lay listening to the slight rasping of her breath, hating to disappoint her, but knowing that she would accept a rational argument.

With a small sigh she said, 'I should have thought of that. One loses a sense of proportion, being alone so much, with nothing to do but think. Poor Elizabeth. She must have realised more than I did. And I've betrayed her confidence.'

'Only with the best of intentions. I understand why she was so eager to leave. I'll see that she does, as soon as spring makes travel easier. Sheriff Hutton should be a haven for her. Meanwhile, I won't inflict myself on her any more than necessary.'

'Thank you, Richard. I wish she could be happy.'

'She will be, one day. I'll find her a good husband.' Another silence, and this time it was Anne trying to order her words. He kissed her to encourage her. What was not said now would probably never be said.

'The boys . . . where are they?' And his answer came without reserve or hesitation.

'They are safe. With Janet Evershed in Bruges.' Her palpable relaxation of tension was reward enough for trusting her with a secret strictly kept. 'They were in great danger in England, and I judged it wisest to hide them, for the present. Mistress Evershed is passing them off as her nephews, I believe.'

'She'll do it well. After all, she has enough real nephews to practise on.' Anne's tone was quite gay; she required no details, and she did not even wonder whether Janet's brother John and her sister-in-law were in the secret. 'From what John and Meg have told me of her brothers, she has at least one new nephew or niece every year! So that is where she was at Christmas. Do you remember when we first saw her, Richard? At Middleham ...' And they reminisced, ranging from that first winter in the draughty hall in Wensleydale, to the happy return in triumph when their son had been installed as Prince of Wales in York Minster. Many memories, none of them bitter, for all the bitterness had dropped from their lives together like sediment to the bottom of a clear pool. The reflection was pure and whole and still, and neither thought, as they talked quietly in the circle of each other's arms, of how soon, and how easily, it would be shattered. At last she sank to peaceful sleep, although there was a clamminess about her brow which would probably turn to fever. Richard did not move, feeling her incredibly slight frame against him, the slender bones seeming to press through non-existent flesh.

In the strange calm which had succeeded to his earlier agonised raging, he knew his grief as a gentle thing, which would dissolve him away without pain as the consumption was dissolving her. It was an illusion, and somewhere the harshness of reality was lurking, but that was beyond this bed where love still held them and protected them. When he left her sleeping, and unlocked the door, it would be the end. She would linger on for a while, divided from him by prohibition, and he would linger on for a while longer – years, perhaps – but it would mean nothing. Generously she had said, just now, that he had given her life. The gift had not been one-sided, and he had not thanked her. It was probable that now his opportunity was lost for ever, for he had little hope of a reunion beyond the earth: he believed he had broken too many of God's laws, which she had kept. The parting would be final.

Outside in Westminster a clock tolled six. Carefully covering his wife, he slipped from the bed and without striking a light he dressed. At the last he went back to her side. He could just make out the white planes of her brow and cheekbones around the deep hollows of her eyes, and her fingers curled on the pillow above where his head had lain. Leaning over her in the darkness, lit by the weird pallid glow from the window, he kissed her lips and left the room.

The pennants were slapping against the flagstaffs above the tiltyard, and the Prince of Wales shot arrow after arrow into the gold of the target. Beside him a little girl in a red cap was jumping up and down in the snow.

'Ned will catch cold,' Anne said reprovingly to her husband, but he shook his head and smiled, and replied, 'No, he won't, he's wearing his fur boots. And he must practise, or my lord of Warwick will never take him into his service.'

'But he will never play the lute as well as Frank,' she sighed, and indeed Lord Lovel was sitting nearby with his foot cocked on a stool and thrumming gently. The sky clouded as if a monstrous storm was impending, and the heraldic gaiety of the pennants vanished. Something brushed across her temples, and she could no longer see her son or her husband but only vague draperies and shadowy faces. Yet the thread of music went on, and drew a little of the bravery of that vision into this sombre present. Her heat came not from the sun but from fever, and while in the place she had just come from she could have run easily across the tiltyard, here she had barely the strength to turn her head and find that it was Margaret who was bathing her with cool water. Farther than that she could not see clearly, for it was night and there were few candles.

'Is it Frank?' she whispered.

'Thanks be to Our Lady you are with us again,' responded Meg. 'You have been away a long time.'

'Don't be sorry. I was at Middleham. Is it?'

'Yes, madame. It was his idea. He thought music might reach through your fever.'

'Will he come?' At once Francis Lovel was there, the lute trailing its pretty ribbons in his grasp. With an effort Anne extricated a hand from the bedclothes and gave it to him. 'Dear Frank!' she murmured. 'David playing to King Saul. If only I were mad, you'd be sure to make me sane.'

He studied their linked fingers for a moment before he said, in a deliberately steady voice, 'If I brought you back from Middleham, perhaps you'd rather be mad.'

'Oh, you were there too –' Talking too much brought on coughing, and when that was over she had no more breath to

344

speak. Meg and other attendants moved about her, straightening and mopping, troubling her for all their gentleness. But the music had resumed, out of sight, soothing her mind despite the unease of her body.

It was a pattern that hardly varied: the vivid, vigour-filled dreams, where winds blew and horses cantered, and her loved ones from all time were around her, mixed and changing, but positive; and the dull struggle of an invalid in a cold damp bed where the warming-pan had no power of warmth over her feet while her head burned, where some of the same people existed but had no vitality or purpose. This curious dichotomy, between a waking without reality and an unconsciousness rich with meaning, was not entirely new to her. Searching in the memory which was so sluggish while she was in·control of it, she found at length the key: Dog. Wretched Dog, the spit-boy, who had shared his food with her, and then abused her, and who had died. Even now, that long-buried recollection had the power to repel her – not the childish groping which had brought him a thrashing and no doubt hastened his death, but the hardly human parcel of skin and bones which had collapsed into the ashes of the hearth, choking up blood. It must have been about then that her dreams took such a hold of her, and the servants of Master Twynyho the grocer faded into grey ghosts seen through a winter fog.

Then Richard had quite literally saved her life. Had he not taken her to St Martin's and given her nursing and a will to survive, she would soon have gone the way of Dog, as little noticed and as little mourned. Paying one of his frequent visits, her husband found the tears running noiselessly down her temples. It was too complicated to explain to him, and the unusual effort of bringing forgotten miseries to mind had sapped her tiny amount of strength. She could only say, with slow emphasis, 'I am one of the most fortunate of women. Richard . . . remember them in your prayers . . . the poor who have nobody to care for them . . . and those who die alone.' He promised that he would; that, further, he would give them whatever relief lay within his royal authority; and he wondered, with more than a touch of mournful awe, at the unselfishness which could bestow such charity of thought at such a time.

It was an unusual display of emotion. For the most part she was a quiet patient, suffering the discomforts and indignities of sickness and its nursing with a kind of absent forbearance. She was very weak now, and between fever and normality the passage of time had ceased to have much meaning. One day she knew that winter must be in retreat, for Katherine brought her a bowl of crocuses. She had them placed next to the rose quartz crucifix which had been one of her son's last gifts, so she could see them whenever she turned her head. On that occasion she asked what the date was, and was told that it was March, just past St Gregory's. So she had survived the death of the year, to see this small evidence of its life returning; that gave her pleasure.

Another day, when the flowers still stood stiff and vigorous in their bowl, her confessor came, ceremonially robed, with some assistants and she realised without surprise that they were here to administer the last rites. Summoning her faculties with all the willpower that remained, she prepared to make her confession; they would not be required again. Father Doget helped her to cross herself, for she could barely move her hand, and she drew courage from the stern controlled face that bent over her. He had heard and absolved her sins many times, and would understand what her infirmity made her omit. But there was little to say. Already he had shriven her of her lesser faults, and in the months of her sickness his discussions with her had shown where the great faults lay.

'I have been weak,' she declared, and although her voice was low it did not falter, 'and a coward. I have turned away from challenge and would have forsaken my duty if I could. Perhaps I could have fought off this consumption if I had been braver. I have questioned God's will and sometimes my husband's. And I have loved people and places on earth too much, more than my love of Our Blessed Lord and His Mother. I ask pardon for these and all other sins and submit myself humbly to my judge.' Through the clouds of exhaustion Anne heard Father Doget telling her that God's mercy was wide enough to embrace even such backsliding as hers, and that He would not condemn her for loving too much.

'For love of His creatures and His creation is love of Him also, and He regards more an excess than a lack of it.' Then he gave her absolution in the name of Father, Son and Holy Ghost, and began the words of the mass. The familiar savour of incense pervaded her nostrils, her son's crucifix was smooth and cool in her fingers, and the reasssuring Latin phrases slid round her, an unbroken chain with all the other masses she had heard. Inside her closed eyes she was far from Westminster Palace, in a convent in Normandy, Angers Cathedral, the chapel at Middleham, the Minster of St Peter in York, in times of stress and distress, serenity and triumph, when the act of receiving the true body of her Saviour had been a refuge from misery, a confirmation of joy. As the transformed bread touched her tongue, she was sure that she would be forgiven.

It was not quite the last call on her strength, she found. With the withdrawal of the priests came the laity, a confusing mêlée of faces who demanded responses of which she was incapable. Though she recognised few of them she could feel their fear and their grief and could not comprehend it. For those she did know there were only broken, useless phrases.

To Katherine, drawn and heavy-eyed with watching, 'Dear Kate ... more than a daughter ... forgive hating your birth ... Tell John.'

To Lord Lovel, 'I hope there is lute music in heaven ... to look for in purgatory.'

And to Elizabeth, her proud Woodville features distorted with weeping, only, 'Trust Richard.'

For him, no inadequate words. He was there, she knew, behind the other supplicants, but not like them clamouring for attention, for consolation. Only when the furore had subsided, the waves of emotion sunk into quiet sobs, her consciousness ebbing, did he appear at her side and take her hand. It was enough, and there was no more need for her to fight. That strong and sensitive grasp had led her through life, and would suffice to send her forth from it. A great quietness fell on her; the breath which had been so hard to draw during her recent exertions became easy again, so shallow that it would not cloud a mirror held to her lips. She could not see him clearly – perhaps it really was growing dusk – but it was not necessary.

There was a light, and very slowly she turned her head towards it. A candle, the blue-hearted flame balanced delicately above the wax, and beside it, glowing with their own and borrowed radiance, the golden flames of the crocuses. Above, surely, not the sombre hangings of a bedchamber, but the washed innocent sky of February, traced with the bare twigs and half-opened blossoms of an almond tree. Next week she would marry Richard and he would take her to Middleham. Suddenly the vision quivered in a rush of grateful tears. Her lips moved, and the kneeling priest and people thought she was praying. But her husband knew, although he did not hear, what she was saying.

'I have been happy. So happy.' Then the sky faded and the candle, and only the flowers continued to glow as her sight was darkened. Those and the man's hand round hers were all that held her to earth, until, easily and without pain, they too drifted away into the waiting dark.

HISTORICAL NOTE

Anne Neville is certainly the only Queen of England ever to have been a kitchen-maid. This surprising fact is contained in a single line of the Croyland Chronicle, a near-contemporary account of the events of her time. Her life is not well documented, except as an adjunct to other people's schemes or actions. No evidence remains of her own opinion of the career which was thrust upon her. That is what this book attempts to supply.

The men who dominated her are slightly better served, and for my knowledge of them – Richard III, Warwick the Kingmaker, Edward IV and Louis XI – I am indebted largely to one historian. Paul Murray Kendall's tetralogy of books on the late fifteenth century has been invaluable, and I recommend *The Yorkist Age*, *Richard III*, *Louis XI* and *Warwick the Kingmaker* to anyone who really wants the facts, as far as we have them, presented in a manner both erudite and readable.

Trying to fill the gaps in Anne's story with intelligent guesswork, I have invented as little as possible. One or two characters asked to be created: Richard's two natural children were acknowledged and provided for, but their mother or mothers have escaped the records. The concept of one mistress did less violence to his rather puritan character than two, so Marja van Soeters came into being; Ankarette Twynyho existed, and if she did not have a brother called Francis, she should have done. Of the Wrangwysh family, Thomas was twice Mayor of York, but Janet and John are mine. Bertrand de Josselin insinuated himself into my mind as he did into Anne's life; I do not know where he came from. Virtually all the others, down to Jane Collins the wet-nurse, are historical.

STRATFORD-UPON-AVON
MARCH 1978

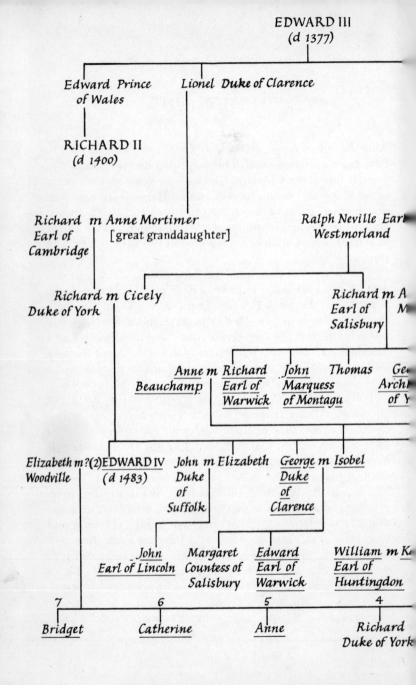

EDWARD III
(d 1377)

Edward Prince   Lionel *Duke* of Clarence
of Wales

RICHARD II
(d 1400)

Richard   m Anne Mortimer   Ralph Neville Earl
Earl of   [great granddaughter]   Westmorland
Cambridge

Richard m Cicely   Richard m A
Duke of York   Earl of   M
                                              Salisbury

                Anne m Richard   John   Thomas   Ge
                Beauchamp Earl of Marquess   Archi
                           Warwick of Montagu   of Y

Elizabeth m?(2)EDWARD IV John m Elizabeth George m Isobel
Woodville   (d 1483)   Duke   Duke
                          of   of
                          Suffolk   Clarence

                John   Margaret   Edward   William m K
                Earl of   Countess of Earl of   Earl of
                Lincoln   Salisbury   Warwick   Huntingdon

7   6   5   4
Bridget   Catherine   Anne   Richard
                                                Duke of York

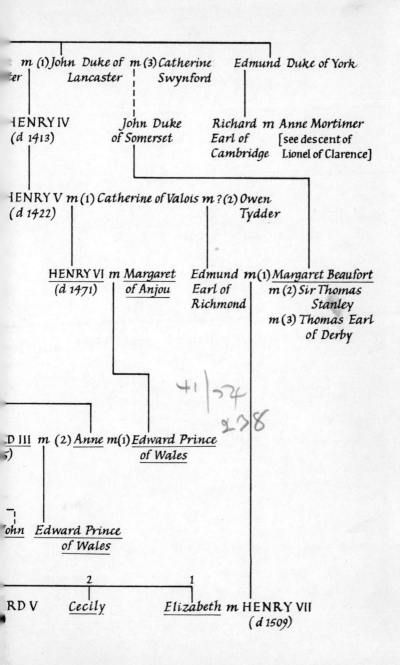

m (1) John Duke of   m (3) Catherine   Edmund Duke of York
        Lancaster   Swynford

HENRY IV   John Duke   Richard m Anne Mortimer
(d 1413)   of Somerset   Earl of   [see descent of
                                          Cambridge   Lionel of Clarence]

HENRY V m (1) Catherine of Valois m ? (2) Owen
(d 1422)   Tydder

        HENRY VI m Margaret   Edmund m (1) Margaret Beaufort
        (d 1471)   of Anjou   Earl of   m (2) Sir Thomas
                                Richmond   Stanley
                                          m (3) Thomas Earl
                                                 of Derby

D III m (2) Anne m (1) Edward Prince
)   of Wales

ohn Edward Prince
     of Wales

              2   1
RD V   Cecily   Elizabeth m HENRY VII
                                   (d 1509)